The Boneyard

KEITH MINNION

THE Boneyard

*This one is still
for Max and Chase*

The Bone Worms
Before • 9
1983 • 41
After • 293

Close the Door
299

Up in the Boneyard
329

Etc.
353

THE
BONE WORMS

GLENDOWER: I can call spirits from the vasty deep.

HOTSPUR: Why, so can I, or so can any man; But will they come when you do call for them?

Wm. Shakespeare
Henry IV, 1597

"A visitor might descend upon this planet a thousand times and never see a tiger. Yet tigers exist, and if he chanced to come down into a jungle he might be devoured. There are jungles of the upper air, and there are worse things than tigers which inhabit them."

Sir Arthur Conan Doyle
The Horror of the Heights, 1913

BEFORE

1323

Lenape Nation, Along the Delaware River
Autumn

The hunter already had two rabbits tied to his gegochbisik when he saw the eagle, the woapalanne, above the Strange Meadow. It was a large male, circling high in the clear azure sky. Too high for even his fastest arrow to reach, he decided. Certainly too high for his sling. He crouched in the shade of a tall chestnut at the edge of the meadow. Like him, the eagle was hunting. Like him, when it found its prey, it would pounce. When it dove, when it grabbed its vole, rabbit or mouse and took to the air again, then his arrow would fly. He squinted, following the eagle as it executed lazy circle after lazy circle, riding the thermals the Strange Meadow produced.

He blinked, and then the eagle was gone. He blinked again, rubbed his eyes with his free hand, but the sky remained empty. The bird, in mid-circle, had suddenly *vanished*.

The hunter stood, and went from the shadow of the trees to the full sunlight. He scanned the entire sky. There were no clouds, no smoke, nowhere for the eagle to hide. A flock of grackles took flight at the far edge of the meadow, but he ignored them. Where had the woapalanne gone?

That evening, when he shared his kills with his family and tribe, he told the story of what he had seen. The tschipelendamoagan hakihakan, the Strange Meadow, they all agreed. Best to avoid it all together.

The following morning was cold and damp, and the lands along the Delaware were shrouded in fog. Anyone near the Strange Meadow would not have seen the shattered, ash-encrusted carcass of the woapalanne pinwheel down from the sky. It fell without fanfare or sound, into the Strange Meadow's tall grass. When the late morning breeze finally blew the fog away, it also blew away the faint, furtive stench of sulfur, of burnt flesh and feathers, of death.

1921

The boy, always quiet, sat on a bench before his easel, painting airplanes. His name was John Randall Pitcairn, and he was six years old today. His grandmother, his uncle, and the house staff were all busy downstairs preparing for his party. Jack (as he liked to be called) heard their hushed voices, silverware and china being placed, chairs arranged; they were familiar, comforting sounds, and the little boy allowed himself a rare, fleeting smile as he painted.

When Jack was three, his mother had died during the stillbirth of his sister. He remembered the screams, echoing up the stairway and down the hall to his nursery, and he remembered when the screams finally stopped. The silence after was almost worse. Jack dipped his brush in the little pot of red paint, imagining all the blood that must have attended his dead little sister's entrance into the world that day, soaking the sheets as his mother screamed above it all. Jack painted an airplane wing bright crimson.

Not even three days after that terrible day, in the rear parlor, in the room always reserved for weddings and wakes, Jack's father had stood over his mother's and sister's shared open coffin and blew the back of his head out with his service revolver, the one he had brought back from the Great War in France. The echoes of the shot had made it seem like many guns discharging throughout the big house. Jack remembered that sound, too. Again, more blood as the fresh, warm corpse of Jack's father fell and sprawled messily over the cold, carefully rouged but wilting corpses of his wife and baby…

A new rug had been procured to cover the stains in the unvarnished pine center of the parlor floor, but Jack found them one day a month later, playing army with his lead soldiers while the rug was out on the line being beaten. He carefully placed his infantry among umber and sienna bomb craters in this splendid, splattered battlefield, and had a wonderful playtime while it lasted.

He chose brown for an airplane's fuselage.

He was a small boy, thin and lightly boned. His grand-mother told him he had his mother's eyes: opaque, flat grey; and his father's thin, serious mouth. His skin was pale, his hair dark, almost black, set high on his forehead, but always falling into his eyes.

He narrowed those eyes as he tried to paint thin black struts for his aerial fleet.

Elizabeth, his nanny, entered the nursery at that moment, blinking in the bright morning light. "Painting time's done now, Master J," she said. "Time to put on your suit clothes for the party."

Jack looked up from his airplanes, frowning at the Negro servant. "But I'm not done yet," he said.

"Done or not," Elizabeth huffed, "your gramma wants you dressed for the festivities." She took up one of the paint pots to cover it as she inspected him. "No time for another bath, but you don't look too bad."

"I don't want to go to my party, 'Lizbeth."

"Oh I know you don't. You made that clear enough. Arms up, now." Elizabeth pulled his painting smock up over his head.

Through the fabric, Jack said, "None of them are even my friends."

"Friends or no, there's a troop of children already on their way. Buttons." Elizabeth leaned down to help him with his shirt, and whispered in his ear, "And every one of them is bringin' you *presents*."

"I wish Billy could come," he said, standing so the nanny could tug his knickers off.

"Billy from the stables? Why you know your gramma don't allow no farm help in the main house."

"But she lets you in here, 'Lizbeth."

"That's cuz I *work* here. My job is in the main house, lookin' after you." She reached for his underpants, but Jack held up a hand.

"I want to do this part myself."

Elizabeth chuckled. "Sure you do. You're a little man now, ain't you." She rose, tousling his hair. "Six years old, almost growed." Then she pushed his hair out of his eyes. "Growin' up too fast, Master J. Much too fast for my money." Then she saw his expression. "Oh! My apologies." She turned her back with a swirl of skirts, and allowed him to change his underpants.

There were six children sitting in the front parlor when Jack came down, four girls about Jack's age, and two boys who were clearly a year or two older. All of the adults were in the larger rear parlor beyond, talking quietly, turning with smiles when Jack appeared. He stood between the sliding doors, forcing a polite smile. "So glad all of you could come to my party," he said.

His grandmother, in front of the crowd in the rear parlor, smiled at him, for he had gotten the words of his little speech just right.

Outside, on the cool autumn breeze, they all heard the sudden low drone of a gasoline motor. Not the sound of an automobile or tractor, however; something different, something rough, something *high*. Jack's Uncle Lucian entered the front parlor and strode to the front windows. "He's early," he said under his breath.

Jack rounded on him, his eyes wide. "*Who* is early?"

His uncle winked. "You'll see soon enough, Jacko."

Jack ran to the windows. After a moment, the other children crowded behind him. Just to be sure, Jack looked first for an automobile on the long, arrow-straight gravel drive that cut a swath through the vast lawn from the estate gatehouse to the circle before the main portico. But then one of the little girls pointed up and said, "Look!"

It was an airplane, a *biplane*, flying high over the trees, lining up on the drive, heading toward the house.

Jack's eyes went wide again, watching it approach. Its body, wings and tails glowed a brilliant yellow in the strong sunlight. It roared over the house, out of view, and the pitch of its motor changed, became less pronounced. Jack turned with dismay to his uncle. "Is it going away?"

"Of course not," Lucian said, grabbing him by the shoulder. Then, chuckling to one of the grown-up cousins standing on the other side of him, "Not for the money I paid him!"

So it *was* for his birthday! An actual airplane, come to his party! Jack pushed through the children and darted through the adults toward the sliding doors leading to the foyer. "I'm going outside!" he yelled over his shoulder.

But his uncle was faster, collaring him before Jack reached the doors, bringing him up short. "It's an airplane, Jack," he said. "Its propeller would cut you in half if you got in its way."

Behind them, Jack's Grandmother gave an audible gasp. "Lucian!"

"Don't worry, Mother," Lucian said, turning. "Everything

will be fine. It's just as we discussed. There's nothing to worry about."

Then a voice, from one of the little girls by the window: "It's landing on the motor drive, Mommy. See?"

The yellow biplane rolled to a stop beyond the empty circular drive. Its engine roared louder for a moment, then throttled back, and coughed to silence. The two-bladed propeller came to rest nearly parallel to the ground.

When Lucian saw the pilot begin to climb out, he let the boy go. Beside him, Jack's grandmother touched his shoulder, "I still don't know if I approve of this."

Lucian watched the boy emerge from the house and run toward the airplane. "Nathan Horrocks recommended him personally, says he's a Princeton man, shot down four Huns during the War."

"That's just one short of a true flying ace, actually," a cousin beside them said.

They all watched the boy duck under the lower wing, missing a hooped bracket there by mere inches, and then pop back up beside the fuselage just as the pilot alighted. The pilot was a tall man, dressed in cotton twill and leather. They shook hands formally, then the pilot knelt, and the two began whispering, already confidants, sharing new secrets.

By this time the other children's parents had given their own reluctant permission, and the six ran across the gravel to the craft. The pilot looked up as they approached, smiled broadly, and stood.

"I say, Mr. Spangler," one of the fathers said behind Lucian as they all moved through the foyer to the portico, "I hadn't planned on my daughter taking an aeroplane ride today."

"He'll only be taking my nephew up," Lucian replied, turning briefly. "Any other arrangements you'd have to make on your own." He saw quick relief on the face of the man's wife. "He comes highly recommended," Lucian told her. "A Princeton man, you know."

With the children in tow, the pilot rounded the wing and approached the adults as they emerged outside. Lucian led them. "Terence Doherty, sir," the pilot said to Lucian, flashing another broad smile. Lucian smelled castor oil and gasoline as they shook hands. "I caught a tailwind. Hope I'm not too early?"

"We're flexible, Mr. Doherty. I'm sure the cake and ice cream are still safe in the ice box."

"Mr. Dougherty says this is a Jenny," Jack said. His face was glowing. Lucian had never seen him so happy. Good, good. "A Curtiss JN-4 Jenny," Jack said.

"A veritable workhorse for the Army during the War," the pilot assured his Grandmother. "So safe they used it for training new pilots."

"Can we go up now?" Jack tugged at his uncle's trouser, jumping from leg to leg. "Now? Right now?"

Lucian shared a glance with his mother, who shrugged resignedly. She said, "I don't suppose you'd like some refreshment first, Mr. Doherty? I imagine you must have flown a distance."

"Not far, actually, madam. Just up from Philadelphia." The pilot looked down to the jumping boy, and grinned. "I think I will pass on the offer, if you don't mind. It looks as though I have some flying to do first."

The noise and vibration of the airplane as it took off was exciting to Jack. There were two cockpits, one behind the other. Jack was strapped securely in a wicker chair in the forward one, so the tremendous prop wind and hot metal smells of the engine washed over him first. Every lever, pedal, and gauge in the pilot's cockpit was duplicated in his, so when Dougherty pulled his control stick back to lift the craft into the air, the control stick between Jack's knees moved the same distance. Like invisible hands were at work; like ghosts.

They roared over the broad roof expanses of his

grandmother's house, and Jack counted six chimneys before the building was gone and tree after tree after tree took its place. Jack felt his seat shift, and out on the upper wings the ailerons tilted, one up, the other down, and the plane banked grandly before Cobb Hill, gaining altitude, returning to the house lawns and the brightly colored ants that were the party guests standing in the circular drive. Then Jack felt a tap on his shoulder. He turned, and saw the pilot point with his gloved finger down to the control stick. "Take it!" he yelled. "Go on, you can fly her for a while!"

Jack hesitated, his eyes wide.

"Go on!" Dougherty yelled through a cupped hand. "We're high enough!"

Jack took the stick, grasping the carved wood grip handle with both hands, and felt the tension in it, the promise. He moved the stick gingerly, just a little bit, and the airplane responded. A sudden feeling of power coursed through the boy. He was flying an airplane! The horizon dipped, and then he felt the pilot at his own control stick, helping him, guiding him, as they banked, and went just a little bit higher.

The hot, sulfurous stench of the engine washed over him, causing him to cough. The sunlight flickered. Then, abruptly, like a train plunging headlong into a previously unseen tunnel, like a powerful knockout punch, everything went totally, utterly, silently black.

To Lucian, it all happened in an instant: he was looking at the miniscule silhouette of the biplane against the brilliance of the sky, then he blinked, and the craft was gone.

Behind him, Lucian's mother gasped: "Oh my! Oh my…!"

"A trick of the sun, Mother, that's——"

But it wasn't. The biplane was gone.

"I say," one of the parents said, standing beside Lucian, "where did it go?"

Lucian's mother grabbed his arm. "What can we——!" she began, then caught herself.

The biplane was there again, a black cutout against the brilliant blue sky, but silent, totally silent now, its engine off, gliding down like some awkward, grotesque yellow bird.

"There must be engine trouble," Lucian said, turning to take hold of his mother's shoulders, "but I'm sure he can bring Jack down safely. Here!" and then he ran to cut off the movement of people toward the motor path where the plane would land, "Stay back! Please, stay back! We must give him room!"

Everyone heard the whoosh of air over the wings and through the struts and wires of the craft as it came down. They strained to see if the pilot and the boy were there, were safe, but the angle of the biplane's descent made that impossible. The craft descended in a wide, wobbling turn, trying to line up on the motor drive. Its spoke wheels struck the gravel hard. The biplane bounced up, then down again, hitting on one wheel hard enough to crumple the undercarriage. The lower right wing dug into the turf, collapsing both it and the wing above it as the craft swung violently about. The propeller caught the ground and splintered, and the biplane came to a groaning halt.

The sudden silence was like a thunderclap.

"Oh Lucian," his mother gasped, a dead weight in his arms.

"Everyone!" Lucian yelled, "Stay back! Stay back please! Annie!" He gave his mother over to his cousin. "Stay with her, take her into the house."

The mothers held tight to their children while the fathers, with Lucian leading, converged on the craft.

"Dear God!" the first man to reach the wreckage exclaimed, stopping within easy sight of the cockpits before swinging about, falling to his knees, gagging. Then Lucian was past him, his hand on the ripped fabric skin of the airplane's fuselage, sliding on it, on something wet. Engine oil? No. Blood. Incredibly, it was blood. It was all along the cockpit's leather collar, dripping down the skin of the plane. Lucian leaped onto the fuselage, using the lower wing for leverage, slipping on the gore and grit that seemed to cover everything, and climbed up to look into the cockpits. The rear cockpit collar was sliced and torn, bloody horsehair padding extruding in several places. In the rear seat he saw red and brown and purple, a mass of raw flesh—like a freshly butchered pig, he described it later to the police It was the pilot, cut so severely and in so many places it was a miracle he was still alive. Lucian saw him move fitfully, his moans causing large pink bubbles to form below his chin. A hand rose up, leather glove sliced through skin and muscle, exposing the very bones of the fingers, then fell back into the cockpit. The moaning ceased, the bloody bubbles filled with the pilot's final breath.

Lucian only had eyes for the front cockpit, however, for his nephew—

But he front cockpit was empty.

Long after nightfall, after the police and the family physician had gone and his mother was finally settled down for sleep, Lucian went out to the airplane in the motor barn where the workers had wheeled it. He saw the stable boy appear at the open door as he approached. "Go on to bed, boy," he said. "It's late, and this is no place for you."

The stable boy hesitated.

Lucian focused on him, a Negro, dark-skinned, wide-eyed, about Jack's age, "You're Gramma Alton's grandson?"

"Yes, sir." The boy ducked his head. "I'm Billy. If you don't mind, sir, I was worried about Master Jack. Have you found him yet? Is he hurt bad?"

Lucian let out a long breath. "He's still missing. We had the police, a lot of people, out searching for him all day. Tomorrow we'll all be out there again."

"I can help look too, sir. He and me, I mean, we…Master Jack plays with me, sir."

Lucian reached out and patted the boy's head, "And you will again, Billy, I promise. Now, would you get the lights for me, please, and then go home to your Gramma and go to bed?"

"Right away, sir!" The boy grinned, then scampered off.

The darkness was suddenly banished as the overhead bulbs snapped on, flooding the motor barn, illuminating the row of automobiles parked inside, and the biplane beside them. Lucian blinked, batted crazed moths from his face, then approached the thing. The pure yellowness of it was loud and crude against the soft blues and blacks of the barn shadows. He reached out and ran his fingers over the painted surface of the still intact lower left wing, and his fingers came away...dirty. He brought his hand into the light; the dirt was actually ash, a pale, grey ash. He walked along the wing, eyes darting. The entire plane was covered with it, a fine, nearly transparent layer of powdery ash. Near the cockpits it was a smeared brown paste where blood had mixed with it. Lucian paused there, noticing the many fine cuts in the fabric of the fuselage, and in the leather collars of the cockpits themselves. Not tears—the crash had made enough of those. These looked like someone had attacked the fabric and leather with delicate blades, surgeon scalpels, a hundred, a thousand of them.

He was tall enough to see inside the rear cockpit. He stared at the leather-covered wooden ring framework for a long moment. Something didn't look right. The leather was stretched over a horsehair padding, and was tacked to the inside every inch around the circumference. Under the leather edge, the wood framework was slightly exposed. Lucian saw something there. He inserted his shoe in a toehold in the fuselage, hoisted himself up on a strut wire, and leaned into the cockpit to get a better view.

The wood frame, purely structural and not meant to be seen or displayed in any way, had nevertheless been elaborately carved. He saw complicated scrollwork, like intertwined vines, but at the same time not like vines at all. More like...*worms*. It was a very odd and disquieting design. Lucian reached in to run a finger along the scrollwork, but stopped himself just short of doing so. A shiver went through him, prickling along the back of his neck, and he jerked his hand back.

Odd. One more odd thing. Lucian dropped back to the barn floor and stood in the raw electric light, not understanding any of it, any of it at all.

He dropped back to the barn floor, finally, and his shoe crunched on something. He looked down. It was a bone, a small, thin, impossibly white bone. Damn rats, he thought, and kicked the fragments away.

Later, making his final rounds of the house before retiring, Lucian found his mother still awake, sitting in the darkness of her bedroom. He walked across the room, put a hand on her shoulder and said in a quiet voice, "I thought you were asleep, Mama."

She shrugged. "I tried, but I can't get this day, this damnable day, to end."

"We all need to get some sleep, Mama. We need to be well rested for tomorrow. When we find Jack—"

She turned suddenly, her face catching the light from the hall, and Lucian saw fresh tears ruining the powder on her cheeks. "He's dead, Lucian."

"We don't know that."

"Even if he survived the fall, even so, the night will be so cold." She sobbed once, then caught herself, pressing her fist to her mouth.

Lucian's grip on her shoulder tightened briefly. "We'll find him. We'll bring him home, we'll take care of him, and we'll make him better."

Her voice took on a hard edge: "I want it taken away, Lucian."

"The airplane?" He nodded. "Of course. I'll take care of it."

"Tomorrow. First thing. Have it burned."

"No doubt the police will still need it for—"

"I don't care about the police! I don't care about any of that!" She turned to face him, and took his hand into both of her own. "Break it up and burn it, Lucian. Burn it to ashes!"

"I promise, Mama. I'll take care of it. But there's nothing more we can do tonight. This day—"

"This day!" She seemed to grow smaller on her settee as she let go of his hand and turned away again. "This day, this damnable damnable day, Lucian, is *done*."

Spangler Estate, Bucks County, Pennsylvania
Friday, October 21

"What's all this, then?"

Billy skidded to a halt at the sound of the booming voice of the head Groom. Marcus, a broad-shouldered Negro over six feet tall, came out of the darkness of the stables. "Master William!" He wiped his big hands with a red-checkered kerchief. "You done your chores already?"

"Yessir Marcus. All done."

"All that cowflop shoveled out those stalls?"

"Yessir. All of it."

The Groom followed Billy's eyes. The fields beyond the blue shadows of the stable yard were bathed in golden morning light. "You be back by supper bell, now," he said, grinning. "Your Gramma don't need a minute of worry outta you."

"Nosir. I'll be back, I promise."

"You see to it." Markus stuffed the kerchief in his hip pocket. "Now get on outta here, sprout, I got work to do."

Billy turned and ran again, out of the shadows, into the light.

Cobb Hill, and the woods covering it, rose beyond the fenced pastures and the high grass fields north of the main house and outbuildings. Autumn had burnt its slopes the color of freshly baked johnnycake. It took Billy a full ten minutes, crossing the fields and climbing over two fencerows, to reach the shadow-line of the trees at the base of the hill. The soft ground was trampled with large, deep shoeprints. The search parties had already come this way, even though the yellow airplane hadn't flown directly overhead here. The parts of the estate where the airplane had actually overflown had been gone over several times during the past week, but Jack was still missing. Billy looked up the slope, into the woods, into the shadows between the trees. Six days was a long time to be lost.

"Well, hello there."

Billy turned.

Lucian Spangler stood at the edge of the last field, half in and out of the tall timothy grass, leaning on a tall walking stick. His clothes were wrinkled and dirty, his hair needed combing, and there were grey hollows under his eyes. He looked like he hadn't slept in a long time. "Billy," he said, "It's Billy, am I right?"

Billy put his hands behind his back. "Yes sir."

"You turned the lights on for me, I remember, in the barn that night." Spangler paused, lowering his head. Then he raised it again. "It's Friday. Shouldn't you be in school?"

"My Gramma teaches me two hours every day, sir, right after supper."

"Ah. Of course." Spangler looked up the slope of the hill. "You were going to play, then, up on Cobb Hill?"

"Yes sir. Jack and me, we, I mean he...he has a tree house up there, sir."

"*The tree house.*" Spangler smiled suddenly, briefly. "That used to be my tree house, you know, when I was a boy. My father had it built for Jack's mother and me, up in the tallest tree at the very top of the hill. We could see for miles up there."

"The leaves hide most everything, sir."

"I'm sure they do. Wintertime, though, that's when you can see things. Far away things."

Billy nodded. "Yessir, you sure can."

Spangler looked back to him, a line of concern creasing his forehead. "The rope ladder must be rotted by now, though. It can't be safe."

"Oh, we put a new rope up, sir. There's knots every foot for easy climbing."

"Good." Spangler nodded. "Good. Well. Don't let me keep you. You be careful up in that tree, now."

"Yessir, thank you sir."

Spangler raised a hand as he turned away. Billy watched him enter the timothy, his face downturned, already looking into the tall grass, looking again for Jack.

Billy ran up into the shadows of the trees. He was looking too, of course. Everyone was, wherever they were. His Gramma had told him just the night before, "If you look where everyone's lookin' and you don't find him, well then, you have to look where folks ain't lookin', don't you. Simple as that."

Billy threaded a path up through the trees and underbrush. The trees gradually thinned, and he blinked in the occasional dazzling patches of sunlight, pausing in them to get warm. At the top of the hill the trees gave way entirely to a crowning field of waist-high yellow grass. The field was empty except for three trees in its center. They were widely spaced, still had half their leaves, and cast three huge patchwork umbrellas of shade. The tree at the very center was the tallest. The tree house was in this one. Billy found the rope looped around a low limb stump, freed it, and pulled it taut. Twenty feet above him were planks spanning two major limbs, and an open trap door.

Billy pulled the rope taut again, and the snapping noise it made caused a flock of grackles to take flight from the dappled shadows above. They dove and swerved in one motion, out into the sunlight.

Lucian stopped walking, swung around on his walking stick, and looked back at Cobb Hill. Its rumpled gold and brown seemed pasted against the chalk blue of the morning sky. He could clearly see the three tall trees in the center of the field at the top. Had the boy reached them yet? Probably.

As he stood, the moment became a minute, then two. Cobb Hill, he thought. The tree house.

The tree house.

He began walking back the way he had come, following his track through the tall grass, back to the hill.

Billy pulled himself up through the trap door with a grunt. The tree house was a large rectangular deck of wide wood planks, with a shoulder-high fence and railings all around. The side against the tree followed the irregular curve of the fat trunk, forming two odd-shaped alcoves at each corner. The alcoves were roofed over with tin sheets, and were as dark and snug as caves. All of their important stuff was in them, safe from the weather: cans of potted meat Jack had pilfered from Cook's larder, a jar of hard candy sweets, a cigar box of marbles, and piles of well-thumbed penny dreadful adventure books.

Billy let his feet dangle over the edge of the trap door as he caught his breath. The floor around him was littered with dead leaves, twigs and cracked chestnuts. A squirrel chattered loudly somewhere above, and a new chestnut fell to the planks. Billy looked up. He found the squirrel clinging to one of the wood ladder cleats that followed the trunk up to the next major crotch of the tree. The squirrel looked down at him with its expressionless black eyes, and scolded him again. Billy grinned. "Think you own the place, do you Mr. Squirrel?" He picked up a chestnut to throw, but the squirrel knew the game, and scampered up out of sight.

Billy got to his feet and went over to the railing. The fields and pastures below were only partially obscured by the remaining leaves. He could even see the main house, barns and stables in the far wavering air. He leaned out, squinting, trying vainly to see Mr. Spangler in the timothy field.

There was a sound behind him, then, a muffled thump. He

turned. Three leaves came spiraling down through the filtered golden light. Was that squirrel throwing more chestnuts at him? Billy grinned again, looking up. Then he went to the railing on the other side. The smoky brown hills of New Jersey seemed to stretch out forever beyond the farms that edged the blue curve of the Delaware.

Another sound, then, to his right. Another thump, but louder this time. Billy turned to it. It had come from one of the alcoves, the one in the northeast corner, the one in the deepest shadow.

"Hey Mr. Squirrel," Billy called out, "You trying to steal our stuff?"

He saw something move in the darkness, and a cold prickling danced up his neck and into his scalp. Whatever it was, it was too big for a squirrel. Much too big. "Hey," Billy called out again, a waver in his voice now, "Who's there?"

He heard another thump, and with a loud rattling a few dozen marbles rolled out into the light.

Billy took a step forward, but sudden movement stopped him as a blur of arms and legs leaped out at him. Billy jumped out of the way, yelling as he saw naked skin, stringy black hair, and crazed grey eyes scramble and scuttle past him to the far corner of the treehouse.

It took a moment for Billy to register what he saw, *who* he saw, cowering naked, filthy skin scratched raw, pushing himself as far into the corner as possible.

"Jack?"

The sun was warm on his neck as Lucian crossed the field to the tree house tree. He followed the trampled path Billy had blazed. Around him, a chorus of cicadas briefly filled the air. He entered the tree shadow and immediately saw the rope, hanging free, with heavy knots every foot, just as the boy had described.

As he grabbed the rope he heard a scream, a ripping shriek through the rustling leaves. He looked up, eyes wide with shock.

Another scream, short, staccato, like a gunshot.

Then nothing.

A shower of leaves fell all around.

Lucian grabbed the rope in both hands and, with a grunt, began climbing.

Jack lay motionless in the center of his bed, head and shoulders propped up by pillows, his small body causing hardly a wrinkle under the richly colored counterpane. His eyes were open, but unfocused. He stared out into the middle distance at nothing at all.

His face, hands and forearms were roadmaps of bright red scars on skin as pale as paper. His entire body was, in fact, covered with hundreds of such scars: thin, precise, brilliantly red, and all of them fully, inexplicably healed.

Seated beside the bed, Lucian reached out and took his nephew's hand. "Jack," he said, gently, for the hundredth time it seemed. "Jack, can you hear me?"

The boy did not respond.

Lucian heard sounds beyond the closed bedroom door, someone ascending the stairs, hushed conversation coming down the hall, then a gentle tap at the door.

Lucian let go of Jack's hand, rose, and went to open it.

His mother stood in the doorway. Beside her was a tall, portly man in a dark wool suit. His florid complexion went from his double chin all the way up and over the crown of his bald head. He carried a black leather bag in one hand, and raised and offered the other. "I'm Doctor Harcourt," he said.

Lucian shook it. "Of course, Doctor. I remember you from last Saturday. I'm glad you could come so quickly." He moved aside to let them enter.

Dr. Harcourt moved immediately to the bedside, sitting down on it, putting his bag beside him. Jack's grandmother stayed back, near the door, a hand to her mouth. "Dear God," she whispered, blinking back new tears as she looked at her grandson.

Lucian put his arm around her. "Perhaps you should go back downstairs, Mother," he said.

"I can't bear to look at him like this, Lucian."

"Then go downstairs. The doctor's here now. Everything will be fine."

She wiped her eyes. "I'll have some tea made," she said, "for later, for after."

"That's a good idea. This shouldn't take long."

"We'll take good care of him, Emily," the doctor said.

"I know you will, John." She braved a smile, then turned, and pulled Jack's bedroom door closed behind her.

Lucian returned to his seat beside the bed. "He's been like this ever since we brought him back from the tree house this morning," he said. "In this...trance."

"Your mother said you heard yelling, screaming, as you approached the tree house?"

"I did hear screaming, but I think it was the other boy."

The doctor looked at him. "The other boy?"

"A child of one of the stable help. A Negro, about Jack's age. I think he may have been up in the tree house with Jack."

"These aren't wounds from a fight between two boys, Mr. Spangler."

"No, of course not. I wasn't suggesting that."

The doctor leaned close, examining Jack's face. "These are surgically precise. Uncannily so." He looked up. "What's the young buck's story?"

"We don't know. He's missing."

"Missing? Didn't you say he and Jack fought up in the tree house?"

"He wasn't there. I only found Jack."

"Well," the doctor said, "little boys like to hide, don't they? Particularly when they're afraid."

Lucian nodded. "I'm sure he'll be found."

The doctor reached out and cupped Jack's chin in his meaty

hand; for an instant Lucian thought Jack would awaken at his touch, but his body remained limp, his eyes empty. The doctor stared into them for a long moment. Then he reached into his bag and took out a small brown bottle. He shook a few drops of clear liquid into his handkerchief, and held the damp portion under Jack's nose.

"What is that?"

"Just some camphor. It might bring a sneeze if nothing else."

But it brought nothing.

The doctor put the bottle away, and extracted a stethoscope. "Would you help me get his nightshirt off?"

"Certainly."

Jack was like a rag doll, neither helping nor hindering, as they undressed him. "Fascinating," the doctor said, his gaze darting over the new patterns of scars revealed across Jack's upper body. He donned the stethoscope, breathed on the nickel-plated disk to warm it, and placed it carefully on Jack's chest.

Lucian watched the doctor intently for some reaction, but his expression was impassive. He only grunted softly as he sat back. "Can we turn him over?" Lucian helped him, laying Jack's head to the side so he could breath unhindered. The scars on his back radiated out from his spine like the wings of a bird.

"They follow the skeleton," the doctor observed. "The scars, I mean."

"I noticed that too," Lucian said.

The doctor bent forward, laid the stethoscope disk on the boy, and listened again. He did this several times, in several different places. Then he sat back, frowning, and put his stethoscope back into his bag.

Lucian couldn't help himself. "Well?"

The doctor looked at him briefly. "He sounds fine. Heart is strong and steady, lungs are clear. Your mother said the boy was washed. Was there any blood? From any of the scars? From any orifice?"

"None. He was very dirty, that's true, but there wasn't any blood. Just the scars."

"Well that's a good sign, then. One might expect some internal injuries, what with—" The doctor stopped himself, his eyes going wide, then narrow. "*Do you see that?*" he whispered.

Lucian began to form a soundless 'What?' with his lips when he saw it too.

Jack's ribs were moving.

Each one alone, not together the way a ribcage was supposed to move, but separately. Each rib's movement was so slight, however, that it seemed almost a trick of the light, a fool to the eye. But Lucian saw it clearly.

The doctor put his hand out and touched Jack's back with just a finger, feeling for the rib beneath the boy's skin as it *shifted*.

"Fascinating," he breathed.

Lucian awoke with a start, blinking in the darkness. He was in the chesterfield in Jack's bedroom, fully clothed. A blanket was on the floor at his feet. Someone must have covered him with it, earlier in the night.

He brought his hands to his face and rubbed his eyes with his thumbs. Dear God, he thought, what time was it?

From the direction of the bed, then, he heard a sound.

He dropped his hands, suddenly, fully awake. The boy was no more than a shadow in the bed. Lucian saw him move under the counterpane, and groan. Lucian went from the chesterfield to the bed in one motion. "Jack," he whispered, finding the boy's hand and taking it up. "Are you awake?"

Jack's breath caught in his throat. He swallowed, then groaned again. "Billy," he said, his voice rasping. "Billy."

"It's me," Lucian said, "Uncle Lucian. I'm here, Jack."

Jack's entire body jerked, and his head came off the pillow. "Don't go up!"

"I'm not going anywhere, Jack. I'm staying right here. You're safe. You're in your bedroom. You're—"

"Don't listen to them, Billy! Don't listen to them! They're lying!"

"*Jack*." Lucian tried to ease the boy back, but Jack struggled against him. "Don't go up! Don't go up!"

Lucian gathered his nephew to him; the boy fought him at first, then surrendered, going limp against his chest with great, heaving sobs. "I told him! I told him not to do it. I told him!"

"It's all right, Jack." Lucian held him close. "Everything will be all right. Everything will be fine…"

The ladder was leaning against the lip of the tree house's open trap door. In the urgency and confusion of getting Jack down safely the previous morning, no one had taken it down.

"Like I told you, sir," Marcus said, gesturing, "It's still there."

Lucian stopped to catch his breath. "Good for us, then. I didn't look forward to climbing the rope." He slapped the head groom on the back. "Let's do it then, hey?" Together, they crossed the meadow to the tree house tree.

Lucian put a hand on one of the ladder rungs. It was wet with dew, and still carried the chill of the previous night. He looked up. The trap door framed golden leaves and a pale morning sky.

"*He went up! I told him not to! I told him not to listen to them!*"

The only sounds Lucian heard were the wind rustling the leaves, and the far-off honking of geese in flight. No voices.

"You sure you want to go back up there, Mr. Spangler? That fool Billy ain't up in this tree. Even if he was hidin', it was too cold and windy up here last night. He'd of come down for sure."

"I agree, Marcus, but there's still something I have to check. You stay down here, hold the ladder for me. I won't be long."

Marcus shrugged. "Whatever you say, sir."

Lucian climbed the ladder slowly, deliberately, aware of the dew-slicked rungs. When he had his head above the lip of the trap door he paused and looked around. The tree house was much as they had left it the day before. Newly fallen leaves covered older, browner ones. Spiny chestnut hulls were littered everywhere. The alcoves on either side of the tree trunk were empty.

He climbed the remaining rungs, clambered onto the floor planks, and stood. The wind rushed through the tree in a constant ebb and flow. Sunlight danced in a dappled pattern across the planks. Somewhere above a chestnut fell, racketing its way down through the branches and leaves. Perhaps because of that, or all on its own, a full yellow leaf spiraled past his face to land at his feet. He looked up into the canopy, cupped his hands around his mouth and yelled, "Billy!"

The tree swallowed his voice.

"You okay up there sir?"

Lucian looked down. Marcus was standing at the foot of the ladder, still holding it with both hands, one shoe on the first rung. "I'm fine, Marcus. This won't take long."

He made a quick inspection of the tree house, verifying that both alcoves were, indeed, empty. He ended up at the tree trunk, where he put both hands on a rung of the rough ladder nailed into it. The ladder went up at a slight angle, following the curve of the trunk, and was quickly lost in the tangle of branches and leaves above.

He leaned on the rung, testing it.

From below, "You want me to come up there, Mr. Spangler?"

"No, Marcus, I'm fine. Five more minutes, that's all." He looked up, listening.

Nothing.

He put his foot on the lowest rung, grabbed the highest he could reach, and began climbing.

Two minutes later, from below, Marcus heard a loud exclamation of surprise, then a grunt, and then silence. He stood rooted at the foot of the ladder as a wave of goosebumps ran down his neck, his back, his arms.

Crisp, burnt-gold leaves came drifting, spinning down.

Then something else fell, making a quiet, pattering sound. Marcus looked down at his arm, at the warm droplets splatting on his skin, and he realized it wasn't rainwater. It was blood.

1922

The one job Louie disliked most as a City Hall janitor was cleaning the pigeon crap off the tower observation deck. He didn't give a rat's ass what those goddamn birds did to Billy Penn above. A commercial company came in once a year with scaffolds and steam-cleaned the statue. Nobody was going to catch Louie hanging off a creaking wooden framework a couple hundred feet over the Broad Street cobbles steam-cleaning Billy Penn's bronze ass-crack, no sir. Cleaning the pigeon crap off the observation deck was high enough, thank you very much.

Goddamn dirty birds, pigeons. Crapped anywhere they felt like it. Dumb as bricks, too.

The trick was to stay ahead of it, put the hog bristle brush and the lye soap to the crap before it got too old, too hard. Smelled worse, the fresh crap did, but it was easier to scrub off the limestone than the old stuff.

Louie did most of the dirty work first thing in the morning, before the tower opened for the tourists. The guards downstairs let them up at ten, so Louie tried to get the scrubbing and the hosing off done by nine to give the place a chance to dry out. Today was cold and windy, so Louie added a little rock salt to his pails. No tourist was going to slip and fall on their ass on his watch, no sir.

He saw the little Negro boy as soon as he set his pails down outside. "*Holy cow*," he exclaimed.

The boy was all curled up in the corner, under the wide, sheltering lip of the stone railing, covered in soot and looking beat-up...and he was naked as a jaybird.

"Holy cow," Louie said again, certain this little boy was dead, frozen solid, out all night up here in the cold with no clothes on. Little naked dead Negro kid and Louie had to be the one to find him. No sir, wasn't me, I didn't beat him up, I didn't kill him. I only found him. I didn't touch him, I swear, I just came out to clean the pigeon crap and there he was...

But when he went over and crouched close, Louie saw with relief the boy wasn't dead after all. He was awake and shivering, blinking at him with wide dark eyes. His lips were purple, and under the layer of ash and soot covering him from head to toe Louie saw scars, dozens of them, a *hundred*, criss-crossing his body. "You poor kid," Louie said, pulling off his coat, reaching forward, covering the boy's nakedness. "You'll be fine, you'll be okay."

He cradled his arms around the boy and lifted him easily—he couldn't have been more than five or six, no meat on him at all—and carried him into the Observation Lounge. As the sudden warmth enveloped them the boy began emitting long, moaning sobs. Then he thrashed about so suddenly and so violently that Louie lost his grip and the boy fell out of the coat onto the green linoleum. "Hey, now," Louie said, "take it easy—"

Making sharp, shrieking noises now, the boy took short, erratic leaps on his hands and knees across the floor to the nearest corner. He pushed himself into it, till yelling, all the while looking at Louie with wide-eyed terror.

"Holy cow, kid," Louie exclaimed, "will you quiet down? What's the matter with you, anyways?"

The boy stopped his staccato screams, his hands covering his face, eyes peeking out between fingers.

Louie went down on one knee. "Hey," he said, "what's your name? You got a name, right?"

The boy panted, like hiccoughs.

"It's okay," Louie said. "You're inside now, where it's warm. We'll get you some clothes, get you something to eat. You're hungry, right?"

The boy said nothing, but his hands slipped down a little, just below his eyes.

"I could get you a candy apple," Louie said. "You want a candy apple?"

"Billy!"

Louie blinked. "Did you just say Billy? Your name's Billy?"

The little naked Negro boy shrieked once, twice, then, "Down!"

"Down? You want to—"

"Down!" the boy leaped forward, grabbing Louie's arm with both hands. "Take me down! Please! Take me *down!*"

1983

1

Holy Rood Hospital, Philadelphia
Sunday, November 20

The Emergency Room duty RN closed the plastic curtain behind her. "And what have we here?"

The intern nurse looked up from taking the patient's blood pressure. "A man in his PJs who took a tumble down the atrium steps in that new skyscraper on Fifteenth Street, if you believe the wagon cowboy's story."

"Ouch. That's a lot of steps. In his *pajamas*?" The duty RN lifted the sheet. "Sleepwalking? That'd be a first."

"It's a clean break of the tib and fib, left leg. Doctor Sharnish already set them. Luis is going to do the pressure cast in a few minutes."

The man on the green-sheeted gurney—maybe 65 or 70, the duty RN noted, slight build, with thinning silver hair—opened heavy-lidded eyes, but they were unfocused and wandering. His mouth moved slowly, as though he was saying something, but no recognizable sound came out. Then he lapsed into unconsciousness again.

He's well shaven, the duty RN saw, and his clothes, such as they are, were top drawer; at least he's not a bum, she thought.

The intern nurse pointed to the old man's forearm resting on top of the sheet. "Did you see the scars?"

The RN bent close. They were old scars, barely noticeable, strangely straight. "Looks like he had some surgery early in life."

"Some? Listen to me, they're all over."

"What do you mean?"

"All over his body. I'm talking *all over*. Arms, legs, fingers." She reached for the sheet hem. "You want to see?"

The RN put her hand on the intern nurse's arm. "Spare me, Anita. Anybody get a number, call the family?"

"No ID."

The RN lifted the chart and ran her fingernail down the patient's particulars. "So what did Sharnish put our mystery man on?"

"You can't read his scrawl either? Percoset. Too much if you ask me." Anita packed up her blood-pressure kit. "His BP's way too low. Still."

The RN put her hand on the old man's forehead. Cold, clammy. She took his pulse, timing it against the sweep hand of her watch. Not NFL material, but strong enough. "You'll do fine, sir," she said softly. "Luis wraps a mean cast."

The old man mumbled something, and then his eyes opened again. The RN saw confusion there, and pain, and fear. No, more than that: *terror*. "The bones," he whispered roughly, swallowing between words. "Don't let the bones get me, please…"

"There's nothing to be frightened of," she said in her best soothing voice. "They were clean breaks, and should mend just fine."

His eyes unfocused again, then closed; too much happy juice indeed; he lapsed back into unconsciousness.

"Has he been saying anything else besides this bones

nonsense?"

"Yeah." Anita shook her head slowly. "Something about the nineteenth floor. 'Don't put me on the nineteenth floor,' something like that."

"Nineteenth?" The RN hmphed, reading his chart. "He gets his wish, then. Says here he's slotted for a bed on one of the Eighteenth Floor wards once Luis gets through with him. Miss is as good as a mile, right?"

When John Randall Pitcairn awoke, it was still night. His left leg was in a cast from his toes to just above his knee, and throbbed dully. He felt a pull on his left wrist, and saw a catheter taped down, its tube connected to a hanging IV half-full of some clear liquid. Soft pastel-green light spilled through the half-open door to the hallway, and after a moment it allowed him to see the room's other two beds were empty, their privacy curtains pulled back, sheets tucked and flat like empty billiard tables. He was alone.

Hospital. This was a hospital. Then the memories came back to him: waking up in that new building wearing nothing but his pajamas and slippers, wobbling at the top of the lobby stairs, unable to gain control, the bones pulling at him, pulling him up—

And then one of his slippers fell off, and he was spinning in space, falling down the hard, marble steps. There was the explosion of pain in his leg and hip as he hit, an agony so intense he blacked out…

He lifted his left hand, careful of the catheter tube, and saw new bandages on three of his knuckles; somewhere down the bed, a sling mechanism cradled a cast on his left leg.

The real pain was there, a whisper of it, a promise, but the bulk of it was…elsewhere. The drugs were like a soft, warm blanket wrapping him snugly in the half-darkness. I'm safe, he thought, as the drugs pulled him back down to sleep, safe…

In his dream, he awoke in the same hospital bed to faint

sounds above him, something touching the foam panels of the ceiling; gentle rustlings, like the scurrying of rats in the dark void above.

Then, directly above him, the scurrying stopped.

He blinked rapidly, staring upward, sudden horror tightening the clock spring of his heart with a single, savage *twist*.

The foam panel moved, lifted at one corner, and a whiff of ash, of acid, of *heat*, drifted down. The panel jerked, then, with a squeak of rigid foam, and a trapezoid of blackness suddenly yawned above him.

Out of the blackness, glinting white, a skeleton claw with talons as large and sharp as strop razors slowly lowered itself, grasping at the empty air.

The longest talon came within inches of his nose. *Whick*, it went, in the still air.

And a voice, a whisper, like a fingernail on wet sandpaper: "*Jaa-ack? Ahhh…Ja-ack?*"

Whick.

He lay transfixed below the claw, crucified to the bed.

Somewhere far away, he heard his clock-spring heart beating. This is a dream, he reminded himself. Just a dream.

The claw came down another inch.

"*Ahhh…*"

Whick.

The urge came upon him then, the old glow, the *fire* from the bones inside him, straining to get out. He knew what it was, and he fought it with everything in him.

"*Uppp.*" The talon beckoned. "*upp…Jack…uppp…*"

He heard himself whimper like a slapped dog.

"*Ja-ackk!*"

New pain began radiating from his chest. He wrapped his arms around himself, and felt his ribs moving, raising themselves, stretching his chest to the tearing point. He pushed at them desperately, but they had a life of their own, a single, compelling purpose: to go *up*. In moments, he was sure, they would rip free.

Finally, miraculously, he found his voice in this nightmare. "NURSE!" he screamed raggedly, "NURSE! NURSE NURSE NURSENUR—!"

The banging of an opening door jerked him awake, and light exploded across the room. Walls, floor, window, beds, all suddenly solidified, and became real.

"SIR!" hissed the duty nurse, silhouetted in the doorway. "Any more screams like that and you'll wake the entire floor!"

"But the *bones!*" Jack shouted, "the bones up there!" Gesturing up to the ceiling. "God help me! The *bones!*"

The nurse followed his wildly pointing finger, and her annoyance only deepened.

"The bones," Jack gasped, sweat running off his forehead and down his wrinkled cheeks. "Can't you see? Can't you...?"

But of course she couldn't, because there was nothing there, nothing at all.

Jack wiped the sweat from his face, panting, swallowing back the terror. His entire body was twitching.

The nurse came over to his bedside. "Lucky for us, the only bones around here are the ones in your dream." She reached over him to straighten his blanket, took his left hand and went over the catheter and tape with practiced ease. Then she said, "Your gown is soaked through. How about a fresh one?"

The gown was suddenly freezing on him. "Yes," he said, "if you would, please."

As she changed him, he kept his attention on the ceiling. "This floor," he said, "what floor is this?"

She paused with the snaps. "The eighteenth. Why?"

"*WHAT?*" He pushed her away, "This is WHAT?"

"Oh dear," the nurse said, "If you're going to start yelling again—"

"You don't understand! You've got to get me off this floor!" He raised himself up, grimacing at the pain shooting through him. Through clenched teeth, "Right *now!* Do you hear me?" He grabbed her arm. "Now!"

"Listen, sir," the nurse began, her voice firm, shaking off his grasp, "First of all it's two o'clock in the morning. There's no way—"

"I don't CARE what time it is! You must put me on a lower floor!" Jack lurched upright again, flung his blanket off, and reached for the sling mechanism. The catheter hindered him, so he grabbed the tube with his right hand and pulled it free, tape ripping his hair, the catheter itself dislodging from his wrist, bright drops of blood landing on the sheets, on his skin.

"Wait! You can't do that!" The nurse grabbed for his arm. "That's a glass catheter! If you've broken it—"

"Wass goin' on here?"

Jack saw a large figure filling the doorway, dark skin, vast mop of greased black hair, broad shoulders and thick, muscular arms pulling taut the sleeves of his hospital scrubs.

"Quito! Thank God you're here! I need help with this one."

"Much too much noise comin' from in here, wake everybody up." The orderly advanced into the room, looming over the bed. "You should be sleepin', hey?"

Jack sat straight up in bed, shaking with fear. He jabbed a finger at the orderly. "I need a phone! I want to call my man. He probably doesn't even know where I am. I need to speak with my man."

The orderly looked at the nurse, then back to Jack. "Your *man?*"

Jack took in a deep, shaky breath. "He's probably still asleep, and doesn't even know I've left the house."

The orderly and the nurse exchanged another look. Then the nurse said, "The phone service is closed this time of night, sir. We couldn't possibly activate service for your room until—"

"Then take me to one, please. You have telephones in this hospital that work, don't you? I need to—"

She raised a hand. "Just give me the number. I'll call for you at the nurse station."

The orderly bumped his knees against the bed frame. "She's doin' you a favor, man."

Jack recited the number, then fell back to his pillow again.

"Stay with him, Quito, okay? I won't be long." The nurse left the room, shaking her head.

Quito grabbed the bedside chair, turned it around and straddled it. The chair creaked under his weight as he sat. He put his elbows on the chair back and cradled his chin in his hands. "Had a bad day, huh?"

Jack only glared at him, wrapping his arms around himself to control his shaking.

After a few minutes the nurse returned.

"Did you—" Jack began.

"I got hold of your William Alton," the nurse said.

"Did you tell him what floor I was on?"

"He asked, and I told him. I also told him we couldn't possibly have you moved until tomorrow, told him there were no visiting hours this late, told him Security downstairs wouldn't let him up here till tomorrow anyway." She turned to the orderly. "Can you stay with him? I'm about to start rounds."

Quito nodded. "No problem," he rumbled.

The nurse cleaned Jack's hand, replaced the old catheter with a new one, and taped it securely. Then she left him alone in the room with the orderly.

Qutio leaned on his chair back again. "Those are some serious scars you got."

Jack didn't reply.

"You must have got them a long time ago, hey?"

Jack turned his head finally and looked at the orderly. "A long time ago, yes.."

Quito nodded. "Badges of honor." Then, "Now you get some sleep, hey?" He settled his chin in his cupped hands again.

Jack closed his eyes and focused on the fresh pain in his hand.

Twenty minutes later, in the silence of the sleeping wards,

the orderly suddenly grunted. "What the hell was that?"

Jack was already looking up at the ceiling.

The orderly stood, following Jack's eyes, but the sound, the quiet, furtive scurrying, scratching, above the ceiling panels, had stopped.

One of the panels was slightly askew, revealing a sliver of darkness. Jack stared up into the sliver of black, unable to take his eyes away. The orderly dragged his chair closer, stood on it, and reached up to maneuver the panel back into its frame. They're going to reach down, now, Jack thought, and drag him up. They'll take him just like they took the others, took *me*...

The orderly had to jiggle the panel a few times before it finally fell into place with a quiet squeak.

"There," he said, as he got down off the chair, "better?" Then he turned at new sounds: quiet voices, quiet footsteps, coming down the hall.

A thin, grey-haired black man in a finely tailored suit strode into the room. A harried doctor followed him in, pushing a wheelchair.

Jack nearly choked in the flood of his relief. "William!"

"I came as quick as I could."

"We've got to get out of here! We're on the—"

"I know." William nodded respectfully to the orderly, then turned to the doctor. "We're leaving," he said. "*Now.*"

Not an hour later, in the dark, empty hospital room, a ceiling panel jerked, tilted, then fell to the stripped bed with a soft, squeaking thump.

And ashes, like soft grey snow, drifted slowly down to smolder on the mattress, then go out.

2

Tomorrow, Detective Sergeant Francis Lomax was going back on the job. His medical leave was over, two solid months of therapy, pills, sessions with the shrink, peace and quiet, books, daytime soaps, walks in Pennypack Park, and his mom's home cooking. Over.

Tomorrow he was finally cleared to strap on his piece, clip his gold shield to his belt, and walk back into the Homicide Unit with his head held up. No shame, Frannie; happens to us all, some a little, some a lot, but we all go through it eventually. Yeah. That was the operative phrase: we all go through it. If we're lucky, we come out the other side, too. Yeah.

Tomorrow, he would sit in on the morning brief and Lieutenant Goaz would dump a new case in front of him. No one else had taken a holiday, not the monsters, anyway. Murder was like garbage, like shit: every time you turned around you stepped in a fresh, steaming pile of it.

But that was tomorrow.

Tonight, one more time, he lived the nightmare that had sent him into medical leave in the first place:

North Philadelphia, American Street, a low, ragged canyon of row houses, half of them either burned out or tinned up; half of *those* shooting galleries or junkie squats.

Early Sunday morning. July. Cloudless indigo sky waiting for the sun. The pavement was still warm from the previous day, dry sandpaper against his cheek as he tried to flip over after the trip and stumble, flip like a fat-assed turtle, grabbing for his weapon as he did so, his fingers jamming into an empty holster even as he heard the sound of running, felt the pounding in the asphalt, coming up against a Belgian block curb as the shadows reached him, surrounded him, covered him.

"Lookin' for this, you fat pig fuck?"

His Browning was in the fist of one of them, a nine-millimeter circle of darkness pointing down at him. Next to it, in another fist, the glint of a steel blade, ready to dig for something deep in his belly. All of them had something in their hands. All of them moved closer.

"You're making a mistake," he said, panting, his eyes jerking from one to the other. "I'm a cop—"

"Oh we're not gonna make a mistake, you big fat fuck *pig*."

The black circle danced; the tempered steel blade flashed.

"We're gonna have some fun."

Over. It had to be over. It had to be done. He found himself yelling: "So kill me, then! Go on, you cocksuckers! Do it!"

"He wants it? Crazy anglo cop *wants* it?"

"Come on!" He was screaming, now, "Do it! What's the matter with you shitheads? You wanna off me, so off me!"

"Go on, Anglo," one of them said, "give him what he wants. Cut off his cojones and shove them in his fat anglo mouth."

"Kill me! One of you! All of you! What are you afraid of? KILL ME, dammit!"

But of course then the cavalry arrived, the three uniforms, one on foot, the others in the bright Rizzo-red cruiser, the gang scattering like vultures flapping off a carcass.

Oh my God, he thought, gasping, pushing up onto the sidewalk, onto his elbows, recognizing the look in the face of the uniform on foot as he approached. What did he hear? The fear was like acid pouring from his brain to his belly. *What did he hear?*

Alone in the bathroom where he had grown up, where he had taken his first big-boy dump on the pottie, where he had spied his first pimple, where he had first discovered the curious, joyless joy of jerking off...in this place with so many memories of life, of *a* life, of *his* life, Fran sat on the toilet seat cover, the pre-dawn light of a Monday morning painting across his lap, and contemplated the plastic bottle of pills he held tightly, tightly, in his big hand.

The bottle was brown, the cap white with little cautionary words in raised red letters; he shook it, rattling the capsules. Take one a day, Frannie, keep you happy, keep you sane.

Don't take them, you could go down that dark road again. Put you back on American Street, in the gutter, begging for it.

Five minutes went by.

You want to go down that road again, Frannie?

A few more minutes passed. Silence, in the big old house. Silence and secrets.

When he shifted his weight, the toilet rocked slightly. Needs a new wax ring, he thought. I could pick it up at Reeds Hardware and do it tonight.

Then he realized he was smiling.

You've still got some things to do, Frannie. Still got some things that need doing. Like fixing the friggin' toilet.

Keep off that dark road, now. Don't take any crazy turnoffs.

There was a quiet knock on the door.

"Fran? Honey?"

He closed his hand over the bottle, popped the lid, shook out a capsule. "Yes, Mom."

"Everything all right in there?"

Fran sighed. *She knows.*

"Kill me! Go on! Do it!"

"He wants it? Crazy anglo wants it?"

"I haven't fallen in yet, Ma," he said, his words hollow off the ceramic tiles of the small bathroom.

"You're going to get hemorrhoids sitting on that throne too long." A pause. "I got your grey suit pressed, so you look good, your first day back."

Fran shook his head slowly, and a faint smile played across his lips. Then he dry-swallowed the capsule, stood, shook the pain out of his knees, and stretched the kink from his back. That's why I'm here, right? So my mom can make sure my suits get pressed. That's why I'm living in this house again. So the little things can get done, all the little cracks can get filled. All the little check-boxes checked.

To stop me from trying it...again. To stop me from...succeeding, this time.

Oh, he thought, *the secrets we have. The secrets we keep.*

He put the little bottle back in the cabinet. He knew his mother was counting the capsules, and today, one more day, she would count one less. He lifted, then dropped the toilet seat lid, then flushed.

"All done, Mom," he said, and opened the door. The look of worry on her face, of concern for her boy, her baby, was enough to make him want to cry. "Everything's fine," he said, gathering her to him. "Everything's gonna be...just fine."

3

Jack awoke to full sunlight painting rectangles on the dark wallpaper of his bedroom. Dust motes danced and drifted through the beams as he realized where he was: in his own pajamas, his own bedroom, his own bed…was it all just—? But as he shifted he felt heaviness in his left leg, and a dull jolt of pain. He cried out—

William appeared in the doorway, and came quickly over to the bedside. "You slept soundly," he began.

"I wasn't dreaming," Jack said, "was I? I wasn't—"

"No. You…went to that new skyscraper they put up on Fifteenth Street."

"But the locks, William! The precautions!"

"You got past them somehow after I went to bed." William stood up straight. "It's my fault. It's all my fault."

"Nonsense, man! You have to sleep some time. The fault was mine." Jack shook his head slowly. "It's getting harder to fight it. I'm not strong enough, anymore." He regarded William briefly. "I've never been as strong as you. I've always been the weak link."

William lowered his head, and said nothing.

Jack cleared his throat. "We will need new locks."

"Already ordered. The security company's coming after lunch."

Jack looked down to the floor beside his bed. He saw a length of chromed steel chain looped out beyond the dust ruffle. "The handcuffs?"

William pushed the chain under the bed with the toe of his shoe. "I don't think we need them."

Jack nodded, feeling weak, awash in the warm, glowing pain in his leg. His hand found William's forearm, and he gripped it briefly. "They took me too high. They took me too damned high."

"They didn't know."

Jack loosed his hold, and let his hand fall back to the covers. "Dear God," he said, "it's begun again. After all these years." He looked up. "Do you think it's begun again?"

William frowned. "I don't know."

"The killing," Jack whispered. "The killing is going to begin again."

William shook his head, slowly. "We don't know that for sure."

"They can't find us, this time." Jack felt like a child, a silver-haired, wrinkled, tiny child, lost in a sea of covers. "They won't find us, will they?"

"No," William replied, rising again to his full height. "They won't. Not this time."

Jack pulled at his blankets, wincing. "I'm helpless with this leg. I feel like such a fool, Billy."

"You're home," William said. "You're safe."

Now it was Jack who shook his head. "No one is," he said. "Not now."

4

Cherry Street, West Philadelphia
Wednesday, November 23

KA-BOOM-KA-KA-BOOM! KA-BOOM-BOOM-KA-KA!

All the old man heard through the walls and ceiling were bass drums, goddamn jungle music pounding away all day long and into the night. He never had a moment's peace. Even when he turned the TV up to drown it out, his neighbors seemed to crank up the volume in response. It made the fillings in his teeth ache, sometimes. Thirty-five years in the Post Office for this? He came down to that thought, every day. *I retired so I could live like* this?

"Drive a sane person to drink," the old man muttered, rooting through his refrigerator for a fresh beer. KA-BOOM-BOOM-KA-KA!

On nice days, when the sun was shining down the airshaft, he would flee the apartment building for the Penn campus a few blocks away. The University's Quadrangle was an oasis in the West Philadelphia slums; it had well-maintained lawns and gardens, and very comfortable, clean benches under the beech trees. The campus security police weren't too shabby, either. He could sit back, watch the last big leaves fall, and read his Daily News in peace. That's where I should be, the old man thought as he grabbed a fresh beer, cold in his hand, and swung the refrigerator door shut. I should be in the Quad reading my paper, if only that damn kid would get back with it.

KA-BOOM-KA-KA-BOOM!

Someone knocked on his door.

"About time!" The old man went to the door, peeked through the spy-hole, then unbolted the locks and swung the heavy metal door wide. A black youth stood there, brown bag under one arm. "Got your stuff, Mr. Copper," he said, and handed the bag over.

The old man inspected the contents. "You got whole milk, right, James? None of that two-percent crap I hope."

"No sir, Mr. Copper. I got you the whole milk, just like you asked. And the paper too. And it's *Jameel*, not James." He dug in his pocket. "Got your change right here too—"

"Keep it." Mr. Copper waved it away. "Your tip."

"Thanks Mr. Copper."

Still peering into the bag, the old man suddenly cursed. "My smokes," he said, looking up, frowning, "didn't I tell you to get me a pack of Pall Malls?"

"No sir, Mr. Copper. That wasn't on the list. Even if you did, you didn't give me enough money for it."

"Here." He dug into his pants pocket, emerging with a five-dollar bill. "Go get me four packs. Unfiltered, now."

Jameel took the bill. "Sure thing, Mr. Copper, I'd be happy to. I'll be right back." The young man grinned. "And it's *Jameel*." He waved, and turned down the hall.

The old man swung his door shut. "Jameel," he said, reaching up with his free hand to turn the locks, "what the hell kind of name is that?"

He sniffed, a waft of burnt, ashy air going past his nose;

someone must have propped the incinerator chute open again. Then something touched the back of his neck, like a bug, a fly alighting. The old man moved his hand from the still open locks to his shoulder to swat it. The bug promptly stung him on the finger in a flare of sudden, intense pain. "Damn it all!" he exclaimed, jerking his hand back as he turned, puzzled at the blood he saw there, so much blood for just a sting, why so much blood—?

Then he saw the thing standing there, gaping at him, reaching out for him. And then it was *on* him, *in* him, and he didn't even have time to scream.

5

Detective Sergeant Fran Lomax walked up the street from his unmarked olive-green Dodge to the tall, ugly project apartment house. There were two red patrol cars parked half on and off the sidewalk, squawking and flashing their jiggle lights. There was also another olive-green Dodge, which was either the Crime Lab team or another dick.

Ignoring the crowd of gawkers on the sidewalk (this was Thanksgiving, for God's sake; why weren't they inside eating turkey and watching the Cowboys kick the Giants' collective ass?), he nodded to the two uniforms standing in sober conversation, then huffed up the steps and through the cracked and taped double doors.

Inside, another uniform saw him, and hung up the receiver of a battered wall phone. *Big guns are here now*, his expression read. You're right there, sonny. Fran spread his hands. "Where is it?"

The uniform nodded up. "Nineteenth floor, Sarge. I hope you skipped dinner. It's a bad one."

"Hell, they're all bad."

"No, I mean it. This one's *real* bad."

"CL's car outside?"

"Yeah. They've been here about twenty minutes already. I was second on the scene."

"Who was first?"

"Kid named Nyland. He's still up there. His first stiff, I think."

"Great. When I finish upstairs, I'll need to talk to you too, so stick around. And I don't want any media past you, understand?"

The uniform shrugged. "I'm not going anywhere, Sarge."

Fran grunted. "Elevator work?"

"In this dump?" The younger man pointed. "Stairs are back there."

Ten minutes and eighteen flights later, Fran paused in the stairwell at the landing to the nineteenth floor, both hands holding the rail, and waited for his heart to quiet its pounding protest in his chest and temples. Got to take off those forty pounds, he told himself, not for the first time. Fifty, actually. This was frigging ridiculous.

He shoved off, finally, and followed the yellow tape to the apartment door where the sound of a vacuum cleaner and the acrid shit reek of a fresh butchering emanated.

Outside the door, leaning against the wall, a young uniform stared blankly at his freshly polished broughams.

"You Nyland?" The patrolman's head snapped up. Fran noticed his eyes right away. The kid was in shock. "I'm Detective Sergeant Lomax, Homicide. What have you got?"

"Uhh, one elderly white victim, an Edward Copper. Death by...stabbing, I think."

You *think*? Fran decided not to hide his frown. He said, "I'll take it from you now."

The look of relief on the patrolman's face was almost

comical. "Should I…?"

"Yeah. Stay out here, keep the other tenants out of the way, but I need to talk to you later."

Nyland straightened. "Yes sir."

Fran turned to enter the apartment, but stopped at the threshold and grinned. "Is that the Laugh-man?"

Jay Lafferty, senior technician of this particular Crime Lab team, turned around, switched his vacuum cleaner off, and grinned back. "Fran Lomax! How the hell are you doing? Shit, I'm glad it's you." He gestured about with the nozzle. "Happy Thanksgiving, eh?"

Fran reached into his coat pocket, extracted a pair of latex gloves and pulled them on, then stepped across the entry tile to the brown kraft paper Lafferty and his partner Bill Sanderson had put down on the worn hardwood floor. "Word I got on the way over was there was only one stiff. What's with this paper shit?"

"We were all out of footsies, sorry." Lafferty pointed the vacuum nozzle to an open door down a short hall past the kitchenette. "It's in there. Bedroom. Bill's taking samples. Photographer and M.E. are late."

He left off the 'too', Fran noticed, bless him. "Ambulance crew coming?"

"Already sent them packing. The M.E.'s meat wagon should work."

Fran winked. "I always said you were the smart one."

"You're just a little ray of sunshine, Frannie. Glad to have you back."

There was minimal blood spatter in the short hall. Fran followed the kraft paper to the bedroom. He stopped at the door, breathing a quiet curse of disbelief. The floor, walls, ceiling, furniture, all were splattered and smeared with congealing blood. Like a monochrome Jackson frigging Pollock. The room was small and its only window was closed tight, so the stench of the butchered body on the bed was palpable in the air. Bill

Sanderson, bent over the corpse, waved a silent greeting over his shoulder. "Welcome back, Frannie."

Fran looked around. "Somebody had some *real* fun in here." He crunched on the paper over to the window, confirmed it was locked. "What did he do, Bill, *flay* the poor bastard?"

"Better." Sanderson straightened. "Sucker de-boned him."

"*What?*" Fran turned, went over to the bed, looked down, then quickly away. "Jesus Christ," he breathed. Then he looked down again. "Where's the head?"

"It's here." He pointed. "Face and scalp there…and there."

"What about the skull?"

"Gone, along with most of the rest of the skeleton, maybe all of it. Besides the skull, every major limb bone, pelvis, rib-cage, spine, all gone, as far as I can see without poking too much." Sanderson pointed again. "See this? This used to be his left hand. A hand's got a couple dozen bones in it at least. You see any?"

It looked like bad hamburger meat with too much yellow gristle.

"And here," Sanderson continued. "See that yellowy-purple-grey mess? That's his brain and menenges. I'm betting the eyeballs and tongue are under it. Took the skull, dumped the contents." He pointed down the bed. "Left all the skin, musculature and viscera too, all cut up. Nothing like a sliced-open gut to scent up a room, eh?"

Fran looked up, caught Sanderson's eye.

Sanderson nodded. "We're talking about somebody who makes Jack the Ripper look like the fucking Pope, Frannie."

Fran dropped to a crouch to get a better look. "Victim was white."

"And old. An old white dude too scared, stubborn or poor—take your pick—to get out of this shithole and live someplace decent."

"Some smack-head took him out for what, his social security check?"

"All this for a score that small?" Sanderson shook his head. "And anyway, Social Security checks don't hit till the first week of the month."

The detective rose, and rubbed his face with his hands. "I had too much turkey, too much pie." He blinked his eyes clear. "Smack-head didn't happen to oblige us by leaving the murder weapon behind, did he?"

"There's a knife set in the kitchenette."

"Used?"

"Go see for yourself. They're not bagged and tagged yet, but we're going to take them back with us."

Fran turned into the kitchenette on his way back to the living room. There was comparatively little blood in here, nothing out of place or knocked over, and no sign of a struggle. He ran a quick scenario through his mind: Smack-head surprised the old man at the front door, danced him into the bedroom, then did the job on the bed. Not too complicated.

He saw the knife set by the sink, black plastic handles in a cheap block of wood. The handles were smudged with blood, and there were a few drops and smears on the counter. He carefully lifted the biggest (a *Psycho* butcher variety) out by the bottom edge of its pommel, and saw the blade was largely clean. Didn't use this one, but he drew it out, got blood on it, handling it. What for? Admiring it? Got a special thing for steel?

"They're all like that," Sanderson said, standing in the hall. "Handled but not used."

Fran dropped the knife back in its slot, then followed the tech back to the living room.

Lafferty was kneeling by the vacuum, tagging one of its large plastic collection bags, 'LVG RM AREA-6'. He rose. "First impressions, Detective Sergeant?"

Fran frowned at the largely blood-free floor. "There couldn't have been any cutting done in here."

"*Something* better have happened in here," Lafferty said, "or I've been wasting my time."

"Sure, but just the meet and greet, and maybe the first disabling blow."

They returned to the bloody bedroom. Fran looked at the body on the bed once more, then turned. "He's lying on his pillow, face up, right?"

"He would be if there was a face," Sanderson said dryly.

"Regardless, he's in bed. On the floor, neatly arranged, a pair of polished brown leather shoes. Hanging just as neatly off the chair, a fresh shirt; and on the chair seat, a pair of pants, perfectly folded, with a belt coiled on top. What does it tell you?"

Lafferty shrugged. "That he was a neat freak, that he had routines, and he stuck by them. And that he could have been asleep when he was attacked."

"Exactly. But this window hasn't been opened, that's plain."

"So the entry had to be by key," Lafferty said, "or the door was never locked in the first place. There's no sign of a forced entry."

"How about the other window?" Fran asked.

"Just like this one. By the look of the dust, they've both been closed since late October at least." Sanderson shook his head. "I agree. No way anybody came in or out by the windows."

Fran frowned again. "So where does that leave us? Was the door locked when the body was discovered?"

"The kid in the hall should know. He said he took some info from the building super."

At that moment, from the next room, all three heard, "Jumpin' Jesus H. Christ!"

They all exchanged a look, then Sanderson said, deadpan, "Otto the Terrible has arrived."

Fran led the move back into the living room. "Otto Gustafson, you sonofabitch." He shook the old police photographer's gloved hand warmly. "I haven't seen you since—"

"Since they carted you off to the booby hatch this summer for some mandatory R-and-R." The old man with his wrinkly pink scalp regarded the detective through coke-bottle glasses. "I don't know…you *look* sane enough."

Okay, Fran thought, here's somebody who is saying it out loud, shooting right from the hip. But that's just Otto. I can take it, can't I?

Lafferty slapped Otto on the back. "About time you showed up, you rude, crude bastard. I was just about to *move* something."

"You moved anything," the police photographer said, "and I'll personally reserve you a third shift beat counting meters up in the farms." He slipped his bulging black camera bag from his shoulder and sighed audibly. "Eighteen flights, can you believe that? Why can't everybody get murdered on the first floor?" He looked about. "And on top of that, I'm going to have to photograph every goddamn square inch of this place! Jumpin' Jesus H. Christ!"

"They don't pay you enough, Otto," Fran said solemnly.

"Now there's a smart man." The old photographer began assembling his tripod. "There's a man with a College Education."

Fran turned to the door. "I'm going to hunt up that building super. Look busy, guys, okay?"

He found Patrolman Nyland still standing outside. "You holding up?"

The young officer nodded. "Everything's quiet, Sir."

"Let's count our blessings, then. Listen, you took a statement from the super? What's his involvement?"

"He was the one who called it in." Nyland pulled out his notebook and flipped it open, his hand shaking. "He said he got word of a disturbance in the victim's apartment, so he went to check it out."

"Where is he now?"

"Down the hall. There's an empty apartment. I told him to stand by. You want me to get him?"

Fran shook his head. "It'll be quieter where he is. Lead the way."

They went down three doors to one that was ajar. Fran

pushed it in, and entered an apartment with the same layout of rooms as the one where the murder had occurred. This one was bare save a slate-blue colored couch held up in one corner with a cinder block, and a Day-Glo poster tacked over it of a naked, statuesque black woman with a huge afro hairdo.

Nyland said, "He might be in the bedroom, or in the john. I'll—"

A deep voice suddenly called out, "Who's that? Who's that out there?"

Fran nodded. "Bedroom." Then, louder, "I'm Detective Sergeant Lomax, Philadelphia Police. I need to talk to you, if you don't mind."

There was a giggle from the bedroom, then a young, comely black woman with long, tousled hair came running out. She stopped short in front of Fran, whose frame more than blocked the door. "I didn't see nothing," she said quickly, her dark eyes darting. "Ask Jimmy. He knows. He knows I didn't see nothing. I wasn't even—"

"She wasn't even around, man."

Fran looked up to the new voice. "You Jimmy?"

"In the flesh." The building super was shirtless, a black man in his late thirties, solid, middle height, well-muscled, with three distinctive knife-cut scars on his abdomen. All of this registered automatically in Fran's brain as Jimmy gathered the girl under his arm and met Fran's penetrating stare with the cold, stony defiance of his own. "I'm serious, man. The lady wasn't even here."

Fran waited for a long enough moment, then stepped aside.

The girl was immediately out of Jimmy's embrace and through the door, yelling over her shoulder, "You call me, Jimmy!"

Jimmy grinned. Two gold front teeth. Jesus Christ, Fran thought, I could probably shake him down right now and score, the cocky bastard.

Instead, he said, "Officer Nyland tells me you were checking on a disturbance in the victim's apartment?"

"That's right. That's my job. We get a problem, I take care of it."

"Did you use a pass-key to get in? A master?"

"Didn't need to. Door wasn't locked."

"But you do have a master key, right?"

"Got a slew of them." Jimmy dug into his back pocket and pulled a full key ring free. "This hell-hole's got twenty-two floors, last time I counted."

Fran extended his hand, and made a gimme motion with his fingers. "Give me one."

"What, for this floor?"

"Unless you want me to roust you every time I want to unlock something."

"Fuck no. Here." He twisted a key free, and tossed it.

"Okay." Fran pocketed the key. "What happened when you got to…?"

"Nineteen-G," Nyland supplied.

"Old white dude named Copper or Cooper or some shit didn't answer the knock. No big deal; he's a wino anyway. So I yelled I was coming in, and I did, and man-oh-man, all that blood in his bedroom, all that stink…shit, man, have you seen it yet?"

"Did you enter the bedroom?"

"What are you, nuts? *Shit.* I took one look then hauled my ass outta there."

Fran pointed to Jimmy's sneakers. "You've been wearing these all day?"

The super looked down, then back up. "Shit yeah. Why?"

"Mind if I look at one?"

Jimmy glanced to Nyland. *What-the-fuck?* his expression said.

Nyland said, "Give Sergeant Lomax a sneaker. What are you, deaf?"

Good boy, Fran thought.

The super slipped a sneaker off and handed it over.

"This is a good basketball shoe," Fran said, hefting it.

"Same as Doctor J's, just not as big. That's real leather, man. Cost me a fucking bundle."

Fran turned it over. There was no blood in the geometric pattern of the tread, no moisture of any kind. And the leather upper was dry. He handed the sneaker back. "Did the old guy get many visitors?"

Jimmy slipped his sneaker back on. "He was a white dude all alone in a building full of niggers. Who'd want to visit him?"

"Did he get along with the other people on the floor?"

Jimmy shrugged. "How the hell would I know? Why don't you ask them? *Shit*," he sneered, "you looking for a nigger did this? Well, Mr. Whiteass Detective, you're probably right. But it wasn't nobody around here. We got families in this building. Families with kids. *Shit*."

"You said you were checking on a disturbance. Who told you about it?"

Jimmy hesitated, then he said, "Just a kid, a little brother lives on Eighteen, does errands for folks for pocket change."

"What's his name?"

"Jameel some shit."

Fran looked at Nyland. "I'm on it," the patrolman said, and took off for the elevators. Turning back, Fran saw the super pulling on his tee shirt. *Dial-a-Beating*, it said, over a graphic of a battered phone, and under that, the number for the Police Roundhouse.

Jimmy saw where Fran's eyes had strayed, and smiled his wide gold smile again. "Want to see the back, Mr. Detective?" He turned.

For Faster Service: 911.

"Cute," Fran said.

"Hey," Jimmy turned around again, thumping his chest with his forefinger, "no fucking Grand Jury's investigated *me* for no police brutality, you dig?"

By the time Fran returned to the murder scene, Otto had finished his work, and the Assistant Medical Examiner had arrived and was already making motions to leave.

"So what's the verdict, Doc?"

The Assistant M.E., a sour-faced skinny type named Koenig, said, "Off the cuff? Acute trauma. Death resulted from wounds inflicted by a sharp instrument. Knife. Sharp one."

"What about the bones?"

Koenig breathed a short, tired sound that might have been a laugh. "What bones, Sergeant? They were all *excised*, then removed from the scene."

"How long would that take? Deboning an entire body, I mean."

"The cuts required were numerous. A few hours, I'd say. Maybe two, maybe more. You ever try to debone a chicken?"

"But the blood is—"

"I know, Sergeant." Koenig nodded his head slowly. "The blood is still relatively fresh. All of this must have happened just a short time ago. Less than an hour, no more than that."

"So how could the killer take two hours to cut out the victim's bones if it all went down in less than one?"

"At least two hours, maybe a bit more." Koenig sighed wearily. "I'll have the report for you in a couple of days."

"Tomorrow," Fran said. "I need it tomorrow."

Koenig regarded Fran with eyes as tired as his voice. "This is my second homicide since shift change, and I'm on my way to a third, so what you need, Sergeant Lomax, and what you get, might be two entirely different things, hm?" He waited for a rebuttal, then waved once, and headed for the stairs.

Lafferty said, "Don't piss off this M.E., Fran, no matter how much of a bastard he is. He's new, but we all have to work with him on this one, you know?"

"He's got a bad attitude," Fran grumbled.

"Don't we all. Anyway, we're ready to bag up whenever you're through. We still haven't moved him yet."

Fran nodded. "Did anybody get coffee?"

"Yours is on the table in the kitchen."

Fran got it. Cream and sugar, and still hot. He took a sip. "Anything extraordinary turn up?"

Lafferty suddenly looked as tired as the M.E.; everything about him seemed to *sag*, just a little. "Not much. So far the place is clean. We still have a few hours of work left, though. Usual bullshit. Take us a week to sort through it all. What we can't do we'll send to Harrisburg, take them a fucking month."

"You up too long too, Jay?"

The technician shrugged. "So what else is new? So many people get bopped in this town it isn't funny. Hell, I got money on us breaking nine hundred stiffs before Christmas. Still, this one," and he looked toward the bedroom, "this one takes the goddamn cake." He pulled a baggy out of his duffel. "We did find this, anyway."

Fran took the plastic bag from him. Inside was a photograph, color, five-by-seven, with a gilt cardboard frame. Seated on a plush burgundy velvet couch by a gold and white end table was an old man with a florid complexion and a full head of white hair. He was wearing a mint-green polyester pants-suit with white stitching, lapels wide enough to land a 747 on, and an emerald tie to match. At his side sat a woman of comparable age, dressed in a more conservative, pale yellow pants-suit with a large white corsage. They were holding hands, and were both smiling.

"Mr. and Mrs. Copper, taken in Atlantic City," Lafferty said. "One of the new casinos." He pointed to a half-finished drink on the end table. "That's a Resorts logo on the napkin under the glass."

"Before they lost it all at the slots, by the smiles." *Before she died and he had to pick up the pieces on his own.*

"Least now we've got a face to go with the chop-meat inside," Lafferty said.

Fran pocketed the photo. "I'm going to keep this."

"Hey, it's your case. Feel good to be back in the saddle?"

Fran grunted. "Let's see what you guys missed the first time around, shall we?" He went over to the living room window. It was indeed closed and locked, and the dust on top of the lower sash and clasp lock was undisturbed. He peered through the dirty glass. The window opened onto an airshaft. The opposite wall was brick, with cinder block filling what had once been windows.

"That's a furniture warehouse," Sanderson said, coming out of the bedroom to peer over Fran's shoulder. "They share a common shaft here in the back."

Fran grunted, pushed himself away from the window, and returned his attention to the blood traces on the living room floor. "The victim has a knock on the door," he said then. "He goes up to it and asks who's there. 'Got some booze for you, old man, got some good stuff, fell right off the truck.' Victim doesn't even think twice about that, since he's probably half in the bag already. So he opens the door and then gets the final surprise of his life. He and the killer dance a little in here, then the killer takes the body into the bedroom, lays him out nice and neat on the bed, and then finishes the job."

Sanderson was skeptical. "Or he had a key, like we were saying before."

"I don't know, Frannie." Lafferty shook his head soberly. "Got any blind luck stored up since you last hit the streets? I think we're gonna need it on this one."

Fran took another sip of coffee. "Gee, kids," he said, "thanks ever so much for stopping by. Just don't trip over your cranks on your way out, okay?"

Nyland appeared at the door. "Sarge? I think we got a witness. That kid who lives in the building, name's Jameel?"

Fran turned. "No shit?" He grinned at Lafferty. "*Luck*," he said.

The Frankford Avenue trolley bus let Fran off at Pennypack

Park with a quiet whine of its electric motors. He walked the rest of the way up the dark, quiet street to the hulking Victorian where he had been born, reared, and now, since his breakdown, he resided once again.

You can never come home again? *Shit.* Have a nervous breakdown, and they hand you the frigging *keys*.

Inside, he debated calling Sarah, to apologize again for screwing up Thanksgiving dinner, but the late hour and his less than rosy disposition put a quick kibosh to that idea. Sarah Blyth Fitzpatrick, the kind, understanding (and probably fast asleep) lady friend, deserved Francis Xavier Lomax, the tired, grumpy, overweight man friend, at only his very best—and right now just wasn't it.

He sat down at the kitchen table for a conciliatory piece of pumpkin pie and glass of milk. "Drink lots of milk," Dr. Feldman had said more than once. "It'll do what's left of your stomach lining <u>and</u> your disposition a world of good."

Outside, the wind suddenly picked up, and the cover from one of the garbage cans blew off and clanged up against the backyard fence.

Upstairs, then, his mother's voice came drifting down: "Frannie?"

"Stay in bed, Ma," he called up. "It's late, and I'm going to bed in a minute anyway."

But he heard her footsteps creak across her bedroom floorboards, then slowly, carefully, down the back stairs, so he reached for a napkin and cut another piece of pie, thin one, just enough.

The old woman in the powder blue robe who entered the kitchen was no more than a quarter Fran's bulk. On her toes she barely topped five feet, and wringing wet, a hundred pounds. Add eighty to those numbers, Fran thought, for that's how old she was. A child of the First World War, and a mother for more than half of that. And sharper, more alert, more alive, than he would ever be. Christ.

"So you finally have a new case," she said, sliding into the chair opposite him.

"Had to sooner or later, Ma. I've been off the horse long enough." He pushed the pie on the napkin across to her.

"What, no fork?" Her eyes filled with quiet mischief. "Where did you grow up, kiddo, Fishtown?"

He rose heavily, and went to the dish drainer.

"Much better," she said, taking the fork from him and digging in. After a moment, with her mouth full, she said, "This is a Rillings. What do you think?"

Fran focused on the plate before him. "It's fine," he said, putting his own fork down.

"You want a turkey sandwich to go with that?"

"God no." He pushed his plate away. "So when did Sarah leave?"

"About eight. We watched *Holiday Inn* together."

He nodded, said nothing.

She studied him. "So this case, it's a bad one?"

"No, actually it's a good one. It's a puzzler. It may actually take some thought."

"Who died?"

"An old man in West Philly. Stabbed. Cut up more than he had to be." He glanced at her pie, then up to her. "It wasn't very pretty."

She followed his eyes. "There's nothing you can say that would put me off food, Frannie. The stories your father would bring home, now, *those* stories were—"

Fran held up a hand. "Please. I heard them too, remember?"

His mother took a reflective mouthful. "Murders in the old days just seemed more...gruesome, you know? Messy."

He pushed his plate away a little further. "That's because the pictures they took of them were in black and white. Grainy; out of focus. Hollywood Technicolor has taken all the imagination away, all the mystery, that's all."

"So what's so gruesome about this one?"

You asked for it, Ma. "Whoever killed the guy...took most of his bones."

His mother paused, her fork halfway to her mouth. "What do you mean, took his bones?"

"The killer flayed and deboned him. All that he left was some knucklebones, little stuff. And the guts, meat and skin."

"So what did he do with the bones he took?"

Fran shrugged, letting his shoulders sag. "We couldn't find them in the apartment, or in any of the public spaces of the building. There's a team of uniforms spiral-searching the trash bins in the area right now."

His mother put the forkful of pie in her mouth and chewed slowly. "I don't think they'll find anything, Frannie."

"Oh? How come?"

"If somebody takes the time to cut out nearly every single bone in a person's body, I don't think they'd just go and toss them all in the garbage, do you? All that work for nothing? No, they'd keep them." She chewed, swallowed. "Trophies, or for something particular, you know?"

Fran scraped the linoleum pushing his chair back, and stood. "I agree with you. But you know the drill better than I do. We have to hit all the marks." He put a hand on the chair back to steady himself.

"You're past tired, Frannie. You go to bed and I'll clean up here."

He started to voice a protest, but she shushed him. "This is still my house, and my rules still apply. Now get that fat rear-end of yours up the stairs and into bed."

He smiled wearily. "Yes Ma."

6

Jack didn't have a name for it, but to William it was *the pull*. The Boneyard, up there, reaching down for them, dragging at them. For decades the pull had been nearly gone. Now, however, since the incident at the hospital, it was back, and with a new, focused purpose. Now, it was *undeniable*.

Downstairs, Jack was safely secured in wrist and ankle leather cuffs, their chrome steel chains bolted securely to the heavy bed frame, and the frame was bolted to the bedroom floor. He needed those chains, on nights like this. But not William. He was stronger than Jack. He had always been the stronger of the two. And the pull, for him, wasn't…But that was his secret. That was his burden.

He lay quietly in his third floor bedroom, on his back, motionless in his own bed, and stared up at the ceiling with a quiet, defiant frown.

Enough.

It was the word he used. A simple talisman.

Enough.

He visualized the word as vast letters carved into a grey-granite cliff, taller than Mount Rushmore, older than the Pyramids. Staring up at the smooth, flat expanse of ceiling plaster above him, staring into it, through it, his lips formed the word without making a sound: *enough.*

He heard a muffled thud, from the direction of the floor.

He sat up, alert, fully awake.

Another thud, definitely from the floor, from below it, from the ceiling of the room beneath his own.

Jack's bedroom.

But the cuffs and chains—

Jack called out, through the plaster, wood, and carpet.

William flung his covers aside and was into the hallway at a dead run, down the front staircase, and was in Jack's bedroom in seconds. He looked at the bed, but it was empty, its sheets and blankets in wild disarray. He saw an empty drill-hole in the closest bedpost where an ankle chain had been bolted. Then he looked up—

"Here," Jack said, faintly, "Up here…"

Jack was huddled up against the ceiling, in a corner, his body pressed against the plaster and cornice molding, bedclothes and glittering chains hanging, swinging free. "Help me," he said, gasping, "for God's sake *help me…*"

7

Ashburner Street, Holmesburg, Northeast Philadelphia
Thursday, November 24

Fran woke up, shouting, tangled in sweaty sheets, after only an hour of troubled sleep. Outside, the stars twinkled furiously in the cold wind. He used the sheets to wipe his face and neck, then flung them from him.

For a long moment he listened, wondering if his shouts had awakened his mother. But all he heard was the quiet sounds of the old house creaking in the night wind.

It had been the nightmare, of course. The same one. Always the same one. The one Dr. Feldman said he shouldn't be having any more. "It's over, Fran; you're past it, now…"

When would it go away? When would it leave him alone?

(*"He wants it, can you dig?"* Yellow eyes, yellow, broken teeth, and rancid, tobacco and weed breath, bearing down on him, smothering him, *"Mothafucka' wants it!"*)

Wasn't the memory bad enough? And the shame?

Then he heard the other voice in his head, his father's tired, quiet brogue: *"You ain't got it, lad."* And the sweat turned cold on his skin.

"Damn it," he whispered, thrusting that voice, that memory, away from him. "God damn it!"

He stared at the shadows of the beech tree branches dancing over the old plaster ceiling, willing sleep to return. Then he cursed again, and swung out of bed. He found his slippers by feel, and eased into the hallway, careful not to make any noise to wake his mother. 'You're like a bull in a china shop, Frannie,' he heard her say. 'Ballet is just not in the cards for you, kiddo.'

He took the rear stairs down to the kitchen, where the overhead fluorescent was always on. He made himself a turkey and stuffing sandwich, poured a half-glass of milk, then sat down at the old chrome and Formica table and wolfed the sandwich down. Then he finished the milk off in a single, brain-freezing chug.

As he put the glass down he suddenly started, thinking he saw movement in the shadows of the back stairs. The darkness of the second floor hallway tumbled down the steps, but there was nothing else there. Fran looked at the odd geometries of the winding steps, their paint worn down to wood in the center of the treads. Should repaint those, he thought. Should do a lot of things to this old house.

Years ago, Fran's father would come home in the evening after his beat on the Avenue and sit there, on the second step, and slowly, carefully, ease out of his uniform greatcoat. All those shining brass buttons, one after the other, pushed carefully through their buttonholes. Fran's mother would be at the stove, making him a fresh cup of coffee, and he would relate the events of his shift, innocuous things, everyday things, never anything like Fran saw on *Highway Patrol* or *Dragnet*, or in the gangster serials Saturday mornings at the Devon. Never any bank robbers, mobsters or shootouts.

Still, every now and then, a six-year-old Fran would be sitting at the same table, in the same seat he was in right now, and he would invariably ask his father, "Shoot that gun today,

Pop?" And every time his father would smile at him, reach into his greatcoat, unbuckle his holster belt and slowly, carefully draw it out. "Thank the Lord, Francis," he would say as he wrapped the supple black leather around the holstered .38 revolver, black on black, oiled and ready, "I did not." He would point a finger meaningfully then, "And if I'm lucky, I never will."

Fran blinked, seeing the old revolver, the oiled leather belt, the brass buttons flashing under the kitchen's fluorescent ring. His father's broad cheeks still pink from the cold. The massiveness of him, black coat, black uniform, black hair thick as a rug. And his china blue eyes. The reality of him, home, safe from another day. Then Fran blinked again, and the step was empty, the kitchen silent. The brass buttons were with the rest of that old coat, packed in mothballs, in the back of an upstairs bedroom closet.

A sunken bloodshot china blue eye, focusing on him from the hospital bed: "*You ain't got it, lad.*"

He heaved himself up, put his plate and glass in the sink, and took the back stairs, back to bed.

8

Arch Street, Center City, Philadelphia
Monday, November 28

The body was in plain sight on the sidewalk, so the police cordon was tight. It was the end of the Monday lunch hour, so the crowd was, too.

Detective Mike Finnean parked his Dodge in the middle of the street and elbowed his way through the gawkers to the sawhorse barricades with all the finesse of a defensive tackle stampeding a cornered quarterback.

He pointed his finger at the patrolman standing over the rumpled plastic tarp. "You first on the scene?"

The patrolman nodded. "I stuck with the body. My partner's upstairs."

Finnean touched the tarp with his toe. "What we got?"

"Hard to tell, Detective. We think his name's Halloran, first name Jeffrey. At first we thought he was a jumper, but the word from upstairs says there was probably a struggle." The patrolman leaned close, and Finnean smelled Brute. "He may have been pushed."

Finnean dropped to his haunches and lifted the plastic. Landed flat on his back, head split open like an overripe melon. His guts must be mush. Probably every major bone shattered too. "How far did he drop?"

"Nineteenth floor. Out of one of those big factory windows way up there." The patrolman pointed; Finnean craned his neck. Another warehouse converted into condos, with all those oh-so fancy and oh-so out-of-code architectural details. Like windows you could fucking *waltz* through.

Finnean returned his attention to the body. "So what's this bullshit about a struggle?"

"Dagliesh, my partner. He's the guy to talk to."

Finnean glanced up at the patrolman sourly. "I'll make a point of doing that. Anything *you* know?"

"Well...the legs..."

Finnean pulled the tarp all the way back. The dead man's pants had been cut, *sliced*, straight down both front creases, beltline to cuffs. Socks too. So had the legs themselves, from hips to ankles, right down to the bone. Surgeon's cuts, perfect, just perfect, like they were trying to—

Then something clicked in the back of Finnean's mind. "We need to get Detective Sergeant Lomax down here," he said.

"Where can we find him?"

"How the fuck should I know?" Finnean dropped the plastic back in place "Just get him here. *Now*."

There was a candy machine in the corner by the stairwell, humming ominously.

Fran paused before it, staring flatly at the selection. Then he dropped in his change and pulled the knob below the Snickers bar, and grunted as he stooped to retrieve the candy from the bin.

He would have eaten it then and there, but being grilled by a force psychologist with chocolate stains on his teeth would probably 'create the wrong impression,' so he dropped the candy in his suit-coat pocket for later.

He went the final few yards down the pale green hall he only saw twice a month, a hall he wished he never had to see again, but that wasn't going to happen anytime soon.

Not if he wanted to remain a cop.

He stood for an extra moment before the door, reading the card in the slot: *J.A. Feldman, PhD, PPD*, then raised his meaty hand and rapped once.

"Come," said a voice from within.

Fran opened the door.

Dr. Feldman rose from behind the rat's-nest clutter of his desk. "Good afternoon, Sergeant Lomax," he said, smiling, and extended his hand. "So it's that time of the month, eh?"

Fran looked at the hand, the immaculately manicured nails, the pink, smooth, probably moist skin, the hairless back, the un-callused palm (the wuss never did an honest day's work in his life), and shook it briefly, then lowered himself into the molded plastic chair beside the psychologist's desk. The plastic squeaked, but held. Doing his level best to hide his irritation and his unease, he said, "How many more of these do we have to do, Doc? I've got three stiffs on my plate already, and there's a full moon tonight."

Feldman sat back, his pasty face falling out of the sunlight. "You don't know how lucky you have it, Sergeant Lomax. Only three? And I'll bet your clients don't even bitch at you about how much work they have, hm?"

Fran grumbled, but said nothing. Instead he stared at his own fingernails, chewed in earnest since childhood, and too far gone now to ever recover.

"There's really nothing wrong with biting your nails, you know."

Fran looked up, folding his hands, hiding the fingertips.

"It's a perfectly acceptable escape mechanism," Feldman continued. "Compensation therapy, if you will. Of course, your fingers look like hell, but that's just the tradeoff."

Fran kept his hands folded in his lap. "I never thought much about it," he said.

"When did you start biting them? Do you remember?"

"I don't know, when I was a kid, I guess. Way back. My dad—"

Feldman raised an eyebrow, just barely, but Fran noticed. "Your father..."

"Nothing," Fran said. "Nothing."

Feldman lightly slapped the clear area of desk in front of him. "Lieutenant Goaz tells me you went back on casework last week."

"I just told you," Fran said slowly, "I've got three stiffs in the morgue right now with nothing solid to bring any of their families for Christmas."

"Two were drug related—?"

"Kid on Locust got a hole in his back the size of a saucer from a .45 slug in the bellybutton over a stinking nickel bag buy. The other was a Main Line idiot in a red BMW trying to score coke in University City at two in the goddamn morning." Fran caught Schuyler's eye. "Psychologist named Serlick. From Bryn Mawr. Big house, in-ground pool, three kids, wife, and a dog who loved him. You acquainted?"

"No, I'm sorry to say I don't know him. *Didn't.*" Feldman spread his hands. "Anyway, and the third?"

"The third." Fran began examining his fingernails again under the edge of the desk, out of the psychologist's line of sight. "The third is..."

"Pretty gruesome, from what I hear. Some sort of cult killing?"

"That's what the *Daily News* says. *Inquirer* hasn't taken up the beat yet."

"Does the publicity bother you?"

"Publicizing an ongoing murder investigation *always* bothers me. It bothers any cop. If there's one thing screws up a case every time, it's the goddamn press." Fran looked up again. "And you can quote me on that."

Feldman laughed good-naturedly. "I'm glad to see some of that deadpan delivery you used to be so famous for is coming back."

"I've got a million of 'em, Doc. A million of 'em." But Fran wasn't smiling.

Feldman said, "Word is you've at least got a suspect."

Fran nodded. "A teenager who lives in the building."

"Strong case, you think?"

"Hell no. He was seen talking to the victim an hour before the murder. No big deal, but that brought him in. Then we matched his hair with some found at the scene. Again, no big deal: the kid used to run errands for the old man, brought him his beer, got him the paper and smokes, all for pocket change." Fran looked sour. "Still, for the moment, he's better than nothing. We've got him locked up, waiting on the D.A. to see if they're interested."

"He proclaims his innocence, I would imagine."

Fran snorted. "He claims the boogeyman killed the old guy, some story about skeleton monsters. Hell, Halloween was just a month ago." He waved his hand. "We'll probably cut him loose tonight."

"Still, you feel you can...handle things?"

"It's my job, Dr. Feldman I come to work every day now and I do my job." He blinked. "I'm fine."

"Lieutenant Goaz's principal concern is, of course, you might not yet be up to the challenge of your casework." Schuyler examined Fran closely for a reaction, but Fran only leaned back and began counting the louvers in the window blind behind the psychologist, squinting into the cold early afternoon light that slanted through. Calmly, calmly.

"After all," the psychologist said, "it has only been a few months since the incident."

"Kill me! Go on! Do it!"

The seven inches of tempered steel blade flashing in the streetlight—
"He wants it? Crazy anglo cop wants it?"
—moving, weaving, headed for home somewhere deep in his belly—

Fran frowned, a line of cold sweat forming at his hairline. The incident. The breakdown.

Feldman was still talking, "—Particularly since the first case to cross your desk is such a...a—"

"Juicy one," Fran offered.

"Exactly so. A *juicy* case, one that—"

"One that should have gone to somebody else, I guess, right?"

"Well."

"Someone who never had a setback, who never stumbled, who never fell off the horse, who never had to prove himself all over again, from square one, with every single member of the force..." Fran leaned forward, wiping the sweat away. "Am I getting close?"

Feldman sighed. "Right on the mark, unfortunately. The reality of—"

"Reality. You want to talk about reality?" Fran placed both of his fists on the edge of the desk. "Reality is having a little bit of self-doubt, just the littlest bit—and to this day I don't even know *what for*—and then having it gnaw at you until it gets big enough and mean enough to turn you into a textbook case of classic depression." His fist rose and lowered: *bam.* "I didn't want to go to work anymore; when I did, I didn't talk to anybody." *Bam.* "Instead, I cultivated this tunnel vision, narrowing everything down to the dead bodies I saw every day, day after day." *Bam.* "I lost weight, the only good goddamn thing to come of this; my skin broke out; I got two ulcers, not one, *two.*" *Bam.* "And one day I just decided that staying home, alone in my apartment, was the best thing in the world for me to do."

"—just do it!"

"—crazy anglo! Can you believe this motherfucker? —"

Feldman lifted his gaze from Fran's fist. "And the Department agreed."

"Yes, yes indeed." Fran wiped fresh sweat from his forehead. "The Department agreed. So they gave me eight weeks to get my act together. I moved back home with my mom, started eating right, took long walks in the park, started seeing *you*, and I waited for the itch to do police work, to get back into my *life*, to come back."

"Which it obviously did."

Fran's grin was macabre. "I was talking about reality, Doc, wasn't I?"

"Yes indeed." Feldman replied quickly. "And that's exactly where I think we should pursue some points today. Why don't you—"

The phone rang.

Feldman raised a finger, and picked up the receiver before the second ring. "Feldman," he said, then, "…Yes, he's here…" glancing at Fran with a raised eyebrow, "… Right now? At this moment…? Of course, I understand." Then he hung up. "They need you at Fourth and Arch."

"Who does?"

"A Detective Finnean."

Fran grimaced as he rose. "I guess you can add another one to my plate, then," he said. "Two weeks?"

Feldman went around his desk to get the door. "Same time, same station."

Fran ate the Snickers on his way downstairs.

Outside, grey clouds gathered over the grey city, and the scummy blood on the sidewalk began to freeze.

From his vantage point nineteen floors above, Fran turned away from the broken window, jammed his hands deeper into his overcoat pockets, and shivered.

Then something caught his eye.

He took his right hand from his pocket and reached out to the molding around the broken window. He ran his fingers down the wood, and felt a subtle, almost invisible carved relief under the glossy white paint.

"That's odd," he muttered. The room, hell, the entire apartment, was decorated slick, with modern laminates, lacquers, glass and tubular stainless steel. No antiques; nothing old.

Except, apparently, for some fancy Victorian (Baroque? Rococo?) molding around one window, the broken one.

File that one away, Frannie, next to the fact you're probably going to have to release your one and only suspect now. Young Jameel's snug as a frigging bug in his juvie holding cell right now. He didn't do this. He couldn't have.

Fran put his hand back into his pocket. Damn, he thought, it's cold in here.

He found Finnean in the kitchen, where it wasn't much warmer. "What did the M.E. say?"

The other detective looked up from pondering the cutlery drawer. "He was probably alive when he hit. Death caused by the fall. Of course, after the other guy got started with his blades, the sorry bastard would have probably bled to death anyway."

Fran nodded to the steak knives, nested neatly in their plastic clips in the drawer, "But he didn't use these."

"There's some blood on them." Finnean pointed. "There, there, and a little bit there."

"But not enough. It's just like the other one. He touched them, *fondled* them, maybe, but he didn't use them." Fran's expression and tone were sober, professional. "He used his own steel."

Finnean pushed away from the counter with his hip. "If this really turns out to be two, that makes it the beginning of a pattern. And if it's a pattern, we're going to have to cut your buck loose. Just what we need, right?"

"Did you hear the story he fed us?"

"Something about monsters?"

"Five minutes in the tank and he starts crowing about ghosts and goblins, skeletons jumping out of closets, in windows from nineteen stories up…. Mulligan was eying him for Detox." Fran sighed. "Is Goaz coming?"

"What do you think? For all I know he's bringing the whole goddamn Seventh Cavalry with him. I think you should stick around. You mind?"

Fran felt the weight of it, the indescribable burden, settle surely on his shoulders; this one, too, would be added to his plate. "Merry Christmas, Mike, a month early."

"Yeah," Finnean said, looking across the vast room with its fancy metal furniture overturned, its glass tabletops smashed, "and a happy fucking New Year to boot."

Lieutenant Goaz pointed a blunt, calloused finger toward Fran, then Finnean, both seated on an uncomfortable black vinyl ottoman already dusted and cleared, as he paced the frigid living room. "They're waiting for us back at the Roundhouse, gentlemen. Halberstadt hasn't come downstairs yet, but if these deaders get to be a habit around here, he will."

"I guess it doesn't take an idiot to smell a connection between the Cherry Street stiff and this one, Lieutenant," Finnean said. He disliked Captain Halberstadt as much as anyone in Homicide.

Fran saw sweat through Goaz's Marine Corps buzz cut, and realized: he's mad; he's *pissed*. Only two deaders and it's already under his skin, here. What gives? He said, "We got Sanderson and Lafferty again from the CL, and Koenig took this stiff too. We've got some continuity right there already."

Goaz snorted a humorless laugh. "We got continuity all right. Jesus Christ, if it's one thing we got, it's fucking continuity." He ran it down on his fingers as he continued to pace: "We got one stiff with all his bones cut out, and the other on the way to the same before he took his dive. We got a murderer—"

"Or murderers," Finnean said. "I can't see one guy pulling this shit off by himself. Two, three, maybe a *team* of them." He chuckled. "Maybe a fucking *coven*."

Goaz clapped his hands together once for effect. "So the Great and Powerful Michael Patrick Finnean introduces 'Religious Cult' to the conversation, does he?"

"Cult murder?" Fran looked skeptically to Finnean. "You really think so?"

The other detective shrugged. "Gotta be more than one doing this, Fran, regardless of how we dress it up."

Fran shook his head slowly, frowning.

Goaz stopped his pacing. "You think it's just one crazy, Fran? We got two stiffs who could have passed for twins: same age, same build, same hair for chrissakes, and how do you get around a complete deboning of a human body? You think that's easy to do? You ever tried it on a goddamn uncooked *chicken*?"

"That's the second time somebody asked me that," Fran said.

"Two guys." Finnean held up fingers. "Two at the most. Any more and we would have found more. This place is as clean as a House Beautiful photo shoot."

"And we're cutting our one loony-bin suspect loose in the morning." Goaz stared grimly at the broken window. Snow had begun swirling in. "We're freezing our asses up here. You!" He pointed to the patrolman standing in the terrazzo marble foyer by the front door. "Get some people up here and seal this window up. A plastic tarp or something."

The patrolman nodded his head without a word and left.

Goaz glanced to Finnean, muttered "Ah, what the hell," then turned to Fran. "I spoke to Feldman before coming down here."

Finnean stood. "I'll…go roust us up some coffee."

"Good idea," Goaz said, not even looking at him. "Make mine black."

"Cream and sugar, Fin-man," Fran said. "Two sugars."

The detective ducked out, into the hallway, and closed the door behind him.

Fran said, "So what does the good doctor have to say, Lieutenant? We didn't really have too long a session today."

"He says I'm crazy if I let you keep your caseload. He says it's too soon."

Bang. There it was. Fran managed a noncommittal shrug. "He's the expert, I guess."

Goaz raised his voice, "So that's it? You're willing to cash in on one shrink's word?"

Fran spread his hands wide. "What kind of clout do I have these days? Hell, I'm walking on eggs every time I show up for work."

"One voice," Goaz said, beginning to pace again, "tells me to leave it alone, to let you and Mike do your thing, get the results you're so famous for. Trouble is, you see, Captains, psychologists and my own goddamn common sense all tell me different." Then he stopped pacing. "So, where does that leave me, Frannie?"

"Backed into a corner as usual, Lieutenant. Listen, without a break, it doesn't matter who's running the show. Without a break, we're all nowhere, you know that as well as me."

Goaz feint-kicked at a shard of glass glinting in the carpet. "Nothing from the street? Nobody's heard anything?"

"Nothing. I don't think these guys are home grown."

"I don't either."

Fran watched him pace, waiting for him to continue. When he didn't, Fran said, "So what's the verdict, Lieutenant?"

Goaz stopped, hesitated, then swung around. "So you and Mike finish up here, then you go home and get a couple of hours sleep. Tomorrow you two jump into it together."

"Teaming us up?"

"Yeah," Goaz said, "the two of you. With both feet."

"Whatever you say, Lieutenant. Actually, when we're done here I was thinking about stopping by the library. Do some background."

"There you go," Goaz said. "The *library*. Sit down with a good book. Clear your brain. Right." He rubbed the top of his buzz cut furiously. "You and your fucking library. *Exactly*."

9

The best time to hit the Periodicals Room microfilm readers was about an hour before closing on a weeknight, Fran had found. There was always a machine free, and the Library Assistant on duty, a furry-headed hippie named Salvador, was always just a step away, big white teeth gleaming from out of his tangled black forest of a mustache.

Tonight, the day of the week and the bad weather (spitting, sleeting snow showers) had both conspired in his favor, because the Periodicals Room was empty when he arrived.

Salvador must have heard the doors bump open, because he was out on the floor immediately, waving a friendly hello. "Hey Detective Lomax," he said, "how come you're not out discoing to the beat?"

"South Street is dead these days, Sal. I don't need to tell you. And anyway, disco is dead."

"I defer to your better judgment." Salvador pulled the dust cover off Fran's favorite reader machine and waited for him to settle himself. "I haven't seen you in a while, figured you took a vacation, or got smart and got your ass out of this city."

"I had some down time, yeah." Fran turned the microfilm machine on to warm up the lamp.

"You're researching another homicide? So what is it, the Arch Street business?"

Fran pulled a notebook out of his coat and fished for a pen that worked. "The newspapers are guessing a suicide, but the guy was cut, knife-cut."

"A struggle upstairs, then?" Salvador made plunging motions. "A crime of passion, perhaps?"

Fran shook his head. "The wounds don't say that." He extended his left leg and ran his forefinger down a pant seam. "Sliced, Salvador, from ass-cheek to ankle, like a flounder fillet. Both legs."

"But he fell nearly twenty stories. That could break a body up."

"*Tear* the skin, maybe, but not cut it, not in straight lines. These were like surgical incisions."

"That wasn't in the article."

Fran looked up, and winked. "Nope, it sure wasn't."

Salvador was silent for a moment, then he snapped his fingers. He looked up into space and quoted, "West Philadelphia stabbing. A sixty-seven-year-old West Philadelphia retired postal worker was found mutilated and stabbed to death yesterday in the 4100 block of Cherry Street. Responding to a call at 11:50 a.m. yesterday, police discovered the body of Edward Copper in the bedroom of his apartment. Copper had been stabbed numerous times, and was pronounced dead at the scene. Police have no motive or suspect in the killing as of late last night." Then he looked down. "Friday, November 25, Daily News, Metro Section, page 2, News In Brief."

"Bravo." Fran clapped briefly. "That one's also one of mine. But Mr. Copper was nothing more than hamburger. Literally. No surgical slicing there."

Salvador blinked, his left hand slowly stroking his mustache. "So this time it's exotic knife slayings?"

"No family disputes, nothing gang related. Maybe youth, but definitely not organized." Fran tapped his pen on an open, empty notebook page, then put it down. "I'm thinking theft related, or cult related: sexual, religious, or fringe-political."

"Old men and their medications." Salvador shrugged.

"Okay, we'll consider a drug angle on the first go-around, but I don't think that will pan out." Fran leaned back, laced his hands together behind his head, and the library chair creaked as he leaned his considerable bulk back. "Glad I showed up tonight?"

"You test my mettle." Salvador rubbed his dark, lean hands together, and grinned. "You are not just my customer, Detective Lomax, you are my *meat*."

Fran rolled his eyes, then unlaced his hands and made shooing motions. "Get out of here before you misquote somebody else, okay?"

Within ten minutes, Salvador returned to Fran's microfilm station with four spools and scribbled location notes on each. *The Bulletin*, 1970 to the day it folded, Fran gathered from the labels. "I haven't touched *The News* yet," Salvador said.

"Don't even bother with the *Inquirer*."

"I hadn't planned on it." Another grin, then he was gone again.

Fran threaded the first spool, spun to the first noted article, read it briefly, then spun to the next. A youth killing, Nazi swastika carved into his belly. Nope. He went on to the last on the spool: barber accident gone suddenly serious, suddenly, weirdly bad. But no, it didn't fit either.

The next spool had only two tagged items, neither of which were any good. As he was reaching for the third spool Salvador arrived with a small cardboard box. "*The Daily News* is always so much fun," he said, setting it down. Fran peeked inside: twelve spools. "No repeats?"

"I'm insulted. I'll go after the ethnic rags next, okay?"

"You are a wonder, Salvador. Has anyone ever told you that?"

"Every night," the young Latino replied, deadpan.

"No, I'm serious."

"So am I." He winked, then was gone again.

A half-hour passed, a parade of twenty-six disfigurements, dismemberments and, more often than not, deaths. But nothing that clicked. Salvador had two other customers, both elderly, matronly women researching old recipes, but he still managed to get Fran back to 1950 with five minutes to spare before the library was to close.

Salvador gathered up the last of the spools, frowning at Fran's empty notebook. "Not even a doodle?"

"Nothing." Fran threw his pen down, and leaned back to massage his eyes.

Salvador began to say something, but hesitated.

Fran focused on him with one bleary eye. "What?"

"You're only interested in recent knifings?"

"What do you mean?"

"I did some work for a Temple economics professor a few weeks ago, got him some source material on the Post World War Two era."

"Post war? What does that have to do with me?"

"Follow me on this, Sergeant, please. There was a string of murders here in the city in 1946." Salvador grinned. "You mentioned hamburger?"

Fran glanced at the clock on the wall. He was supposed to meet Sarah at 9:30. "Bring 'em on, what the hell."

Salvador hefted the cardboard box, snapped his fingers, and was gone.

Behind Fran, almost immediately, the doors to the Periodicals Room opened. He glanced back, and recognized the Head of the Reference Section, a stout, middle-aged black woman with orange hair and freckles, and huge, conical tits that stuck out to *here*. She surveyed the room, then came over to him. "Is Mr. Melendez available?"

"He's in the back," Fran pointed, "getting me a spool. He should only be a few minutes."

"We *close* in just a few minutes." The librarian tapped her watch.

"I won't be long," Fran said. "I promise."

The librarian looked briefly toward the back, frowning vaguely. "Very well, then," she said, and turned back to the doors. "Don't forget to turn the Reader off when you are through, hm?"

"I promise," Fran said again, but she was already gone.

Salvador emerged moments later, whistling, holding two spools.

"Your boss was looking for you," Fran said, taking them from him.

"Ah, Mrs. Franklin. She loves me. They *all* love me."

Fran snorted. "So what's on these?"

Salvador handed him the location notes. "They called him 'The Slaughterhouse Killer'. Never caught."

Fran chuckled. "Hey, I like him already."

"When you read what he did," Salvador said soberly, "you just might change your mind, Sergeant."

Behind Fran, from the vicinity of the double doors, someone cleared her throat. Salvador looked past him, and Fran saw him hesitate. He turned; Mrs. Franklin was standing there, tapping her low pump on the linoleum tile floor. At that moment, the overhead lights blinked once, twice. "I think it's time to leave."

Salvador took back the notes and the spools. "I will keep these for you. Next time, then, Detective Lomax."

1946? That was what, thirty-seven years ago? Still, Fran filed it away. He heaved himself up, nodded to Salvador, and passed the librarian with his best courtly smile. "Have a good evening, madam," he said, and followed the rest of the library patrons streaming to the front doors.

"Three or Four will take you up tonight, Detective Lomax."

Fran nodded silently to the Court House Annex night guard seated comfortably behind his semi-circular security station. In his immaculately tailored uniform and shock of thick, dark hair, he looked better than Fran ever had, or ever would. "Makes twice your salary, too," Sarah had commented once.

Fran's footsteps echoed sharply in the vast, empty lobby atrium. He felt like a mouse in a last, desperate dash for the next shadow, knowing the hawk had him dead in its sights. On either side, huge expanses of glass held the darkened city at bay. This was a truly inhuman place, as inhuman as the courtrooms filling its upper floors. "Nice place you work in," he had observed, the first time Sarah had shown him around. "Real...homey."

"There's a doughnut shop in the basement gallery," Sarah had replied dryly.

"Oh very funny. Very funny indeed." Pause. "Do you think they have coconut creme?"

He reached the bank of elevators at last and depressed the polished UP bar between Numbers Three and Four. The two doors immediately chimed and rumbled open. He stepped into Three. The walls of the elevator were beveled stainless steel, polished to a mirror finish. Jesus Christ, he thought, is my bald spot *that* big?

He touched the button for the twelfth floor where Judge Harris (and a certain auburn-haired Legal Clerk named Sarah Blythe Fitzpatrick) had her office. The doors rumbled closed.

Eleven floors later they opened on soft darkness. Through several transparent walls and occasional oases of ferns, the only pool of light on the entire floor seemed to be in Sarah's area. Fran followed a cautious route across silent seas of beige carpet and between island workstations of walnut and brass, all empty, all shrouded in dust covers emblazoned with the city seal. Then he saw her, bent over a wide, tilted library table, pouring over a jumbled array of papers. Tonight she had on the green two-piece he liked, with a lacy white blouse, opened low, and her auburn hair was down in soft, loose waves. Her face and body simply drove him nuts, always had, always would. The fact that a stunningly beautiful, intelligent, funny and caring person like Sarah Fitzpatrick had fallen, and by all indications fallen very hard, for an overweight, frumpy police detective was one of life's mysteries Fran hoped would never be solved. She was far better than he deserved, but so far anyway, he was managing to get away with it.

She saw him approaching, finally, and straightened with a welcoming smile. "Just in time, Sergeant. I'm almost done."

He slipped his hand around her impossibly slim waist and pulled her to him for a lingering kiss.

"I thought you said on the phone you were feeling depressed," she said with a giggle.

"I did. I am. Are we alone?"

She looked over his shoulder, into the dark sea of workstations. "Yep," she said then, and reached across to turn off the light over the table. Then she hoisted herself up onto it, and proceeded to pull her skirt up over her hips.

Fran whistled low. "Does the Judge know you come to work dressed this way?"

"I took them off a few minutes ago, smarty, on a *whim*." Her smile turned downright naughty. "This sturdy enough for you? Or we could use the floor…"

Fran found himself fumbling with his belt like a teenage kid. "Just move the stapler. I bruise easy."

10

Some might have called them recluses; hermits, even. In the world that was 512 Delancey Street, there was only the two of them. Beyond the motley succession of day help through the years, there had always only been the two of them. There could never have been anyone else. Structure and strict regimen meant safety in their lives...even normalcy, to a degree. There was too much insanity around them, too many enemies, both real and unreal, to ever let the rest of the world in. Every salesman who knocked on their door, every passerby who brushed against William in the street, every face staring blankly back across a crowded store or subway car...everyone was suspect. Any one of them could be one of *them*.

And now, there was only one certainty, one deadly fact: *they* were coming down again. *They* had been reawakened, had noticed, had refocused, had been stirred and angered (was it anger, though? Was it anything he could explain, or rationalize? It was just so confusing), and now *they* were coming down, entering the world, any way *they* could.

Now, at long last, it was only a matter of time.

Their home, their brownstone on Delancey Street, was a fortress. It was a fortress not only against the world, it was a fortress against *them*.

Jack was content with his thick walls, his locks, his newspapers and books, painting skyscapes in his studio, content to be a perpetual observer, a rare animal in his own personal zoo. If the front door to 512 Delancey Street were suddenly locked forever, Jack would only mourn his newspapers, perhaps, or the last tube of oil paint; for the most part he probably would not care; he might not even notice.

"My supplies at Utrecht's is in today, I think."

William, across the dining room table, said nothing.

"New brushes. Winsor & Newton. Special order." Jack looked at him expectantly.

"I don't..." William began. He put his coffee cup down on its saucer with an audible click. "I don't think this afternoon is a good time to go out."

"But the London papers are in today. I thought you could do both in one quick trip."

Why am I hesitating, William wondered. We both know only I can do this. He picked his coffee up again. "I'm sorry, of course, I'll go right after dinner."

The lines of concern on Jack's forehead cleared. "Utrecht's is open till nine. Could you get me a large tube of burnt umber as well?"

Outside, a strong but cold sun cast long, dark shadows across the sidewalks. Utrecht's Art Store was on Walnut Street, and three blocks east was the international news kiosk, where Walnut intersected Broad. A ten-minute errand, at best. William knew the route by heart. The passersby crowding the sidewalk were mundane, easily dismissed. This will be fine, he decided. This will not be a problem.

But instead of crossing Walnut and turning left, he found

himself continuing north, to Chestnut, weaving his way through the crowds of shoppers there, then to Cherry, where the crowds thinned and the shadows gathered. What is this? Why am I doing this?

A bitingly cold wind struck him, enveloped him. He closed his eyes, and pulled his coat lapels up against his cheeks. When he opened them, he found he was on Arch Street at the place where the Lennard Building had once stood, where a doorway to The Boneyard had once been opened, and now was apparently open once more. The murder scene.

He stopped next to a bus stop shelter, out of the flow of the early evening pedestrian traffic, and looked across the street at the empty lot, a large flat rectangle of gravel and broken brick covering the foundation of the old Lennard Building, then up at the apartment building next to it, the converted mill. A sudden thought erupted: We should have bought this property also. We should have leveled it like we leveled the Lennard, and kept it all, both the ground and the volume of air above, all of it, *empty*.

They were up there; he knew it, felt it like an itch in the center of his brain; *they* were up there, watching, waiting. He dug his hands deep in his overcoat pockets, clutching them into secret fists (Enough!), and counted the stories of the apartment building. He stopped at the nineteenth floor, and his eyes traveled across to the window boarded up with two full sheets of plywood. Large, star-shaped bolts protruded, holding the plywood in place.

Come up, The Boneyard whispered, through that itch in the center of his head. *Here, Billy...up here.*

My GOD! Why did I come here?

The traffic in the street slowed and stopped for a red light. A country-western Christmas song blared from a half-open car window. Someone on the sidewalk yelled for someone else to slow down, dammit, or they were going to have a goddamn coronary. A truck horn blatted; bus brakes gasped and hissed. The light changed, and the country-western song moved on down the street.

William remained beside the bus stop enclosure, looking up, oblivious to it all.

"Hey, man, what you looking at?"

Someone stepped up to stand beside him, a bum, dishwater-colored hair spiked below a raveled knit watch cap, the rest of him bundled in grey, ratty clothes. He rubbed his stubbly chin with red, raw hands, half-moons of grime beneath cracked fingernails, his eyes moist, rheumy, faded green. He coughed, cleared his throat, and looked up too. "That's where he jumped from, man," he said.

William ignored him. In his mind, he saw the victim leaping, twisting, falling...and he saw what peered out past the broken window glass, watching him go down.

"Suicide," the bum continued. "You know, man, the jumper. Swan dive to splat." He pointed to the sidewalk in the blue shadow of the building. A knot of yellow crime-scene tape still fluttered from a sign pole. "Right over there, man. That's where he hit." The bum coughed again, hawked, and spat into the gutter. "Swan dive to splat city."

William looked down finally, and gave the bum a brief, appraising look before turning and walking quickly away.

"I saw the whole thing!" the bum yelled after him. "I saw when he hit!" His hand went to his chin again, rubbing. Then he looked back at the patch of sidewalk across the street. "Saw the whole thing," he repeated, to himself, drawing down to a rough whisper. "Swan dive to splat city, man. Swan dive to splat."

Directly across the street, a dark figure, a man, detached himself from the deepest of the building shadows. As he reached the curb, a brass bar of remaining sunlight struck him, illuminating his dark, oddly cut clothes, his long, unkempt, chestnut hair, his pale, mottled face. He entered the street, walking through the traffic as though it wasn't there. Brakes squealed; a motorist cursed him loudly. The dark man reached the other side of the street untouched, directly in front of the bum in the grey clothes. For the briefest moment their eyes met, then the dark stranger was gone, into the pedestrian crowd, in the same direction William had taken.

"Hey," the bum called after him, reaching for his chin, "cool tats, man!"

By the time he reached Walnut Street, William knew he was being followed. A dark figure, long dark coat, dark hair, always too far back to see clearly, but following him, definitely following him.

He stopped at a store window, pretending to look at the display of woman's clothing and handbags there, but really watching the reflections of the passing pedestrians behind him. His eyes darted, moving from face to face. The dark figure, the stalker, wasn't among them.

He continued walking, aware of how long he had been away, how long he had left Jack alone in the townhouse. You fool! What were you thinking? When he reached the international editions newsstand on Broad Street he stopped and waited his turn. His unplanned sojourn up to the scene of the Arch Street murder had been a stupid, stupid mistake. William spied a dark figure a block away, in the shadow of a marble doorway, watching while a man in front of him bought a Cairo paper printed in scrolling Arabic.

"Same old same old, sir?" The news-seller lifted a short stack of different newspapers tied with twine and dropped it on the narrow plywood counter. William handed him a five-dollar bill, took the bundle, and shoved it securely under his arm. "Thank you, Fred," he said. "Please, keep the change."

It was five blocks east to Seventh Street, then three blocks south to Pine. William hurried in the gathering twilight, losing most of the pedestrian crowd as he moved from commercial to largely residential streets. At every corner he paused to look back. Only once he thought he glimpsed the dark man, but the lengthening shadows under the violet sky were nearly impenetrable, and the figure who emerged was just a balding man in a brown overcoat, walking home from work. William passed an elderly woman dragging a supermarket-shopping cart filled with bulging plastic bags, and a tall man with a silver handlebar mustache carrying an expensive leather briefcase. "Excuse *me*," the mustached man said, as William brushed past him.

Approaching Locust Street, he thought he heard footsteps behind him, matching his own. This is ridiculous, he thought. Who was this person? Why would he be following me? Not a mugger, surely, all this way. A policeman? A detective? But that made no sense either. No one knew. No one *could* know. You *are* a fool, he scolded himself. A scared, stupid fool.

Still, while he waited at the corner for the WALK sign to flash, he grabbed his bundle of newspapers with both hands and whirled around, quickly scanning the dark street behind him. The people there either studiously avoided his gaze, or looked at him like he was a crazy man. But the dark stranger was not among them. Crazy man indeed, he thought, turning back.

The light turned green, and the WALK sign glowed. Stopping a turning cab with a look, he crossed the street.

Pine Street between Sixth and Seventh was largely deserted. He hurried down the sidewalk, avoiding the icy patches, warmed by the pools of yellow light spilling down the brick and marble steps of the townhouses, and the occasional display of Christmas lights framing front doors, or blinking out from behind the old, wavy glass panes of tall front parlor windows. He saw a police car cross the intersection ahead of him, going south on Sixth, and that warmed him as well. There were no following footsteps here; there was no dark figure, standing at the corner. Home was in sight.

When he reached Delancey he went past the front door of Number 512 to the barrel-vaulted side passage that led to the rear courtyard. There were wrought iron gates at either end. William unlocked, entered, closed and relocked the front gate with a quick, practiced motion. He looked back through the bars to the street. No one was there. No dark figure. Just a plastic Santa Claus, glowing in a window across the way. You old fool, he scolded himself yet again, and turned to walk down the dark passage.

The inner gate screeched as it swung open. William turned as he passed through, his eyes registering the brick walls of the courtyard, the snow-dusted ivy, the pale grey cobbles, the black, glittering Bentley parked facing the alley gates, all this in the moment it took to get beyond the swing of the inner gate and begin to push it closed.

But then he stopped, and turned toward the steps leading up to the back door of the townhouse.

The dark man stood there at the bottom of the steps.

His hair hung in oily strings, obscuring his face, spilling down over a black, ragged, threadbare suit coat. His pants were baggy, caked and shiny with grime, ripped in one knee, and raveled over black, scuffed boots. His filthy hands hung loosely at his side, their long, thin fingers with yellowed fingernails curled slightly into his palms. He couldn't have been more than thirty, but he looked...*old*. It's the clothes, William realized, and the filth. A bum, probably a drug addict. A mugger after all. Then: *can I take him?*

William took a step forward, raising his voice: "This is private property! You're trespassing!"

The dark figure slowly shook his head.

William dropped the newspaper bundle and grabbed a broom leaning against the rear stoop, and used it to point to the alley gate. "I don't know who you are, but I want you out of here now!" He took another step forward, raising the broom. "I said—"

"You don't know me, Billy?"

The sound of the intruder's voice stopped him in mid-stride. It was a bare whisper, paper thin; its tone spoke of infinite loss, infinite sadness, age beyond counting. The figure raised his hand, pointing a pale finger at him. "But I know you," he said, and swung his arm to point, now, at the back door of the townhouse. "And I know *him*."

William stared at the intruder's hand with sudden, startling recognition. The exposed skin, bloodless, wrinkled parchment, had *scars*. Impossibly thin, impossibly straight. Dozens of them.

"Little Jack," the intruder whispered. "Little nephew."

William lunged with a cry, swinging the broom to knock him down, but the intruder eluded him, sliding to the side with surprising speed. William fell heavily, cracking his elbow on the cobbles. Ignoring the flaring pain, he rolled to his knees, then back to his feet, and raised the broom again.

"They resurrected me, Billy," the dark man said, his face free of hanging hair now, his cheeks and forehead a patchwork of scars and wrinkles, a young man's face, but so very old, used, dead. "I'm just their messenger. I'm paper, I'm wind. I'm nothing, any more. I'm just a voice, a message." He raised his arms, his elbows at an impossible angle. "I can't hurt you."

"Get away from the steps!" William lunged again, missed, again.

"End this," the dark man whispered, "Return to them, both of you, or they will surely come for you, take you, *reap* you." He shook his head again, and a tuft of hair fell to his coat front. "The deaths, Billy, the deaths of the innocent. Their blood is on you. It's always been on you, and on Jack."

"It's not Jack's fault!"

The dark man looked at him. "You're right," he said. "It's *you*. It's always been you. You failed, Billy. You failed us all."

"No!" William raised the broomstick and held it poised like a baseball bat. "I *won!*" He lunged and swung the broomstick one more time; this time the dark man did not elude him but took the blow on his side, a solid hit. He made a soft, huffing sound, and small clouds of what looked like yellowed cellophane, a confetti of desiccated flesh, erupted from his collar and cuffs. He staggered back, collapsing, and William saw more dried flakes of skin on the cobbles, spilling out from under the stranger's pant legs. "My God," William gasped, "*who are you?*"

A whisper, a sigh, dissipating in the rising cloud, lost in the darkness: "*Lucian.*"

The tattered black clothes folded in on themselves, and fell in an empty heap on the courtyard cobbles.

Jack roused from his nap at the sound of William's steps, coming up the stairs. The daylight was gone, and it was dark in his studio. He reached to pull the chain of the floor lamp beside his chair, flooding the room in warm yellow light. William appeared in the doorway. "You're late," Jack said, reaching for the copy of the London Times William held in his hand. Then he noticed the left elbow of William's jacket was ripped, and his shirt as well, spotted with blood. "What happened?"

William put his hand over the elbow. "A bit of ice," he said. "It's nothing." He paused. "I'm sorry for taking so long."

Jack snapped the newspaper flat, laying it in his lap. "I was napping anyway. Did you get the package from Utrecht's?"

"No. I forgot. I'm sorry."

"Well, it's too late to go back for it now." Jack waved his hand. "Nothing that can't wait till tomorrow. Go take care of that elbow, will you? We can't afford to have two cripples around the place."

William hesitated.

"Was there something else?"

"No," William said. "Pork loin for dinner tomorrow."

"And carrots. I feel like having carrots."

William nodded. "Carrots it is, then."

11

"Hey," the blonde said, as her bra and panties hit the carpet, "you weren't shittin' me; you *can* see Independence Hall from up here."

The old man on the bed said, "Well I can see heaven from where I'm sitting, sweetheart. Screw Independence Hall and come over here."

She turned from the glittering evening cityscape outside, smiling, "Did somebody say *screw?*" I've got my work cut out for me tonight, she thought, glancing at his white, flaccid penis. She shook her breasts, her smile turning hot and full of promise, but the old guy's prick didn't even stir. Oh yeah, time to earn it, girl. But the insistent pressure of her bladder said otherwise. "Listen, honey," she said as she swung around the bed and gave him a quick, licking kiss, "I've got a minute of business in the little girl's room. You think up all the ways I'm gonna make you scream tonight, and I'll be right back." She quickly entered the bathroom and closed the door behind her.

As she discarded her panties and sat down on the toilet, she heard the bed on the other side of the wall creak, then heard a quiet, muffled curse from the old man. In the silence that followed, her streaming piss in the tiny room sounded like Niagara Falls. "I'm almost there, baby," she said through the door. She reached for the toilet paper, then heard a sudden intake of breath, and a short, gurgling cry. "Oh my God," she whispered slowly. What's he having out there, a heart attack? "You okay, baby?"

On the other side of the wall, then, there was the quiet sound of wet ripping, of sucking...of something very, very bad.

The blonde grabbed a rough bath towel from the wall rack and threw it around her, then wrenched the door open and stumbled into the bedroom. She immediately slipped on something warm and wet, and fell flat on the carpet.

The towel dropped away as she twisted around. She grabbed for it as she looked up, and there on the bed...

There on the bed...

She saw the john, lying on his back, arms and legs splayed out, jerking, writhing, splattering blood and bits of raw and glistening meat and tissue, and something was crouched on his chest and belly, a writhing mass of something white, working on him, working *into* him, ripping, slicing, sucking—

She scrambled to her feet, slipping again on the blood pouring off the bed. She made little mewling sounds, and swung awkwardly around to get to the door, to get the hell *out* of—

And fell headlong into something slime-soft, a wriggling knot of snakes with open, gaping mouths rimmed with razor teeth, just like the nightmare things furiously working their way into the john's body on the bed.

She screamed, flailing her arms, knocking the things away from her, and felt something sharp, a sudden burning on her arm. Looking down, she saw blood pulsing out of a deep slice in her flesh. Then the white worms were at her again, and she felt another explosion of heat and pain as she spun about, shrieking, and slammed herself against the door to the hall, fumbled for the knob, grasped it, and pulled desperately as the nightmare things pursued her. A razor mouth reached her, bit her, slicing effortlessly into her left hip. Blood, warm and thick, sheeted down her thigh.

Then she was in the hall, sprawled on the worn, Oriental rug runner. She got to her knees, choking, then to her feet, and careened down the hall to the elevators.

There was a bank of three, and the center one was open. She grasped at the rubber gaskets of the door edges and threw herself inside. Hauling herself up by the side rail, she pounded at the floor buttons. There was a scrambling, slapping sound outside, coming down the hall. "Oh God damn it!" she cried, slamming the flat of her blood-slicked hand on the buttons. The air smelled like dust frying on an old light bulb, like something scorched to ashes, and she knew it was just six feet away, then two...

Then the elevator chimed, and the doors rumbled shut just as a spray of worms appeared, their open mouths biting at the edge. The door dragged their teeth along until only one tooth protruded into the car, caught fast in the rubber gasket. It was small and flat and impossibly sharp, twisting about like a bug on a pin. She crawled backward to the rear of the car, staring at the tooth in horrified fascination, knowing that as the doors settled shut they would sense it, and would open again, and she started screaming again.

But the doors remained shut, the elevator engaged, and the tooth snapped free, falling harmlessly to the floor. She looked at it, in a growing red haze of pain, all the way down.

On the first floor, the night security detective managed to grab her in her gibbering waltz toward the lobby doors. She collapsed into his arms, and he was able to wrap his big suit-coat around her to hide her bleeding nakedness. "My God, little lady," he gasped, "you're really—my *God!*"

The Thursday night shift was half gone. Fran sat alone in his cubicle, mulling over the assembled facts of the two murders, and what he could cull from all of it, which was a suitcase full of nothing.

That prick Koenig had squeezed a preliminary autopsy report out of his ass on the Arch Street stiff only after Fran's fifth call, and it wasn't worth any more than the one he'd done on the West Philly stiff. And the Crime Lab duo of Lafferty and Sanderson had likewise come up short: no other blood types found, no fiber samples that sat up and wagged their tails, nothing that didn't belong, or couldn't be explained outright or rationalized after five minute's of sober thought. Two complete neighbor canvases had been done, both locations, and except for the Jameel statement, Nobody Saw Nothing. Nobody Heard Nothing. None of his snitches had anything either, which in itself was a little weird, and someone in the Homicide Squad Room said they'd seen Captain Halberstadt nosing around just before shift change. Great.

There was the historical info Salvador had dug up for him Monday night that he still had to go back to see, the Slaughterhouse Killer who had apparently raged up and down the rags for a few weeks in the mid 1940s, but it was a nearly forty year gap between those homicides and these. Forty years might as well be forty *light* years. Fran made a mental note, anyway, to go back to the library to check it out.

Great. Just great.

"You still here, Fran?"

Fran looked up. John Moyer, Dick Second, stood by in the doorway with a Styrofoam cup of coffee in his hand. "I decided to do a double, Johnny," Fran said. "Why the hell are you still here? Don't you have one of those things they call a 'family'?"

"They're at the Civic Center." Moyer grimaced. "Sesame Street On Ice." He took a sip of his coffee, and grimaced again.

Fran chuckled. "Suddenly it all becomes clear."

"Listen." Moyer rapped Fran's desk with a free knuckle. "I

ran into Otto in the john. Says he might have something for you and Mike."

"Otto?" Fran reached across and lifted a heavy manila file. "We've got all his pretty pictures right here. What else does he have?"

"Didn't say. I think he must have hemorrhoids or something. Does most of his best bullshitting sitting on the can." Moyer pushed off. "Hey, don't kill yourself on this, okay? Anything surfaces, it'll still be there in the morning."

Fran began to reply, but then his phone rang.

Moyer paused at the door.

Fran lifted the receiver to his ear. "Lomax."

"Sergeant Lomax? It's good you're still here. This is Officer Mallon in Ops. Detective Finnean wants you at the Ben Franklin on Chestnut ASAP."

"Crap," Fran said, straightening. "What have we got?"

"Another one, Sarge. Two, actually."

"I'm on my way." Fran dropped the receiver back in its cradle.

"Don't tell me," Moyer said, "number three?"

"And maybe four." Fran rose heavily, reaching for his coat.

"What'd you and Mike step in," Moyer said as he passed, "to get so goddamn lucky?"

There was a TV van parked at the curb, Fran saw, Channel Six, The Action News Van, but it was too late for a crowd in this part of town, thank God. He breezed past the van, but the soundman sitting in the open back recognized him, and yelled to the reporter on the curb.

"Excuse me!" the woman reporter called out, running around the van in a sequined evening dress and high heels. They must have rousted her from someplace nice. Fran motioned to the nearest uniform and rolled his eyes in the direction of the reporter, and the broad young cop stepped smartly across the sidewalk to intercept her. "Nobody past the lobby doors," Fran said to the other patrolman by the entrance.

"Detective upstairs already laid that one down, Sarge," the officer said. "We'll keep them out of your way; don't you worry."

He raised the yellow tape, entered the lobby, closed the doors firmly behind him, and looked around. Only two things were of obvious interest: the trail of bloody footprints across the gaudy carpet from the center elevator, and a lumpy yellow plastic sheet on the lobby floor where the prints ended. Fran recognized the patrolman standing by the sheet. "How goes it, Woz?"

Corporal Wozniak nodded to him. "Couldn't be quieter, Sarge. Not a peep out of our young lady here." He nudged the sheet gently with his shoe.

Fran squatted, lifted the plastic, and surveyed the corpse. "One hooker, down for the count. I see three significant blade wounds: arm, thigh and lower abdomen." The abdomen cut was ragged, could be multiple cuts, but the other two were clean. The carpet had taken a lot of blood. "She bled out here."

Wozniak nodded. "In the arms of the house dick, by the looks of his clothes. He's in one of the offices behind the main desk, with the night manager and the desk clerk. Do you want me to get him?"

"Let him keep for now," Fran said. "The other body's upstairs?"

"Room 1934, an out-of-towner called Silborough. I tell you, Sarge, fifteen years on a beat I never seen anything like it."

Fran's expression was impassive. "CL done with the elevator?"

"Just a cursory. It's still off limits, but there's nothing in it except her blood. She came down alone, or so the house dick tells it."

"Is it locked?"

"I don't think so, Sarge."

"Shit. Anyone else been down?"

"Except guests we put in the bar or sent outside? Not since

I've been here."

Fran went over to the center elevator, avoiding the blood and footprints, and pushed the UP button with his longest fingernail. The doors chimed open immediately, and a breath of rich, slaughterhouse air enveloped him. He gave the carpet inside a serious look, and after a moment noticed something white against the blood-soaked burgundy and cream of the pattern.

A small flat tooth.

He donned latex gloves from his left coat pocket, and took a plastic baggie from his right. Stooping, he reached into the car, picked the bone up with one swift motion, and deposited it neatly into the baggie. He held up it to the light. It looked definitely like a flat curved tooth. Except for a little pink smudge of blood on one end it was a pure, desert-dry white, straight out of a cartoon or a B horror flick. "What the hell," he whispered.

Then he reached into the car and touched the edge of the DOOR CLOSE button. The elevator chimed, and the doors closed.

Behind him, Wozniak said, "Find something in there?"

Fran ignored the question. He said, "Tell the manager I want this car locked immediately." He gestured to the elevator on the left. "This one cleared?"

The patrolman nodded.

Nineteen floors. The stairs would probably do him some good. That, or kill him.

He took the elevator.

Emerging into the nineteenth floor hallway, Fran was immediately assailed with more slaughterhouse air, heavy, nauseating. He took in a shallow breath of it, and proceeded down the hall, not needing the room number to find where he had to go, he just followed the blood.

The door to 1934 was wide open. Two patrolmen stood outside it, and they nodded to him as he swept past. Inside, the Crime Lab team of Lafferty and Sanderson was standing by the big king-sized bed. Across from them was Mike Finnean.

"Welcome to the party, Frannie," Mike said. "Have a look at our guest of honor."

"Nobody locked the elevator," Fran said.

"Oh holy crap—"

Fran raised a hand. "Forget it; it's done." He approached the bed, gripped Lafferty's shoulder briefly as he reached his side, then looked down.

Silence for a moment, then another. Then Fran said, "They didn't finish with this one."

"Either that," Lafferty agreed, "or they're just playing a new game."

"Don't quote me," Sanderson said, "but I think all of his skeleton is still here. The major bones, anyway."

The bones, all glistening red, brown and purple, were neatly piled up conical fashion in the center of the bed, surrounded by a lake of blood and tattered, shredded viscera. On top of the bone pile, perched neatly, the skull leered.

Fran frowned, his eyes darting. "Where's the rest of him?"

"Over there." Mike motioned to the gap between the side of the bed and the wall. Fran trod the brown paper to where the other detective pointed, and found the victim's skin, organs and major muscle groups lying like a discarded suit of clothes on the sodden carpet. Marbled yellow fat and darkening blood. "It's nearly complete," he said, "isn't it? The vic's skin? In one piece?"

Lafferty said, "When the M.E. gets it back to the Morgue we'll spread it out, get some prints to you. But I think you're right. The cutter's a genius with a blade."

"There's so much blood," Mike mused," "you'd think there would be more than one set of footprints exiting the room, but there's just the hooker's, and some odd smearing. If I wasn't numbed by all this shit I'd be royally pissed, you know?"

Fran looked to the window, wide sash, old-fashioned double-hung, unbroken glass. Except for some air-flung blood splatter, the sill was unblemished. Cream-colored enamel, several layers thick. The casings were heavily carved: scrolls and whorls, a snaky, wormy pattern. That rang a bell. Where had he seen this before? Arch Street. The broken window. He said, "No one's come or gone through this window?"

"Working hypothesis for the moment," Mike said, "the killer took the same elevator down after the hooker did, and in the confusion in the lobby he got away."

"And left no prints?"

Mike spread his arms. "Left *nothing*."

Sanderson cleared his throat.

"Preliminary," Mike said, giving Sanderson a wink, "of course."

Fran pulled the bagged tooth out of his pocket, and tossed it to him. "Except this. It was in the elevator."

Mike gave it a quick scrutiny, then handed it to Sanderson, who shook his head dubiously. "This is too clean. And what's it from, anyway, Dino the Dinosaur?"

"You found this in the elevator?" Lafferty took the bag from his partner. "We're gonna need another CL team."

"Dream on, guys," Mike said.

Fran said, "Wozniak downstairs mentioned a house dick."

Mike gestured at the pile of flesh on the floor. "You want to do him?"

"Not unless you'd rather."

"Nah," Mike said, "I'll stay up here. I'm already used to the stink."

The hotel security head's name, Fran learned from the night manager, was Evan, Frank Evan. He was in his late fifties, a bit overweight, and he was still smeared and soaked with the hooker's blood. He looked pale enough for a transfusion.

Evan cleared his throat, nodding to acknowledge Fran's shield. "I guess you want to talk to me, Detective?"

Fran looked over to the night manager in his ill-fitting suit. "Is there someplace private where Mr. Evan and I can talk?"

"Yeah. Sure, sure. My office?" The manager, his perfectly round bald spot gleaming under the naked fluorescents, led them down a short, cluttered hallway to a small cubbyhole of a room with printed paneling and no window. He quickly cleared his desk of the remains of a Burger King dinner, dumped a pile of catalogs and *Penthouses* off the room's only chair, then exited with an odd, nervous little bow.

The door closed. Fran motioned to the chair, and the hotel security dick dropped into it.

"So, Mr. Evan," Fran said, leaning back against the desk, pulling out his notebook and pen, "you were in the lobby when the victim exited the elevator?"

Evan nodded. "I do a sweep every hour or so. I try to mix it up."

"What time was this particular sweep?"

"Around ten-thirty. The place was pretty dead. I guess it was lucky I was there when she came out. She was bleeding pretty bad."

"So what did you do when she came out, Mr. Evan?"

"Well, she was naked, and I saw right away she was hurt, so I took off my suit coat and wrapped it around her, you know, to cover her."

"The body is only a few steps away from the elevator. How did she end up there?"

Anger flashed briefly in Evan's eyes. "Because she *died* there. She just started going limp, and I couldn't hold her up. She just slid to the floor and then didn't get up."

"I see." Fran made a few bullshit notes, giving him a chance to calm back down. Then, "Did she say anything before she died?"

"Only crazy stuff. She was raving."

"Crazy stuff." Fran tilted his head, pen poised. "What crazy stuff?"

Evan rubbed his forehead. "Something about worms."

Fran looked up. "Worms?"

"Yeah. That's what she said. She said the worms were coming. She said the worms were gonna get her." Evans spread his hands. "See? Crazy."

12

Downstairs in the rear parlor, William heard something fall in Jack's studio a floor above, then the sound of a heavy chair being pushed back, and erratic footsteps, the bump-step of cast and shoe, entering the upstairs hall. *Where is he going?* William put the newspaper aside and pushed up from his chair. He heard Jack on the stairs to the third floor. *He's going to the roof!*

He took the back stairs, past Jack's living quarters on the second floor, and his own on the third. A flood of cold air engulfed him as he made his way up the empty back hallway; the blue night glow of the city flooded the narrow staircase at the far end. Jack had somehow made it up them already.

He emerged onto the roof, his slippers sinking into a thin crust of old snow. The townhouse roof was flat, graveled, with a gentle pitch to the rear. There were two brick chimneys and three pipe vents. A clear path of footprints and a dragged cast led around the front chimney north and east to the cornice wall overlooking the street.

He found Jack leaning against the front cornice wall, staring out over the buildings of Old City toward the clock tower of Independence Hall and the taller buildings along Chestnut Street. William came up beside him, and they both stood with their arms wrapped tight, shivering in the night air. "They're trying again," Jack said in a strained voice, after a moment. "The pull. Can you feel it?"

William was silent.

"Someone just died."

William only nodded.

"I didn't use to care, in the beginning, when it was new, when I was strong." Jack looked at William. "It was a war, you know? Them against me, against us. And wars meant casualties."

William said nothing. He saw Jack's grip on himself begin to relax. The worst of it was over. This time.

"I'm tired," Jack said. "Of this. Tired of all this."

William turned, seeking out his footprints in the snow. "So am I," he said.

"It's time to do something," Jack said.

William stood perfectly still. "What do you mean?"

"Time to stop hiding. Time to take the war to *them*."

"It all began at the tree," William said, after a moment.

"Yes. That damned tree." Jack shivered. "We'll start there."

Fran counted two ace hookers and four drunken pigshitters littering the Operations Room as he walked through it with his case box under his arm. It was a little past three in the morning. Hello, Friday. "Kind of slow," he said to the duty sergeant as he passed him, who shrugged. He kicked the first tank room door open, slapped the light switch on, dropped the box on the table, and then swung the door shut. He dumped the box over, and spread its meager contents out before him.

Four deaders, now. And the night wasn't over yet.

He put the photographs of the victims who had retained

their faces in death in the center; on the left, he put the Atlantic City photo of victim number one, blown up and sans the wife; beside it, a portrait photo of the Arch Street jumper, found in a drawer in his apartment. On the right, he laid down a fresh composite drawing of the face that had gone with the pile of bones on the bed at the Ben Franklin. They looked like triplets.

He hesitated, holding the morgue shot of the hooker. She obviously didn't fit. All of the others had been males in their mid to late sixties; all had had a full head of white or silver grey hair; all had been six feet tall or taller. The hooker, blond, thirtyish, five-four, had just been in the wrong place at the wrong time.

Fran put her photo to the side, and pushed the composite drawing over toward the center. Three dead old men, the first a retired Postal worker, the second an investment banker, and the third a sales rep from Milwaukee, in town for a concrete aggregate convention.

Murder number one—Copper—had occurred in the morning hours of November 24, death by stabbing and evisceration. Murder weapon, a blade of some kind, currently unaccounted for. The victim's bones (all of them) had been removed from the scene as well.

Murder number two—Halloran—had occurred around noon on November 28, a stabbing complicated by a probable escape leap out a nineteenth story window. Murder weapon, a filleting knife or worse, was likewise missing. The victim had jumped before his bones could be excised and, presumably, removed from the scene.

Murder number three, in an Old City hotel room late on December 1. A Joseph Silborough. The bones had been cut out of the body, but they had not been taken. The victim's skin and musculature had been left nearly intact, though the viscera had been dealt with almost carelessly; still, this time there had been less of the frenzied slashing and chopping exhibited by the first murder. Bladed weapon, once again, nowhere to be found.

Murder number four, the hooker, was apparently incidental,

but death for her had also come by way of a blade. Everything pointed to a very sharp deboning or filleting knife, but the kitchen staff at the hotel (all three of them, at that time of night) had no such knives missing as far as they could determine. Everything they did have, of course, had been confiscated for tests.

Fran stared dully at the four piles. The connections, the threads of a common killer, were clear enough, but not enough to hang anything on. There were no fingerprints, and no blood other than that of the victims. No consistent hair or fiber samples. Nothing on the bodies, under fingernails, or in what was left of their mouths, or in their bowels. Nothing on their clothes. Nothing foreign, except perhaps the weird little claw or tooth in the elevator, had been left at the crime scenes to indicate any avenue of investigation whatsoever.

No leads. No meat. Nothing to chew on, or even to gnaw at.

There was nothing but gruesome, inhuman, incomprehensible slaughter.

There was, of course, the two statements made by the witness Jameel at the Copper scene and the hooker at the Silborough scene. About the monsters, the skeletons, the worms. The bones and the worms were coming to get them.

The fucking *bone worms*.

Fran's fist came down with enough force to hurt.

Good, he thought. Maybe I broke something.

Grimacing as he flexed the hand, he stared again at the faces, the lists, the reports. There had to be something here, something he was missing. Maybe the M.E.'s report on this one would—

The door behind him opened.

Fran turned. "Who the hell—!"

It was Otto Gustafson, the old police photographer.

"Otto, it's past three o'clock in the goddamn morning. What the hell are you doing here?"

"I'm saving your fat and sorry ass, Frannie, that's what I'm doing." The old man plopped into the tank's only other chair. His coke-bottle glasses flashed under the fluorescents, and he smelled like he needed a shower. In his hand was a Xerox of a newspaper clipping. He pulled a Mars Bar out of his shirt pocket and threw it across the table to Fran. "Here. Breakfast's on me."

Fran smiled in spite of his mood, grabbed the candy up, ripped it open, and bit off a substantial chunk. "So," he said, chewing, "what've you got there? A signed confession?"

"Funny man." Otto spread the paper out flat on the table. "After that first homicide, the one I covered, I got this thing, this memory, nagging at the back of my brain. 'Jesus H. Christ,' I say to myself, 'there's something funny about this, something goddamn funny,' you know?"

"This whole thing's a regular riot, Otto." Fran took another bite. "So what did you remember?"

"An old friend of mine, real old, another cop crime scene photographer, you know? Name of Lester. Lester Blue. Did his best work early, during Prohibition, followed Legs Diamond around before the bastard went up to New York and got famous, all that crap, but Lester was just a snot-nosed kid back then, sniffing out crime scenes, using a big old Leika four by five he'd gotten out of hock." Otto tapped the Xerox with his forefinger. "He eventually joined the Force, got to do his photography legit. He and I crossed paths, back in the 1950s, before he retired. He told me a story once, about a string of homicides he covered after the War, World War Two, 1946." Otto raised his finger to his head. "I remembered this. I said to myself, Fran Lomax maybe could use this. So I figured what the hell, I've got a few breaths left, I'll do some digging."

1946? Those last two spools of microfilm Salvador had found for him...The Slaughterhouse Killer...the ones he hadn't had time to look at before being kicked out... "So what'd you dig up? An engraving of Ben Franklin bopping Betsy Ross?"

"Shut up and read this, you ungrateful sonofabitch." Otto shoved the paper across the table.

Fran picked it up. It was a clip from the *Bulletin*, circa October 1946. "'Slaughterhouse Killer' Mystery Deepens" was the headline. Under it: "Police baffled by brutal murders." His eyes jumped to the first paragraph, and he read the piece line by line with increasing intensity. When he was done and looked up, his face was pale. "It's the same as our killer. The same."

Otto nodded soberly. "Damn right. Same damn thing all over again. Only back then the bastard confined himself more or less to one building."

"The Lennard Building on Arch. I don't place it. What's it called now?"

"It's not called anything now. It got torn down that same year." Otto leaned forward. "Next door to the warehouse condo where your Number Two took his nose dive on Monday. It says there the murders in the Lennard all took place in apartments on the highest floors, some on the nineteenth floor, did you notice? The investment banker in the co-op on Arch lived on the nineteenth floor, didn't he? Coincidence?" He looked at Fran carefully through his thick-lensed glasses. "As for me, I'm going to remember those never-ending goddamn flights of stairs in West Philly for the rest of my *life*. Nineteenth floor there, too, if I'm not mistaken." He sat back. "So what floor did tonight's little surprise happen on?"

Fran put the Xerox down. The hotel room number had been 1934. So all of the murders could have occurred on the same floor, different sections of the city, but all on the same floor. What the *hell*?

Otto said it for him: "Our darling boy only offs people at two-hundred, two hundred fifty feet in altitude. Nineteenth floor thereabouts, whatever. Then *and* now." He shook his shiny bald head in disgusted wonder. "So how's that for a new, sick wrinkle?"

Fran's full, sleepless twenty-four hours caught up with him then, hard. He sagged in his chair. "I appreciate the help, Otto," he said, "but how is this supposed to save my ass? Did they catch this Lennard Building bastard? I mean, even if he was still alive he'd be in his late sixties or seventies now, right? Does he have a whacko son, maybe, or has he come back from the goddamn grave, or what?"

"Very funny, Fran. You look like you could use some sleep, you know that?" Otto reached into the same pocket he had pulled the candy bar and came up with a pen. Taking the Xerox back, he scribbled on the back of it briefly. "I have a name and address for you."

Fran dragged the paper back. *Lester Blue. Holmesburg Retirement Annex, 8223 Frankford Avenue.* "He's still alive?"

"Still kicking, last time I checked."

"Eight-thousand block of the Avenue, this place is up near me."

Otto rose. "So here you've been living near probably the only surviving connection to the Lennard Building murders all this time, Francine, and you didn't even know it? What the hell kind of detective are you supposed to be, anyway?"

"Hey Otto?" Fran raised his hand, palm forward.

The old man high-fived it with a passing slap. "I'm too old for this crap," he said. "I'm going home to bed." He patted Fran on his bald spot. "Follow my example, kid."

13

As Fran walked down the second floor hall of the retirement home he smelled sweat and piss, but mostly he just smelled old things: old clothes, old perfumes, old muscle ointments, old skin creams. Old *people*. People old enough to make this place one of their last stops, probably The Very Last Stop. His mom, he promised himself, wrinkling his nose at a heady waft of Ben-Gay and hair-perm from an open door, would never end up in a place like this. No frigging way.

There were several residents standing idly or shuffling along the hall, wrapped in ratty bathrobes, mumbling quietly at the floor, eying him suspiciously or longingly as he passed. Because I'm young. Younger than them, anyway. Young enough to be just a visitor, passing through. Somebody who could walk out the front door. Someone who still had options. Not a sheep down the last shoot, with no option left but the final one. Shit.

He reached the room number the nurse downstairs had supplied him, squinted at the names scribbled on the card in the slot on the door, then knocked, and pushed the door slowly open.

He counted two beds, two bureaus, two mirrors, two closets, and a single, small, black and white TV on a wire stand between the bureaus. *Good Morning America* was on, droning through an erratic snowstorm of static.

An old man in pajamas and robe sat on the side of the bed nearest the TV, his bare white legs dangling down, swinging slowly. His watery eyes reflected the glow of the TV screen.

"Excuse me," Fran said. "I'm looking for Lester Blue."

The old man either ignored him, or hadn't heard him, because he continued to stare at the TV.

Fran went over and turned the set off. David Hartman became a white line, then a white dot, then faded to nothing.

The old man looked up, vaguely vexed. "Who the hell are you?" He pointed. "That's *my* TV. *Mine.*"

Fran said, "I'm looking for Lester Blue. Are you him?"

"Lester? Lester? Hell no." The old man reached for his pillow, then slowly, slowly, swung his feet up and folded his body into the bed. "My name is Derwent. Laurence Scattergood Derwent. I work for the phone company. PA Bell." He groped for the blanket edge. "Are you having a problem with your telephone service?"

Fran reached over, pulled the blanket to where Derwent could grasp it, and said, "My telephone is doing just fine, thanks. Do you know where Lester is right now?"

"Probably in the lounge, or the crapper. Breakfast isn't till eight." Derwent pulled his blanket up to his chin, and grinned with a mouth largely devoid of teeth. "Lester's got the hots for that newsgirl on the *Today* show. Can you believe that? Me, I'll take Jessica Savitch any day. Any day of the *week*."

"Where's the lounge, Mr. Derwent? Is it on this floor?"

"If you've got a problem with your phone, now," Derwent continued, "I have only one piece of useful advice."

Fran hesitated. Ah, what the hell. "And what's that, Mr. Derwent?"

The old man closed his eyes. "You shove that receiver of yours right up the old bunghole. Shove it up *tight*. And you tell the bastards downtown Lawrence Scattergood Derwent told you so, you hear?" Then he rolled his face into his pillow.

Fran stood quietly for a moment, then he said, "Do you want the TV back on, Mr. Derwent?"

"Hell no," the old man said, muffled in his pillow. "Can't see the damn thing anyway."

Fran reentered the hall and started walking. The lounge was at the far end, a large square room with windows on three sides. It was filled with unmatched stuffed furniture, two ping pong tables, and a few bookcases stacked with old paperbacks, dog-eared magazines and box games. Someone had begun putting up Christmas and Hanukkah decorations in the windows, and a still bare artificial Christmas tree had been erected in one corner.

A large console television dominated the room, however; indeed, most of the chairs faced in its direction, and nearly all of them were occupied.

And, as promised, Jane Pauley and *The Today Show* held sway, babbling on about holiday cookie recipes with the overweight weatherman.

Fran surveyed the assembled crowd. The women outnumbered the men two to one. The men all seemed to be wearing something blue; the women, something pink. Like babies, he thought. Like they're all little kids again. And they probably didn't even realize it.

He tapped the nearest man on the shoulder. "Excuse me, I'm looking for Lester Blue."

The resident, short, thin nearly to emaciation, turned his shiny, liver-spotted head with a single raised eyebrow. "Well now," he said in a high, whistling voice. "I guess you found him, then."

"You're Mr. Blue?"

"The name is Lester. Philadelphia Police, retired. I knew Jack Diamond, way back when." The old man nodded to himself for a moment, then focused again on Fran. "His friends called him Jack, you know. Only his enemies called him Legs. Them and people who didn't know any better. Who are *you?*"

"My name is Francis Lomax, Detective Sergeant, Philadelphia Police." Fran put out his hand. "I'm pleased to meet you, Mr. Blue."

Blue pressed a business card into it. "You got a card yourself?" he demanded archly.

"I'm a detective, Mr. Blue. Of course I have a card." Fran pawed his suit-coat pocket, pulled one out, and surrendered it into the old man's waiting, trembling fingers. Then he glanced at the card still in his own hand. *Lester Blue*, it read simply, in black blocky letters. *PPD, RET.*

Blue squinted at Fran's card. "What's this number, Homicide?"

"Yes. I've come—"

"Oh I know why you've come." The old man winked. "I can still read the papers. I know what's going on. I figured it was just a matter of time before one of you got to me, or me to one of you." Blue rose, using Fran's arm for leverage. "Come on," he said, dropping Fran's card in his bathrobe pocket, "let's go to the back. We'll only ruin the gang's day if we jaw it up too near the boob tube."

They moved to a sofa set against the rear wall. Fran watched Lester settle himself, unaccountably fascinated. Just how old was this old guy, anyway?

"I'm ninety-three," Lester said in his airy, whistling voice, apparently reading Fran's mind. "Born in Fishtown in 1889. Can you believe it? Crapped across two centuries, and still kicking. And after the God almighty life I led, too."

"Your family…must be very proud of you, Mr. Blue."

"Family? Hah! I've outlived them all! Two sons lost in the Second World War: one in Tunisia, the other on some Godforsaken Pacific island that didn't even have a name, not one I could ever pronounce, anyway. A daughter, too. Cancer got her in the 50's." Lester looked down at his hands, then laughed. "And two wives to boot. Used them up like firewood, zip zip!" He laughed again. "But you didn't come here to talk about my love life; you came to talk about those murders. About the Slaughterhouse Killer. They call him The Butcher, now, of course. At least the *News* does."

The Slaughterhouse Killer. Oh yes. "Your name was given to me by Otto Gustafson."

"That young bald-headed bastard still kicking?"

Fran smiled. "We can't seem to convince him to retire."

"Retire him," Lester declared, "and you'll kill him. Might as well shoot a guy like that in the temple as retire him." He closed his eyes for a moment, then, abruptly, opened them again. "So. You want to talk about The Butcher? That's what the papers are calling him today. The *Daily News*, for one." He said the words again with relish: "The Butcher."

"A little, Lester, sure. I also want to talk about the murders you were involved with, back in the 1940's. The ones that occurred at the Lennard Building. The Slaughterhouse Killer, just like you said." Fran took out his notebook." Do you remember any of the particulars?"

Lester nodded slowly, looking down at his hands again. "How could I ever forget? How could anyone forget what we saw?" He looked up. "Who made the connection?"

"Otto."

"Good for him." Lester leaned toward Fran. Then, slowly, distinctly, he said, "They're the same, you know."

"The same? In what way?"

Lester leaned closer. "The same *killer*."

"We're talking nearly a forty year gap, Lester. How can the killer be the same?"

Lester sneered. "You found bones?"

"The bones of the victims were——"

"Not *those* bones. I'm talking about the *other* ones. The little white ones." Lester glanced at Fran slyly. "You didn't find any of those, did you?"

The tooth in the elevator. The little white fang. "What about them, Lester?"

"You watch where you take those bones; you watch how *high* you take them." Lester raised a withered finger. "Mind me, now. You take them too high and you're a dead man," he swung his finger like a rapier, "just like the rest."

High. Nineteenth floor. Two hundred-plus feet. Fran tried to keep his expression passive, his voice calm. "What does how high they are have to do with anything, Lester? I'm not making the connection."

Lester shook his head. Mournfully, he said, "I'm an old, old man. I'm so old nobody believes what I say anymore. Nobody believes old Lester's stories."

"What stories? I came here to listen, Lester. What stories?"

The old man leaned toward him again. "Stories about the place where the bones are." He lowered his voice. "Where they come from. And who *made* them come."

"The place where the bones come from? I don't follow."

"You go up twenty stories, maybe nineteen, maybe twenty-one, depends on the building, how high the ceilings are, you know? If they're hungry, or if they're looking for something, or if they're just plain mad...*they'll get you!*"

Oh Christ. Fran felt something fall, inside himself. Fall and break. Lester was one step away from a trip up the Avenue to the Byberry nuthouse. "Who are 'they,' Lester?"

"They don't have a name." Lester shook his head suddenly, violently. "Never did, never will. The Butcher, they call them now, because they think it's a *him*, because they think it's a *human being*, a garden variety *murderer*. Someone they can pinch, someone they can stick behind bars." The sneer returned. "But we know better, don't we, Detective?"

Fran cleared his throat. Time to steer this boat back toward shore. "Otto said you were directly involved with the killings, back in 1946?"

"Damn right I was. On the payroll, *my job* to be there, document it, the visual evidence. I used a large format Leika. Those goddamn Nazis could make a damn fine camera, I'll say that for the bastards." Lester paused, blinking, then took in a long, deep breath. "I took every picture the detectives told me to, and I saw...I saw..." He swallowed, coughed, then coughed again. "Damn," he said then, patting his chest, "it still gets to me. After all this time."

Slowly, patiently, Fran said, "Do you remember anything about witnesses, Willy? Other people who were there, who might have seen something important?"

"Witnesses?" The old man looked up, fingers to his mouth. "No witnesses. Everyone there was dead, cut up, and their bones..."

Fran waited him out.

"Gone," Lester said finally.

"Gone," Fran repeated. "You mean they were missing? The killer took them? Took the bones?"

Lester nodded slowly. "Every one. Only left the meat, the skin, the guts." His voice dropped. "Like they were collecting them."

"Did anybody have any idea who they were, these bone collectors? Something that didn't make the papers?"

"The inside scoop, you mean?"

"Yeah," Fran said, "something only a cop like you would know."

Lester narrowed his eyes. "They had a suspect, early on, didn't pan out, though. Never got to the papers. A person of interest." Willie narrowed his eyes even more. "Alton was his name. Bill, William. He was a domestic, a valet, I think. A black man. Young. Looked like he'd been hurt in the war. Scars. Scars all over his face and hands."

Fran wrote the name down in his notebook. "That's good," he said, "that's helpful. Anything else?"

A sly smile played across the old man's lips. "There was

another one."

"Another person of interest?"

"Someone who came every day, after the murders, stayed down in the lobby, asking funny questions."

"Who was he? He have a name?"

"Made a regular pest of himself, in his fine clothes, his Main Line airs." Lester nodded to himself, his gaze wandering. Then he turned back to Fran. "Terribly scarred, though, just like that Alton fella."

"Scarred?"

"I'll always remember those scars."

"No name, then?"

Lester smiled again. "He knew about *them*."

Fran felt like a parrot. "He knew about them?"

Lester looked around the room, then he leaned very close, and whispered: "The Bone Worms." He paused for effect. "The Bone Worms from The Boneyard. It was them he was interested in."

"Bone worms," Fran said. "Boneyard." So this guy had the same crazy story as Jameel and the dead hooker. But none of that information had been released to the press. The kid must have blabbed to his friends and neighbors, the little shithead, and the *Daily News* must have sniffed it out and printed it. And Lester here must have read it. He said he read the papers, didn't he?

Shit.

Fran said, "These bone worms are what are killing the people now, too?"

Lester nodded slowly. "I think they're *becoming* something, now, or trying to. A creature. A person. So they can *be* here, you know? So they can be *down* here, among us." He kept nodding. "They want to *do* something, down here. Or they want to *get* something." He paused. "Or get someone. They need the bodies, the bones, to get down here."

Fran closed his notebook with a snap. Everything inside him

felt cold, cold and tired. In a neutral voice, he said, "A creature, Lester? A monster of some kind? Something…supernatural?"

Lester must have sensed the wall Fran had just dropped between them, because he pulled away a little, and shrugged defensively. "You've seen what it did. I can read between the lines; I know what you've seen." He nodded, more for his own benefit than for Fran's. "Nothing on this earth could have killed those people. Nothing on God's earth. That's why you're stumped. That's why you're going nowhere." He nodded again. "I know why it's started again; Christ, I knew why it started back then, too. Because of that goddamn building they built, so damn high. But back then you could count the number of buildings with twenty floors in Philly on just your two hands. They were up there, and we were down here. We were safe. But then there was that damned building."

"The Lennard."

"Of course the Lennard! Twenty-two stories high they built it, just shy of Billy Penn's hat."

"But how can a building—"

"It wasn't just the building, dammit! The Lennard was just *the door*, the way down to get *him*. *He* woke them up, damn him! *He* got their attention, got them *mad*. *He* was the reason for it all, back then. He's probably still the reason for it now!" Lester began coughing again.

Fran gave him a moment to calm down. Then he asked, "Who is this person you're talking about, Mr. Blue?"

Lester wiped his mouth, and looked away. "You know who." His voice was now just a whisper. "He's the one. He's the one they want."

"I'm sorry, Mr. Blue, but—"

"And now, *Christ*, it's just a million times worse!" Lester suddenly waved his arms about. "I picked this place because it's down by the river, and it only has three floors. I've never gone any higher than this, not since that day in that damned building when I had to take the pictures. I've never been in an elevator, never in an airplane, ever since. They'd smell me, I know they would. *Smell me*, because of what I know. Just like they smelled *him*. So I've never gone higher—"

"Than two hundred feet," Fran finished for him. A haunted monster with a taste for blood. High-flying worms from Hell with a good sense of smell who collected bones. And some unnamed schmuck who was responsible for pissing them off.

God help me.

"Damn right," Lester said. "I was up there. I *know*."

"You still haven't told me who this person is, Mr. Blue. The one who started it, the one who stirred up the…bone worms."

Lester looked at him defiantly, but his voice trembled, "I don't have to tell you anything, Detective."

"No," Fran said, heaving to his feet, "No, Mr. Blue, you don't."

In the lobby on the way out he noticed a table filled with amateur ceramic bric-a-brac. Beside it, in a glass wall cabinet, were samples of macramé, embroidery and crewelwork. A matronly woman, as wide as she was tall, sat by the ceramics table, her hands cradling an open cigar box. She caught his eye and smiled. "Store's open," she said in a friendly, musical voice.

Fran's eyes wandered briefly over the pieces, the ashtrays, Santas, teddy bears, flower vases and napkin rings. Then his hand darted down, and he picked up one of the pieces.

A skull. A white ceramic skull with its crown missing, but a skull nonetheless. "Who made this?"

The woman frowned. "Why, that would have to be Mr. Blue's work. We can't seem to steer his creativity into doing anything but…skeletons."

Fran turned it over. Scratched in its base were the letters WB/PPD/RET. He put it back down. "Sell many of those?"

She shook her head, smiling. "Only around Halloween, I'm afraid."

My only lead, he thought, who turns out to be nuttier than

a maple walnut sundae. With extra walnuts. He thanked the woman, and exited to the sidewalk. The roar of traffic on the Avenue washed over him, filled him up, consumed him.

And almost, but not quite, drowned out his single, raw, frustrated bellow.

The clock on the partition in his cubicle office said 8:35. Fran looked at it, following the second hand as it slowly swept around. Is it slower going up, he thought, swinging past the nine? Is it faster going down the other side? Looked like it, anyway. He rubbed his eyes. Somewhere in the building, an electronic horn blatted. End of Roll Call; Day Shift beginning. Rise and shine, you sorry excuse for an asshole. Time to roll into your third eight.

"Hey Sarge."

"Yeah." Fran cleared his throat, blinking. Heckleman was at the door, an open bag of bagels in his hand. He gestured with it. "You want first dibs?"

"Hell no. Thanks, but no."

"I just made a fresh pot, anyway."

"Thanks, Heck. Maybe later."

The Ops Officer hesitated. "You've been here all night?"

"I'm fine, Heck." Fran waved him off, shooing him like a fly. Then he exhaled through his nose, looking blankly at the file piles on his desk. On the left: the Butcher cases; on the right: everything else.

He looked up at the clock again. 8:47. What the—?

"What the hell are you doing here, Frannie?"

Fran swung his head around, and found Mike Finnean, freshly shaved, in a new bad suit, standing in his doorway. His partner said, "Have you been here all *night*? You look like hell."

"I had a lead. From Otto. I just interviewed somebody up Frankford Avenue, old guy at a retirement home. Lester Blue." Fran rubbed his eyes. "It didn't pan out."

"Retirement home on Frankford? Isn't that up near your

mom's house?'"

Fran leaned back in his swivel chair, nodding.

"And then you came back down *here*?'"

"Go figure, Mike."

"Did I mention you look like hell?"

"I love you too, Sweetpea."

Mike pushed off the doorjamb, came in and sat on the edge of Fran's desk, spilling a file pile in the process. In a low voice, he said, "You're no use to me like this. Why don't you just go home, get a few hours' sleep? I'll cover for you."

"I should." Fran found himself nodding again. "I know I should." But he found himself looking at the files before him. "We're going nowhere, Mike," he said.

"Bullshit." Mike punctuated the word with a sharp wrap of a knuckle on the desk. "It's still early. We've got time. Plenty of time." He stood back up, pulled the wrinkles out of his suit coat, and shot his cuffs. "We've still got a window, as long as we stay sharp."

"Optimism," Fran grunted. "I love it."

"I just had five hours of sack time, Frannie. I'm a little frigging ray of sunshine this morning." He rapped his knuckle on Fran's desk again. "I'm going back to the Ben Franklin today, do some re-interviews."

"That's good. Re-interviews." Fran yawned. "Good."

"You gonna be okay?"

"I'll be fine. I'll probably red out, like you say, go home for a few."

Mike pointed a finger at him. "When I come back I better not see your sorry fat ass in here." Then he was gone from Fran's doorway.

Fran leaned back, staring dully again at the case files stacked and spilled before him, at the victim faces tacked to the wall. Outside his little office, the rest of the Homicide Unit was just background, white noise. He closed his eyes for a moment, for just a moment, and when he opened them again fifteen minutes had passed. "Shit," he muttered.

His phone rang, the red light of Button Number One flashing. Lieutenant Goaz. He pushed the button and picked up the receiver. "Yes sir," he said, rubbing his eyes with his free hand.

"Go home."

Fran opened both eyes, blinking. "Sir?"

"Go. Home. Mike Finnean tells me you've been at it all night. Get some sleep. Hit it fresh your next shift."

"But—"

"Mike's had his, now you go get yours. That's an order, Sergeant." Goaz hung up.

Fran placed the receiver back in its cradle. Then he heaved himself up, and grabbed his overcoat. "Red me out," he told Heckleman as he passed his desk.

"Already done, Sergeant," Heckleman said. "See you tomorrow."

Goaz leaned back in his swivel chair, rubbing his eyes with the palms of his hands. He said, "You worked with Lomax before, Mike, right?"

Across the desk, hunched in his own chair, Mike Finnean nodded. "Couple of times, yeah."

"So?"

"So what, Lieutenant?"

"So what's different?"

"What do you mean?"

Goaz looked at him. "You know what I mean, Detective."

Finnean's expression was pained. "The other cases were cut and dry, nothing out of the ordinary. We had victims, we had evidence, leads, suspects. We did what we needed to do and got our collars. I remember Fran had it all in his head, all of it, every time. He was always two steps ahead of everybody else."

"And now?"

Finnean leaned forward. "There's no comparison, Lieutenant. None of these homicides are normal. Hell, they're anything but. We've both been working our asses off—"

"You think it would be better if you were Primary?"

The words hung in the air between them. Then, "No sir. I think Fran should remain Primary. He had the first case. He's the senior officer. He should be Primary."

Goaz reached across his desk and pulled a file out of the litter. He set it in front of Finnean, unopened. "This is the latest report on Lomax from Psych."

"Really, Lieutenant, that's none of my goddamn—"

"I'm not sharing the damn thing with you, Mike, except for one of the recommendations. That *you* be Primary."

Finnean looked at the file. "I think," he said, "it's too early for a switch like that. I think everybody needs to give Fran and me more time to work it." He looked up. "That's what I think."

"Okay then." Goaz pulled the file back, and nodded toward the door. "So go work it."

14

The doorbell chimed.

Fran awoke on the couch with a start; evening shadows resolved themselves as living room came slowly into focus.

His mother called from the kitchen, "Frannie…?"

"*Ahh, lad…*"

The doorbell chimed again.

"*You just ain't got it.*"

"I'll get it Mom." He rose, shook himself like a big dog, and rubbed his face with both of his meaty hands. He lumbered into the hall, the foyer, and into the cold vestibule. Through the wavy glass he saw an elderly woman, bundled up tight against the evening, clutching a handbag. He shivered suddenly, shedding the last vestiges of sleep, and opened the door. "Yes?"

"Mr. Lomax? Detective Lomax?"

"That's me."

"I'm not interrupting your dinner…?"

"Not at all." Fran shifted his weight to his heels. "Is there something I can do for you, ma'am?"

His mother crowded into the vestibule behind him. "For goodness sake, Frannie, invite the lady in! It's positively freezing!"

Fran held the door for the visitor, flashing his mother a disapproving look over the woman's hat, which she batted deftly away with a more potent look of her own. He followed them both back to the living room.

"Can I make some coffee?" he asked when they were seated on the sofa.

"It's already made," his mother said, "and I'd love a cup." She turned to their guest, "Mrs. ...?"

"Miss. Grundy. Ruth Grundy." She offered Fran a tentative smile. "I'd love a cup also." She included Fran's mother in the smile, "If it's not too much trouble."

"No trouble at all," his mother replied. "How would you like it?"

"Black's just fine."

"Two black coffees coming up." Fran retreated to the kitchen to fetch them.

When he returned, not a minute later, his mother and Miss Grundy were whispering to one another, their knees nearly touching, like long-lost friends.

Grunting as he bent, he placed their cups on the butler table before them, then settled into his overstuffed chair.

"Miss Grundy," his mother explained, "is a volunteer worker at the Holmesburg Retirement Annex on the Avenue."

"Oh?" Fran tensed slightly. "I was just there this morning, interviewing a resident."

Miss Grundy nodded vigorously. "Lester Blue, I know. Lester Blue is the reason for my visit, Detective Lomax." She picked up her coffee, hesitated, then put it back down. "Lester is one of my personal projects."

"Projects?"

"We play checkers, I help him with the crossword, get him

a snack from the cafeteria, read the paper to him when his eyes are tired, that sort of thing. We discuss politics and the news of the world. He's come to trust me about certain things."

"Well I think that's very nice," Fran's mother said, beaming.

Miss Grundy put her handbag on her lap. "Earlier this afternoon Lester gave me something to give to you, Detective Lomax." She reached inside, searching, then took out a folded handkerchief, and placed it carefully on the butler table before her.

Fran leaned forward, as his mother moved the coffee cups out of the way.

Miss Grundy unfolded the handkerchief. "Lester wants you to have these."

Nested in the center of the cloth were two objects: a business card, and an empty key chain. Fran reached out and picked up the key chain. Dangling from it, pierced through with a dull brass ring, was a tiny yellowed tooth. It was curved slightly, thick at its pierced end, thinning almost to a point at the other. It was nearly a twin to the one he had found in the elevator at the Ben Franklin. He touched it, and a *tingle*, a *sizzle* went silently up his finger.

He found his voice. "You say this is…Lester's?"

"He kept it, but I don't believe it was his. I think he was just…holding it for someone. The *right* someone."

"Holding it for you, Frannie," his mother said softly. "Maybe."

Fran dangled the chain, let the tooth dance on its ring. Lester had gone out of his way to warn Fran about things like this, teeth, bones. Be careful where you take them, he had said; be careful how *high* you take them. Yet here he'd had one in his possession all along?

Fran's mother picked up the business card and read it, then she handed it across. "Philadelphia, Penna. I haven't seen 'Penna' used in years."

Fran looked at the card. It was for a photography studio on

Walnut Street. He knew that block of Walnut; there was no photography studio there, not any longer, anyway. The card was thick pasteboard, fuzzy around the edges. He flipped it over. There, written in blue-black inkwell ink, neatly printed, a name: 'John Randall Pitcairn.' It was underlined twice. "Mr. Blue had this in his possession, you say?"

Miss Grundy nodded vigorously. "Lester is past ninety. He's collected quite a lot of things over the years, business cards in particular. He has quite a number of them in shoeboxes under his bed. This one, for whatever reason, he singled out for *you*, Detective Lomax."

"Does this photography studio mean anything to you, Miss Grundy?"

"No, not particularly. I'm sure it's been out of business for many years."

"How about the name on the back? This John Pitcairn?"

The old lady hesitated. "Lester talks about a lot of people, Detective Lomax. He has lived a long life, after all."

Fran closed his big hand over the card, the key chain, and the tooth. "Has Lester ever told you...*stories*, Miss Grundy?"

"Stories?"

"Strange stories, stories like you'd read in pulp magazines, or the *Daily News*, the *Tribune*..."

She looked at him shrewdly over the rim of her coffee cup. "Are we talking about The Boneyard, Detective Lomax? The Bone Worms?"

The Boneyard. He let that resonate in his head. *The Bone Worms.* He let that resonate too. "Yes," he said, gently. "We're talking about The Boneyard. And The Bone Worms." As he spoke the words an odd thrill went through him, another hot sizzle. "Do you believe them?"

"The stories? Of course I do." Miss Grundy put her coffee down. "Lester's a policeman, just like you. He's dealt in facts his whole life. Of course I believe his stories about The Boneyard."

"But—" Fran groped for the proper way to frame a next

question. But he came up empty.

Miss Grundy smiled again, and stood. "You believe the stories too, Detective Lomax."

"I never said—"

"You don't admit it, but you believe them, all right." Her smile was positively righteous. "Anyway." She took Fran's mother's hand and squeezed it kindly. "Thank you for your hospitality, Mrs. Lomax."

"Please stay," Fran's mother protested, "at least to finish your coffee."

"No, I really have to go. I don't like walking the streets during the evenings. Drivers are just so crazy these days, you know? And the seedier elements…" She turned to Fran, who had risen with her. "That's not a reflection on the police, Detective Lomax; you're all doing the best you can, I know. It's just the world in general these days."

"Going to hell in a hand-basket," Fran's mother agreed. "I know what you mean, dear." She touched Fran's shoulder to stay him. "I'll see her out."

"Thank you, Miss Grundy," Fran said, feeling as inadequate as his words sounded.

"Don't take Lester's things lightly," the old woman said. "Certainly, Lester doesn't."

"I won't," Fran said.

Then his mother led her into the hall.

Fran opened his hand, regarded the card, the chain, the tooth on its brass ring.

When his mother reentered the room, he asked, "How late does the library stay open?"

"The branch on the Avenue closes at four on Fridays."

He looked at his watch, then reached for the phone anyway. It turned out the Free Library on the Parkway in the city, the Mothership, was open till nine, and yes, Salvador Melendez was indeed on duty in Periodicals. Could he be connected? Certainly.

"Detective!" Salvador's voice sounded genuinely surprised.

"What can I do for you this fine evening?"

"I have two names for you: John Randall Pitcairn, and William Alton." Fran spelled them.

"Pitcairn," Salvador said. "Alton. Got it."

"When can I stop by?"

"Monday morning, first thing, okay?"

Fran frowned into the phone. "Nothing quicker than that?"

"I can work this tomorrow, Detective, no problem, but we're closed Sunday."

"Maybe I'll stop in tomorrow."

"I'll do my best, Detective."

"Thanks, Salvadore." Fran hung up, and saw his mother looking at him.

"So how did Miss Grundy know where we lived?"

"Probably from this Lester Blue. He's still got connections, don't you think?"

"I left him my card," Fran said, then, "Otto," and grinned briefly. "I'm going to head out tomorrow, see about finding this Pitcairn character."

"Of course you are," his mother said, nodding. "But first I want to hear about this Boneyard." She pointed him toward his chair. "And Salvador."

In the dark, an hour after lights-out, Lester heard something that nearly made him wet himself: the faint sound of tiny claws, mouse claws, scrabbling on metal. His roommate Larry was asleep, snoring quietly. Lester lay on his back in the center of his bed, motionless, his top cover pulled up to his chin. He stared up at the ceiling, at the ventilation grate that punctuated the otherwise unrelenting pattern of acoustical ceiling tiles.

The noise was coming from up there.

His bed was not directly under the grate, but it was close enough for him to see two strands of cobweb hanging down, drifting gently in the air currents.

The scrabbling noise came again, louder this time, from out

of the grate. Rat claws, now, echoing down the shaft.

His breathing quickened. Blood began pounding in his head.

The scrabbling stopped.

He held his breath.

Lester.

His eyes went suddenly round. Pain flared in his finger joints as he clutched the blanket. The pain spread, running up his left arm. Hard pain. It reached his chest and *punched* it.

Lester. A whisper from up the ventilation shaft, no more than that. The cobwebs hung undisturbed.

Commming, Lester.

The pain in his chest grew, became unbelievable. Lester lay heavily in his bed, unable to move.

Soooon, Lester. The whisper was less than a breath, lighter than the cobwebs, dancing across his consciousness. *Sooonnn.*

Lester's mouth opened, slowly.

Gget ours, Lesterr.

His eyes did not blink.

You thiefff you.

A thin dribble of saliva poised at the corner of his open mouth.

Ahh…. The whisper trailed.

The scrabbling began again, retreated, became fainter.

Below, in the dark, Lester's open eyes began to glaze over, and dry. His blood, no longer pounding, no longer flowing at all, began cooling, coagulating, seeking its own level.

In the other bed, snoring lightly, Laurence Scattergood Derwent dreamed of telephones.

15

"Do you remember the way?"

William glanced into the Bentley's rear-view mirror. "Yes," he said, answering the question for the third time since leaving the sanctuary of their townhouse courtyard. It was near midnight, and the roads leading out of the city were mostly empty. The luxury car cut through this cold end to the night with a subdued, steady growl. "I'm more worried about the deer," William said, peering ahead beyond the sweep of the hi-beams.

Jack sat back with a quiet grunt.

Deer in the road were the furthest thing on William's mind. He saw instead a huge, leafless tree crowning an otherwise bare hilltop. And he saw *them* intertwined in the upper branches, hiding, waiting. Sixty-two years waiting.

The northern neighborhoods of the city merged seamlessly with the suburbs beyond. William drove steadily through nameless housing developments punctuated by anonymous strip malls. In many intersections the traffic lights blinked yellow, allowing them to drive through unchecked. The only indication that this had once been farmland was the occasional produce stand, crowded now with Christmas trees. Everything was dark; everything was closed. Starlight on tinsel and dirty snow. Nameless. Anonymous. Still, the old roads remained, and they led eventually to a sprawling upscale suburban tract of quarter-million dollar homes scattered among twenty-year-old maples and birches in discrete, curving cul-de-sacs.

Somewhere among the houses and trees beside the road the Spangler estate had once stood. All the property had been sold except for one tract. All of their childhood haunts were gone. Except for Cobb Hill.

At the end of one of the peripheral streets in the development, a hundred yards or more beyond the nearest back yard was an old, spiked, iron fence with a gate hung between massive fieldstone pillars. William brought the Bentley up to it, its headlights pointing into dense woods beyond.

Jack said, "You have the key?"

William raised and shook his key ring as he got out of the vehicle. "This won't take long," he said.

He saw Jack shiver in the invasion of cold air through the open driver door. There was a strong wind blowing. He closed the car door with a quiet thump, then trudged up the gravel to the gate. When he reached for the padlock he found it dangling on a broken chain. He looked closely and saw that someone had worked very hard to bend and break one of the links. He pulled the chain through the bars and heaved it into the weeds, then pulled the gates open, one after the other.

"Odd," he said, sliding back into the driver seat, and closing the door.

"What do you mean?"

"The gate. The chain's been broken, a while ago by the looks of it."

"But you could open it. I saw you open it."

William nodded. "We can get through."

"Well then let's get going. After we finish this I won't give a tinker's damn about the gate or the property or any of it. They can build a bowling alley here for all I care."

William nosed the Bentley through the stone pillars. The headlights immediately found the graveled ruts beyond, and they proceeded up the long, high hill.

The surrounding woods were still there, older, taller, and still impenetrable but for the road; and the field still crowned the top of the hill, a tonsure of tall grass, the wind moving it in silver waves.

And the huge, ancient chestnut tree, in the center of the field—that was still there as well.

There had once been three Chestnuts in this clearing, and William had held a vague hope that the Blight before the Second World War had taken all of them down, but the biggest tree had survived.

The damned tree house tree had survived.

But so have we, he said to himself as he turned the vehicle around to park it.

"Not too close," Jack said. "We can't be too close."

"I know." William parked the Bentley about fifty feet away from the tree, well beyond the outermost perimeter of branches. He got out, came around, and opened the rear passenger door for Jack. "Do you want to come out? I can get the wheelchair from the trunk."

"No, not the damned chair. I think I'll just stand by the car. I can see everything from here."

William helped him down, his grip firm on Jack's arm. When he was safely on his feet, balanced on the ball of his leg cast, Jack shrugged out of William's grasp, and leaned back against the car. Together, they looked up at the tree. It was an ill defined, shifting mass against the blustering night sky. The cold, twinkling stars peeked and hid beyond its clacking branches and flexing limbs.

"Listen to it groan," Jack said quietly. "You'd almost think it was alive."

William's eyes never left the tree. "It is alive."

"I meant *alive* alive."

"I know what you meant."

Somewhere in the darkness, a flock of Canadian geese honked faintly as they passed overhead.

Jack said, "Let's do it, please. Before someone comes."

William went to the rear of the Bentley, unlocked the trunk, and lifted out a full, sloshing gasoline can.

"The whole tree, William," Jack said. "All the way around."

"I know," William said patiently, taking off his overcoat, replacing it with a knee-length yellow rain slicker, then a pair of rubber gloves that reached to his elbows. He picked up the can with both hands and stood there for a long moment.

"Hurry!"

Still, William hesitated.

The Bentley rocked slightly as Jack pushed himself upright. "William!" he hissed.

William grasped the can tightly, in both hands, and trudged through the tall grass to the tree. He worked methodically, dousing the trunk, splashing gasoline as high as he could swing the can. He returned to the Bentley, pulled a large plastic trash bag out of the trunk and stuffed everything into it: can, slicker, gloves. Then he took out a newspaper section already rolled into a tube and secured with a rubber band. He raised it to show Jack, and returned to the tree.

"We're shutting a door," he muttered aloud, remembering that time in 1921 when this door had first opened, in the cockpit of a Curtiss Jenny biplane, when they had taken Jack, fouled him, *raped* him. And then again, when *he* had been taken, broken, consumed by them just as Jack had been... And yet again, finally, when Jack's Uncle had climbed up this same tree, and had never come back down. Gone, taken, eaten by The Boneyard. This won't be enough. The thought twisted through him. This won't be enough.

He stood off a few feet as he lit the rolled newspaper, waited for it to take flame, and then threw it down among the gasoline-soaked roots of the tree.

There was a soft but powerful WHOOF, and he staggered back, silhouetted against a sudden wall of lemon and blue fire. He turned and ran back to the car, grinning, rubbing at his forehead. "I think I may have lost my eyebrows!" He saw twin, growing fires reflected in Jack's eyes.

Together, they watched the flames ringing the tree, but its progress upward was slow.

Jack gripped William's arm. "What if it's not enough?"

"I used the whole can," William said. "It'll have to be enough." He finally turned away. "This is bound to draw a crowd. We need to go."

Five minutes later, they were out of the housing development and back on the public road. Up in the darkness to their right, the glow of the fire was like a new moonrise. Jack put his hand up to the glass. "It's working," he said. "The entire tree must be on fire."

"I think so," William agreed, nodding. "We did it."

He saw Jack looking at the old scars on the back of his hand. "What a team we make, eh?"

"We're just a couple of fools," Jack said, looking up, staring out, "a couple of old fools."

"Yes," William said, quietly. "We are indeed."

Entering the city limits, the Philadelphia skyline spread out before them like jagged, jeweled teeth. William drew an imaginary line across the buildings, dividing them into the real world below, and the Boneyard above. Suddenly, the act he and Jack had just accomplished seemed hollow, useless, and pitiful. Jack seemed to read his mind. "We should take all of that down," he said, a statement rather than a question, "shouldn't we. All of it."

"No, not all of it," William said. "Just what's on the list."

Jack nodded. "I hope it will be enough."

William tightened his hold on the lacquered walnut grips of the steering wheel.

Jack said, "After we're done, we need to leave Philadelphia. We need to leave for good."

"I know," William said, staring ahead. "That's on the list too."

The sound of a ringing phone first entered Frank Evan's dream, then woke him up from his nap. He dropped his feet from his desk with a crash, spilling some papers, and got to the phone by the fourth ring.

"Evan!" the voice at the other end barked, "Were you sleeping?"

The head of hotel security wiped spit from the corner of his mouth. Shit. "No way, Mr. McDermott, I was just across the office getting some—"

"Save it. The police just called. They're done with the room. I need you up here before I get a crew in."

Evan rubbed a finger in his left eye to clear it, and stifled a yawn. What the hell, was it past midnight? "They done with the elevator too?"

"Thank God yes. Take down the signs and unlock it on your way up."

"Yes sir, I—"

But the night manager had already hung up.

Sally, the weekend temp, smiled sheepishly as he passed her. "Sorry, Mr. Evan," she said, snapping her gum. "I was in the little girl's room."

"Not a problem, sweetie." He turned, still walking, "How's the tie?"

She gave him a thumb's up, then pointed, "Shirt tail…"

"Oh, right." He tucked as he turned back, down the short hall to the lobby. He crossed it, giving Manuel behind the reception desk a nod, and another to George at the Concierge station, and approached the bank of elevators. There were three, and the middle one had a magnetic Out-Of-Service sign, dead center on the doors. Squaring his shoulders, he took down the sign. Then he pulled his key ring from his belt chain with an audible zinnnggg, and unlocked the car. The doors hesitated a moment, then slid open. Even with the carpet removed ("Evidence, my man," the crime scene technician had said, through his paper mask, "it's all evidence.") he could still smell it: like rot, like roadkill. The clean-up crew would have fun in here, oh yeah.

He rode the car up to Nineteen, holding his breath most of the way.

The entire nineteenth floor had been vacated the morning after the murder. All of the guests had been moved to other floors, upgrades for the most part, the costs of the remainder of their stays eaten by the hotel. A nightmare and a half, in other words.

Evan saw broken crime scene tape hanging from an open door halfway down the corridor. As he approached it, still holding the magnetic sign, he heard voices. McDermott was already inside, along with Harry Chung, the head of Maintenance. They were both standing in the middle of the stripped and empty room. The exposed hardwood floor had a multitude of old stains and cigarette burns, and one new stain, in the corner by the window.

"Do you smell that?" McDermott demanded as he entered.

Evan pointed to the manhole-sized bloodstain by the window. "You mean that?"

"No goddammit, the smoke! Can't you smell the smoke?"

Then he did, faintly, but definitely: wood smoke and ash, like from a fireplace, but there were no fireplaces in this hotel. Something was definitely burning, though. "Oh no," Evan said, "A fire?"

The little night manager flung up his hands. "Goddammit! What *else* can go wrong around here?"

16

Mayfair Diner, Frankford, Philadelphia
Saturday, December 3

The Mayfair Diner on Frankford Avenue was packed solid with the weekend breakfast crowd, but the hostess knew Fran—once, in high school, they had even had a date or two—and without even a glance at the line going out the door, she got him the first open window booth at the preferred northern end. "The usual, Frannie?"

"Make it two, Faye. I'm expecting a friend of mine."

"Dirtbag or cop?"

"Who else would associate with a mug like me?"

She winked, ordered him a coffee with a glance to one of the waitresses, then plowed back into the crowd.

Fran watched her for a moment, then turned to stare outside. There were new Christmas decorations hung from utility poles at regular intervals along the Avenue: plastic Santas, plastic Christmas trees, plastic candy canes, courtesy the Mayfair Merchants Association. It still didn't feel like the Christmas season though, he decided. Even with the decorations, it didn't feel like Christmas *at all*.

The waitress for his table, a new one, young and pretty, with a tight flat belly and fingernails long enough to need registration, delivered his coffee. "Your order'll be up in a minute, Hon," she said.

"No problem."

She turned with a flip of her bangs (the young ones were always on stage) and he watched her ass wiggle back into the crowd. Oh Sarah, he thought.

Then Mike Finnean slid into the seat opposite him, rubbing his hands together. "Christ," he grumbled, "it's colder than a witch's tit out there. Clouding up, too."

"They're talking about snow tonight," Fran said. "Real snow. First real accumulation of the season."

"Just what we need." Mike reached for a menu, but Fran stopped him. "I already ordered."

"You ordered for me?"

Fran grinned. "You getting particular?"

The young waitress returned then and placed a coffee in front of Mike. He frowned into his cup. "This'll be my fourth coffee already today," he said.

The waitress put a hand on her hip, "You want I should take it back?"

Mike looked at her for the first time. "Nah," he said, "it's fine."

"Your orders'll be here in a minute." She turned—*footlights*, Fran thought, *spotlights*—and shimmied back into the crowd. He said, "You look like you could use some good news, Fin-Man."

"I don't know why I let you drag me up here on a perfectly good Saturday morning." Mike shivered. "This part of the city gives me the creeps. Too many damn trees."

Fran said, "I've got a John Randall Pitcairn."

"A John Randall who?"

"Pitcairn. A lead."

"John Randall Pitcairn is a lead." Mike regarded him across

the booth. "So who is John Randall Pitcairn?"

"Well," Fran began.

As if on cue, the waitress returned, and placed a platter in front of each man.

"What is this," Mike said, his frown returning.

"Hash and eggs," the waitress said. She put both hands on her hips now (*weapons at the ready,* Fran thought), "You want me to take this back too?"

"No! Hell no. Leave it here." Mike waved his hand over his plate. "It smells great."

"Best in the city." Fran dusted pepper over his, sampled it, and nodded.

The waitress looked from one to the other. "You guys set, then?"

"We're fine," Fran said. "Thanks."

Mike waited for her to leave, then pushed his plate away from him. "Who eats hash any more?"

"You should," Fran said, mouth full, "It's good for you. You're a sorry excuse for an Irishman, you know that?"

Mike picked up a piece of toast. "So this character Pitcairn, what's his story?"

Fran proceeded to tell his partner about his interview with Lester Blue, and Ruth Grundy's visit to the house. Mike was silent throughout, then he asked, "Are you going to reinterview this Lester Blue?"

"He's on my list. I'm following up on that Alton name too." Then Fran laid two plastic baggies on the Formica tabletop between their plates. One held the keychain and its sharp little tooth; the other contained the old business card. Mike wiped his hand, and picked up the one with the keychain and tooth. "It does look similar," he said. "It could be from the same animal. I had Freddie run the first claw over to the Penn Zoology Department on Friday. We should have something back from them on Monday." He put the baggie back down, wiped his hand again, and grabbed another piece of toast. "Monsters?"

He said then, chewing. "Monsters…"

"Bone worms, specifically."

"Bone worm. That's a new one. Is that a real animal? Is the report back from Penn going to say 'species identified as Bone Worm'?"

"I doubt it."

"That kid from Cherry Street you collared talked about bones."

Fran nodded.

"So did the dead prostitute, if you believe the hotel dick's statement."

"I know," Fran said.

"*Daily News* and the *Bulletin* both ran stories just as crazy."

"I know that too."

Mike picked up the baggie with the business card inside. "So Lester Blue thinks this guy Pitcairn is the key?"

Fran mopped his plate with his own piece of toast. "That's what I plan to find out."

East Bringhurst Street was a quiet, one-way residential side street off the granite cobbles of Germantown Avenue. At the corner was a storefront where used books, used appliances and used bicycles were sold. Along with the usual garden-variety of pills, herbs and powders, Fran decided, evaluating the quality of the clientele hanging out on the store's corner-facing door and three-quarter-round steps. He raked his hardest gaze across the motley collection of kids and teenagers. They stared back with equal defiance. Screw 'em.

He turned to look up the street, then back again. The defiant eyes still blazed, daring him, daring him…

He dismissed them, and started up the side street.

Halfway along the unbroken wall of brick row homes, by an ancient abandoned Buick, he came upon the correct address. He stamped his feet on the marble stoop steps, found the front door unlocked, and quickly escaped the cold for the close, cabbage-smelling air of the grimy vestibule. There was a haphazard list of names taped beside the mailboxes and doorbells. Fran quickly found what he was after:

J. R. Pitcairn / 1-D

He pushed the button next to it.
Silence.
He tried the inner door, found it also unlocked (Jesus!), and went down the short hallway to 1-D. He knocked on the tired old door, waited, then knocked again.

The door to 1-B back by the vestibule opened slightly, and a wrinkled, grey-haired black woman peeked her head around the jamb. "Mr. Pitcairn doesn't live here any more," she said in a loud whisper.

Fran took a few steps toward her, so she could see his badge in the dim light from the front door glass. "Do you know where he's gone?"

The old woman blinked behind round, rimless glasses. "You're the police?"

"Yes ma'am, I am."

She blinked again, and chewed softly on her dentures. Then she said, "Mr. Pitcairn went to live with his family. He broke his hip, you see, on those steps outside. When the stone gets a slick of ice on it, it can be dangerous."

"Do you know where his family lives?"

"Near Latrobe, I believe, west, on the way to Pittsburgh. They were out not too long ago, collecting his things."

"Mr. Pitcairn's first name, is it John?"

"Yes. John Russell Pitcairn. He liked to use all three names. He was always trying to impress people."

Russell. "He's an older man?"

"Older than you, younger than me." She touched her finger to her temple. "He was simple, if you know what I mean. He bagged groceries at the Acme down the street on the Avenue.

When he broke his hip, he couldn't take care of himself any more." She nodded her head contemplatively, still chewing on her dentures.

Russell, not Randall. And borderline retarded? A red herring, Inspector. Nothing to see here.

"I appreciate the information, ma'am," he said as he passed her for the front door.

"Oh," she replied to his back, "Some of us are still civilized, Mr. Policeman," blinking behind her glasses. "Some of us still care."

According to the mainframe computer in the Roundhouse basement, and a dog-eared set of telephone directories in the Ops Room, there were fourteen other people named Pitcairn living in the Philadelphia area, but only one more John R. Pitcairn, this one an MD, with a Merion exchange for both his office and home.

Fran dialed the doctor's office number first, and got a machine. The doctor was not in, apparently. He tried the home number next, unlisted, of course, but that had never been a particular problem for the mainframe's data files. He got another answering machine, and hung up on the taped message.

"Crap," he said.

He sat for a moment, drumming his fingers, then he dialed the doctor's home number again. He waited through the message, then said, "Detective Sergeant Lomax, Philadelphia Police…it's Saturday, December third, nine-thirty in the AM. We…need to talk." He rattled off his number, then hung up. *God*, he thought, I hate those machines; 'We need to talk'? Christ.

His hand was still on the receiver when the phone rang, and he picked it back up. "Lomax here."

"Detective Lomax? This is Doctor Pitcairn, returning your call. Sorry I didn't pick up right away." Same voice as the one on the tape. Young, late twenties, no neighborhood accent to speak of. *Too young*.

Fran leaned back in his chair. "Good morning Doctor. Thanks for getting back to me so quickly. I'm conducting a homicide investigation, and I was wondering if you'd mind helping me out?"

"Homicide investigation? Well, sure. I guess. Sure. What about?" Caution, more than there should be. What was he afraid of?

"Real simple, Doctor Pitcairn. It may even sound a little off-the-wall, but here goes anyway: is there anyone else in your family with the same name as yours?"

"You mean another John Pitcairn? No, I'm afraid I'm the only one."

"No uncle? Grandfather? Great-grandfather, even? Someone, perhaps, no longer living?"

"No. I'm sorry Detective Lomax, but I think you've got the wrong Pitcairn. There must be twenty or so—"

"Fifteen, actually. You were just second on my list." Fran hesitated. "You're…still at the Merion address, correct?"

"Yes. Home and practice."

"Okay. Fine." Fran sighed through his nose. "Thank you for your time. Sorry to have bothered you."

"Don't mention it, Detective. Goodbye." The doctor hung up.

Still that trace, that little trill, of fear. Even in his goodbye. Fran held the receiver in his hand for a moment. Probably running a little pill game on the side. Probably gave him a good, healthy shot of the guilts. Or at least the panics.

But he's not the one.

He hung up the phone.

That left the other thirteen. No more Johns or J.P.s, but Pitcairns nevertheless.

He reached across the desk, pulled the printout to him. "Crap," he said again, and began dialing the next number on the list.

17

"A ticket to the top of the City Hall costs two bucks," the man in the booth said around the fat, cold stub of a stogie. "That'll get you to the Observation Deck. They only open the stairs to Billy Penn's hat in the summertime."

"The Observation Deck's high enough for me." William pushed his money under the glass, and the man handed him a blue ticket.

"Any of the corner stairs will take you up to the concourse level." The man shifted his stogie to the other side of his mouth. "They got elevators there, take you the rest of the way. Just follow the signs."

William held the door at the northwest corner stairwell for a mother and three little children. "Mommy," one of the children said, "that's an old black man!"

Another whispered, loud enough for William to hear, "Look at his scars!"

"Hush, Aaron." The mother gave William a brief, embarrassed face. "Now hurry up. We have a lot of stairs to climb."

William followed them at a respectful distance. When they all reached the concourse level the mother herded her children toward the elevators. William continued up the stairs.

Halfway up he stopped to rest. The window was set deep in the wall, its panes translucent, with embedded chicken wire. How high was he? He closed his eyes, smelling the air. Nothing. A door squeaked somewhere above, its echo magnified off the stone and tiled walls of the stairwell. Like a little scream, he thought.

He continued up the steps to the Observation Level.

A cold wind blew into the Lounge every time someone opened one of the doors to the deck outside. Inside, the air was thick with the smell of hotdogs and popcorn from the concession counter, and cigarette smoke from the young mothers shepherding their children about. The smell William was seeking wasn't there either, however. Not inside, anyway.

Stay calm, he told himself, making a conscious effort to let go of the railing by the stairwell doors. There's nothing to be afraid of, here.

He crossed to the glass and metal windows on the western side of the lounge, and looked out. The deck was about ten feet wide, and ran completely around the tower. The waist-high wall and ledge was topped with six feet of black iron fence, which was itself topped with a battlement of iron spears curving inward, like talons.

A janitor had found him out there, in one of the corners, under the stone ledge, sixty-three years before. Somehow, some way, he had escaped The Boneyard, had escaped *them*, and ended up there, in one of the corners, under the stone ledge. His memories were clouded. After so much time it was hard to remember what had been real, and what he might have imagined. He remembered the cold, though, after so much heat. And he remembered the *smell*.

Outside, a dozen or more people leaned up against the wall,

looking out through the iron bars, peering down at the streets. Little children bundled in winter coats and brightly colored knit caps and scarves ran about, dodging between their mother's legs. William could hear their screams and laughter through the thick glass.

Go out, he told himself. Out there, with the people. Look at them. It's safe enough.

He went to one of the doors, grabbed the brass handle, and pushed. A flock of pigeons outside took sudden, startled flight. He stepped back, bumping into a little boy in a brown corduroy coat behind him. "Hey!" the boy protested, "Watch where you're goin', willya?" He went around William, giving him the eye, then pushed his shoulder against the door and went outside.

William smiled, and rubbed his cheek. Go on, go out there with the people, with the children, with the brave little boys in their corduroy coats. *It's safe.*

He went out onto the deck.

The sudden sunlight made him blink, and the cold wind made him dig for his coat pockets. Children ran by him laughing and chattering. Mothers glanced his way, then turned their heads. He went to the wall, his hands surrendering the warmth of his pockets to grasp the cold iron bars. Center City spread out below, and West Philadelphia beyond. He saw the 30th Street Railroad Station, the Art Museum, and the succession of bridges marching up the Schuylkill River into the hazy distance.

Nothing. He felt...nothing. He took in a lungful of air through his nose, searching for the acrid, sulfurous stench of that other place, of The Boneyard, but all he smelled was...popcorn. A little girl had come up beside him with a greasy bag of the stuff clutched in both hands. Behind her, several pigeons waddled over. "Leave me alone!" she yelled down at them. Then she looked at William. "They won't leave me alone!"

William found himself smiling again. "They only want some popcorn," he said.

"Well they ain't getting any." She frowned, then pointed at

him. "You ain't either."

"That's okay," William said, "I don't like popcorn anyway. Sticks in my teeth."

"Huh!" The little girl turned, ponytail flying, and skipped away. The pigeons followed her.

William began walking, his fingers trailing along the limestone ledge of the wall. He felt an odd, undulating pattern in the surface of the stone, hardly noticeable except by touch. He stopped, and bent to examine the surface.

Hey...Billlly.

William ignored the voice, someone calling for a child with the same name as his own. He hadn't been called Billy since he was a little—

Hey. Billl...llly.

He straightened. The voice, low and rough, no more than a stage whisper, was behind him.

Then he smelled hot metal, like a motor about to burn out, and a warm thread of air caressed the back of his neck.

He spun around.

A little boy in a blue and white ski-jacket stood there, holding a half-eaten hotdog.

William gaped at him for a moment before finally finding his voice. "What did you say?"

The boy screwed up his face. "I didn't say nuthin'."

"You said 'Hey Billy'."

"No I didn't."

William went down into a crouch to get on eye-level with the boy. "Is Billy a friend of yours?"

The boy took a step back. "I'm not supposed to talk to strangers—"

"*Excuse* me."

A woman in a green wool coat came up behind the boy, and put her hand on his shoulder. The vivid red of her nail polish matched the red on her lips. Her voice was as cold as the day. "Can I help you?"

William rose. "I'm sorry, ma'am. Someone called my name, and I thought it was your boy here."

"I doubt my son knows you."

The boy grabbed the edge of her coat. "I didn't say nuthin' Mom, honest!"

"Didn't say anything, dear." She turned him. "Come along. We'll go finish that hotdog inside."

"My apologies——" William offered, but the woman had already dismissed him, and they were moving away.

Hey, the voice said again, behind him, again. *Billlly*.

He turned, fists clenched.

No one was there.

A fleeting whiff of ash, of sulfur, the cold breeze laced with heat.

Up...uppp here Billlly.

The hair under his knit cap stiffened, and his entire scalp began to itch.

He pulled the cap off and looked up, and his breath caught in his throat.

The huge bronze statue of William Penn, the crown of City Hall, loomed above. During the summer months tourists could take a winding staircase up through the statue to an observation room inside the hat. There were windows in the wide band, just visible above the indent in the brim. William saw pigeons up there, wheeling against the bright sky.

Something leaned out from one of the windows, something angular, and white.

We misssed you, Billlly. We want...

His entire body jerked, and he took two steps to the doors and the stairwell beyond, leading *up*, up to *them*, before he even realized he was doing it. He stopped himself, but only with great effort.

We waaant.

He uttered a gasping moan.

DD-down.

Not yet! Not...yet!

SSSoooon.

His left leg wrenched, dragging him a step forward. Just as slowly, he dragged it back.

"ENOUGH!"

Several people nearby him stopped, looking at him with startled expressions.

William ducked his head, took determined steps, his *own* steps, to the Lounge doors, into the lounge and across it, bypassing the elevators, to the stairs that only led one way. Down.

18

The young black woman, wearing nothing more than an old Shaft tee shirt, a cheap gold-plated necklace and a naughty, naughty smile, dangled a coffee mug from her finger. "How you want your coffee, hon?"

Jimmy, the building super, chuckled quietly from the couch. "Same as I like my women...with just a little sugar." He spread his arms wide. "Fuck the coffee, come over here and gimme some."

She placed the cup on the kitchenette counter with a coy expression. "You want something from me, Mister Jimmy?"

He patted the cushion beside him. "You know what I want, baby."

Her hands strayed to the hem of her shirt. "And you think I got some of what you want?"

"You got more than you need, baby, so get your sweet ass over here and share a little bit of it with Mister Jimmy."

She raised her tee shirt slowly as she walked the short

distance across the living room to the couch. First her belly was revealed, then the smooth, chocolate-cream curves of her firm, upright breasts. Her nipples were tight, erect, anticipating the pain/pleasure of Jimmy's lips, tongue, and teeth.

As she pulled the tee shirt past her head the material got caught on the pendant of her necklace. "Give me a hand with this, won't you, Jim—"

A sudden hot, dry wind rushed past her. "What the—" she began, but a sound, a strange, furious *slapping, sucking* sound, interrupted her.

She wrenched the shirt free, scratching her cheek with the pendant, and flung it from her with one hand while she pulled the necklace chain from her face with the other.

Then she screamed.

And in the few remaining moments left of her short, sweet life, she saw:

Jimmy prone on the couch, straddled by a mass of creatures without skin, without meat, just dead white, looping, writhing worm-snake limbs and flashing, strop-razor teeth and claws, thrusting, slicing, pounding to a beat rat-tatting in eerie syncopation with the final, futile hammerings of her heart.

In those same few moments, Jimmy's struggles were futile. The weight of the things, and their twisting knots of roping limbs, held him completely immobile. His eyes rolled, and a single, wailing cry escaped his mouth, even as the beasts burrowed into his face, jamming claws and chalk white flesh down his throat to silence him forever.

Another one of them, a nest of hot fluid movement engulfed her, overpowered her, pushed her to the floor. The nightmare beasts covered her, and she found herself staring into empty black eye-sockets with nothing behind them but death.

She tried to scream again, but the writhing white worms stuffed themselves into her mouth, down her throat, jammed tight, *slicing* as they went.

She struggled desperately, tried to jackknife her body, anything to free herself, to get the things out of her throat, anything to breathe.

But it was useless. She grew weaker, more disoriented with every second…suffocating, filling up with them, with the unbelievable pain.

As the red rimming her vision darkened to brown, then to violet, the very last thing she saw, the last nightmare, was Jimmy's ribcage ripping free from his torso, the worms coiling in his open body cavity, and his organs spilling like shiny new toys onto the blood-soaked carpet.

The red light on Fran's office phone started blinking at 8:05 on Monday morning. Fran allowed himself one heavy sigh, then punched and picked up. "Yes sir."

"Come on in, Frannie," Goaz said.

Fran walked across the Homicide squad room. Goaz's door was open, but he knocked on the doorjamb anyway, then entered.

Lieutenant Goaz's desk was even more cluttered than his own. Goaz looked up from an open file, his reading glasses perched at the bottom of his nose. He took them off.

"Sorry I missed Roll," Fran said.

Goaz waved his glasses dismissively. "Finnean tells me he's off doing more canvassing and re-interviews at the Cherry and Arch Street scenes."

"He's got more energy than me, Lieutenant."

"What are you bringing to the party this morning?"

"I'm running some leads." Fran pointed over his shoulder with his thumb, in the direction of his cubicle. "Putting some pieces together."

Goaz nodded, looking at him steadily. "You feeling okay?"

"I'm fine." Fran straightened. "Just peachy."

"Halberstadt gets his weekly update on our major cases Wednesday morning. I'd like to have something to give him."

"I understand, sir. We'll do our best."

"Good enough." Goaz put his glasses back on.

That was the signal. Fran turned and left. As he passed Heckleman's desk he said, "Where the hell is Harold? I sent him downstairs half an hour ago."

Heckleman only shrugged and grinned.

After two coffees and a stale Tastykake lemon pie, a short, fireplug-shaped man appeared in the doorway of Fran's cubicle office with a pushcart piled high with official-looking but dusty cardboard boxes.

"Harold! It's about frigging time!" Fran rose to inspect the boxes on the cart. He lifted the top off the top one, smelling dust, mildew, and stale cigarettes.

Harold, with an Edward G. Robinson face and matching scowl, said, "I've been down there in that goddamn hell hole since Roll, Lomax, digging this shit out."

Fran began leafing through the files inside. "You got them all?"

"I got crotch rot is what I got." Harold wiped his hands ceremoniously.

"Every single one?" Fran persisted.

"Yeah yeah yeah. 1946. A clean sweep."

"I'm only interested in October, actually. Maybe a little September, maybe November too."

"*Now* you tell me?" Harold gave Fran a disgusted look, then a dismissive wave. "Watch out for the silverfish, Lomax. They're monsters." Then he was gone.

Fran hated bugs, especially the quick ones like silverfish. Nasty, sneaky little bastards. Like tiny versions of the thing from that *Tingler* horror movie he had seen when he was a kid. He gathered up all of the open-case files on his desk and piled them on the floor in the corner by the beat-up metal file cabinets, not out of sight, but out of the way. He found the two file boxes covering the months in question and, watchful of critters, set them out on his now bare desktop.

There were twenty-seven homicide cases here, all unsolved,

all still technically open. Cold cases, as the civilians liked to say. A very low number, considering the city was nearly as big in 1946 as it was now, thirty-seven years later. The only real addition to Philly since then had been the Great Northeast, the neighborhoods sprung up along Roosevelt Boulevard, known internally as 'The Farms' if you were unlucky enough to get assigned to one of the precincts up there.

But the murders Fran was interested in could never have been committed in the sleepy Podunk streets of the Great Northeast; there were no hills to speak of (you had to go farther north into Bucks County for those) and no tall buildings. Certainly no skyscrapers. He began arranging the files chronologically. Nope, if you were interested in finding the Slaughterhouse Killer's work, you needed to look in Center City, where the tall buildings were, buildings with at least nineteen floors. *Like the Lennard.*

There were six unsolved homicide case files for the month of September 1946, and five for October. In November, thankfully, none. Fran quickly eliminated all six of the September cases, because none of them fit the profile even remotely, and piled them in an empty chair beside his desk. The first October case did, however. October 18, the remains of a body with massive blade trauma discovered on the observation deck on top of City Hall. Fran placed the October 18 homicide file in a place of honor on his desk. Get back to you in a minute, bud.

The second case, a day later, was a rape/strangulation. He tossed it on the pile with the September cases. The third case was a robbery/shooting, also on the 19th. Must have been a full moon that day. It followed the previous file onto the reject pile.

The fourth case, October 21, was a knifing dismemberment homicide in an apartment of a new building on Arch Street. The Lennard Building. Eighteenth floor. Fran sat up straight. Here we go. Glancing through the yellowed forms and photo-stats, he felt a surge of adrenalin, but he held off the war dance and put the file with the first one at the corner of his desk, arranging it neatly on top.

The fifth and final file was also the thickest. On October 24 there had been a multiple homicide at the Lennard, in an apartment on the nineteenth floor. Four members of a family killed, their bodies flayed, bones excised, internal organs and viscera thrown about. "An active search of the building and surrounding streets and alleyways was conducted to determine the whereabouts of the skeletal remains," Fran read aloud. He stared at the descriptions, went slowly through the crime scene photographs, noting Lester Blue's faded attribution stamp on the backs of them.

There had been no witnesses, but several 'persons of interest' had been interviewed: Miss Suzanne Button the day maid and Mr. William Alton the valet, had been principals; then building maintenance staff and the super, just to hit all the marks. The murdered family's residence had taken up the entire nineteenth floor. The floor above had been empty, not yet rented, and the floor below—considering the homicide there the previous day—unoccupied at the time of the crime. The only person re-interviewed had been Alton, a young black man, a World War II veteran. He had been out having the family car serviced when the murders took place, and the alibi had been verified by the auto repair shop on Second Street. Alton was one of the names Fran had given to Salvador. He looked forward to stopping by the Free Library later to hear what his young Latin Sherlock had dug up on this William Alton.

Fran spent nearly as much time reviewing the City Hall Observation Deck case and the single homicide on the eighteenth floor of the Lennard, scribbling notes, making a list of every aspect all three cases shared, filling several pages of his notebook. He also made a list of the names of the primary detectives involved in the three cases; then, rather than get his fat ass up out of his chair and walk across the squad room, he picked up his phone and called Heckleman at the Ops Desk. If anybody would know, it would be him. "Heck," he said, "I'm gonna shoot some names at you. Breton, Martin C."

There was a pause. "Former detective on the squad, right?"

"Right. Is he still around?"

"He died back in the '50s. One second." Fran heard a book being pulled, some pages turning. "Yeah, 1959. Car accident."

"Okay, one more: Edels, Alvin D."

"Another oldie." More pages turning. "And another deceased detective. 1962. Cancer, I think."

"Last one: Weinstein, Leon, no middle initial."

"I went to his funeral five years ago. You did too."

"Shit, you're right, I forgot. You're a regular font of knowledge, Heck."

"Any time, Sarge."

Fran put the phone back in its cradle. "Crap," he said. He sat silent for a long moment, then picked the phone back up and dialed. "Yes," he said to the voice that picked up, "Periodicals, please." Three voices later, he finally got Salvador on the line. "You got me going crazy up here, Detective," Salvador said, "All that action you got going on and I'm stuck here helping old ladies thread microfilm for apple pie recipes, you know?"

Fran grinned. "You get anything on those two names I gave you?"

"Give me a little more time, okay? I got some good stuff, but I know I can get more."

"Can you have something for me tomorrow?"

"We open at eight thirty, Detective."

"I'll be there, thanks."

Five minutes later, with his leather case in hand, Fran passed Heckleman on his way out of the squad room. "Red me out, Heck," he said.

Heckleman rose to mark the In/Out Board. "Where to?"

"City Hall, Office of Records, Office of Deeds, Office of Whatever The Hell They Got that's gonna help me with this goddamn case."

"Any place in particular where somebody can reach you?"

Fran stopped. "If I told you that, then somebody could reach me, right?"

Heckleman grinned. "Be careful out there, Sarge," he said. "Snow's starting to build up."

I'm out of my league.

Mike Finnean stood in his disposable paper booties just inside the door of the Cherry Street apartment, the unoccupied one down the hall from the Copper crime scene, feeling oddly calm.

Odd, because what he saw before him should have scared him shitless on several levels. Odd because, like Fran Lomax, the future of more than just his career depended, *depended*, upon solving this case, this insane, endless case.

Instead: calm. Calm acceptance.

I'm out of my league, he decided. Way, way out. Then: Where the hell is Fran?

On the couch was the open, empty skin of a black man.

Note that, he thought. A *black* man, medium height, aged around thirty-five. Not white, not tall, not in his sixties. Not, in other words, at all like the others.

This victim had been cut open the way a tailor would cut along the seams of a garment, so neatly, so precisely, that the skin and attached fatty layers laid out on the bloody cushions were easily, instantly recognizable as human, as a man, as a particular man. The building super, a man called Jimmy.

Like a Halloween costume, Mike thought. Better, like a Sunday suit, neatly arranged to avoid wrinkles. Hell, I can even see old knife-slash scars on his belly.

Scattered about the room, some of it on other furniture, the rest on the floor with the majority of the pooled blood, were Jimmy's musculature and viscera. In the corner, the liver, lumpy and purple; the large intestine was looped over the couch arm, brick red and puss yellow, pruned at the anus; he glimpsed a dirty pink and blue lobe of pebbled lung peeking out from under a side chair.

Next to his left shoe, almost touching the kraft paper: the heart, large and well marbled.

Mike stooped to study the organ close up. The artery edges and ligature looked...*torn*, not cut.

Torn. That was odd. Considering the care given to the victim's skin, very odd indeed.

What's the conclusion to that?

Delicate (Christ: *inspired*) blade work on the skinning, right down to the asshole, yet the organs were haphazardly ripped out and scattered?

And where-oh-where, of course, were the bones?

The killers (for it had to be more than one, *had* to be) had plenty of time with this one. Obviously. Not like the messy, interrupted work done down the hall a little over a week before, or across town at the Ben Franklin, or on Arch Street. For this one, they had time. Time to take the bones, all the bones, and time to take a peculiar, special care with the skin. No frenzied ripping, slashing or tearing here, at least not at first.

And those crazy, crazy prints in the bloody carpet near the couch. Repeated looping smears, like a kindergarten finger painting. What the hell kind of shoes did they wear? At least the ones leaving the apartment were normal footprints; bloody, maybe, but normal.

Mike rose. It was just five days since the hotel slayings, nine days since Arch Street, and two weeks since the first one, poor widowed Mr. Copper, right down the hall.

I'm out of my league.

Then, again: Where the hell is Fran?

He heard a sound at the door, and turned. "Well? Where did our bloody footprints lead us?"

Nyland, the same officer who had been first on the scene for Homicide Number One, pointed down the hall with his night stick. "Downstairs. 9-N. They refused to open the door. Said they didn't know anything about…this."

"So what are you waiting for, my personal permission to bust their fucking door down?"

Nyland colored. "We got in, Detective. A couple of ace teenagers gave us a little hassle…" The young officer gestured again with his stick. "You better come see for yourself, though. Looks like we got a witness, if she lives."

Finnean was suddenly past him at a dead run. "Nine what?" he flung over his shoulder.

"N!" Nyland leaned against the doorjamb, closing his eyes. "9-N."

The nervous young man with the black-rimmed glasses and ill-fitting plaid sport-coat peeked out of his office for the third time in as many minutes. "We really do have to close up for lunch now, sir," he said. "Really."

Fran sighed, spun the microfilm handle a final time, then turned the machine off.

"You can leave the spool in the Reader," the young man said. "I'll take care of it."

Fran regarded him as he would a bug in a jar. "One last time: all your records are on microfilm, Mr. Yurt?"

Yurt nodded, his head moving like a bobble-figure. "We're very proud of the fact that the Office of Deeds was the first in city government to—"

"Nothing left on paper? All the way back?"

Another bobble-head nod. "All the way to March 1949. After the fire. Everything before that, though, *pfft.*"

"Pfft." Fran got slowly to his feet. "I'm keeping you, I know," he said, gathering his notes up. "It must be past noon; I'm sorry."

"That's all right, Detective." Yurt watched him as he stuffed his papers into his leather case. "Sorry you didn't find what you were after."

"The fact that what I was looking for was conspicuous by its absence is almost as important as finding it, Mr. Yurt."

"Really?"

Fran hefted his case. "Thank you again, and now I will get out of your hair." He left young Mr. Yurt and the Office of Deeds and entered the cavernous third floor west hallway. City Hall on the outside was a Second Empire fruit-salad bordello eyesore of an architectural landmark. On the inside it was shaped like a square doughnut, with wide staircases at the corners, so either a left or a right would take him where he needed to go. He looked at his watch. Ten minutes past the time he was supposed to meet Sarah. "Who is always late anyway," he said to the anonymous stream of people in the hallway. Three gave him a funny look, like he was a bug in a jar. Perfect. He looked out one of the tall corridor windows at the steadily falling snow. Just perfect.

"We got a meat-wagon coming—" the officer at the door of 9-N began, but Mike brushed past him, following the footprints into the apartment. At the door to the bathroom beside the kitchenette was a group of three black youths yelling and shaking fists, and two more officers trying unsuccessfully to shout them down. But Mike shouted louder than all of them put together. He *roared*: "Everybody SHUT UP!"

Sudden, blinking silence.

Then a soft, moaning cry from inside the bathroom.

One of the three youths, a skinny teenager with a bad case of acne darkening his cheeks, puffed up his chest and said, "So who the fuck are *you*, you whiteass moth—"

Mike picked him up by the front of his shirt with one hand, slammed him against the wall and said, distinctly, "I'm the *man*, you little cocksucker. I'm in *charge*." Then he let the kid's Converses touch the floor. "Now get the fuck out of this apartment and take your smartass pals with you."

But the teenager persisted. "I live here, goddammit! And that's my *sister* in there! You got no right busting in our place telling me—"

"I got every right to bust your candyass young butt into a Holmesburg cell with a fucking *river* view if you don't back off and back off NOW!"

"Paulie," said a quavering voice, a mother's voice, from inside the bathroom, "do like the policeman says. There's nothing you can do in here."

"But Mom—"

Quavering more, "And take your friends with you. Like he says. Mind me, now."

"There's an ambulance coming," one of the officers said. "Your sister's going to get all the help she needs."

The teenager opened his mouth to say something, but Mike beat him to it: "Out," he said. "Now." Then he muscled past everyone and opened the bathroom door. "Oh my God," he said then.

On the floor, on a crumpled blanket and scattered towels, was a middle-aged black woman crouched beside the naked body of a young black woman.

The mother was crying, daubing futilely at her daughter's body with a washcloth, trying to staunch what appeared to be a countless number of deep cuts, cuts in a pattern that...(*Jesus Christ*, Mike thought, realizing)...that were exactly the same as the dead man's ten floors above.

Like the neat, regular seams of a garment.

Like the killer wanted to take her bones out too.

But this one, this one...

Finnean dropped to one knee, felt the girl's neck. "She's still alive."

"She's got to be alive! Dear Lord, even with all this blood, she's *got* to be!" Raising the blood-soaked washcloths she held in her hands, she pleaded with Mike, "You've got to help her! You got to!"

Mike and the officers behind him exchanged bleak looks, then he said, "Go get a sheet; we'll rip it up into strips, and make some tourniquets. Those goddamn ambulance cowboys could take forever to get here in the snow."

There was a gallery of stores and restaurants below street-level that connected the City Hall subway station with the Suburban Railroad Station on JFK Boulevard. On a snowy day like this one, it was a good way to avoid the weather. Under the Court Annex Building was Fran and Sarah's 'special secret little place,' the Penn Donut Hole. Sarah was already in a booth when Fran got there. She had a coffee and an open box of donut holes waiting for him. Her coffee, he noticed, was already mostly gone. "So," he said jovially, throwing his case onto the seat opposite and sliding in after it, "how's the most beautiful woman in the Penn Donut Hole doing this fine day?"

"She's mildly miffed," Sarah said, but gave him a quick kiss anyway. "I only get an hour, you know. And your coffee is probably cold."

"I was upstairs for the past three hours spinning bureaucratic wheels." He took a sip. Yep, cold. Think: iced coffee.

She pushed the box of donut holes toward him. "That serial case? It's been, what, only a week or so? There's some sourdoughs in here."

"Since Thanksgiving, actually, the one we missed having together because of Victim Number One, remember? And I've spent most of my time on it, too, letting my other cases slide."

"Is letting those others go such a good idea?" She finished off her own coffee. "What about Mike Finnean? I thought he was the co-primary."

Co-primary. Fran got a kick out of Sarah throwing police procedural jargon around. "Yeah," he said, "he's in it up to his eyeballs too. More so, really, since he was first on scene for the last two. He's got three bodies to my one. Plus he's dogging the crime scene evidence tracks, doing all that bullshit slog work." He regarded his coffee. "But I'm still the Primary, unless you heard something."

She popped a chocolate glazed donut hole in her mouth.

"So what are you doing, then, Mr. hotshot Primary?"

Fran took a swallow, and grimaced. Iced coffee my ass. "Chasing after ghosts."

"Ghosts?"

"Two people. Two mystery men. The first one is named John Randall Pitcairn."

"Who is John Randall Pitcairn?"

"That, my darling dear, has been the question of the day. I haven't been able to find him. Anywhere."

"Is it a pseudonym? A fake name?"

"No, it's real enough. Two different sources told me so, anyway."

Sarah frowned. "I don't get it. If he's real, then he has to be in the system somewhere."

"You'd think so, wouldn't you? I checked every city agency, every record archive back to 1949."

"Ahh. The City Hall fire. What about state and federal, then? Social Security?"

"Never signed up for it."

"But that's the *law*."

Fran grinned briefly.

"IRS?"

"Never paid any taxes, either. They never even heard of him."

"*That's* illegal. DMV?"

Fran shook his head.

Sarah clapped her hands together. "I know! FBI! They've got a file on everybody! You know that guy, what's his name—"

"Sarah, I made that call this morning. No soap."

"I can't believe the IRS had nothing."

Fran spread his hands. "Why would they lie to me? I'm such a lovable shamus."

"A shamus is a private detective, babe, like Sam Spade. You're just a cop."

Fran had a pretty good Bogart impression in him, and

Sarah knew it, but he let the moment pass.

She said, "So what is John Randall Pitcairn's connection to the serial murders?"

"Well, nothing, really. At least, not to any of the current cases."

"The current cases?" She put her hand over his. "My God, a spider just crawled up my back! There were other murders?"

Fran nodded. "In 1946, one on the observation deck below Billy Penn's feet, another in an apartment in a building on Arch, then four more next day, same building. The Lennard. It got torn down right after."

"Six people murdered?"

He lined six donut holes on his napkin. "Yep."

"Six in a month? And they all died the same way? Same MO?"

MO. She killed him. He said, "Evisceration and deboning; the bad guy actually took off with the skeletons of two of the last four. They were never recovered."

"What about that other name you were chasing?"

"Alton. William Alton. He was associated with that last multiple murder at the Lennard. He was the family valet, a black kid, right out of the Army, taking a job to shine whitey's shoes."

"It was in the '40's you said, right? That was pretty common then."

"I suppose."

"Don't tell me: you can't find him in the system either?"

Fran shook his head. "You'd think so, with the Army connection, but not yet. I've got some calls in, but Uncle Sam can be slow. At the moment it looks like he dropped from sight too, just like Pitcairn."

Sarah put another donut hole in her mouth, and chewed slowly. "Thirty-seven years is a long time to get lost... or dead."

"Maybe. No death certificates, though. Couldn't hide one of those."

"Maybe the current killer is the original killer's son, you

know, carrying on the family tradition, revenging the father..."

Fran snorted a chuckle. "That only happens in bad books and movies-of-the-week."

"You know me. I'm a sucker for a good potboiler." She toyed with one of his donut hole victims. "So we've got our William Alton possibly at the scene of the old Lennard Building murders, that's clear, but how was this Pitcairn dude connected?"

Fran told her about the Lester Blue interview, and the subsequent visit by Ruth Grundy. "And," he said, rummaging in his case and pulling out his notebook of scribbles, "the detectives in the last two cases from 1946 list a John Randall Pitcairn as being at or near the scene of the crimes."

"As a material witness?"

Fran smiled again. Material witness. God, he loved her. "No, honey-bunch, just a plain old garden variety 'citizen at or about the scene of the crime.' A face in the crowd, one of dozens."

"But these detectives made a point of noting him down."

"Yeah." Fran glanced at his notes. "They did do that."

"So maybe he's not a red herring after all. Maybe he's connected to this Alton character."

"Maybe." Fran scooped up the last of his donut holes and crammed them into his mouth, then washed them down with the last of his cold coffee.

"So what are you going to do now, Mr. Detective Sergeant?"

"Now?" Fran reached across the table and took Sarah's hand back. "Now I'd like to take you out to some nice place for lunch."

"Lunch? Babe, I just ate a dozen donut holes! *This* was lunch. Plus I have to get back—"

"Come on. A nice, leisurely lunch."

"But Judge—"

"Screw the judge. I'll bet she'll understand. She's got a boyfriend or two, doesn't she? And boyfriends take their girlfriends out on dates, right?"

"You mean this…" Sarah pointed to the empty coffee cups and donut holes box, "This isn't a date?"

"You're a killer," Fran said, "you know that? A real killer." He looked around, saw a phone booth hanging on the wall, and started to get up. "Just let me call in, let them know where I am, okay?"

Nyland, a young police officer with traces of Academy soap still fresh behind his ears, a twenty-three-year-old kid from a good Irish family in Kensington where everybody's uncle was a cop, or wanted to be; a beat cop who in the last few weeks had seen more blood, more gore, more *death*, than most twenty-year pension veterans would ever see, was about to see a little more.

He rode in the back of the ambulance with the victim and a para-medic policeman named Wilson, lending moral support to his meat wagon brother in blue, if nothing else.

"I don't get it," Wilson said for the third time since their mad race for the hospital had begun.

Nyland raised his own voice above the wail of the siren and the roar of the tires on the wet pavement. Outside, the snow was picking up. "Don't get what?"

Wilson spread his arms to encompass the victim strapped to the folded gurney. "This girl is alive and dead at the same goddamn time."

"Dead?" Nyland sat up. "What do you mean?" Christ! This was the witness, *the witness*. She couldn't be dead. "She looks the same…she's looks—"

"I know. She's taking the IVs; she's working with the respirator. Hell, there's probably some brain activity—won't know that till we unload at Hahnemann and get her up to the ICU. But, jeez, there's still no heartbeat, there's no—"

Then the girl on the gurney groaned.

Both men flinched.

Then Nyland said, "Dead, huh?"

The girl groaned again, and shifted.

Then she screamed.

"Jesus!" Wilson yelled.

The girl spasmed, then spasmed again. In spite of the straps her body under the blanket seemed to leap into the air in a messy, confused bundle, like a marionette having all of its strings pulled.

"Help me restrain her," Wilson shouted, moving over her, reaching out to contain her movements.

But Nyland hesitated, and at that moment there was an explosion of blood from the girl's mouth: dark, sticky blood, cold and thick, *gobbets* of it, flung everywhere. "JESUS!" Wilson yelled again, his hands on his face, wiping the gore out of his eyes.

But Nyland's eyes were clear, wide, broadcasting his fear like lighthouse beacons, and he saw what happened next.

He saw the thin blanket they had wrapped the girl in *move*, move in a hundred separate places. Like there were rats under there, crawling all over her, he thought, his fear turning into pure terror. Rats! God help us, what is going on here? What is going on?

Wilson's face was finally clean enough for him to see, and he immediately reached to uncover the bloody blanket.

The ambulance skidded, slowed, and the driver yelled through the door, "You guys okay back there?"

"Drive, goddammit!" Wilson shouted, "just drive!"

The ambulance lurched forward again; the siren wailed and warbled.

"Don't—" Nyland began, but Wilson already had the blanket in hand, pulling it free from the straps, exposing the strangely undulating girl...

19

Standing in the falling snow on the front steps of the West Philadelphia apartment building, one of the patrolmen, a 20-year beat veteran named Carroll, hailed Fran. "Sarge! You ready for this one? It's pretty bad."

"They're all bad, Sammy. Anyway, I'm late. Detective Finnean upstairs?"

"Yeah." Carroll grinned. "Detective Finnean said something about having your gonads filleted on a plate or some such."

"Wonderful." Fran let his breath out like a steaming locomotive. "So I missed the whole party, eh?"

"Well, you got two crime scenes, one on 19, the other on 9."

"Yeah, I heard."

"Body of the deader from 19-G is gone, and they took the girl from 9-N to the hospital. Hahnemann, I think. And the Crime Lab crew just went out for some chow."

"Good." Fran slapped Carroll on the shoulder as he passed him. "I don't like crowds anyway. And get the hell out of the snow, will ya?"

Inside, he glanced at the door to the fire stairs, then saw a kid kneeling with his nose pressed to the cold glass beside the front doors. "The elevators work yet?"

The kid turned, appraised him, then pointed. "Lef' one does. Not the rest."

Fran went over to the bank of three double-doors and was about to press the UP button when the doors on the left buzzed, and then chunked open. Mike Finnean came out of the car, looking beat, but his expression lightened when he saw Fran. "Well it's about fucking time, Detective Lomax! I pull you away from something important?"

"I wish it was." Fran pointed up. "Anyone left upstairs?"

"Just some uniforms. Otto's done and gone. Sanderson and Lafferty will be back, but they're pretty much done too."

"What about the M.E.?"

"Koenig? He came and went like his friggin' pants were on fire." Mike ran a hand through his hair. "He's as much under the gun for that Major Cases brief tomorrow as we are. Listen, I'm headed over to the hospital, maybe get something out of this girl if she ever wakes up. You want to come?"

"I'll go through both scenes with Lafferty and Sanderson first. Maybe I'll meet you there. Hahnemann, right? Why the hell did they take her all the way over to Hahnemann?"

"God knows." Mike raised his hand, then made for the front doors.

The elevator had closed, so Fran pushed the UP button, and it chunked back open. He entered the car, wrinkling his nose at the sour, vomity smell. Lovely, just lovely. He brought his finger to the '19' button, hesitated, then pressed it. *God*, he thought, as the doors closed and the smell pressed in, *I hate elevators*.

As the car began its slow, groaning ascent, he sorted out everything that had happened in this apartment building: first, the Copper murder in 19-B, back on Thanksgiving. Now the building super, Jimmy, gets the same treatment in 19-G, and in the process, some teenage girl gets cut up bad enough for a hospital run. What had Finnean told him on the phone? She had made it down to her parent's apartment on the ninth floor, where Finnean had found her in the bathroom. Jesus. The witness at the first homicide, the kid Jameel, lived where? Eighteen?

He looked up, saw the floor indicator flashing through the floors, and suddenly punched the button for Eighteen. First things first.

In the hallway on Eighteen he had to step over a sleeping wino before he reached the door to Jameel's apartment.

He knocked.

Inside, a door slammed.

Fran waited a moment, and knocked again.

Then, from the opposite side of the door: "Whatyouwant?"

"This is the police. I'm Detective Sergeant Lomax." He pulled his badge free of his belt and held it up to the peephole. "I want to speak with Jameel."

"Jameel ain't here."

Sounded like an older woman, mother, aunt. "Do you know when he'll be back? I need to ask him some questions."

"Seems you whiteass policemen asked him enough questions already. Seems like you already had your chance on that poor child."

"Listen." Fran leaned against the door. "There are still a few things that need clearing up. If you could just tell me—"

"You got a warrant?"

"Of course not. I'm not here to search the place or arrest anybody. I just—"

"Jameel," the voice yelled, "ain't here! He's innocent! Now get the hell outta here and leave decent folks ALONE!"

Down the hall, a door opened, and a huge Hispanic man in a tight white tee shirt and black pants stepped out. "You gotta problem?" he said, rumbling the words.

Fran turned to him. "Not yet," he said, cheerfully. "Why?

You thinking about giving me one?"

The big man squinted in the dim light of the yellowed, buzzing fluorescents. "You a cop?"

"Detective Sergeant." Fran showed him his badge. "Homicide."

"Shiit." The big man reentered his apartment, and the slamming of his door reverberated down the hallway.

Fran returned his attention to the door before him.

From within: only silence.

He turned, finally, and went back to the elevators. Dumb idea, anyway. Seemed like he had a million of those, lately.

On the nineteenth floor he went left, *away* from the scene of the newest murder. *Second things second*, he thought. He went to the other apartment—19-B—where crime-scene tape was still draped across the door like a crazy yellow spider web; he went to the place where another unconscionable atrocity had been committed, where the first murder had occurred a week and a half before.

He tried the door, then used the copy of the floor master the now-departed Jimmy had given up when it had been just one death, just one old man hacked to smithereens.

The door swung open on grey shadows. Fran pushed the tape aside, bent, and slipped his considerable bulk through. His shadow ran across the empty hardwood floor, up the far wall, and was lost in the dark rectangle of the window. Outside, steady snow drifted down the airshaft, softening the warehouse wall opposite.

He found the light switch to the overhead fixture and flipped it on.

The apartment was empty of furniture, and the pale brown stains in the wall paint, stains no amount of Spic-N-Span or elbow grease would ever get out, were the only visible reminders of the crime.

He went into the bedroom. There was no overhead fixture, but even in the dark Fran could see it was as bare as the living room. There was only close, rank air, a closet door, and the single empty window.

What are you looking for, Fran?

He found he had no answer to that question.

What would be left, now, for you to find?

He took a step into the room, letting his eyes adjust to the dark.

Something.

Then he went over to the window. Outside, across the airshaft, the wall of brick and cinder-blocked windows stared back at him through the snow. What a view.

He tried to open the window, and succeeded only when he slammed at the top of the sash with both palms. No screen. He leaned out, into the cold, moaning wind. The snow swirled down. He breathed in its clean smell, filling his lungs with it. There was an old newspaper on the fire escape grate, a complete Sunday *Inquirer*, by the looks of it, but so sodden by wet weather that the pattern of the grate showed through its solid inch of newsprint and thick icing of snow.

Fran shivered, leaned back inside and pushed off the windowsill with his belly. In doing so, he put a hand on the side of the window, grasping the trim molding for support.

Then he stopped.

The moldings. They were nondescript, featureless, with numerous coats of white enamel on them, grimed, chipped and scored with years of use. But under all the paint, carved into the wood, was a subtle, swirling pattern.

In his mind, then, it came jarringly together. In all the rooms where people had been murdered, the moldings of the windows had been the same. Arch Street, then at the Ben Franklin, and now here: all the same. He ran his hand along it, lightly. It was an organic, flowing pattern of complex twists and curves. Down the hall, in the newest butcher shop, he wondered if he would find the same pattern in the window molding there.

"But that's just crazy," he whispered, as his fingers followed the patterns beneath the chipped paint. Coincidence? It couldn't be. You didn't just walk into a lumberyard and order this. Fran doubted that it was sold at all; the pattern wasn't even a pattern; it seemed completely random.

But then how…? And why…?

He reached into his pocket and pulled out the little bone on the key chain, the gift from Lester Blue. He rubbed his thumb over it…

Something.

A warm, furtive gust of air touched his face, smelling vaguely of ashes, of burned metal. Must be the incinerator, was his first thought.

He reached up to pull the window sash back down, and then before him, like a flickering TV screen changing channels, the wall across the airshaft faded and disappeared, and in its place was a bottomless black abyss filled with indistinct movement. The movement was…ominous and *wrong*, just *wrong*. Fran blinked, trying to focus his eyes. What the hell was going on here?

The movement focused on its own, then, and came forward from out of the black distance, growing, approaching like the front grille of a semi, like a steaming, sparking, screaming locomotive: a huge, writhing mass of white, of open mouths, razor teeth flashing, slicing the air—

Coming straight for him.

The bone between his fingers was suddenly burning. The heat and stench of sulfur was overwhelming. The bone turned white-hot. He yelled, flung the bone and key chain through the window toward the onrushing nightmare, slammed the window down and staggered back as large shards of glass fell, shattering, at his feet.

He scrambled, stumbled out of the bedroom, careened through the living room and flung himself headlong into the web of yellow tape in the front doorway. The plastic resisted for an instant, but his weight and bulk prevailed and he fell free, into the hallway, slamming into the opposite wall, rolling, coming up on his knees, finally pulling his Browning free and thumbing off its safety.

"Hey! Who the hell's that?"

Fran swung the gun about. From down the hall, out of the darkness, a familiar figure approached.

"Fran," the figure said. "Fran Lomax? What the hell!"

It was Lafferty. Fran swung the gun back to the open apartment door. Within: light, shadow, and silence.

No monster at his heels. No mouths reaching to bite his face off.

No foul breath of hell.

The Crime Lab technician saw the gun then and froze in mid-stride. *What?* his eyes said, as he fumbled his own weapon free.

Fran took a breath, then another.

Silence, light, shadow. The apartment was empty.

He rose slowly to his feet. The yellow Crime Scene tape hung from his coat like party bunting. "I'm going back in." He pointed his gun at Lafferty's. "You know how to use that?"

"Shit yeah." The lab technician tried a grin. "Always a first time, right?"

"Just stay in the hall. It's probably nothing. Okay?"

Lafferty nodded.

Fran went back into the apartment.

The living room and kitchen were empty. In three steps he was at the bedroom door. It was half-closed. He gripped the Browning with both hands, listening.

Silence from within. Through the broken window, only the muffled sounds of the city, and a cold draft of air.

No movement.

Nothing.

Fran lunged, kicked the door and then was in the room, pointing his gun quickly to the window, the closet door, then to each corner, to each shadow.

Empty.

Cold air, broken glass, grey shadows. The window was empty. The jagged glass in the sash frames echoed the teeth that had filled the darkness there only moments before. Now, beyond the sill, only the blocked up windows of the empty warehouse stared back at him, through the falling snow.

The closet was in the corner opposite the window. In two steps he was there, again, listening.

More silence.

He grabbed the knob and pulled the door open.

Empty. As empty as the room. Not even a coat hanger.

Then the hairs on the back of his neck prickled, and Fran spun about, both hands gripping the Browning again, a full pound of pressure on a trigger that didn't need much more, pointing to the broken window.

There was something on the sill. Something he hadn't noticed.

Fran advanced until he could see.

It was the key chain, the one the old lady had given to him, the one that Lester Blue had carried, down through the years. The key chain with the small white bone. What had Lester said? Watch out where you took the bones? Watch out how *high* you took them?

Fran advanced another step, then stopped.

The bone was gone. The ring that had held it was broken, blackened, and twisted open.

And the bone was gone.

Out in the hallway again, Lafferty barely contained his relief. "So what the hell were you doing in there, anyway? The new scene is down the hall."

"Just a loose end." Fran holstered his gun with a single, savage movement, then wiped his hands on his coat. "You know me and my loose ends."

"Like Columbo."

Fran laughed hollowly, "yeah, like Columbo. Look." He

took in a long breath. "Can you do me a favor, Roj? A big one?"

Lafferty hesitated, then pulled a piece of tape off Fran's coat. "I'm the only one up here," he said. "I'm going to close it up for the night. Right? I can close it up?"

"Good," Fran said. "That's good."

"What about the uniform downstairs?"

"Carroll? He's an old pal. Beat days. You know. Anyway, I'm supposed to be down the hall, right? The murder of the building super? I'm just late, that's all."

Lafferty balled up the tape in his hands and gestured with it to the open apartment. "What about here?"

Fran looked in again. Silence, shadows. He pulled more tape off himself. "A broken window. That's all. Vandals."

"Okay." Lafferty accepted the rest of the tape, and balled it up with the first piece. "Can't help break-ins from the fire-escape," he said, pulling the door shut, locking it, "right?"

"Right." Fran turned down the hall, stopped, turned back. "I owe you one," he said.

"Oh yeah." Lafferty dismissed his very presence with a wave of his hand. "Now," and he ducked around Fran's bulky figure, "if you like, I'll give you the tour of the new scene, then you better get your fat ass over to the hospital before the girl kicks it."

Hahnemann Hospital was full of ghosts for Fran. Personal ghosts. Bad memories. His father had died here, after all. As he approached the ICU he remembered the last time he had walked down this same corridor, hesitated in front of these same ICU doors, knowing that his father lay dying beyond them. The line of orange plastic chairs were still there in the lounge, bolted to the wall. He dropped heavily into the first one, closing his eyes as he leaned his head back against the wall.

The ICU nurse came out to the lounge area and touched the young man on the shoulder. "Mr. Lomax," she said quietly as he started, eyes blinking, coming out of his doze. "Sorry to wake you, but you wanted to know when your father—"

"He's awake?" The young man rubbed his face with quick, rough motions, clearing his throat as he unfolded his tall, thin frame from the lounge chair and stood. His long hair fell briefly over his eyes, but he brushed it back, and cleared his throat again. "He's conscious, then."

"Yes. And he's asking for family."

He followed her into the ICU. The semi-circular arrangement of patient bays was low-lit and half-empty. He kept his head down, trying not to look into the occupied bays, afraid he would see one of the patients awake and looking back at him, awake and alone with the quiet machines, looping plastic tubes and flickering screens. *This is the real deal, Frannie, he told himself. This is the real shit. Dad's in here.*

When they reached his father's bay Fran looked up for the first time, and for an endless moment he did not recognize the pale, collapsed old man in the bed. *This isn't him, Fran thought, this can't be him. You brought me to the wrong patient—*

But then the man in the bed opened his eyes and looked at him, and attempted to raise a hand stuck with catheters and tubes. Fran went forward, and took the hand into his own. "Dad," he said.

His father smiled. "Hey laddie. How's the boy?"

"I'm fine. How are you?"

The smile again, tired, all-knowing. "There's no pain, just achy, just a bit. Where's your mother?"

"I sent her home. It's really late. I told her to go home and get some sleep."

"How late is it?"

Fran looked at his watch. "Past two-thirty."

"Two-thirty in the morning? Christ-on-a-stick. You should be home too, sleeping. You've got school tomorrow."

"I can sleep any time." Fran let go of his father's hand, and sat in the armchair beside the bed. "I wanted to be here when you woke up."

"Always the optimist ain't you." His father arranged his hand so the catheter tubes hung freely, taking his time, frowning with the effort. "So," he said then, "what's the verdict?"

"Verdict?"

"*The pain in my chest before I blacked out and woke up here. It was like a locomotive hitting me square on. What does the doctor say?*"

"*I haven't spoken with one in a couple of hours, but they said it was another coronary. Heart attack. Another heart attack.*"

"*Ah.*" *His father nodded slowly.* "*Three strikes, lad. Next one takes us into extra innings.*"

"*You'll be fine, Dad.*"

"*Nah.*" *He looked at the machines beside his bed.* "*I don't think so. I think it may be over.*"

Fran knew what his father said was probably true. How many times can you break? How many times can they put you back together?

"*Dad…*"

His father looked back. "*Yes, laddie?*"

"*I was going to wait until they released you, but I wanted to tell you something. News.*"

"*News, eh? Good news, I hope.*"

"*Yeah.*" *Fran hesitated, then in a rush of words:* "*I signed up for the exams.*"

"*Exams. Not the Academy exams?*"

Fran dropped his eyes. "*I figure I have a good shot at it.*"

"*You're a college kid, Fran. You're gonna get that sheepskin, go be something. You want to waste it on being a fugging policeman?*"

"*I want to be a cop, Dad. Like Grandpa. Like you.*"

"*Ah, lad.*" *The old man in the bed sighed. Silence lengthened between them.*

"*Dad—*"

"*You ain't got it!*" *His father spit the words out.*

Fran felt a sudden coldness wash through him. "*What do you mean?*"

"*You just ain't got it, lad.*" *His father raised his hand, tubes trailing, to cover his eyes.* "*Be something else. Be anything else.*" *His hand came down, and Fran saw tears on his cheeks.*

You ain't got it, lad.

You ain't got it.

"Sergeant?"

The place where the ICU gurney should be was empty. They'd taken the girl down to the morgue already.

"Excuse me, Sergeant?"

Fran looked around. A young uniform was in the corridor. "Yeah. What's up?"

"You okay, Sergeant?"

"Yeah." Fran rubbed his forehead briefly. "Just wool-gathering. I'm fine. You find Nyland?"

"He's downstairs. Outside the ER, in one of the cruisers."

"Good. Good." Fran went past him. "Thanks," he said.

There were two cruisers parked in the circular drop-off by the hospital's ER. Fran nodded to the officers standing by the first one, the one with someone in the back seat cage. Even through the snow and the glare off the glass, he recognized Nyland. "Can I have a few minutes with him?"

"We were just waiting on you, Sarge, then we're taking him home."

Fran slid in, and pulled the door shut.

The young patrolman looked up at him. "Now we're both trapped in here," he said.

"How's it going…Dan, isn't it?"

"Dave. David Quentin Nyland." He looked away with a crooked smile. "Third generation of Nyland blue."

"Me too. My dad was a cop, my grandpa too."

Nyland stared out at the snow as it hit and melted on the glass.

Fran said, "You were at the Cherry Street scene, the deader on the nineteenth floor, Thanksgiving. I remember. Quite a day that was."

Nyland was silent.

"So what happened today?"

"In the ambulance?"

"Yeah. What happened in the ambulance?"

"You wouldn't believe it, Sarge."

"You sure about that? Try me."

Nyland looked at him, then back to the snow. "The girl, she had cuts all over her body. All over."

"Regular incisions? Straight, clean?"

"Yeah, like a scalpel, like a surgeon did them. They followed the pattern of her—"

"Bones. Her skeleton."

"Yeah." Nyland frowned at him. "Exactly. They followed her skeleton." He rubbed his hand over his forehead, scrubbing it. "But the cuts were mostly closed, hardly bleeding at all. Just marks, lines."

"Scars," Fran said.

"Yeah, scars. At least, after a while. I mean, she was bleeding a lot in the apartment, in that bathroom her mother had her in, but in the ambulance Wilson put on some pressure bandages—"

"Wilson's the EMT?"

Nyland nodded. "I took the ride in the back of the wagon with him."

"So Wilson had her bleeding in check."

"Yeah, but like I said, the cuts were all practically closed by the time we got her on the gurney and into the back."

Wounds that healed before they had any right to. Fran said, "Then what happened?"

"We weren't in the wagon more than a few minutes, tearing down Walnut over the river, not sure why they picked Hahnemann over Penn, but that's where we were headed, when the girl started jerking at the gurney straps, making choking noises, convulsions, you know?" Nyland paused; he rubbed his lips with the back of his hand. "The sheets started moving, like there was something under them besides her. Like rats scurrying around, under there. Then the sheets started showing blood, like the cuts had opened back up." He looked at Fran again. "Then the bones came out, Sarge."

"Her convulsions caused her bones to be exposed—"

"No, they *came out.* All on their own, wriggling around like *snakes.*"

Like worms, Fran thought.

"They came out of her body, Sarge, ripping through the sheets, shooting up into the wagon, hitting the roof and then back down on the deck. There was blood everywhere."

"So what did you do?"

"Besides freaking out? Besides screaming our fucking heads off? Wilson worked on the girl, more bandages I guess, while I grabbed the bones and put them in a nylon bag that was back there. Some of them were still moving, right in my hand, *moving.* The driver had us here in less than five minutes, don't know how he did it, but he did. The ER crew took over with the girl. I hung onto the bag in the back of the wagon until some other uniforms showed, then Detective Finnean."

"Were they still moving, the bones in the bag?"

Nyland shook his head. "They were just bones again, bloody and slimy, but just bones."

"Anything else?"

"When I picked them up off the deck, they were hot."

"The bones were hot?"

"Almost too hot to touch. And they had a smell."

Ashes, Fran thought. Ashes and sulfur.

"Like ashes," Nyland said. "It filled the whole wagon. Ashes and sulfur. I remember that same smell." He looked at Fran again with bloodshot eyes. "From the Copper crime scene."

Later, Fran found Mike Finnean in the hospital's ICU lounge, nursing a machine-dispensed cup of coffee. "Sorry I'm late," he said, collapsing into a seat next to his partner.

Mike put his cup down and leaned back. "They'd already tagged her and taken her to the morgue by the time I got there. Lafferty walk you through the scenes?"

Fran nodded. "Nineteen and nine, yeah."

Mike rubbed his eyes, opened them, blinked. "Did you hear

about what happened in the ambulance?"

"I just spoke to Nyland. Watson and the driver were already discharged."

"You believe that shit?"

Fran spread his hands in a shrug. In his mind, he saw the window, the teeth-filled writhing locomotive roaring at him. "He seemed okay to me. A little shell-shocked, maybe. What happened in the girl's apartment on Nine? Lafferty didn't have the details."

Finnean told him. When he was done Fran said, "I interviewed them, both of them, the girl and the Super, after the first homicide. And that Nyland kid was in on the first one too, the Copper homicide, first on scene."

"I know." Mike grimaced, stretching. "You two got the touch of death, Frannie."

"Gee, thanks. Wanna shake on it?"

"Please. No comedy. I'm too depressed."

Fran was quiet for a moment, debating what he should say about what *he* had seen in that Cherry Street apartment house, in that window. His shoulder still throbbed where he had hit the hallway wall. He said, "What about you? You believe Nyland's story? And the other two in the wagon?"

"The three accounts corroborated. I *have* to believe them. Either that or two uniforms and a licensed EMT driver are certifiable."

Fran hesitated, still seeing the bones, the teeth, rushing toward him. He thought about the pattern of the homicides so far. The pattern of them. He also remembered what Lester Blue had said, about *them* trying to get down, using victim's bodies like clothes so *they* could operate at ground level, to do whatever it was *they* wanted to do. Then he said, "I've got an idea. A theory."

"A theory." Mike looked at him. A silent moment lengthened between them. Then he said, "You going to share this theory or are you just gonna sit there on your fat ass?"

"That's the second time today somebody's made a

comment about my ass." Fran winced as he stood. "Let's see what the M.E. has to say about that girl and those crazy bones of hers first. Then we'll talk." He shifted his shoulder, wincing again. "For now, I'm going home. It's been another long day."

Some nights he got off the 66 trolley bus at the corner of Ashburner and Frankford and walked the short block to his mother's front door. Other nights, like tonight, he got off a stop back, south of the Pennypack Park bridge, and walked in the slush along the Avenue the few blocks to the park, then taking the back way home in the woods that bordered the creek. The snow had stopped, and the moon was out, but it was still a dark night. Any city park after dark was a gamble, but sometimes Fran needed the smells of the woods, the tree sap, the decayed leaves that still littered the path in soggy piles under the new snow. He even liked the sound the empty tree limbs made in the night wind, their groaning, clacking and cracking, high above.

He stopped on the path, halfway from the Avenue to the dead-end of his street, and looked up at the full moon through the trees. It seemed to be playing hide and seek, racing from one ragged cloud to the next. The wind was a clean cold sting on his cheeks. He heard something else, then, high in the moving branches: the fluttering and flapping of wings. Must be bats, he thought. Birds are all gone south; must be bats.

Or dark angels, watching over him. Dark angels to help him fight the demons. The demons that were *real*.

He turned, finally, and looked through the woods to find the glow of the back porch light his mother always left on. With that as a beacon in the darkness, and with his angels on high, he continued along the snow-filled park path.

When Fran entered, he saw his mother at the kitchen table in a bathrobe and curlers, nursing a big mug of tea. He stamped his shoes of clinging snow in the mudroom before entering the welcome warmth of the kitchen. He tented his overcoat over the chair opposite her, and dropped into it. "Long day, Ma," he said, rubbing his face with both hands. When he brought them down, he found a fresh mug of tea on the table in front of him. "That was quick," he said, blinking. "Thanks."

"At least the snow stopped," she said. "No more than an inch or two around here."

"Yeah." He stared down into his tea, breathing in the steam.

He pushed the mug forward an inch, then looked up. "Ma...do you believe in the supernatural?"

"You mean like ghosts? Like the Bermuda Triangle?"

"I'm serious, Ma."

She sat silently for a moment. Then, quietly, "You think it's monsters, doing those things to those people? Like what that Miss Grundy said?"

"I...saw something tonight Ma."

Even more quietly, "What did you see, Frannie?"

Oh you sorry sonofabitch, he realized then, you're breaking her heart.

Again.

He said, "I think I know who's responsible. I think I know who's been killing them."

She nodded slowly. She nodded the way a cop's widow would, like a cop's *mother*. "So...have you told your partner?"

"I can't, Ma. I just can't. Not yet."

"What about your Lieutenant? What's his name, Goaz? He put a little bit of himself on the line, putting you back in rotation, didn't he? What's his take?"

"He's been supportive," Fran said, not looking at her. "More than I would be, if I was in his place." The window, the onrushing madness there, flashed across his mind's eye; the ache, still, in his shoulder, where he had slammed against the hallway wall. "I'm not going to him until I have something solid, something I already run past Mike Finnean." He looked up at his mother, finally. "Hard evidence. Prosecutable evidence, you know?"

She nodded again. A cop's widow knew what to ask, and what not to. So did a cop's mom.

And Fran loved her all the more for it.

Instead, she said, "Then you'll work this angle yourself, for now."

Yeah, he admitted to himself. He'd have to work it himself. Yeah.

Crazy as it was, it wasn't *him* who was crazy.

He had seen what he had seen.

Crazy as it was, people were still dying.

And he had met the beast that was doing it. On that nineteenth floor, in that window that looked out into… what had Ruth Grundy called it? *The Boneyard.*

Crazy as it was, somebody had to stop it.

"Yeah, Ma," he said. "I'm gonna work it myself, for now."

20

Free Library, Center City, Philadelphia
Tuesday, December 6

The Free Library opened exactly on time Tuesday morning, and like a customer on a Strawbridge's Clover Day sale, Fran was waiting at the front doors when the guard unlocked them.

Salvador was at his desk in Periodicals wearing a Cheshire smile when Fran arrived. "I'm glad you made it, Detective Lomax," he said.

Fran dropped his leather case on an empty table by his favorite Reader, and then sat down heavily in front of it. "I have been busy."

"I saw it on the news. What's going on in this town? Two more murders? Same location as Number One?"

"Not exactly the same location. Same building, same floor, but different apartments." Fran opened his case, took out a legal pad, and slapped it down next to the Reader. "Now, about those names I gave you?"

"Ahh." Salvador stood, his smile a slash of white under his mustache. "John Randall Pitcairn, the mystery man. Shall we do him first?"

"By all means."

"What do you already have on him?"

"Well, he's never voted, never owned property, doesn't own a current passport or credit card. He doesn't pay utilities, or taxes, was never in the military, never arrested, and never signed up for Social Security." Fran smiled briefly. "And he doesn't have a library card."

Salvador laughed. "That narrows it down a bit."

"So." Fran laced his fingers together like an expectant student. "Wow me."

Salvador brought over a small sheath of papers, waving them. "Lucky for us," he said, "that 1949 fire in the City Hall Annex didn't spread up the Parkway. Here." He handed Fran the top sheet, a Xerox of a newspaper clipping from the Bulletin, late October 1937, a society column called 'About The Town.' "I highlighted the important part."

Fran read: " 'Spangler Heir Comes Home to Roost. John Randall Pitcairn, grandson and heir extraordinaire to the Anthony Spangler coal and railroad millions, has recently returned to our shores courtesy the HMS Queen Mary from a succession of private schools in Merry Olde England. The squeak on the street tells us this very private Master Pitcairn will not be attending the Philips Beaux Arts gala in Bala this weekend, much to the dismay of the eligible damsels up and down the Line.'" He looked up. "Gala in Bala?" Then he continued, "'The squeak does tell us John Randall has forgone the materfamilial pile in the fair Upper Makefield hills for some bright light townhouse digs in Old City.'" Upper Makefield. That was in Bucks County. "There's a Pitcairn estate in Upper Makefield?"

Salvador nodded. "Spangler estate, actually. The father married up. Sold and subdivided in the 1950s. But it did lead me to these." He handed Fran two more Xeroxes. "When I found them yesterday," he said, "even *I* got the chilly willies."

Fran laid the copies out side by side. Both were articles from the old *Sun* newspaper, the yellow rag of its day, both circa 1921. The first was from mid-October, about an accidental death and disappearance at the Spangler estate. The victim was a barnstorming pilot performing at the birthday party of a certain six-year-old John Randall Pitcairn. The disappearance was of the Pitcairn boy himself. Fran read aloud, " 'The Spangler Pitcairn Machine attempted to whitewash the horrible yet suspicious tragedy, but this reporter garnered an exclusive interview...'" He read intently for almost a full minute, then looked up. "This pilot was hired to perform for his sixth birthday, and killed himself in a crash?"

Salvador pointed to the other Xerox. "Read on."

The second *Sun* piece was just a snippet from one of its gossip columns called 'Whistling Down The Lane', this one a few days after the first *Sun* article: " 'Who was it taking a ride in that doomed biplane with the recently deceased aeronaut Terence Doherty? Every man, woman and child in the Spangler and Pitcairn clans are mum on the subject, and a certain investigating sheriff at the Newtown Barracks isn't dishing. Why, then, hasn't a certain birthday boy come out to play since his recent soiree?'"

"And then this." Salvador gave Fran another Xerox. "*Bulletin* this time, a week after the pilot's death."

Fran read this one silently. 'Police Baffled by Spangler Disappearance' was the headline. The article concerned itself with a Lucian Spangler, (cousin or uncle to John Randall?), a resident of New York City who made frequent visits to the family estate in Upper Makefield. It was during one of these visits, not four days after the death of the barnstormer pilot that Lucian had disappeared without a trace.

"Anything further on this Lucian character?"

Salvador shook his head. "As far as I could tell they never found him, if that's what you mean. There must have been a missing person's report; maybe you got something, some record at the Roundhouse?"

"I doubt it. Unless they cross the line into the city, we tend to leave county business alone." Fran continued reading. "Nothing more on our birthday boy I see."

"There is a mention of another kid, though, see it? In the second to last paragraph."

Fran skimmed down. "The son of one of the estate staff, went missing around the same time as Lucian. No name, though. Huh." He raised his hand and waffled it. "Maybe this Lucian had a thing for little boys?"

"They did that sort of thing back then?"

"They've always been doing that sort of thing, Salvador my friend." Fran assembled the Xeroxes, laid them down in a neat pile, and sat back. "So in October 1921, in the space of a week, we had a bizarre death and two unexplained disappearances, and in the midst of it all, a six-year-old named John Randall Pitcairn goes incommunicado, soon to be packed off to school across the Atlantic."

"Dicey stuff," Salvador said.

"Then things go quiet until 1937, when John Randall returns, aged, what, seventeen?"

"Just eighteen. Birthday in mid-October, remember?"

"Okay, so our John Randall returns home, of age. Anything on him after that?"

"Nothing in the society pages beyond what you already read, which is a little odd, don't you think? A young rich playboy, you'd think there would be more."

"What about college?"

"Ahh. He did spend some time at Penn, and the Pennsylvania Academy. But he was just a face in the crowd there." Salvador produced another Xerox.

"College yearbook page...which one?"

"There." Salvador pointed. "The Art League."

"Very blurry."

"It was the only photo of him I could find. For a society

dude, that's an interesting fact all by itself."

"Camera shy…" Fran studied the tiny smudge of a face. The detail was atrocious. "So he just made his grades at school and moved on." He put the paper aside and tapped his finger on the first Xerox. "This one from 1937 mentions a residence, a townhouse, somewhere in the City, where he went to live. You got anything on that?"

Salvador made a 'tsk, tsk' noise, shaking his head. "Again, why didn't you just come to me?"

Fran eyed the final piece of paper in the young Latino's hand. "That it?"

Salvador read from it, "From 1937 till 1946 there was a B. Spangler on the deed to a property in the five-hundred block of Delancey. Number 512."

"Old City," Fran said. "Someone on the mother's side of the family, the Spangler side. Not an uncommon name in this city, though." He pulled out the *Bulletin* article. "This one mentions a grandmother on the Spangler side."

"Bertha Spangler. In November 1946 the deed was re-administered, signed over to a holding company, which I traced back to a conglomerate of mid-level financial firms owned by—"

"The Spangler family, again?"

Salvador smiled appreciatively. "You got it, Sergeant. They obviously tried to hide the link, but it wasn't hard to figure out. After 1946, though, I didn't see any other activity for that address."

"1946…"

"You said you already got stuff about the murders at the Lennard Building in 1946, right? I can pull that microfilm again."

"No need. An old friend at the Roundhouse gave me a copy of a clipping, and I got first hand info from the case files. Late October 1946, one homicide in the City Hall tower, then multiple homicides at the Lennard."

"And one month later, the name Spangler is taken off the deed to 512 Delancey. Coincidence, sergeant?"

"So, unless he moved—dear God please tell me he never moved—our Pitcairn character has been living anonymously on Delancey Street since 1937."

"Looks like it."

Fran felt a quiet, familiar surge, as the case took a sudden, definite step forward. "Okay," he said, "now that second name I gave you. William Alton."

"This one was easy. An African American. We already know he was employed as a valet by the family killed at the Lennard in October 1946. He was in the military, drafted in 1942. Served in Europe in an EOD company, that's Explosive Ordnance Disposal, apparently nobody minded having a mixed race company when you were probably going to be blown up anyway. He got discharged in 1945 and then dropped off the radar for a while. Except for the Lennard business, I found nothing in the rest of the '40s or '50s, you know, the last days of the Era of Cash. When credit cards started kicking in, though, he started leaving trails."

"You found him again, then?"

Salvador nodded, grinning. "I've been sitting on this since closing time last night. Are you ready for this? Home address is Delancey Street. Number 512."

Fran's mouth dropped open. "Pitcairn and Alton live *together*?"

"Looks that way."

"But why? What's the connection?"

Salvador shook his head. "I don't know, Detective."

"I don't know either," Fran said, rising, "but I think it's time I find out."

The front door knocker boomed once, twice, then three times. The sound echoed throughout the house.

William left his work in the basement, leaving his gloves and leather apron on the workbench, and went upstairs to answer it. He looked through the peephole of the front door and saw a large man in an overcoat, holding up a police badge. Adrenalin shot through him, making him shiver. He reached up, disabled the alarm, then opened the locks, one by one, and swung open the front door on a brisk, biting wind.

The plain-clothes policeman was large, solid, with florid cheeks, prominent nose, and receding brown hair. He filled the doorway. He was wearing a cheaply cut khaki overcoat, his pants had lost their crease, and his shoes needed shining. "Good morning," he said, smiling. "Are you William Alton?"

Another shot of adrenalin washed through William. "Yes," he said, "yes I am. Is there something I can do for you, officer?"

"Detective, Mr. Alton. I'm a detective sergeant with the Philadelphia Police." He showed his badge again, then pocketed it. "Can I come in?"

William gripped the edge of the massive door. "What is this about?"

"I'm gathering information related to an ongoing investigation, and I thought maybe you could help me." The detective's friendly demeanor shifted, and his smile disappeared. "If only to get me out of the cold for a few minutes?"

William stepped aside, and the detective entered the vestibule. William swung the door shut, turned one of the locks, then gestured the detective into the foyer. "You're a detective? What kind of detective?"

"Homicide. We investigate—"

"I know what 'homicide' means, Detective. You investigate suspicious deaths." Be careful, William told himself. This may be nothing.

The detective nodded, his whole body moving with it. "Yes, that's it exactly. Suspicious deaths." He looked about, and saw the short sofa and armchairs in the alcove. "I've been hoofing it around town all morning. Do you mind if we sit down?"

"Be my guest." William led the way, indicated the sofa for

the detective, and took the closest armchair.

The detective suddenly thrust his hand out for William to shake. "My name is Lomax, by the way. Francis Lomax."

"Pleased to meet you, Detective Lomax," William shook his hand. Contribute nothing, he thought, and soon he will be gone.

The detective looked about, his gaze lingering on Jack's large atmospheric paintings that dominated the walls. "This is an amazing house, very impressive."

"Thank you, Detective Lomax."

"Is Mr. Pitcairn at home?"

Another shiver went through William. Just how much did this detective *know*? "No," he said, "I'm afraid Mr. Pitcairn is not available."

"Not available," the detective repeated.

"He suffered a fall recently. His left leg was fractured. He's resting and in no condition for visitors."

"That's a shame. A recent fall, you say? Around Thanksgiving?"

"Just before, actually. But what—"

"I suppose he was taken to Jefferson?"

"No, Holy Rood."

"Ah." The big detective nodded vigorously. "Jefferson's closer, of course, that's why I asked. I take it he's recovering well?"

"As well as can be expected." William folded his hands in his lap. "You said you were investigating a suspicious death, Detective Lomax. How I can help you?"

The detective smiled again, open now, affable. "Do you know a Lester Blue, Mr. Alton?"

"Blue? No, I'm afraid not."

"How about a Ruth Grundy?"

William frowned politely. "Sorry, but that draws a blank too."

"Your scars." The detective pointed to the back of William's hand. "I'm curious. Stop me if I'm getting too personal, but when did you get those? It must have been a terrible ordeal for you."

William covered his left hand with his right. "I'm afraid you *are* getting a bit too personal, Detective Lomax."

The detective leaned forward, gesturing with his finger, "Remarkable work, though, you have to admit, what the doctors did for you."

"I beg your pardon?"

"The scars. They're so straight and regular. I've never seen scars so perfectly straight, so perfectly healed before. Old, though. They look like they happened a long time ago."

William was silent.

"Forgive me, Mr. Alton," the detective sat back, "You must think I am a very rude person."

"I know it's your job to ask questions, Detective Lomax. It's what you do. Though I still don't see how scars from a childhood accident relate to a homicide you are investigating."

"Really? The local papers and TV news have been full of it."

"*It?*"

"'The Butcher' slayings, Mr. Alton. Six homicides, the first on Thanksgiving, the last two just yesterday." The detective leaned forward again. "Surely you've heard about them?"

William cleared his throat. "I'm sorry, but I have better things to do than read newspapers."

"I imagine it must be particularly upsetting to you, Mr. Alton."

"What do you mean?"

"They are so much like those other deaths, back in 1946. At the Lennard Building on Arch Street. Surely you remember."

William fought to remain calm. "1946 was a very long time ago."

"The family murdered there, at the Lennard, very well-to-do, had the entire top floor to themselves. They had a valet, a young fella, right out of the Army." The detective paused, watching him. "That valet was *you*, wasn't it, Mr. Alton?"

William said nothing.

"You probably escaped being killed yourself by sheer dumb luck, I imagine. I mean, the killer murdered everybody who was in that apartment. What was it, you were sent out on an errand? Had the afternoon off? The Slaughterhouse Killer—that's what they called him back then—cut those poor people up, *flayed* them, took their bones, left just their flesh, their guts, spread out all over the place. A regular abattoir, or so the case reports say. 'slaughterhouse' made for a better headline, though, just like the 'Butcher' killer now. Just like today. They're still abattoirs, though." He pointed at William. "There's a connection, Mr. Alton, between those murders at the Lennard back in 1946, and the ones happening now. I think that connection has something to do with you. You and John Pitcairn."

"Mr. Pitcairn has nothing to do with that."

"Oh yes he does, Mr. Alton, yes he does. When he was six years old he had a birthday party. We're talking 1921 here. They hired a pilot, to give party rides, I suppose. That pilot crashed his airplane, got cut up, sliced and diced, just like your former employers at the Lennard. Pitcairn's uncle disappeared around the same time, as well as one of the estate staff's children."

This was too much. This was much too much. "I think, Detective," William said, rising, "it is finally time for you to leave."

The detective spread his hands as he stood. "I've gone too far. I've been rude and inconsiderate. I'm so sorry."

William gestured to the door. "Good day, Detective Lomax."

The detective followed him out. "And I didn't even get to ask you why you've been hiding in this townhouse here, this big, impregnable castle," he paused, "all these years."

William opened the front door. The cold morning air was like a slap in the face. "Good day, Detective," he said again.

"Again, really, I'm sorry if I upset you." The detective

reached into his coat pocket and produced a business card. "You can contact me any time," he said. William glanced down at the card, then back up. The detective seemed to grow larger, silhouetted against the open door. He looked to his left, saw a narrow side table there, and put the card on it. Then he was gone, down the stone steps, back into the hard morning sunlight.

William swung the door shut with a solid slam, reset the locks and the alarm, then went straight upstairs to Jack's studio. "Did you hear?" He tried to keep the anger out of his voice. "Did you hear what he said?"

Jack was seated before his newest painting, two small biplanes in a huge bank of clouds. His face was grim. "I heard everything," he said. "Just what we need. The police finally getting smart."

"I don't want to rush our plans," William said, "but we may have to."

Jack slumped in his chair, looking tired, older. "There were two more murders yesterday?"

William nodded. "*They're* getting better at it. *They're* rushing us, too."

"When is your meeting with your old army contact?"

"This morning. I'll be leaving shortly."

"Good," Jack said. He looked at his painting on the easel, and rubbed his cheek wearily. "Good."

"The murders will stop," William said. "We'll make them stop."

Jack turned back to him. "Will we?"

William nodded decisively. "We have to."

William had never been to this part of town. There were neighborhoods where it was an advantage being black, and there were other neighborhoods where being black was a distinct *dis*advantage. This neighborhood was one of those. When the Colonel told him on the phone the location where they were to meet, William had hesitated. The Colonel did not tolerate hesitation. "Wait," William had said, hearing his former commanding officer begin to hang up, "I'll be there."

Now he stood outside the narrow storefront bar, The Star Tavern. Neon ads for Budweiser and Yuengling flickered in its two high, grimy windows. Rowhouse trinities surrounded it, filling the rest of the block, each one in its own unique state of disrepair. He looked at his watch, then at the group of white youths adorning a stoop down the block, looking back at him. He reached for the door handle and went inside.

There was an old mahogany bar on the right, three men on stools there, nursing beers, and five booths on the left, red naugahyde, all of them empty. To the rear he saw a pool table in the shadows. The bartender was young, white shirt rolled to his tattooed biceps, long brown hair pulled back in a ponytail. As William moved toward the booths the bartender said, "Morning, Chief."

William turned. "Good morning."

"What can I get you?"

"A coffee?"

"Coffee it is. Cream and sugar?"

"No, just black."

One of the old men at the bar sniggered into his beer. The bartender gave him a look. Then, to William, "You got it, Chief. I'll bring it over."

William sat down in the last booth, the one furthest away from the men at the bar. He ran his fingers over the patchwork of graffiti carved into the surface of the old wood table: LOUIE & ANGIE, Star-T ROX, BILLI LUVS BETTI, PHILS SUX.

The bartender delivered his coffee. William slipped his hands around the thick ceramic mug, enjoying the warmth. As he brought it to his lips he heard the front door open. He put the coffee back down.

"Good morning, Colonel," he heard the bartender say.

Then a voice he remembered, a voice tangled in dark memories of frozen mud, barbed wire and bloated corpses:

"Hello, Dennis. I'm expecting someone."

"Last booth, sir."

Firm footsteps, then the Colonel put a hand on William's shoulder, squeezed, and took the seat opposite him. "Billy," he said, "I'm sorry this is so early in the day, but I have another engagement later that I simply cannot avoid."

"I'm glad you could see me, sir," William said. The man across the table from him was in his mid-seventies, but looked much younger. Lean, tall, ice-blue eyes, a full burr-cut of silver hair revealed as he took off his pork-pie hat and laid it carefully on the seat beside him.

"It's been too long," the Colonel said, smiling.

"Yes sir," William said, "I suppose it has. Much too long."

"You're looking well, Billy."

"So are you, sir."

"Thirty-nine years, or is it forty? Is my arithmetic correct? You dropped off the face of the earth for nearly four decades. Until I took your first call, I thought you might have passed on."

William smiled into his coffee. "I've managed to avoid that, sir. You know me."

"Still getting the nightmares?"

"I'm still working on them, sir," William said, his smile fading.

"That nighttime Goony Bird flight we took from Tunis to Sicily…"

William closed his eyes, remembering.

The bartender approached. "Something for you, Colonel?" William noticed, then, one of the young man's bicep tattoos was the battle slogan of their old battalion, black gothic lettering on an unfurling red banner. A Vietnam vet; the newest generation. The ponytail had thrown him.

The Colonel pointed to William's coffee. "I'll have the same, Dennis, with a splash of Dewars." He rubbed his hands together as the bartender retreated. "It gets more and more difficult to keep warm as we get older, don't you think?"

The bones in William's fingers throbbed suddenly, and his grasp on his coffee mug tightened. The bones craved warmth. In his mind he smelled hot ash, dry, searing heat sucking at him as he gasped—

Enough.

The bartender returned with the Colonel's coffee. "Thank you, Dennis," the Colonel said. He took a sip, then put the mug down. "So, Billy," he said, "Let's get down to cases, shall we? What do you need that you couldn't tell me on the phone?"

William leaned forward, and told him.

The Colonel said nothing at first. He looked past William, his gaze lingering on the men at the bar, then back again, meeting William's gaze finally, his expression calm, impassive.

"A favor given, sir," William said.

"Is a favor owed. I know." The Colonel continued to look at him. "You would be handling this…personally?"

William nodded. "I haven't forgotten what to do."

"I could get one of the young bucks like our Dennis here to—"

"No." William placed both of his hands on the table. The scars were mirror imaged. "I have to do this myself, sir."

The old officer across the table frowned. "Forty years ago we put our lives in each other's hands. Forty years ago we had the smarts, the talents, the *youth*. Forty years ago, Billy."

"I haven't lost anything," William said, fighting to keep his voice calm. "Not the talent, or the touch. Or the nerve."

"I'm not questioning your courage, Billy. I'm just being realistic."

"So am I, Colonel. No one else can be involved."

The Colonel nodded. "Very well, then. You said today, correct?"

"Yes sir. It has to be today."

"Very well. It will take a few hours. There's a small park at the corner of Seventh and Lombard. Be there at noon." The Colonel rose, took up his hat, and put it on. "Call me before that, if you change your mind."

William began to rise himself, but the older man stopped him with a wave. "Stay, finish your coffee." He turned. "Dennis? The corporal's tab is taken care of."

"Yes sir," Dennis said, from behind the bar.

Favors owed, favors paid. William stared down at his hands. The Colonel had seen it, of course. They were still shaking.

21

"Where the hell have you been?"

Fran collapsed in the chair next to Mike Finnean's desk. "Out," he said. "Out and about, working a lead. Why?"

"Goaz has been on the rag since Roll Call, that's why. Says we've been dodging him about tomorrow's brief—"

"Uhh…we *have* been dodging him, Mike."

"He says if we don't have a sit-down with him before lunch he's going to have our asses *for* lunch."

Fran laughed. "He better be hungry then, because people tell me I've got a big one."

"Wait a minute." Mike peered at him. "You look like Sylvester right after he gobbles Tweety. You got something? That Pitcairn guy?"

"I got the address this morning, actually—"

"*Finally*, Christ." Mike leaned forward.

"He lives on Delancey, five-hundred block. Old City."

"Money," Mike said. "Old money. So what is he, sixty, sixty-five? A bit too old to be doing the work we've seen."

"I didn't actually meet Pitcairn, I met his sidekick, William Alton."

"William Alton." Mike blinked once. "You're starting to lose me. Who is William Alton?"

"Crap. Okay." Fran took three minutes to fill him in, finishing with, "...And he had *scars*, Mike, straight ones, down his hands and fingers. They were old, probably from childhood, but I could still see a distinct pattern across his face."

"You mean like the cuts on our last victims."

"*Exactly* like the cuts on our last victims."

"Shit-on-a-stick." Mike sat back, blinking rapidly, his hand on his chin. "So he was a part of those old homicides you and Otto dug up, then."

"More than just a witness at the scene? Had to be."

"The two of them, Pitcairn and this Alton guy, living together like Frick and Frack all these years?"

"Since before the Second World War," Fran said, nodding. "Like two peas in a goddamned pod."

"We need a warrant." Mike slapped his desk. "Get back in there, do some digging. Pull this Pitcairn out of whatever closet he's hiding in and shine a big light up his ass."

"No good. I just asked one of the ADAs to go to bat for us, and she turned me down."

"Who'd you ask?"

"I tried Przybylski."

"You tried *who*?"

"The blond, always wears the short suit-dresses."

"She's too new. We should try Selheimer. After his lunchtime martians he doesn't give a shit what he goes to bat for."

"Maybe you can try Selheimer while I——"

Mike's phone rang. "That's Goaz," he said. "Ten spot?"

Fran snorted.

Mike picked it up on the third ring. "Homicide, Finnean." He sat up. "Yes sir." He put out his free hand, palm up, which

Fran ignored. "Yes, sir…yes, no, he's right here." Mike rolled his eyes. "Yes sir, we'll be right over." He dropped the receiver in its cradle. "Lieutenant's in the Morgue with Koenig. We've been summoned."

The basement corridor under Eighth Street connecting the Roundhouse with Administration Building Two was long and straight: twenty fluorescent pools of light on eight-by-eight grey wall tile and putty-colored terrazzo, the air dank and piney like a cold, recently flushed public toilet. The main City Morgue was under Admin Two, a left turn off the main corridor, grey wall tile turning to white, stainless padlocked cabinets punctuated by old gurneys substituting for tables, piled high with medical-related supplies and hardware. Fran and Mike pushed through the double doors of Examination Suite D, a large, square room with two tanks and four drain tables, two of which were occupied.

"God I love the smell of this place," Mike said under his breath.

Lieutenant Goaz and Koenig, the Assistant Medical Examiner, stood over the nearer of the two stiffs. "You were there for this one, Mike," Goaz said, motioning them over, "but I don't think you'd recognize her now. Fran? Meet Victim Number Six."

He made room for them. Fran's belt buckle clicked on the zinc table edge. "I met her," he said. "Thanksgiving. Girlfriend of the super, Jimmy."

Koenig pointed to one of the meat lockers set in the far wall. "We have the building super filed over there. What's left of him, anyway."

Goaz spread his arms. "Your case seems to be taking up most of the real estate down here, gentlemen."

Fran and Finnean were silent. No sense belaboring the obvious.

Fran looked down at the corpse of the girl. He bent close, saw fresh, perfectly straight scarring that transformed to torn flesh. Like she had been made whole, and then ripped back apart, from the inside out. She looked flat, deflated. "No skeleton," he said.

"It's over here." Koenig nodded to the other occupied drain table, to an odd assortment of humps and lumps under a cloth sheet. "According to the scene report, the victim's bones were somehow pulled out of her body."

"This kind of ripping," Fran pointed. "Does it look like the bones were *pulled* out?"

Koenig looked momentarily uncomfortable. "I...haven't made that determination yet."

"I'm only asking because of the officer statements, the ones in the ambulance. They didn't say 'pulled.' They said 'pushed.' They said the bones came out by themselves."

"One reason why Officer Nyland and Officer Wilson are on administrative leave," Goaz said.

"Nyland said that the bones came out of the victim's body on their own," Fran repeated, looking from Goaz to Koenig, then back again. "Wriggled out on their own, he said, like *snakes*."

"Which, I say again, is one good goddamn reason why he's cooling his ass," Goaz said, "till we straighten this shit out."

Fran went over to the other drain table and folded the sheet back. A chalk-white skull leered up at him. Below it, a pair of collarbones, shoulder blades, spinal segments stacked together like toy blocks. He pulled the sheet all the way back, revealing the entire skeleton. He turned to Koenig. "Were these cleaned? There isn't a bloodstain on any of them."

The Assistant M.E. shook his head. "That's how they were delivered. The CSU harvested them in exactly that condition from the ambulance. Officer Nyland had put some of them into a plastic bag."

"Well doesn't this seem weird to you? I mean seriously, seriously frigging weird?"

"It's on my list, Sergeant," Koenig said, "yeah."

Fran turned back to the skeleton. He looked for a long moment, then he said, "I don't know much about anatomy or biology, but there's something else here that doesn't look right."

Goaz came over to stand beside him, and Mike Finnean followed. "What do you mean?"

"Take a look yourself, Lieutenant. The ulna and the radius of her left forearm, they're supposed to match, right? Same approximate length? Do these look like they're the same length to you?"

Goaz frowned. "Doctor Koenig?"

Koenig crossed his arms. "I was not aware that your detectives were trained anatomists, let alone certified forensic pathologists."

"Look," Fran said, warming, "if something doesn't look right, we question it. That's something we *are* trained for. It doesn't take a Doctor Frankenstein to see that these bones are screwed up. They're steam-cleaned first of all, goddammit, and they don't *match*."

"Calm down, Frannie," Mike said.

"Actually," Koenig said, his eyes averted, "there does seem to be a...slight confusion in that area."

Both Fran and Goaz said at once, "A slight confusion?"

"The...ah, pelvis." Koenig pointed. "It's...male."

"It's *what*?" Goaz's voice ricocheted about the room.

Fran bent close. "He's right. See where it's fused? In a woman it's flexible here...and here. Two pieces." He looked up. "So what's a male pelvis doing in a female body?"

"Holy shit," Mike said. "So she was really a he?"

"No." Koenig raised his hands as he shook his head. "This victim was female. Naturally female. I suggest re-interviewing the three uniformed officers—"

"The Medical Examiner's Office fucked up," Goaz said.

Koenig's face flushed. "I hardly think—"

"You can't keep your stiffs straight down here, you're mixing up evidence bags, and you're compromising these cases. What the hell are we supposed to do now, Doctor?"

"We collected and tagged every bone from that ambulance," Koenig said frostily. "We accounted for every single one, and they are all here, on this table."

"So these bones came out of this girl."

"We don't have any other explanation at the present time."

Goaz flung his arms up, and began pacing. "What about the meat wagon? Maybe it wasn't clean. Maybe somebody left shit from some other run back there."

"We only collected one pelvis from the ambulance, Lieutenant. And the victim on the table is missing hers."

A sheen of sweat had formed on Fran's forehead as he stared at the skeleton, and it went clammy in the morgue's cold atmosphere.

Bones from The Boneyard, he thought. These had to be bones from the Boneyard. The bad ones. Keys to the Kingdom. An unbidden shudder ran through him, and he touched the edge of the metal table to steady himself.

Mike saw his face. "You okay, Fran?"

"Yeah," Fran said. "I'm fine. The smell of this place gets to me after a while, that's all."

The Assistant Medical Examiner drew the sheet back over the dead girl's bones. "Are we done here, Lieutenant? I have to be in court at two, and I have a lunch appointment with the District Attorney before that."

Goaz looked from Fran to Mike, then nodded. "For now, Doc," he said. "We look forward to your report."

"I'll have Featherston take care of these. Just let him know when you're done here." Koenig left without a further word. The tapping of his shoes receded down the hall.

"Odd stuff, Lieutenant," Mike said after a moment.

Goaz pulled the sheet over the bones back a few feet. "Odd's putting it a bit mildly, Mike. I mean, shit, look at this. Since when have any of us seen a fresh skeleton taken out of a dead body before? Why is it so goddamn clean? And how can parts of it not even be *hers*? She was whole at the apartment," he looked at Mike, "right?"

"Yes sir. Bleeding, cut up, but that's all. Multiple witnesses, family, two uniforms, including me. She was hurt, but she was whole."

"But when the wagon unloads at the ER, we end up with three gibbering idiots, and this. It's a fucking horror show."

"All of them were horror shows," Fran said, quietly.

Goaz looked at Fran, then at Mike, his expression grim. "You guys have still made no progress on the other cases?"

Mike glanced at Fran, who said, "A few leads, nothing big. There's a possible I'm starting to lean on."

"I heard you tried to get a search warrant out of Judge Przybylski."

"We're going to Bill Selheimer after lunch," Mike said.

"Bill should work with you." Goaz flipped the sheet back over the bones. "I'll put in a word to expedite it." He turned back to face them both. "Listen, here's the deal. Halberstadt's had it. He dumped his pail of shit on me last night when I told him we probably wouldn't have anything fresh for the Major Case brief tomorrow, and now I'm dumping my own pail of shit on you guys. Starting tomorrow, Abbey Fogel and Joe Kandetzke are on the case with you." He looked at Fran, then Mike. "Mike, I'm making you Primary." He waited two beats. "Questions?"

"No sir," Mike said.

Koenig looked at Fran. "Lomax? Questions?"

"No sir," Fran said.

Goaz strode to the door, paused, turned back. "Tomorrow morning, eight A.M., dog and pony show for Major Crimes, you know where, then again for the entire Unit. Get all your turds in a row, gentlemen."

The door swung shut behind him.

Fran and Mike exchanged glances, then Fran went over to the drain table holding the victim's remains. "They shouldn't leave her out like this," he said.

"What, it isn't cold enough in here for you?" Mike came over to stand beside him. "Anyway, we'll tap Featherston on the way out, like Koenig told us."

Fran took his hand out of his coat pocket and offered it. "Congratulations, asshole," he said.

Mike grimaced, then shook it. "Big fucking reward, right? Now it's *my* ass. Should have been yours."

"We'll get it done."

Mike looked at him.

"Really," Fran said.

They both heard someone coming down the hall.

"One other thing," Mike said, "before they chase us out of here."

"Yeah?"

"Somebody broke into the other West Philly apartment last night, the one where the first homicide went down. Broke a window in the bedroom; broke all our 'keep-the-fuck-outta-here' tape from the door." A wary smile played briefly across Mike's lips. "You hear about that?"

"Nope," Fran said, "not a word. Everything was quiet when I was there."

The doors to the hallway swung in, and a uniform Fran didn't recognize stuck his head in. "One of you guys Finnean?"

Mike raised his hand. "That's me."

"Detective Fogel sent me looking for you, Detective."

Fran and Mike exchanged a look. "It begins," Mike said.

Fran chuckled. "The life of the Lead Dick." He patted Mike on the shoulder. "I'll catch up."

Mike left with the officer.

Fran looked at the clock on the wall, then went quickly over to the table that held the skeleton. He lifted the sheet, hesitated, then selected a bone from one of the feet and picked it up. He expected a reaction, like the electric shock he had experienced when he touched the bone on the keychain, and the claw in the elevator, but he felt nothing. This one was small, thin…and human. He couldn't be scientifically sure, but he was sure nevertheless. Those skeletons that had been taken, that they had never recovered, he was certain he was looking at bones from them, reassembled in that poor girl's body. These weren't Boneyard bones, they were human bones, put back together in a jigsaw pattern *they* were still trying to figure out, still trying to make work. No, these weren't Boneyard bones. These weren't the keys to anything.

He put the bone back, replaced the sheet, adjusted it, then turned around and leaned against the table edge.

Then, directly behind him, faintly, something *clacked.*

He spun around. The room was empty. He looked down at the sheet-covered skeleton. He stood motionless five seconds, ten, staring at the sheet. Nothing moved. He took in a long breath. *Crazy.*

He left the examination room, and didn't look back.

He got two hotdogs and a soft pretzel from a cart vendor parked at the curb at Pine and Sixth and called it his lunch. "Plenty of mustard on all three," Fran told the little Korean man in his chrome and Plexiglas cubicle, "And knock off some of the salt, okay?" Then he took up station on one of the benches installed when this portion of Pine Street had received its recent facelift. He had a perfect view of the west end of Delancey. Fran checked his watch. As soon as he finished his meal, it would be time to call in to Mike to check on the warrant. The next time he went into that townhouse, he was going in with ammo.

He demolished the second hot dog, and was about to take a big bite out of the pretzel when he saw Alton turn the corner off Delancey, and head down Sixth, right toward him. Fran threw the pretzel in a waste bin as he rose. Alton came up to the intersection, looked up and down Pine Street, then crossed to join the sidewalk traffic heading south. Fran came up beside him. "Glad to see you're getting out of the house, Mr. Alton."

Alton startled, glaring at Fran with alarm. "Have you been

following me?"

"I had a few more things to discuss, didn't think you'd mind. I figured you might want to talk outside, you know, without Mr. Pitcairn around to listen in."

Alton turned from him, and plunged into the crowd. Fran hurried to keep up. "Just a few questions, Mr. Alton. What can it hurt? Surely you want to help us catch whoever has been committing these murders."

"I'm not answering any questions, Detective," Alton said, dodging between slower pedestrians. "We—I...have nothing else to say to the police."

They had to go single file under a construction awning of steel pipe and wooden planks. Fran was directly behind Alton. "I understand your reluctance, Mr. Alton," he said. "I've been to all the crime scenes. I've seen what this 'Butcher' has done to those people. I know that you saw it too, that terrible day in 1946. With all due respect, you're the only witness we have of those murders who is still alive."

"I wasn't there when it happened," Alton said over his shoulder. "I didn't see anything."

They walked the next block in silence. Alton turned right at Lombard, heading west. One of those quaint little Old City block parks was just ahead, at the corner. "Five minutes, Mr. Alton," Fran said, coming abreast. "Just listen to a theory I've got." Fran used his bulk to herd Alton toward the park entrance. Okay, trump card. He reached into his overcoat pocket, found what he was looking for, and pulled his hand back out, palm up, right under Alton's nose. "A theory about this."

The claw bone from the elevator at the Ben Franklin, in its little evidence baggie.

Alton saw it and stopped short with a gasp. "*What is that?*" He took a small backward step, glancing upward as he did so; he couldn't help himself, Fran saw.

Fran said, "You know what it is, Mr. Alton. Probably better than me."

"Where did you get it?"

"Now look who's got questions all of a sudden." Fran closed his fingers over the baggie and put it back into his pocket. "Well?"

Alton's expression changed from alarm to anger. "Mr. Pitcairn and I are innocent! We didn't murder anybody!"

Fran gestured to the park's open gate. "Shall we? Five minutes. I promise."

Alton turned into the park, sought out the nearest empty bench, brushed a thin crust of old snow off it, and sat down. A crowd of pigeons scattered. He crossed his arms, hugging himself, and looked down at his shoes.

Fran took a seat at the other end of the bench, one ass cheek on, one off. "Okay," he said, "My theory. First of all, I don't think you or John Pitcairn committed these crimes either." He brought the bone claw out again, and took a deep breath. "I don't think anyone did...anyone *human*. I think the murderer came out of The Boneyard."

Alton looked at the bone sideways, smiling suddenly, coldly. "The Boneyard? Is that what you call it?"

"Hey, if you've got a better name——"

"You sure you know what you're holding there, Detective?"

"This?" Fran picked it up with his other hand, holding the baggie between thumb and forefinger like a bug. He studied it, frowning slightly. "I think I do."

Alton huffed softly, turning his eyes away again.

"Here's what I think, Mr. Alton. And please, stop me if you think I'm wrong. I think something woke The Boneyard up just before Thanksgiving, about the same time John Pitcairn had his accident and broke his leg. Whatever it was, this...trigger, I think it was the same sort of thing that woke The Boneyard up in October 1946 too. Not to mention 1921. Whatever it was, The Boneyard got antsy. They got *active*. They *wanted* something. They'd do anything to get it. But they were up there," he pointed, "and they couldn't get down here to get it. Why? I don't

know. But a real conundrum, hm? So what do they do? They try
to figure out a way to get down, of course. How? Same as in the
good old days: get themselves *into* someone, into a body, walk
around in it, *use* it, *own* it, like a suit of clothes. At first, though,
they're clumsy, not very refined. It's been a while, right? Maybe
they lost their touch, maybe it's a new crowd. So they butcher a
victim or two, getting back their chops, so to speak. They get
better at it, though. They get so good, in fact, that they actually
manage to get into one of my victims without killing her, not at
first, anyway. They even manage to get her down to street level,
and still she doesn't die on them. But in the end it's no good; they
still don't have it right, not like they used to. In the old days."
Fran paused, watching white breath escape Alton's nose. "Even
so," he continued, "it was hard. They had to take out the victim's
bones, not hurting the muscles, the flesh; they needed that, you
see. Then they tried to fit their own bones in, and that raised a
whole new set of problems." Fran shifted on the bench,
redistributing his weight. Damn it was cold. "You ever try to use
Chevy parts in a Ford engine? Car's a car, right? Engine's an
engine? Might work, right?" Fran shook his head. "Nope.
Doesn't work. Didn't work for them, either. Victim still fell apart
in the end. Left an entire skeleton behind, can you believe it?
Must have made them very angry, angrier than before, don't you
think?" Fran held the claw up. "It's so white and chalky, hardly
bloody at all. Like something you'd see in a cartoon. Crazy, eh?"

"I think," Alton said, turning back finally to look at him,
"you need help, Detective Lomax. Serious psychiatric help.
Nothing you just said makes any sense, not to a sane person,
anyway. If there's anything crazy here, it's you."

Fran chuckled, pocketing the bone once more. "I have my
days, I admit it. But if anybody really needs help, Mr. Alton, *real*
help, it's you and John Pitcairn. We both know what they're after.
Sooner or later, unless we stop this, they're going to get it. No
matter where you hide, they'll find it. They'll find *you*."

Alton opened his mouth to reply, but then Fran saw something catch his eye, something over Fran's shoulder. He turned, and saw a young man in a faded Army foul weather jacket, an olive colored canvas satchel under his arm. As he turned away, Fran saw he had a ponytail. He returned his attention to Alton. "Friend of yours?"

"I don't know what you're talking about." Alton stood. "I want you to leave me alone, Detective Lomax. And I want you to leave Jack Pitcairn alone too. That's all I'm going to say." He began walking, out of the park, into the crowd of pedestrians on Seventh Street.

Watching him go, Fran said under his breath, "Hate to disappoint you, then." Mike would have the warrant in an hour, maybe less. He rose, saw a bank of telephone stalls by the bus stop on Seventh, and scattered pigeons on his way over to them.

22

The townhouse, Number 512, looked formidable from the sidewalk: three stories of solid stained limestone block topped with a medieval-inspired crenellated cornice, wrought iron bars across all of the deeply recessed first floor windows, and a massive planked oak front door atop a high grey granite stoop. This block of Delancey was not a thoroughfare; it was a quiet residential street, empty of both traffic and pedestrians. Except for the occasional tourist in a rental Chevy searching vainly for a parking space, visitors to the five hundred block of Delancey only came because they had a reason to be here, because it was a destination.

There was no one, therefore, to stand on the sidewalk and look up at the imposing façade of Number 512, no one to admire the row of fine copper-sheathed casement windows arrayed along the second story, no one to stop and look at the third window from the left, one of two that punctuated the western wall of the master bedroom within. There was no one to see Jack Pitcairn, shoved up against the glass like a bug on a windshield, his feet dangling at least a yard above the expensive Kazak rug, struggling vainly against a force that had grown too powerful and compelling to resist.

Finally, someone turned off Sixth Street, entering Delancey at a brisk clip: William, returning at last with the canvas satchel cradled in both arms. When he glanced up at the townhouse he stopped short, momentarily startled. Then he broke into a run across the street, clutching the satchel to him, to the courtyard gate.

Fran heard Mike Finnean when he was still halfway down the hall. He heaved himself up from his desk, shoved his clip holster back down where it belonged, and grabbed his coat just in time to hear Mike give a loud hoot as he entered the Operations Room, with Detective Abbey Fogel in tow. He waved a folded blue paper. "Got it, Francine! For everything that's not nailed down at 512 Delancey Street."

"About frigging time," Fran said. "Who's driving?"

Upstairs, he heard the muffled sounds of chains rattling, of wood creaking.

Downstairs, flashing red lights on the parlor ceiling drew William to one of the front windows. He saw three police vehicles—two cars and a van—double-parking at angles to the curb, effectively blocking the street to traffic. He took an aborted step toward the rear parlor, then another back toward the hall stairs, then startled as someone knocked heavily on the front door. William made another aborted step toward the hall stairs as the door knocker sounded again. Finally, he went to the hall and the vestibule, stood behind the door, and looked through the peephole.

Lomax, the big, broad detective who had accosted him on the street earlier in the day, was standing on the top stoop step, shoulder to shoulder with another detective. Both of them held out their gold badges. "Sergeant Lomax," William said loudly, to the peephole, "we are not entertaining visitors this afternoon."

The detective's voice boomed back through the heavy oak door, "We're not here on a social call, Mr. Alton. We have a warrant to search your home." He held up a blue paper.

William saw typewriting, signatures, and an official seal of some sort. He looked over his shoulder, back to the basement staircase in the hall, a sheen of new sweat appearing on his forehead. Then, reluctantly, he turned off the alarm, undid the locks, and swung the door open. Detective Lomax pointed to the detective beside him, "This is Detective Finnean. Behind us are Detectives Fogel and Kandetzke." Lomax handed him the blue document. William held it in both hands, the typed words blurring as he scanned down to the signatures, and the judiciary seal embossed through them. He looked back up. "Search our home? Search for what?"

"It's all in the warrant, Mr. Alton." The other detective named Finnean touched his shoulder. "Now will you excuse us please, by standing aside?"

William fell back as the other two detectives, one of them a woman, followed the first two into the house. Three uniformed officers crowded in behind them. The third male detective said, "Abbey and me will take the upstairs, Mike."

"Upstairs!" William turned to intercept them. "But you can't go upstairs. Mr. Pitcairn is sleeping. You can't disturb him."

One of the uniformed policemen grabbed him from behind and pulled him up short. "There now, Pops," he said evenly.

"We have authorization to search the entire house, Mr. Alton," Detective Lomax said. "All three floors, basement too." Then, to the policeman holding him, "Let him go, Bernie." The officer released him. Lomax said, "Officer Bernard here will stay with you, keep you out of harm's way."

"But you can't just barge in on Mr. Pitcairn unannounced!"

"Oh we'll announce ourselves all right," the woman detective said, grinning.

Detective Finnean gave her a look, and the grin vanished. He turned to William. "Is this Mr. Pitcairn the only other person at home?"

William nodded. "It's just us. The cleaning woman comes on…" He let his words trail off because he saw that none of them cared what day the house was cleaned. This is madness, he thought. This is wrong.

The detectives split up, two and one uniformed officer proceeded up the stairs. Detective Lomax and the detective named Finnean took the remaining policeman with them down the hall to the kitchen.

Officer Bernard said, "Why don't we go into the living room and have a seat? This may take a while."

"It's a parlor," William said, his eyes cast to the floor. "The front parlor."

"Okay, then why don't we go into the front—"

Someone shouted from the second floor, "MIKE! FRAN! GET UP HERE!"

"Oh my God," William whispered, collapsing into the nearest chair. The sound of people pounding up the staircase vibrated a china dish on the table beside him.

Moments passed…a minute… William heard steps coming back down, and Detective Lomax appeared in the doorway. His expression was set, sober. "Mr. Alton," he said, "would you please come upstairs with me?"

Jack was just as William had left him when the police arrived: in pajamas and an open robe, spread-eagled on his bed. He had stout leather shackles strapped to his wrists and ankles. The shackles were chained to the bedposts. "They didn't believe me when I told them, William," Jack said in an exhausted voice.

"What the fuck!" the woman detective said to William, holding up the chain for his cast leg. "What the *fuck!*"

"What is going on here, Mr. Alton?" Detective Lomax asked.

The story. William's mind raced, trying to remember it correctly. This was the first time they ever had to use it. "Night terrors," he said. "Mr. Pitcairn has chronic severe night terrors. He sleepwalks to escape them." He pointed to the leg cast. "He's harmed himself in the past."

Detective Finnean said, "It's two o'clock in the afternoon."

"I was taking a nap," Jack said. "We do this as a precaution."

The woman detective, the one with the foul mouth, tapped his leg cast. "That how you got this? Fell down walking in your sleep?"

"Exactly, madam," Jack said. "That is exactly correct."

Detective Lomax cleared his throat. "Mr. Pitcairn, are you being held here against your will?"

Jack turned his head first to William, then to Lomax, and a weary smile played momentarily across his lips. "No, Detective," he said, "I'm not." He nodded toward the warrant William still had clutched in his hand. "You have a search warrant, I see."

"Yes sir," Detective Finnean said. "We're investigating the Butcher slayings. As I'm sure you know," he added.

"The Butcher slayings." Jack cocked his head slightly. "And you've come *here*?"

"He's tired," William said. "We should leave him alone."

"We go where the investigation leads us, sir," the other male detective said.

"Very well then, execute your warrant. Make your search. Just try not to break anything, please." Jack's head fell back into his pillow. "Obviously, we have nothing to hide."

Except what I have secreted in the basement, William thought. "I'm staying here," he said to Lomax, coming up beside the bed. "I'm not leaving this room until you're done."

Detective Lomax looked to Detective Finnean, who shrugged. "Sure," he said. "No problem. Bernie?"

Officer Bernard came into the room, found a chair, and sat. "I got it covered, Sarge."

Entering the kitchen, Fran felt like he was walking into a *Leave It To Beaver* episode, or an old black and white movie. Everything in the room was 1950s era, or earlier.   Chrome appliances and white-painted cabinets and furniture pre-dominated.   The countertops were grey soapstone.   The officer with him stooped to open a floor cabinet. "What are we looking for again, Sarge?"

"Photographs, documents, diaries, journals." Fran opened an upper cabinet: stacked plates. "And bones."

The officer shook his head as he crouched with his flashlight. "Crazy."

"You have no idea," Fran said, opening another cabinet. Cups and saucers.

Ten minutes later, in the pantry, Fran heard raised voices upstairs. Somebody was shouting. "You keep going," he said to the officer, and hurried up the back stairs.

Mike and Abbey were in Pitcairn's bedroom, trying to calm Alton down.

"What's going on?"

"Nothing, Fran," Mike said. "Abbey was just trying to——"

"I was trying," Abbey interrupted, "to ask a few simple questions here to Mr. Pitcairn. When Mr. Alton decided they weren't going to cooperate I suggested we might all be better off uptown at the Roundhouse."

"Mr. Pitcairn is injured! He has a broken leg!" Alton looked at each of them, still clearly furious. "He can't be moved. I can't allow it. I won't allow it."

"See," Abbey said with a hard smile, "There you go again issuing ultimatums."

"I think we should all just calm down for a bit."   Mike turned to Officer Bernard.   "Bernie, why don't you go down-stairs and work the kitchen with what's-his-name——"

"DeWald."

"Yeah, work with DeWald in the kitchen, okay?"

"You got it, Detective." Bernard exited gratefully.

Mike said, "I think if we all just take a second, sit down for a bit, maybe get a few general questions out of the way—"

"I've already been interrogated once by this detective," Alton said, indicating Fran with a jerk of his chin.

"I'll stay out of it," Fran said, raising his hands, "I promise."

"I don't think they are going to arrest us, William," Jack said.

"Who said anything about—!" Abbey began, but Mike cut her off with a raised hand. "No," he said, "We're not going to do that."

Abbey muttered something under her breath that Fran couldn't catch.

Mike rounded on her. "Something, Detective Fogel?"

She gave him another one of her hard smiles. "Not a thing, Mike."

Mike turned back to Alton and Pitcairn. "We just have some blanks that need filling in, that's all."

Alton glared, and folded his arms, but Pitcairn nodded. "Of course, Detective," he said.

"I'll get some more chairs," Fran said.

One of the officers working the second floor, Winships, nearly collided with him at the door. "Got something from the art studio down the hall," he said, holding up a tooled leather scrapbook.

Fran took it, turning back into the bedroom as he opened it. Only the first ten or so pages were filled, all of them with recent newspaper clippings of the Butcher homicides. He looked up as Mike and Abbey gathered around, and met Alton's eyes. "So you really have been following the case, Mr. Alton?"

"Um, Sarge?"

All three detectives turned.

"That's just the newest one," Winships said. "We found a whole shelf full of them, scrapbooks just like that."

Fran closed the scrapbook, and handed it to Mike. "Lead

on," he said.

They brought cardboard boxes in from the van, and Fran volunteered to do the inventory list and receipt. Abbey came with him, clearly still angry with the two old men Mike was riding herd on in the bedroom up the hall. "'If we're not under arrest,' she mimicked Alton, 'Then we have nothing to say.'"

The studio room took up the entire rear of the house. There were several large, heavily constructed easels positioned about the room, all of them holding big canvases in various stages of completion. A huge window took up most of the rear wall, framed with thick curtains. "Huh," Abbey said. "Faces east. Aren't they supposed to face north?"

"North wall's a common one with his neighbor." Fran saw the shelf where Winships led him, and whistled. "Beggars can't be choosers, I guess." He and the two officers started taking scrapbooks down, one by one. He decided to inventory them by the first and last clipping date. "I want to do this in order, now," he said. Then, over his shoulder to Abbey, "You really see these two doing the homicides?"

"Nah." She was looking at the paintings on the easels. "Nick themselves shaving, maybe, but that's about all." Fran saw her stop before the largest unfinished painting, four feet by six feet easy, taller than her, monumental towers of cumulus clouds, brilliantly white on top, a sick greenish grey below, with just an indication of a tiny airplane flying through them, a tiny yellow biplane. Fran grunted. Probably a Jenny.

Winships handed him a scrapbook. "This one's May 1957 through February 1963, Sarge."

"I said in order, dammit, in order. Don't just hand me the first thing you pull."

Abbey said, "This Pitcairn character really likes to paint clouds, you know?" Where he can never go, Fran thought to himself, making an entry in the inventory form.

She went up to the big canvas and reached out to touch it. "Fuck," she said, grimacing at her finger. "Still wet."

"Goddammit."

Mike followed Fran down to the first floor. "Let it go, Mike," he said.

"All of this bullshit, and we end up with some scrapbooks and no statements?"

Fran stopped, turned. "You want to bring them in?"

"On what?"

"Exactly." Fran continued down the stairs.

Kandetzke met them at the bottom. Mike asked, "Anything in the basement?"

"Spiders, dust, cartons that haven't been touched in years it looks like. Whole lotta nothing, Mike."

Mike looked at Fran, who only shook his head.

The resounding slam of the front door was gone from the hallways, but it still echoed in his head as William went slowly up the stairs. When he reached the top he grasped the carved mahogany eagle that crowned the newel post, and paused. The house below was indeed silent. The loud, tramping footsteps and foul, common language of the police were gone. They had only spent a short time in the basement, and they hadn't uncovered the satchel. That was the only good thing out of all of it. The only thing.

In the hallway before him he heard the quiet slide of chain, and the gentle creak of a bed. "William," Jack called out into the hall, "Is that you?"

He pushed off the eagle, and went down the hall to the open bedroom doorway.

Jack seemed lost in the vast bed, the pile of pillows and colorful, quilted counterpane. "They're gone?"

William nodded. "They'll be back, though."

Jack closed his eyes. "There's nothing wrong with keeping scrapbooks, no matter what the subject. If there were, they would have arrested us."

William went over to the bed. He untangled one of the leg chains. "The pull," he said. "How is it?"

"It's…bearable." Jack gave a sudden, odd laugh. "All these years, we never had visitors, not so many, all at once, anyway." He raised his shackled arms. "I was hardly the gracious host, eh?"

"You had no reason to be gracious. They came in here with their muddy shoes and trashy mouths and violated our house, our home. Violated it."

"You're angry. I haven't seen you angry in years."

William took out his key ring. "Do you want me to unlock you? Do you need to use the—"

"No, I don't think so. Not yet. Maybe later."

William reached over and rearranged the pillow behind Jack's head. Jack looked up at him. "We might have a long evening ahead of us. A long night too. Don't you feel it?"

William ignored the question. "Can I get you anything, then?"

"Maybe some tea, and later, the evening newspaper."

"Of course." William turned and went to the door.

"We didn't do it," Jack said. "We're not the murderers."

William was silent.

"We're trying to stop them," Jack persisted, "aren't we?"

"I'll go make that tea," William said.

The voice on the phone said, "I'm sorry, Detective Lomax, but Mr. Blue passed away over the weekend."

Fran's fist came down slowly, silently, on his desk. "I'm sorry to hear that," he said.

"We're all a little sad, actually. Mr. Blue was a real sweetie. He'll be missed around here."

"I'm sure he will be."

"Is there anything else we can do for you?"

"No. Thank you for your time." Fran dropped the receiver back in its cradle. He looked at it for a moment, then reached to pick it back up. Mike Finnean appeared at his cubicle door at that moment. "We're in Conference Room One, Fran," he said.

Fran waved the receiver. "I'll be there in just a minute." Mike nodded, and was gone.

Fran dialed quickly. Sarah didn't pick up. "Crap," he muttered. He thought for a moment, then dialed again. Someone picked up on the second ring. "City Courts," someone young and female sang out, much too cheerily for this hour of the evening. "Yes," Fran said, "I was looking for Sarah Fitzpatrick. She works in the same office as—"

"As me. We both work for the same judge. Sarah's not here. She's upstairs with one of Judge Kohler's law clerks."

Sarah worked on the twelfth floor of the Courthouse Annex. The Annex had twenty stories easy. "Can you tell me what floor that is?"

"Where Judge Kohler has her offices? Sure, let me look it up."

Fran gripped the receiver, closing his eyes.

"Here it is," the chipper young voice said. "She's in Suite 1805. Eighteenth floor."

The eighteenth floor of the Courthouse Annex was laid out in long perimeter corridors, floor-to-ceiling windows, and private office suites. The corridor leading to 1805 followed the north perimeter of the building, offices on the right, a wall of glass panels on the left. It had begun to sleet outside, and the runnels of slush blurred the view and smeared the evening lights of Spring Garden, Vine and North Philadelphia beyond. Fran imagined he saw bones out there through the vertical streaks, a vast sea of them, moving with him in waves as he went along the corridor. Stop that, he told himself. This is the eighteenth floor. It's just the eighteenth floor, goddammit. It's not high enough for that. Maybe.

Suite 1805 was one of three off a little waiting-room-like square of carpet filled with vinyl-upholstered chairs, department-store paintings, and dusty broad-leaved plants. Fran went through the double doors into an outer office, where he found Sarah and what looked like another lady law clerk—middle-aged, blue pants-suit, graying hair in an unraveling bun—huddled over a collection of open loose-leaf binders.

Sarah looked up and smiled. "Francis! Cindy said you called. What a nice surprise! You could have waited downstairs, honey. Gwen? This is Francis Lomax, a detective in the Philadelphia Police Department. Fran, this is Gwen Quoyle."

"I'm one of Judge Kohler's clerks," Gwen said, rising, offering her hand. "Nice to meet you."

"Same here," Fran said, shaking briefly. To Sarah, "I was just, you know, wondering if I could take you home."

Gwen said, "Listen Sarah, I can finish this myself. Why don't you and Detective Lomax get going?"

"You sure? Fran won't mind—"

"Go. Skidaddle. Get outta here. Shoo!"

"I think she means business," Fran said. Eighteenth floor. The urge to *go down* was rising in him, pounding in his skull.

"Well...okay." Sarah stood, and gave Fran a quick kiss on the cheek. "I'll be in early tomorrow," she said to Gwen. "Any loose ends, just give me a call."

Gwen pointed a stern finger toward the doors.

They exited into the perimeter hallway.

The sleet streamed down the wall of windows; the imaginary army of bones marched past in the blurry night.

"You're worried about something," Sarah said, looking at him sideways as they walked.

"I'm always worried about something."

She squeezed his hand.

Halfway to the elevators, Fran suddenly realized he still had the evidence bag with the little white claw bone in his overcoat pocket, the one from the Ben Franklin, the one he had used to try to get Alton to open up in the park. He shoved his free hand in, groping, and closed his fingers over the baggie. It felt warm, unaccountably, tangibly *warm*.

Be careful where you take it, Lester Blue had warned him. Be careful how *high* you take it.

He tightened his other arm in Sarah's, pulling her along.

"Hey, what's the hurry, officer?"

Fran quickened his pace. The little baggie in his left hand began to feel hot. The army of imaginary bones beyond the glass rippled, followed, kept pace. Sleet. It's just sleet on the glass, goddammit. It's not—

They came to the elevators. Fran freed his right arm to push the Down button, but stopped, suddenly aware, suddenly certain, that if the elevator doors opened, beyond them would be the gaping jaws of—

"Here." Sarah reached forward and pushed the button. "Won't work if you don't push it."

The bone in Fran's left fist pulsed with intense, flaring heat. He nearly cried out—

The elevator doors opened.

An elderly gentleman in a blue suit stood in the corner of the car, blinking hugely behind oversized black-rimmed eyeglasses. "I'm going down," he said in a reedy voice.

Sarah stepped in, smiling politely. "So are we," she said, and turned back to Fran. "You coming, sir?"

Fran followed her into the elevator.

The doors closed behind him.

The elderly man blinked, and turned his head away.

As Sarah pushed the button for Twelve, Fran took his left hand out of his overcoat pocket and turned it over. There was no burn. There was just the indentation of the bone where he had gripped it.

The elevator hummed quietly, and began its descent.

He put his hand back in his pocket. The little claw was still there, safe in its baggie. No heat now, though. No nothing.

"You hungry?" Sarah looped her arm through his, giving his hand a secret squeeze.

"Yeah," he said, squeezing back. "Starved. But I have to get back. I can't let this one go."

"Of course you can't," Sarah said, and smiled.

23

Nurse Gayle Garabedian glanced again at the clock. One A.M. Three hours till shift change. She sighed. Slow, quiet nights were both a blessing and a curse. Except for a few consulting third-years walking the ward like the zombies they frequently became at this late hour, she might just as well have been tending the stiffs filed away in the drawers of the hospital morgue twenty floors below.

She glanced at the clock again. Thirty deadly minutes till a bedpan round and comatose shuffle. Dear God, what a life. Maybe that cute intern with the dark eyes would stop by...

Then, so quietly she barely heard it, there was a sound behind her, from the direction of the staff hallway. A quiet clicking. She began to turn, feeling sudden warmth on the back of her legs. Then she felt a tugging at her neck, just under her jaw.

More warmth, then, as she continued to turn, wet warmth flowing down the front of her uniform, and a red, pulsing fountain spray as her carotid suddenly jetted fresh, oxygen-rich blood onto the station desk before her.

OHMYGOD, she thought, incredibly, with no vocal chords left to scream with, *I'm dying, aren't I—*

The thing that had once been a young and pretty nurse named Gayle Garabedian shambled out of the elevator and down a third floor corridor of administrative offices nearly to the end, fumbled, managed to fit a key into a set of double doors on the right, and stumbled through. The doors closed behind it. This was the Central Records Room, where all the clerks and medical secretaries had their desk cubicles clustered around the inner room holding the hospital's lone, bulky computer mainframe. At this hour, there was only one clerk on duty, a young one, Anne Verallo, blonde and almost as pretty as Nurse Garabedian once was. The dead thing saw her turn at the sound of its entrance. "Hello?" Anne's voice was high and sweet. "Larry? Is that you?"

The thing that had once been Nurse Garabedian opened its mouth. "It's meee," it whispered. Then, louder, trying not to spray, "It's jussst Gayle."

"Well howdy-doo, girl!" Anne rose from behind her desk terminal. "I didn't know your break was so—" She stopped, seeing what was standing there in the shadows: a naked woman, bent in an odd way, and strangely misshapen. Her eyes were dull and flat, and her black hair hung in wet strings, individual droplets of dark moisture hanging off the ends of each one. But it was more than her nakedness that caused Anne's eyes to go wide. It was her wounds, fresh, still suppurating blood-red incisions criss-crossing her skin. And the *smell*… "Oh my God," Anne gasped, finding her voice at last, *"Gayle*—?" but the dead thing was already on her, its hands on her mouth, throttling her under her chin. Anne gagged, and her eyes started to roll up under her eyelids. The thing shook her, "Don't ffaint on me, dear hhheart," it crooned in a quiet, airless wheeze. "Don't leave quite yyet. Wwwe have wwork to do first, darling."

It pushed the young woman back into her seat, still holding her throat. "I nnneed an addressss," it said. "I nnnneed to *ffffind* ssomeone."

Anne made a muffled sound, but the thing kept its hands firmly on her mouth. Maroon congealing blood oozed out between its fingers, and splat like jelly on her pastel print tunic. "I'm in a hhhurry," the thing said, its mouth against Anne's ear. "I nnneed the address for Pitcairn. Fffor Alton. They wwwere hhere two wwweeks ago. Thhey left a record." The hand on Anne's throat tightened. "Pitcairn, dear hhheart. Shall I *ssspell* it?"

Anne put her hands on the terminal keyboard and began typing furiously. In moments the screen showed the main address database, and a blinking cursor at the search query field.

The dead thing smiled, and a little string of pink spit drooled off its lip, down to the keyboard below.

"Type it," it said.

Anne hesitated, and the hand tightened about her throat again. "*Type it*," the thing said again.

Anne entered the name, then the search string.

The thing moved its hand from Anne's throat to put a cold, dead finger on the monitor glass as Anne slowly scrolled the list, each name jumping up in turn over the carefully manicured fingernail, now bruised purple and puss yellow.

There was no Pitcairn listed. Anne made a mewling sound, and rolled her eyes.

"The little *sshit*," the dead thing said over her shoulder, "thinks he's sso sssmart, does he? Type Altonnn, dear hhheart." The bloody drool was all over her shoulder now, dribbling down to her elbow. Anne did as she was told, and the information scrolled down the screen anew.

"There," the dead thing said then. "Ssstop it there."

The name and address the dead thing wanted glowed in white phosphor letters. It smiled again, and more bloody drool dribbled out of its mouth. "Yesss," it whispered gutturally, in a voice that had once been female, had once been alive. "*Oh yesss.*"

It put its hand back on Anne's throat, and turned her around in her chair. Anne's eyes were bulging, her skin bloodless. She struggled mightily, but the thing's grip was overpowering. "Now, dear hheart," it crooned, leaning close, "there is just one more thing I nneed."

Before it left, wearing its better fitting new skin and damp clothes, it spent a few moments caressing the smooth, blood-slicked curves and dark, empty orbits of the young clerk's skull…then dropped it on the stinking pile of offal littering the floor. "Promises to keep," it muttered in its new voice as it moved out of the office and down the dark hallway, "Promises to keep, Jack…"

The dark-eyed, second-year intern paused before the nineteenth floor west wing ward doors, stretched mightily, adjusted his tie as he got his newest, smoothest come-on line for Nurse Garabedian ready, then pushed the doors open.

Beyond, in the half-light, the nurse station was empty.

What a dramatic letdown: a great line, a killer routine…but no audience.

As he went through the doors he slipped on something wet, cartwheeled his arms, and managed to avoid falling on his ass only by grabbing the handicap rail on the wall. "What the hell—" he began, pulling himself upright, looking down.

Blood. Splatters of it. Streaks of it. *Lots* of it, like the ER floor between moppings.

He should have called hospital security at that moment, but he didn't. Yes, the police detective told him later, grim-faced, you certainly should have done that. Instead, he followed the blood. To the nurse station, to the half-round blue counter.

And what was piled up on the floor behind it, grinning up at him.

Another four hour night, another scalding, needle-sharp shower to wash away the cob-webs, then a hurried, sloppy cup of coffee, waving off his mother's admonitions for something solid for breakfast, a few pieces of toast at least, Frannie, take me two minutes to get for you; then an awkward, lumbering trot down Ashburner to catch the 66 trolley bus he saw showering sparks from the overhead lines as it slid by St. Dominic's in the violet, pre-dawn gloom. New ones, Mike had said on the phone. Holy Rood Hospital this time. A *hospital.*

He slipped on some ice and nearly landed on his ass boarding the bus. As he fished in his pocket for his TransPas the SEPTA driver said, "I saw you running. I woulda waited."

Yeah, Fran thought, finding the TransPas at last and flashing it, sure you would.

There was always a seat on the trolley bus this early, and on the Elevated train as well, rocking, shrieking, more sparks showering down to the shadowy streets below the tracks. He stared out at the second floor windows flashing past the rumbling, shaking train, and wondered for the millionth time how people could stand living so close to the goddamn El tracks.

In the lot outside the Roundhouse where he had told Mike he would wait, a cruiser rolled to a crunching stop in front of him. The passenger window came down and one of the uniforms inside said, "Detective Lomax?"

Fran leaned on the doorframe. "You found me. You my ride?"

"Homicides down at Holy Rood? Pile in."

Fran opened the back door and climbed into the cage. "Don't tell me," he said, "Nineteenth floor?"

The driving officer glanced at his partner, then back to Fran. "And the third floor too. How'd you know that?"

"I'm a psychic." Fran sat back, sighing. "Let's go."

All of the West Wing patients on Nineteen had already been moved to other wards by the time Fran got there, "And none of them saw anything," Mike Finnean said, "Can you believe it?" He pointed to the open doors. "They had over a dozen customers up here last night too." He paused. "Nineteenth Floor, Frannie."

"I know, Mike. I just got off the goddamn elevator." Fran's hand was in his coat pocket. The claw bone in the baggie was cold. He gave the closest rooms a cursory inspection, then turned his attention to the station counter, a half-doughnut of blue Formica up against the end wall of the ward, accessible from either side. Sanderson was working there. Fran noted the arterial spray on the left side, soaked into the papers, files and open binders. "This happened after midnight," he said, getting a pair of latex gloves from his suit coat pocket and pulling them awkwardly onto his hands.

Sanderson handed him a pair of booties. "I'd guess most of the patients would have been asleep, with their doors closed or curtains pulled."

Fran stepped carefully behind the counter. "Asleep or drugged, take your pick, so I'm not too surprised no one saw anything." He looked down. "Still. How could this be quiet?"

"I know what you mean," Sanderson said, looking around. "This took a lot of work."

Fran saw a jumbled pile of bones on the floor, freshly excised, and pieces of cut, shredded and sodden clothing. Lafferty, the other half of the CL team, was crouched at the other entrance to the station, making notes on a clipboard. "I'm counting just about all the bones of a typical skeleton, De-tectives," he said.

"They're all here?"

"Until we start moving the clothing, I can't be one hundred percent, but all the major ones are in plain view."

The skull leered up, cradled in a bloody bra cup.

"No skin, though," Mike said. "No meat, no guts. Just bones and fluids. A neat flip-flop of the Copper scene, you know?"

It found a new suit of clothes, Fran said to himself. And

tried it on. This time, apparently, it looked like they had gotten it right. He turned to his partner. "They told me downstairs there was another one?"

"Yeah." Mike pointed to a side door, smear of blood on the handle. "We got a blood trail through there, into a staff elevator. The other crime scene is in some admin offices on the third floor."

"We haven't processed that scene yet," Lafferty said, "but it's been secured."

Fran said, "I think I'm gonna head down." Then he remembered that Finnean was the Primary. "Okay with you, boss?"

"Sure." Mike squatted with Lafferty. "I'll meet you in a bit."

"Me too," Lafferty said, "So don't—"

"Touch anything, jeez." Fran saluted in their general direction, and left.

The trail of blood and fluids (lymph? bile? piss?) showed long, confused smearing. Fran made out a recognizable footprint three times in the back hallway leading to the elevator, along with extra blood and handprints on the wall, where the thing had apparently stopped to rest, or regain its balance. Getting a feel for the new body. Was it so slow and weak that it might still be in the hospital? The thought hurried him into the elevator. A uniform he didn't recognize was inside, standing on a kraft-paper square. He straightened when he saw Fran. "Going down, Detective?" As the doors closed Fran hesitated over the bloody button for the third floor. He knew whose fingerprint it was, goddamn it; he had just left her piled bones down the hall. He punched it. The uniform behind him didn't say a word.

Fran recognized the uniform in the third floor hall standing guard outside the elevator. There was hardly any blood on the floor down here. "Gibbons," he said, "Where am I going?"

"Down this way, Detective Lomax, last set of double doors on the right. God forgive me, you can't miss it."

Fran started down the hallway, saw the open doors on the right, yellow tape beyond.

Gibbons called after him, "The other detectives are already there!"

Fogel and Kandetzke raised their hands in greeting when Fran entered. Abbey said, "After yesterday with the S&M twins on Delancey, I thought nothing could surprise me." She spread her arms. "What the fuck, Fran, you know?"

"The bloody key is still in the door lock," Fran pointed behind him. "The killer had a key. You know what that could mean. Has the—"

"Hospital's in lock-down," Joe Kandetzke said. "All the ER and walk-in traffic is being routed to Jefferson."

"How long before management starts squawking?"

"They already are. The Hospital Administrator hasn't shown up yet, though. It'll all hinge on him."

"So which one of you two is better at shmoozing?"

Abbey laughed. "That would be Joe."

"Hey, I'll trade ass-kissing to spilled guts any time." Joe snapped his gloves off and tossed them, then clapped Fran on the shoulder as he left.

"You've seen this shit before, Fran," Abbey said, motioning him to follow her, "so I'll skip the fucking preliminaries."

They reached the computer terminal desk. Abbey stooped, pulled the yellow plastic tarp aside, then rose again and put her hands on her hips. "I say again: what the fuck?"

Fran took in the pile of flesh, viscera and bones, realizing almost immediately that he was looking at a complete body, or all the pieces of one, anyway. The skin cuts were very precise and methodical, no ripping, no tearing. Used, he thought, realizing then *precisely* what he was looking at. Used, then tossed aside. Replaced by something newer, something better. Something that *fit* better.

Abbey dropped to a squat, balancing on the balls of her feet. "I see an entire body here," she said, "but it's been, what, taken apart? All the meat, all the skin, all the guts, all the bones..." She looked up. "I don't fucking get it."

"This flesh belongs to the bones upstairs," Fran said.

"They *what*? That doesn't make any goddamn sense! There are bones right here, Fran, hundreds of the fuckers."

"Two hundred and seventy." Fran looked at the terminal screen. "This thing's been on the whole time?" The dark green screen had a short string of letters glowing in the upper left corner. The last character, an underline, was blinking. "You know how to work one of these?"

"Computers?" Abbey shook her head. "I have a hard enough time fucking with goddamn Selectrics."

Fran turned toward the door. "Gibbons!"

The uniform ducked his head in. "Yeah, Sarge?"

"I need somebody who knows how to use computers. I need to get them in here pronto."

"Gimme a minute." Gibbons ducked back out.

Abbey asked, "Why the interest in the computer?"

"The victim was at this desk, in front of this screen, when he—"

"She. Anne Verallo. Blonde, blue, five even, one-oh-five, age twenty-three. Member of the hospital Administrative staff."

Fran smiled. "Very good. So Miss—" He paused, looked at Abbey, "She was a Miss, right?"

Abbey nodded with a sour expression.

"So our Miss Verallo was at her desk, doing her third shift administrative job, probably something to do with computer input and output, when she was killed."

Abbey shrugged. "So?"

"So I think it might help to know what she was working on just before she died." He pointed to the glowing characters on the screen. "It might be important."

Abbey shrugged again. "Fair enough." She saw something past Fran's shoulder, and motioned with her hand. "Over here!" Then she quickly bent and flung the plastic tarp back over the pile of remains on the floor.

Fran turned to see Gibbons shepherding a middle-aged man—balding, glasses, loosened tie and open vest—through the maze of desks.

"I think I'm going to be sick," the man said.

"This is Mr. O'Toole," Gibbons said. "He raised his hand when I asked if anybody knew anything about the hospital computer system."

Mr. O'Toole's eyes darted to the cubicle wall, the desk, the darkly glowing screen, everywhere where the blood had splattered. His gaze settled on the yellow tarp. "I really don't want to be here," he said.

"This will only take a minute, Mr. O'Toole." Fran pointed to the screen. "What does this tell you?"

O'Toole swallowed, pushed his glasses up his nose. "This is the Financial Records database. It's waiting for a command."

"What, like 'save'?"

"No. It's in the middle of a search string. It's waiting for the next search command, or a return to the main menu."

"Miss Verallo was searching for something?"

O'Toole looked at the tarp again. "Dear God, That's *Annie*?"

Abbey took his arm. "Focus, Mr. O'Toole. Don't look at the floor, okay?"

Fran said, "Can we tell what she was looking for?"

"You mean her last search string?"

"Yeah. Her last search string. Can you bring it back?"

"Well, certainly, but…" He pointed to the blood-spattered keyboard.

"Here, I've got gloves on." Fran got in front of it, fingers poised. "What do I type?"

O'Toole told him. Fran punched the sticky keys.

"Now hit Enter," O'Toole said. He pointed. "That big key over there."

All three of them watched as the white phosphor characters

unrolled across the screen.

ALTON_WILLIAM_A_//_512_DELANCEY_ST_//_P HILA_//_PA_//_19002

"Wow," Abbey said, "That's our favorite citizen, Fran."

"Payment records," O'Toole said, nodding. "Looks like address information for someone who paid a patient's bill. Hit that arrow key."

Fran did, and new information scrolled into view.

"Paid with cash," O'Toole said.

Fran stared at the address. The urge to leap up and run for the door was overwhelming. It had what, a one, two hour head start?

O'Toole said, "We can find out who this Mr. Alton paid his bill for by—"

"Thank you Mr. O'Toole, but that won't be necessary." Fran caught Gibbons' eye. "The officer here will escort you back out. Thank you for your help." Both he and Abbey watched as he was led back out into the hall. Then Fran said, "I've got to go," and started pulling off his gloves.

Abbey gave him maneuvering room as he rounded the chair. "Go? You're bailing on us *again*? What the fuck, Fran!"

Fran pointed back to the screen. "I'm not bailing. I'm going back there. Tell Mike where I'm going." Then, over his shoulder as he hit the double doors, "And I need at least two units to meet me, okay?"

24

In his dream, someone whose face he couldn't see poured molten lead into the marrow of his bones. The pain was so sudden and so unbelievably intense there was nothing for him to do but grab his head in his hands, curl into a fetal position and scream.

The door of his bedroom banged open, a spear of hallway light parting the darkness, and William was at his side, urging, "Don't move, just let me—"

He felt a pinprick in his arm, a tiny spark of pain in the agonizing conflagration, and then the injection took effect, banking the flames, deadening him, dulling the pain of the throbbing, rebelling bones.

When Jack awoke he found himself slumped in his wheelchair, fully dressed, wearing his winter coat, as William pushed him down the first floor hallway toward the rear of the house. "Where…?" He muttered, slurring the word, "What is this? Where are we going…?"

"It's time to leave," William said. "We have to go now."

Jack blinked away at the blurriness in his eyes. He tried to raise his hands to wipe them but they weighed far too much, were too far away, a stranger's hands at the end of someone else's arms. "I can't—" he said, feeling saliva leak from the corner of his mouth. "I'm not—"

"Don't try to talk," William said. They reached the end of the hallway, and William maneuvered the wheelchair carefully through the rear entry. The back door was already open, and the storm door was unlatched. William swung the chair around to take the three steps backwards. At each step, each thudding bounce, Jack grunted at the dull throbbing in his head. Then they were down, outside, bouncing on the cobbles of the rear courtyard in the violet pre-dawn light. The tall brick walls hid the neighboring courtyards and the back alley. The ivy covering them was dusted with frost.

Jack shivered, blinking away new tears. "I'm cold," he said.

"I'll have you in the car in just a moment."

On the right side of the courtyard he saw the hulking dark shape of the Bentley, parked outward, facing the alley gates. It grumbled quietly, wisps of white exhaust escaping its twin tailpipes.

Jack tried to focus. "But where are we going?" It didn't make sense. Was William taking him to the hospital?

William didn't answer his question. He opened the rear door of the car, put one foot inside to brace himself, and with Jack's fumbling help, lifted him safely into the rear compartment.

Jack slid across the warm leather, grimacing with the effort.

"I just need to lock up," William said. "I'll only be a moment."

"I'm fine," Jack gasped, leaning back, letting the soft leather cradle him, closing his eyes on his dizziness.

William shut the car door, and in the sudden silence Jack repeated his words aloud: "…Only a moment…" He was barely awake now, the effects of the drug injection beginning to take full effect. Somewhere, inside, the pain waited. Under his folds of flesh, nestled in the warm, wet darkness, the bones stirred again.

Only a moment!

With great effort he brought his hands up, fingers trembling, and pressed them to either side of his head as new pain, fresh cracks across old, scarred surfaces, opened inside him.

Only a moment! William! Where was he?

He saw movement out of the corner of his eye.

He turned—

A hand slapped against the glass of his door window.

He stared at it: long, tapered fingers, manicured nails, soft, pale palm...a woman's hand. It left trails on the glass as it dragged slowly down. It left smears, dark and viscous.

He saw a face then, forming out of the half-light as it came up and close to the glass. It was a young woman, her blond hair stringy with blood, her forehead and cheeks streaked with it, her skin freshly sliced and put back together in the same scar pattern he had seen in the mirror every day of his life since he was six.

Oh God no, he thought, before he realized he wasn't just thinking it, but was screaming it aloud: "NO! NO!"

The thing on the other side of the glass said in a gravelly, guttural voice, "Sshut up and open the door, you little shhhit."

He looked wildly at the door locks. It couldn't get in! He was locked inside and it couldn't get in! He was safe! He was—

"Open the door," the thing said, grinning, teeth and jawbones stretching dead lips tight, "or I'll break the fucking winnndow and open it myssself." It raised a bloody cobblestone into view.

Jack saw his arm jerk, then, saw his hand extend, straining toward the door handle. Ohmygodno—

Behind the thing, then, he saw movement in the yellow glow of the kitchen. William!

"WILLIAM!" He screamed the name even as his hand grasped the door handle—

"WILLIAM! HELP ME!"

Grasped, and *pulled*—

William was in the house less than two minutes, but it was enough. When he came out onto the back steps, canvas satchel in hand, he saw the alley gate open, a scuffled trail through the dusting of snow on the courtyard cobbles, and someone crouched at the open rear door of the Bentley.

He put the satchel down, then came down the stoop steps in a dead run. The figure by the car turned, arms out, head thrust forward. It was a young woman in a pastel tunic and pants, a hospital worker of some kind. In the few second it took him to cross the courtyard William saw the bloody matted hair, the gore splattered across her clothes, and the fresh, red incision scars across her stretched and grinning face. It brought him up short, gasping.

In a low, rasping voice, it said, "Wwe *smelled* you once, didn't weee, dear heart?" She raised her nose, sniffing like some feral beast. "Yesss! We *did*! We——"

With an inhuman cry William leaped to tackle the thing——

The cruiser bumped the curb, then Fran was out, across the sidewalk, taking the front steps of Pitcairn's townhouse two at a time. The rotating jiggle-lights strobed the still sleeping street in red-blue, red-blue, eclipsing the scattering of Christmas lights that had been left on to twinkle through the night. Narrow windows flanked the massive front door, and Fran could see through the thick, wavy glass that there were lights on somewhere in the rear of the house. He took hold of the heavy iron knocker and slammed it down, then again.

Echoes from within, but no approaching footsteps. He squinted through the glass, but didn't see anyone coming.

Beside the house was a brick tunnel alley leading to the rear of the townhouse, but the iron-bar gate was locked. Three doors east was Fifth Street, the shortest way around to the alley backing the townhouses on the south side of Delancey. Fran took it at a steady trot, respectful of just how easy it would be to slip and fall flat on his ass on the icy pavement. At the corner he saw two thin smears of blood on the side wall of the corner property, two fingers dragged across the marble facing. On the sidewalk—he crouched briefly, huffing—oval drops. Not many, but a trail nevertheless.

He stopped at the entrance of the alley, caught his breath, reached into his overcoat and unsnapped the strap over his Browning. He pulled the weapon free, thumbed the safety, then turned quickly into the alley: brick walls eight feet high, car-sized and door-sized gates punctuating them all the way down to Sixth Street. The alley was just wide enough for a garbage truck, and was lit in five places, evenly spaced. A door-sized gate looked open four properties down on the right. Oh shit, he thought. He approached it on the balls of his feet, and as he got close he heard the low idle of a large automobile. Nearer, he caught the smell of exhaust.

He reached the half-open gate. More finger smears of blood, this time in kindergarten abandon. Someone had bludgeoned the gate open. Using his foot, he pushed it out of the way and took two impossibly long seconds to take in the scene before him:

A large, square, cobbled courtyard; on the right, a body thrown up, sprawled against the ivy on the side wall, either unconscious or dead—light spilling down steps from an open back door was enough for Fran to identify him as William Alton; large black luxury vehicle on the left, rear door open, some movement in the back seat.

Fran swung his aim in the direction of the open car door and braced. "You in the car! I'm a police officer! Get out now! Get out now!"

The figure inside paused.

"Out slowly!" Fran took two steps into the courtyard proper, and braced again. "Get out of the goddamn car! I want to see both hands!"

His commands echoed down the brick canyon of the alley.

Then, from inside the car, low, throaty and wet: a giggle. "*Frannie? Isss that you?*"

Fran hesitated; it was a female voice, rough, slightly slurred; *how the hell did she know my name?* He took two more steps toward the car. Inside, he could make out a young woman in a hospital tunic splattered with both fresh and dried blood. Gore-soaked blond hair plastered her face, obscuring her features, but underneath Fran saw a grin.

She giggled again. "I wasss hoping it would be you, dear heart. Come hhere, lllook at my toys."

Fran trained his gun on the center of her chest, breathing through his nose, forcing calm, forcing focus. "I said out of the vehicle! On the ground!" Another step; he could see something in her lap, roping, glistening purple and cream coils of someone's intestines. His voice rose, "Out of the car now! On the ground!"

"On those ssstone cobbles?" Her grin fell into a mocking pout. "But they're ssso hard, Frannie. They'll *huuurt.*"

Fran took a final step, less than five feet from the open door, and he saw the raw red seams in her skin, the weeping slices, the dead white flesh beneath the slopped and splattered gore. This wasn't a *her*, this was an *it*; this was something *dead*—

The thing in the car leaped.

Fran saw a snapshot of arms, legs, hands like claws, flashing, flailing, then the weight of it hit him, knocking him back. He staggered and fell, his head striking the cobbles with a sharp, resounding *crack*—

Blackness for a beat, blessed silence, blessed *nothingness*—

He opened his eyes, staring up into the patchwork face of the dead hospital worker, gasping in the rank stench of its grinning mouth just inches away from his own. The thing was straddling him, dripping, drooling on him, whispering: "Crazy anglo cop wantsss it? Can you believe thiss fucker? *He wantsss it?*"

Fran stared up into those eyes, those dead, soulless eyes. His gun was still in his hand, caught between them, pointing up, pointing under its chin...or his own.

"Do you, Fran?" The thing on him crooned, dripping black blood, tracing cold fingers on his cheek. "Do you rrreally want to die?"

Brass buttons. Brass buttons flashing on his big black greatcoat. Brass buttons flashing like gold. *So, Frannie my boy*, his father said, smiling, unlacing his broughams in the yellow light of the warm kitchen, *what's it to be, eh? Have you got it?*

The thing looked at him, its eyes all yellow and bloodshot, all pupil, black, black. Nothing there but death. Nothing there but *release*... "You *like* my brasss buttons, don't you, boy," it whispered. "You *like* my big brasss buttonss!"

But have you got it, lad?

Fran pulled the trigger of the Browning, hard.

The discharge flashes were so close they raked his chin, but three 9mm hollow point slugs ripped up through the drooling grin, passed behind the dead, soulless eyes, and blew the top of its skull off in an explosion of brain matter, bone and flesh.

The body sprawled on top of him, jerking, spasming. A mewling noise came out of the ragged purple and pink hole that had once been its face. Fran tried to roll it off, but its arms still clung to him, squeezing tight. There was enough room to twist the Browning outward, force the muzzle into its sternum...he pulled the trigger again, three more slugs into its ribcage, and more flesh, bone and blood fountained up and out.

Sudden dead weight as the echoes reverberated, then the quiet splatter of falling fluids and flesh...then there was just the muted rumble of the Bentley.

Fran pushed the remains of the body off him, rolled onto his knees, and threw up.

Beside him, what was left of the hospital clerk still twitched, still spasmed. Fran wiped his mouth with the back of his hand, then reached down, found the Browning in the puddled gore and vomit, and pointed it at the jagged splay of ribs, steaming flesh and entrails. Six shots fired, right? Six? That meant he had eight left, eight more slugs to disintegrate the fucking thing. His mouth was still drooling, and he wiped it again with his free hand. Eight more would shut it down, right? Fuck yeah.

"Detective Lomax."

Fran jerked his head to the right, to the sound of the voice, but his gun didn't waver.

He saw William Alton standing a few feet away, alive after all. The old black man held his right arm in his left, swaying slightly. "Are you hurt?" he asked. "Did it…get you?"

"No." Fran realized he was breathing again, and able to speak. He gestured with his chin at Alton's arm. "How about you?"

"I'm cut, but not bad. I may have sprained my arm when it threw me, I'm not sure. I blacked out. It was leaving me for seconds, I think."

They both watched the jutting, jagged ribs of the thing wave feebly, like fingers, like worms. "The bones," Alton said, "they're still alive."

Fran staggered erect. He wiped his Browning clean on the sleeve of his overcoat, then fumbled to holster it. "We need to get them all together. All the pieces. All the bones."

He saw Alton hesitate, so he raised his voice a notch: "Listen to me. You know what we need to do."

The old black man looked at him with hollow, tired eyes. Then he nodded. "I know," he said. "I know what has to be done. I was trying to do it, as a matter of fact, before I was interrupted by…that."

On the other side of the alley, several windows now glowed yellow.

"We don't have much time." Fran took off his overcoat and laid it out on the cobblestones, then turned to the body of the hospital clerk. "Help me with this."

Together, they put it on the overcoat. "Every piece," Fran said then, even though he knew he didn't have to, "every bone." He grabbed a skull fragment slowly humping its way into the shadows. It squirmed weakly in his grip as he dropped it into the open body cavity. Alton found another, and threw it in as well. When they were done, when they had found every gory piece, Fran wrapped the overcoat around the body like a present, using the sleeves to tie a clumsy knot.

Fran grabbed the arms. "A little help, here?"

Together, they staggered to the Bentley and heaved the body in, onto the rear compartment floor.

They both looked at Pitcairn's body in the back seat. It was flayed open, organs and viscera sliced, ripped, and thrown about, exposing major portions of his skeleton. Even in the poor light they could see Pitcairn's individual bones moving, undulating slightly, weakly. Alton said, in almost a whisper. "I should cover him up."

Fran hesitated. The back-up unit would be here in minutes, probably Mike and crew right behind it. "Leave it," he said. He opened the Bentley's front door. "Open the gate, then get in. We have a delivery to make."

"Where do you think you're going?"

Fran wiped blood off his eyebrow with the flat of his hand. "You know where."

Alton leaned against the car, closing his eyes. Then he opened them again, and pushed off. "I need to get something first." He started off in a shambling gait across the courtyard, back to the stoop steps.

"We have to leave!" Fran looked again at the lights on in the houses across the alley, moving shadows behind shades. Far off, he heard the warble of a police siren.

Alton stumbled up the steps and grabbed a canvas knapsack there. He shouldered it, returned to the car, put the pack carefully on the floor of the front passenger seat, then went to pull the gates open.

Fran started the Bentley forward before the old man even had his door closed. As they barreled down the alley Fran said, "What's in the sack?"

Alton looked at it, wedged safely between his feet. "Something I was afraid you would find yesterday."

They reached the end of the alley and lurched out onto Sixth Street. Fran said, "You ready for this?"

Alton nodded. "Sixty years ready."

25

To the east, across the city, across the Delaware, somewhere past Jersey and the vast Atlantic beyond, the sun was rising. As they followed the blue-shadowed one-way streets around Rittenhouse Square, Fran glanced across to Alton. "Can I ask you a question?"

Alton shrugged, keeping his eyes forward.

"How did this all begin? How did you and Pitcairn meet?"

"We knew each other as children. My family was part of the staff at his grandmother's estate."

Fran nodded. "There was a mention in one of the newspaper articles, after the plane accident, when his uncle went missing—"

"Lucian Spangler. That was his name."

"Yeah, Lucian Spangler." Fran swerved to avoid two Orientals pushing a food cart up onto a curb. "The article mentioned a stable boy who also went missing."

"That was me."

Fran glanced across to Alton again. The old man was still looking straight ahead, ramrod straight in his seat. "So you went up...there."

"Yes, Detective Lomax, I was up there." The old man turned to Fran finally, and his eyes looked dead. "I was only six when I was taken, and nearly eight, I found out later, when I returned. But I remember it, I remember all of it, like it happened yesterday."

Fran slowed to avoid a SEPTA bus pulling out into traffic. They crossed 23ʳᵈ Street. The bridge over the Schuylkill was just ahead. Across the river the top of the huge bulk of the 30th Street Train Station caught the first rays of sunlight.

Fran said, "But you escaped."

Alton nodded. "Yes, I did."

"How?"

"It's not a prison, Detective, it's a place, a world as big as ours, it's own...reality. There are roads from there to here, and many doors." He turned to look at Fran again. "And I was *strong*. Stronger than *them*, anyway."

The bones in the back seat stirred. Alton turned to look back at them.

Fran managed a quick look himself. "How are we doing back there?"

"It's fine." Alton turned back.

"So you and Pitcairn managed to hook up again, after the Second World War."

"He found me, after the publicity of the murders."

"In the Lennard Building. The family you worked for."

"They wouldn't listen, taking that new apartment on the nineteenth floor. They wouldn't listen to the boogeyman stories their black valet told them." Alton shook his head slowly. "But Jack knew. He had been up there, just like me, after all."

"Something happened in November, started this up again. Jack Pitcairn got out of the house, got, what, too high?"

Alton was silent.

Fran didn't look at him this time. "You let that happen. You caused it. You wanted it to be over."

Alton let his breath out. "I'm tired." His hands were loose in his lap. "I'm just so tired."

Fran let it go. He took a right onto a cross street, then a left onto Cherry. "We're getting close."

Alton looked into the back seat again. "*They* know that too."

Cherry Street was already busy with early morning commuter traffic. There were no parking spaces in front of the project apartment house, so Fran swung right into a short, dead-end side street, and bumped the Bentley up onto the curb. Fran got out first, and opened the back passenger door. Inside, the thing that had once been the hospital clerk had managed to partially work its way out of his overcoat. It lay in the flayed corpse of Pitcairn, nestled in his open gut, undulating fitfully as it tried to burrow in. He put his hand over his mouth to gag, but he didn't throw up.

Alton came around the car to stand beside him. "We should get them inside."

"No argument there." Fran reached in and pulled the half-headless body off the corpse of the old man. It came away with a wet, sucking sound. He retied the overcoat, pulling savagely at the knots. The thing was too weak to put up a fight. He dragged it out onto the sidewalk, then leaned his back against the car, panting steam into the cold air. He looked up and down the empty side street. "We need something to wrap Pitcairn in."

"There's a blanket in the trunk."

Fran tossed him the keys. In minutes, there were two bloody bundles on the sidewalk.

Fran looked at the old black man standing there, his hands smeared with gore, his face a blank mask. "You okay?"

"Yes, Detective." Alton nodded slowly, deliberately. "I'm fine. I'll be fine."

Fran noticed the canvas satchel slung over his shoulder. "You going to tell me what's in that?"

"You don't want to know."

Fran looked at him for a long moment, then he gestured to the blanket containing Pitcairn's remains. "You want to carry him?"

"No. You take him. I'll carry the other one."

Fran bent and hoisted Pitcairn in his arms. "You sure you're strong enough to do this?"

Alton lifted the other body in both arms. "Yes, Detective Lomax," he said. His smile was brief, cold. "I'm more worried about you, actually."

Fran gestured up the side street with his chin. "Let's go, finish this thing."

They approached the intersection cautiously. It was about ten yards from the corner to the front entrance of the project apartment house, and they had to pass several pedestrians to get there. All of them hurried by with heads down except one, an elderly lady in a wool coat, pulling an empty shopping basket. "Oh sweet Jesus," she gasped, seeing the blood on them, the limbs sticking out from what they carried. Fran managed to grab his shield from his belt and shoved it in her face. "Police business," he grunted, "move along, please."

Then they were up the concrete steps and through the cracked and taped glass doors into the lobby. Fran led the way, giving the elevator doors a look before lurching toward the stairwell in the rear, wondering how the hell they were going to get up eighteen flights with what they carried. Then one of the elevator doors chimed, creaked open, and a young black man with a full fro emerged, whistling. He stopped in mid-note. "Hey, my brothers," he said, "that's gotta hurt the little ladies, am I right?" Then the blood registered, and the gore. "What the hell—" he began, but Fran shouldered him aside, and he and Alton crowded into the elevator car. The young man took a step after them, yelling, "Wait one god damned minute you honky motherfuck—!"

The elevator door closed with an audible CHUNK.

Fran reached out to press the button for Nineteen, but stopped. "Question," he said.

Alton looked at him.

"You've got scars," Fran said, "just like these two. How come you're still whole, still…in control?"

The old black man was silent for a moment, then he said, "When I was taken, Detective Lomax, I was the same age as Jack. We were the same height, same build. If I wasn't black we could have been twins."

"What does that mean?"

"It means, Detective, *they* put Jack's skeleton in *me*. I've had it inside me since 1922, ever since *they* sent me back, to do this job, this *task*." He gestured with his chin to the bundle Fran held, "To get them their damned bones back."

Fran looked at him, horrified. "You've lived your whole *life*—"

"Yes." Alton leaned back, clutching his slowly squirming bundle. He nodded to the elevator panel. "Nineteen, if I'm not mistaken?"

Fran reached out and pushed the button.

Eighteen endless floors later, the glowing number 19 on the button panel finally went out, and the elevator doors opened on shadows. A lone fluorescent light flickered and buzzed a dozen yards down the long hallway. Halfway there, on the left, broken yellow tape hung from the doorframe of the Copper apartment, the scene of the first murder, and the place where Fran had first seen the door to The Boneyard through the bedroom window.

The dead body of Pitcairn had begun moving slightly inside the blanket like the thing that had been the hospital worker, but he knew it was just the bones. They twitched feebly with each step they took down the hallway. No problem, he thought, gripping the bloody bundle more tightly against him, swallowing back the hard lump that had risen in the back of his throat. Speedy delivery, door to door. No extra charge.

Alton was quiet until they reached the apartment, then he said, "It's probably locked, isn't it?"

"Better be," Fran put his burden down, and fished in his pants pocket for his keys. The master he had taken from the late great Jimmy the Super was still on the ring, and it slid cleanly into the deadbolt. Turning the knob, he pushed the door in an inch. Then he picked up his bundle once more, and looked at Alton. "You ready?"

The older man nodded.

The door swung inward with a push of Fran's knee, and he did a once-over assessment by reflex:

Living room clear, empty of all furniture, single window in far wall; hallway, closet and kitchenette on the left, light from the airshaft the only illumination. There were brown stains on the walls and floor, splatter patterns of old blood. No one home.

Fran entered the apartment, frowning at the memory of his last visit. No freak out now, Fran, right? You got it, lad, you got it. Keep the brass buttons in the closet, right? Behind him, Alton sniffed the air. "Do you smell that?"

"Industrial disinfectant, bleach, mildew…old blood." Fran shifted his hold on the blanket as the body inside it squirmed anew. "Just smells of an old crime scene."

Alton went past him. "No," he said, moving toward the short hallway leading to the bathroom and bedroom, "something else." He stopped just short of the hallway, and as he turned back, the remains of the thing's head in his bundle struck the wall with a dull thump. "Like an old fireplace. Like ash, something burnt."

Then Fran did smell it, and with it, a quiet, sickening thrill, a little Fourth of July sparkler flaring in his gut. "That's the smell of The Boneyard," he said. "Right?"

Alton nodded. "It's close by," he said. "The door must be open."

Fran looked again at the living room window, its pale, watery light steady, unchanging. Then he turned to the dark hallway. The bedroom had a window, too. "Bedroom," he said. "Let's go."

But Alton suddenly cried out, dropping the hospital worker's body on the floor. "Sorry. It bit me."

The body in the overcoat shifted, and Fran saw the half-face, and the slowly working jaw. It humped on the floor, twisting.

Alton bent, re-gathered his bundle, and picked it up once more. He kept the corpse's head as far away from him as possible. Its jaws opened, then closed with a click.

Fran nodded toward the bedroom door. "I'll go first," he said.

The bedroom was square, empty, small closet in the wall on the right, single window in the far wall, blue light from the airshaft filtering in over a square of plywood lag-bolted into the lower window sash. It was an odd blue, nothing like the grey light coming in the living room window. The stain evidence of Copper's murder was everywhere, on the splattered walls, and in the dull grey carpet. The only clean areas were the rectangles where furniture had been originally positioned. The smell of ash was strong in this room. Like dry, hot metal, Fran thought. Like an empty pot left on the stove too long.

"It's coming from the window," Alton said.

"We'll put them down there, under it."

The hospital worker's jaw snapped one more time as Alton laid the body out. "Damn you," the old man muttered, rising, stepping away. Fran put Pitcairn's corpse down next to it, then he stepped back as well. He put a blood-smeared hand on Alton's shoulder. "Thanks," he said.

Both bundles jerked. Then, as one, they dragged themselves toward the baseboard under the window.

Fran felt it too: a tugging, from his overcoat pocket. *Of course!*

He reached in, pulled out the baggie containing the little claw bone he had been carrying around since the hotel slayings.

The bone writhed inside the plastic, anxious, impatient. It was almost too hot to hold.

Fran flung the bone at the window glass with all the strength that was in him.

Several things happened all at once. A gravelly sound rose, a popping, crackling static, but rougher, harder, angrier, rapidly filling the room. The wall around the window frame wrinkled like skin, and long, sinuous welts rose slowly out of the plaster, ripped wounds sutured clumsily back together. The molding and casement of the window itself began changing as well, that all-too familiar pattern of curves and whorls rising up, twisting, writhing, as old paint cracked off, revealing the living grey wood beneath. The plywood patch in the lower sash suddenly caught fire and fell out, into the airshaft.

In moments, the window wasn't a window any longer, but it wasn't a doorway either. The former moldings were now a living, undulating frame of a thousand moving worms. The paling blue-violet light inside it flickered, then turned grey, a cold, dry, dead grey as the brick wall with its cinder-blocked windows across the airshaft melted into a vast *distance*, moving irresistibly away, yet at the same time rushing just as irresistibly forward. There was movement where nothing moved, but *something* was there, coming at them at a terrible, impossible speed. A roaring gust of hot wind slapped Fran's face, searing past his cheek, into his ear, down his neck, smelling of ashy, burnt acid and sulfur, growing stronger with each passing second.

He heard Alton yell something, but the rising static and onslaught of light and wind and the rushing, cresting movement drowned him out. Fran almost took a step back, almost put his hands to his face and closed his eyes to block everything. Almost.

Cut and run, Frannie, he thought…you don't have to stay here…you don't have to face this… But instead, he stood fast, like he was supposed to, both eyes open, a hard smile slowly forming, his fingers spread and curled slightly, arms away from his sides, ready. Ready for anything. He considered pulling his weapon, but only for a moment. No. Leave it holstered. He didn't need it.

Like an old-time locomotive, then, like a huge steaming, screaming train, all pipes and pistons, drive-shafts and wheels, impossible shapes doing impossible things at impossible speed: a cacophony of bones erupted out of the static, vomited out of the frame, the mouth, and Fran had less than a second to brace for a collision that…never came.

A low, draining hiss of air, trailing off to silence. The wind in his face: gone, replaced with a faint touch on his cheek, a soft breeze…

Fran suddenly realized his eyes were closed, and he opened them with a startled jerk.

Darkness lay beyond the window mouth, utter blackness, so close he felt he could reach out to touch it, yet at the same time infinitely distant, a yawning, bottomless, endless chasm of absolutely nothing. Fran tried to focus his eyes, but there was nothing there, nothing at all.

Fran turned to Alton to say—

But Alton was already stooping, picking up the bloody bundle that had once been Jack Pitcairn. Before him, the other bundle had already humped itself to the lip of the mouth, and was nearly over it. Alton gave it a kick, and it fell over to the other side. A cloud of ash dust rose and drifted into the bedroom.

There was a sudden, distant screech, then something huge and heavy, moving.

The wind rose.

"Get out of here, Detective," Alton said. He put a foot up on the slowly moving lip's edge.

A vast, endless sound blasted from the blackness beyond, popping Fran's ears. He saw the small drab-green canvas satchel then, Army issue, still slung over Alton's shoulder, and then he remembered what Alton had done in the war, and he knew what was in it. "That's—" he began, pointing to it, but another ear-drum-popping sound followed the first, all bass in a complex, infinite chord, much stronger, and he stumbled back, grabbing at his ears.

Alton was over the lip, now, trudging into the blackness, his face contorted in obvious pain.

The wind rose to a howl, and Fran saw vast movement in the darkness behind him, a sense of something coming again, something huge, irresistible, unstoppable. There was ash in the wind now, swirling out into the bedroom like hot black snow.

Alton stopped and turned. "GO!" he screamed, now nothing more than a ghost in the infernal blizzard. He had dropped Pitcairn, and was fumbling with the satchel. "Get out of here!"

The ash hit Fran's skin and sizzled. He staggered back, fell to his knees, but somehow found the door to the darkened hallway. He stumbled, lunged out of the bedroom, and stopped against the far wall to draw a heaving, ragged breath. Then a vast, low sound, something immense and heavy slowly falling, shook the air of the open doorway. Without even thinking of how useless it was, Fran reached into the storm of burning ash with a free hand, grasped the doorknob, and yanked the bedroom door shut. The sounds inside continued, and the walls continued to shake. Fran ran out of the apartment, careened off the opposite wall, then down the hall to the elevators and the fire stairs.

The sounds and vibrations followed him. Up and down the hall, residents opened their doors in alarm and anger, yelling, clamoring, "What the hell is going on here?"

"Everybody!" Fran's voice was raw. "Everybody get out! GET OUT OF THE BUILDING! NOW!"

Then the first explosion came, and Fran was thrown violently to the wall, the side of his head connecting solidly, sickeningly. He slid to the floor as everything began to turn red. *Oh God*, he thought, feeling his consciousness slip, *I gotta get out of here, I gotta—*

Then he felt someone's hands grab him by the armpits, and Fran looked up, focused on an anonymous resident, his face streaked with blood, pulling him into the fire stairway. "I got you!" he yelled. "I got you!" Then a second, larger explosion detonated, and a furnace-blast of air lifted them both into the air, and Fran tumbled down the metal and concrete stairs and into blessed, painless unconsciousness at last.

On Arch Street, in Center City, every nineteenth floor window blew out of the condo conversion next to where the Lennard Building had once stood, and huge splintering sheets of glass fell on the morning crowds below. Two pedestrians were decapitated, between words, between gestures, between breaths. Four more bled out on the sidewalk before ambulance crews could fight their way to them. Gas, everyone said, milling about, ogling the death and destruction. Goddamn Gas Company screwed it up royally this time, didn't they…?

Holy Rood Hospital was across the street from a fire department pumper company, so they were able to bring the fires caused by apparent gas explosions on one of the upper floors under control with a minimum loss of life. Fortunately, the entire wing floor had already been evacuated, and nearly all of the police and two Crime Lab teams were together on the third floor in the Administrative offices at the time and out of immediate danger.

Eastern Airlines Flight 179, its landing gear buttoning up, climbing past two hundred feet and just beginning to bank over the Jersey side of the Delaware before it turned its nose south, and exploded in a massive, thunderous fireball, raining wreckage, luggage and flaming body parts into the cold river water below.

The top of City Hall lit up like a Fourth of July sparkler, and as the crowds in the streets below dodged the rain of stone and terra cotta fragments they all heard the groan of the huge bronze statue of William Penn as it tilted precariously with nearly a quarter of its foundation suddenly gone.

Frank Evan, the house detective at the Ben Franklin, snorted awake. "What the hell was that?" He lurched out of his chair. "Sally? Sally? What was that noise?"

The temp at the desk outside his office was already on the phone. "Yes sir," she said, "Yes Mr. McDermott, right away, sir." She hung up the phone, eyes wide. "You have to get up to Nineteen right now, Mr. Evan! There was an explosion, and now there's a fire!"

"Did somebody call the Fire Department?"

"Yes sir, it was the first thing I did—"

"Nineteen!" Evan shook his fists in the air as he passed her desk and banged out of the office, "What the hell is it about Nineteen, anyway?"

The temp watched him go. "And it's Lois," she said to his retreating back, "not Sally. Lois."

High in the cold, clear air above Cobb Hill and the blackened stump of an old Chestnut tree, in a place where, minutes before, a V-formation of honking Canadian geese had just flown by, another fireball erupted, a huge, deafening blast, a blue-white to yellow to orange to ruby red glow inside a rapidly expanding cloud of greasy black smoke. Hot black ash rained down on the hill, on the remains of the chestnut tree, hissing as the hot flakes melted into the snow. Dogs living in the homes at the bottom of the hill began barking and howling as the echoes of the explosion reverberated through the development. Somewhere, a home burglar alarm was set off, adding its klaxon horn to the cacophony.

Standing behind the cracked glass of his French doors in nothing but pajama bottoms and slippers, one homeowner looked up the slope, through the empty trees, his fist raised, cursing a blue streak.

His wife sat up in the bed across from him. "What the hell are you yelling about, Harvey?" She rubbed her eyes. "Those damn teenagers playing with firecrackers in the woods again?"

"That's it," Harvey said, throwing his hands down in disgust, "that's the last straw." He turned, looked down, cursed again, then began stepping carefully through the glass fragments. "Gladys," he said, "You got your wish. We're moving to Myrtle Beach."

AFTER

On the TV, George Bailey ran through the Bedford Falls town square, staggering through the falling snow with new-found joy and hope, waving wildly, yelling sappy hellos to everyone he met. That looks just like real snow, Fran's mother thought, taking a sip of tea from her favorite mug. Jimmy Stewart must have frozen his you-know-whats off doing that scene.

Overhead, then, she heard a quiet creaking. Her bedroom was over the living room.

She put her tea down, got up off the couch, found her slippers under the coffee table, and shuffled out into the hall. She paused at the bottom of the front stairs for a moment, listening, then went up.

All of the doors in the rear of the second floor hall were closed, and the windows in the front and back had their shades drawn low, so the top of the stairs was shadowed. Only one door in the front of the hall was open, and that only barely, casting a sliver of light across the carpet runner. Her bedroom.

Her slippers made no sound on the runner as she went down the hall. She paused at the door to her room and listened for a moment, then she pushed it in and said, "What are you doing out of bed?" She entered the room. "And what are you doing in my closet for heaven's sake?"

Fran turned, his face flushed against the white of the bandage gauze. "Guilty of breaking and entering, Sarge," he said. "I thought you were watching an old movie downstairs."

"You thought I wouldn't hear you sneak in here and root around in my closet? What's that you have in your hands, anyway?"

Fran tried to push a plastic garment bag back in, but it caught on something and ripped. A dozen or more mothballs spilled out, bouncing and rolling every which way on the hardwood floor.

"Damn," Fran said, watching them go.

"Don't you even think about trying to pick them up!" His mother came around the bed and took the garment bag from him. "You should be lying down in bed! You want those stitches to pop? It's two days till Christmas. You want to spend it back in the hospital?"

"I'm fine, Ma. They sewed me up pretty tight."

"And you had a concussion! You shouldn't be walking around. You should be lying down!"

"Yes, Ma."

"So what is this, anyway?" She unzipped the bag, and pulled out a bulky wool coat, coal black, with wide lapels and large padded shoulders; its sixteen brass buttons caught the afternoon light. "Your father's greatcoat?" She looked at him, then laid the coat out on the bed, letting the garment bag fall to the floor.

They both regarded the coat. Fran's mother reached down, smoothed out a lapel. "Your father wanted to be buried with this," she said.

"His dress-blues were enough."

"Yeah. He looked good in them."

"I'm glad you kept it," Fran said.

"Me too." She sniffed, then adjusted the lapel again. "You know, your father—"

Fran stopped her with a raised hand. "I know, Ma," he said.

She looked at him. "Do you?" Her expression was plaintive. "Do you really?"

"Yeah." He reached out, grabbed her shoulder, and gathered her in. "I really do."

She sniffed again, and gestured to the hallway door. "They got the 'It's A Wonderful Life' marathon going on, all day. New one's starting up any minute now. Want to come down with me? Sarah said she'd be here by five, didn't she?"

"That's what she said."

"Good. I could use an extra pair of hands with dinner." She took his arm, and the two of them went around the bed, mindful of the mothballs.

"You can help too," she said, "by laying your fat ass down on the couch and staying put!"

"Gee, thanks."

Moving carefully, they left the bedroom and went slowly down the hall.

CLOSE THE DOOR

This story is a coda of sorts, the chapter after the final chapter of the novel **The Bone Worms**.

"Close the Door" takes place a few decades after the end of that book. Detective Sergeant Francis Lomax is retired now, at the rank of Lieutenant; he is an old man with a bad back, and bad but fading memories of that time in the city when he solved a series of grisly murders by closing the doors of The Boneyard, and banishing the monsters who dwelled there, forever.

Or so he thought.

1

Watching the little red Subaru come up the road, the real estate agent dropped her cigarette, stepped on it, and nudged it into the mulch beside the front porch step. She popped two breath mints, put on a brave smile, and strode briskly down the path. The elderly man who got out of the car was bald, middling thin, well over six feet, and wore a cheap suit. "Sorry," he said in a high voice, grasping the door for support as he stood, "bad back. Have to take it slow." He closed the door with a grunt, then offered his hand. "Fran Lomax."

She gave him a firm handshake. "Mr. Lomax! So nice to meet you at last. You have a darling daughter, but then I don't have to tell you that!"

"She's a pistol, for sure." His eyes narrowed just enough to notice. "You didn't—"

"Tell her about your visit? Of course not! I followed your instructions to the letter. Frankly, I think it's best for all concerned." She produced a set of keys. "Shall we go in?"

"In a minute." He squinted past her for a few seconds, then stepped around her, and walked slowly up the flagstone path. His entire attention was on the house.

"Wonderful landscaping," she said, following, noting a squashed marigold, "as you can see." She stopped behind him as he looked left, then right. And was he…sniffing? She took a quiet sniff herself, filling her nose with the Rose of Sharons crowding both sides of the porch steps.

He took out a handkerchief and wiped his face, then the pink dome of his head. "Is there a way around?"

"To the backyard? Only through the house, I'm afraid. The back is entirely fenced in and the gate is locked on the inside. Great for children and pets."

"I'm sure." He went up onto the porch and gestured to the front door. "I guess it's inside, then."

She jingled the keys. "Just follow me!"

She was glad she had stopped by earlier to air the place out; empty houses in summer got musty so quickly. And here of course was this odd old man, sniffing around like some big gangly bloodhound! She said, "The living room is on the left, kitchen and utility rooms behind it. Morning room here on the right, wonderful light, don't you think? Dining room is behind, right across from the kitchen, just down the hall."

They went into the empty living room. He stood in the center, his eyes darting, taking in the fireplace, inglenook, plate rails, and the bank of three windows overlooking the front garden.

She watched him go over to them, and run his hand up the side molding. "All original fumed oak woodwork," she said, "never painted, which is rare."

Lomax only grunted, feeling the moldings, still sniffing.

The agent finally could not help herself. "I'm sorry Mr. Lomax, but is there some particular odor…something you are smelling you find offensive?"

He looked at her at last. "Something I am *not* smelling." Then he winked at her. "That's a good thing." He pointed to the floor. "Is there a basement?"

"No, just a crawlspace. Solid fieldstone foundation, recently repointed."

He nodded. "Upstairs, then? I didn't see a stairs when we came in."

"It's just down the hall, tucked away. A bit out of the ordinary, but Craftsmen style homes can be like that."

As she followed him up she thought again: Odd old man! At least I'm selling this house to his daughter and not him!

2

Once more, it took him half a day to drive from Harleysville in the Philadelphia suburbs to his daughter's home in the upstate New York Catskills. It took that long because he once again chose to take the long way, Route 209, a narrow two-lane road that wandered through artsy little towns like Jim Thorpe and Mil-ford, and dead little towns like Stroudsburg and Port Jervis. That, and he always pegged his top speed at five over the posted limit, no more. Screw 'em.

He started in mid-morning because the pills for his back had kicked in by then, and because he needed to drive during the brightest part of the day. In the nighttime his cataracts turned oncoming headlights into hurtling, exploding supernovae. To hell with hitting some idiot leaping doe in the dark, he worried more about a head-on collision.

"We'll make it a late lunch," his daughter Rebecca had said on the phone, trying vainly to keep the concern from her voice. "Just take your time Dad, okay?" Then her husband Kevin had grabbed the receiver. "I can come get you. I don't mind. Really."

A few hours alone in a car with Kevin. Coming and going. Yeah. Sure.

With every moment of every mile, his thoughts, like the landscape fleeing on either side of him, began to blur. He felt like he was disappearing, like this was his last trip, full of anticipation and promise at its start, but empty and dark facing him at its end. Ever since he had lost his Sarah, ever since everything had gone grey. Not even the birth of his first grandson could shake it. I'm over, he said to the rising wooded foothills before him, to the patched strip of asphalt curving up into their dark green and solid shadows. I'm done. I don't want to be, but I am. He realized he was longing, no, desperate for this visit to revive him somehow, to slap him in the face, give him a reason to...

You old fool. You pathetic old fool.

Ten minutes into New York State he glanced into his rearview mirror and saw a police cruiser behind him just as its jiggle lights turned on. "Goddammit," he muttered. He pulled over at the first safe place for two vehicles, and opened the glove box for the little leather case where he kept his license and registration. "Goddammit," he muttered again, dropping his window.

The trooper took about five minutes to run his plate. Then he got slowly out, put his Stetson squarely on his head, and walked up the driver side. He was tall, broad and young, and all of his creases were perfect. "Detective Lomax," he said, almost making it a question. "Lieutenant Francis Lomax?"

"Retired," Fran said, squinting up at him.

The trooper's sunglasses flashed under the wide brim of his hat. "You kind of rushed the traffic light back there, Lieutenant."

"Bastard went red on me?"

"Apparently so."

Fran offered his leather case, but the trooper waved it off. "That won't be necessary sir."

"I appreciate that, Corporal."

The trooper nodded to the wrapped present on the passenger seat. "Headed to a birthday party?"

"Sort of. My daughter just had a baby boy. This is my first time seeing him."

"Congratulations. I won't hold you up. Just no more running lights, please, at least in my county."

"Thank you Corporal," Fran said gravely. "I will do that."

He followed the cruiser all the way to the county line, and kept his distance as the trooper did a tight u-turn, nodding soberly to Fran as he passed. Then Fran was alone to drive on this dead little road through all the remaining dead little towns and empty hours still before him.

Stone Ridge, the upstate village where his daughter and son-in-law had settled, was of the old artsy variety. The malls and big box stores in Kingston were close enough, so the town's main street remained just a collection of eighteenth and nineteenth century rubble stone and white clapboard homes, with a sprinkling of antique shops, galleries and cafes thrown in for character. Plus one local brand gas station, which was a blessing because Fran rolled into it on nothing more than vapors and a prayer.

He was getting his gas at one of the inside pumps ('Pump 'n Pay is OK!' said a little hand-lettered sign taped on it) when a dark blue pick-up pulled into the spot on the other side. Fran didn't pay this any mind until the driver got out and came around to open his tank cover. Then every hair on the back of Fran's head rose, and a thousand imaginary spiders commenced to march down his spine. Something about the driver of the pick-up. Something...

He didn't show his hand, however, just gave the driver half of an old police detective's attention, keeping the remainder on the flashing numbers in the pump display. Male, mid to late 60s, five foot eight or nine, 260, bald on top, died black hair cut short, clean shaven, short brown corduroy jacket, plain blue cotton shirt, tan trousers with cuffs, black oxfords, well maintained. His pick-up was a Dodge Ram, two-seat cab, late model. New York vehicles had license plates on both ends, and he memorized the tag without even thinking about it.

Fran's pump dinged and chunked. Moving methodically, he returned the nozzle to its cradle, twisted his gas cap until it ratcheted, then closed the cap cover until it clicked. The pump on the other side continued to thrum, filling a tank considerably larger than his Subaru's. He walked the short distance to the mini-mart, and handed a twenty and a ten to the middle-aged woman behind the register. "You know the guy out there?" He pointed over his shoulder with his thumb. "Guy driving the Ram pick-up?"

The woman looked past him, squinting. "That's Phil Gully," she said.

"Local guy?"

She turned her squint on him. "Yeah. There a problem?"

"No, no problem."

She rang him up, and handed him his change with a brusque movement. "Have a good rest of your day," she said.

The old house his daughter and Kevin had purchased was located on a winding road halfway up what was officially a Catskill mountain, but was really nothing more than a glorified long, tall hill. The house was surrounded by gardens and old-growth conifers and maples, and was in easy shouting distance to the nearest neighbors on either side and across the road. From the right angle, though, the deep gabled, bracketed, mossy old house seemed to be alone in the woods, like something out of a spooky Grimm fairytale. But this little Brothers Grimm bungalow was clean, he knew. Safe. No Door. No Boneyard. He had made sure of that.

He parked in the wide driveway, next to Kevin's glossy black A-6 Quattro, and was in the slow, painful process of getting out of his front seat when the front screen door banged open and his daughter Rebecca bounded out onto the wide porch, grinning with both arms outstretched. "Daddio!" she cried.

He smiled, and finished their old mantra: "Ready to rock and roll, Sweetpea."

3

They sat him down in the old oak and blood leather Morris chair he had bought for them specifically so he could sit in it when he visited. Becky patted his shoulder. "Comfy?"

"Oh boy," Fran said, sinking in.

"Be down in a jiffy."

Fran watched her cross the room to the hall.

Kevin took the sofa opposite him. "Max normally naps in the afternoons," he said. "So that's when Beck and me try to grab one too."

"I'm sorry you're missing your nap."

"Ah." Kevin waved a hand. "No big deal."

They both heard the ceiling creak as Becky entered the nursery. Quiet sounds. Fran felt suddenly nervous, anxious, and gripped the solid armrests too tightly perhaps, but his son-in-law didn't seem to notice.

Then Becky came downstairs. Entering the living room, she was smiling brilliantly, carrying a baby bag over her shoulder, and a small bundle of pastel blankets in her arms. In the middle was a tiny pink face with a furrowed brow, a full head of wispy dark hair, and huge blue eyes looking directly at him.

Hello Max.

Fran made motions to rise.

"Oh no," his daughter said, "don't get up." She bowed over him, her long hair brushing his cheek, and laid his swaddled grandson in his arms.

"Oh my goodness," Fran said. "He's so tiny. In the pictures he looks so big."

"He's over ten pounds already," Kevin said. "Eats like a horse too."

"Don't I know it." Becky hugged herself. "He's got Mom's eyes."

Kevin said, "Don't all newborns start out with blue eyes?"

Fran could tell that was not the first time his son-in-law had said that.

Becky gave him a look. "Not this blue."

"You never met my Sarah," Fran said. "Becky's right on this one." He gently stroked the top of his grandson's tiny clenched fist. "Max," he whispered. "The mighty Max." He looked up. "I promise not to call him Maxwell."

Becky barked her signature laugh. "Well that's a relief! Anyway, he's just Max."

"Only three letters to learn in preschool," Kevin said. "M, A, X."

The infant studied Fran intently. Fran didn't say anything to him, just offered his forefinger, which Max grasped in his left hand. Then he abruptly smiled, and Fran found himself smiling back. "Hey," he whispered, "hey there, Leftie."

"My dad is left-handed," Becky informed Kevin.

"Top ten percent," Fran said, glancing up at them both. He pulled his finger, just a little, but Max held on. "Quite a grip." They both smiled at one another, enjoying the wrestling match. After a few more seconds, though, Max decided the fun was over, and it was time to get cranky.

"Here," Becky said, as the mewling rose to a full-fledged howl. She rose from the couch, but Kevin got up first. "I'll take him. He probably wants his binky."

Fran lifted the infant into his son-in-law's arms. "What's a binky?"

"A pacifier. You know. Teething ring." Becky rummaged in the baby bag at her feet. "This." She held it up, and as soon as Max saw it his cry stopped with a hiccough, replaced with wide-eyed, open-mouthed expectation. Becky put it in his mouth and he sucked it right in, settling contentedly in Kevin's lap. "It's like magic. Anyway, we need to get you settled in. Where are your bags, still in the car?"

"There's just the one."

"I'll get it," Kevin said. Max moved from Daddy to Mommy, who put him on her knee.

Fran tossed his son-in-law his keys. "It's in the back seat, thanks."

"We can't put you in the spare bedroom," Becky said. "That's the nursery now."

Fran shrugged. "Sofa looks comfy."

"Oh no. We fixed up the little porch room next to ours upstairs. Come on, I'll show you."

Fran followed down the hall and up the stairs. Max peered at him over Becky's shoulder, all the way up.

The room they entered was just at the top of the stairs, on the right. It was small, as advertised, a corner room, with solid banks of windows on both exterior walls. Everything was painted a pale butter yellow. The first time he had seen it, it had been pale green. "I think they used to call these sleeping porches," Fran said. "Good place to catch a breeze on hot nights."

"Well, it's got a good firm bed for your back, and shades so you don't have to shock the neighbors."

Fran only saw maple leaves beyond the windows. "Feels like we're in a tree house."

Becky laughed. "Yeah, it does kinda. You like it?"

"It'll be fine."

Kevin came banging up the stairs. "This is heavy," he said, heaving Fran's suitcase onto the bed. "No problem though, glad to help."

Fran looked at him briefly.

"Well," Becky said, "it's time to give this young man something to eat, then maybe get him back down to that nap I woke him out of."

"That sounds good," Fran said. "The nap idea, I mean. I think I'll do the same."

"Dinner's around six, okay?"

"I'll be there."

Kevin took Max and started down the hall, but Becky lingered at the door. "I'm really glad you could come," she said.

The memory of the man at the gas pump flashed through

him. "Me too Sweetpea."

She kissed him on the cheek, then left him alone.

He closed the door and stood quietly for a moment, listening to the whispering maples outside, and his daughter tending to his grandson two rooms down the hall. Then he shook his head quickly, vigorously, and bent to open his suitcase. He hung the two suits, still in their dry-cleaner bags, in the tiny closet, then the suit-coat he was wearing, on a thick hanger he had brought just for that purpose. Everything else from the suitcase fit easily in the top two drawers of the dresser. His latest Ed McBain paperback went on the bedside table along with his reading glasses.

That left the Browning. Never leave home without it.

It was snapped tight in its old leather belt holster. It held a full clip, with nothing in the chamber. After a moment of deliberation he wrapped it in a clean undershirt and put it in the closet on the high shelf, just out of view. Then he closed the closet door.

He sat on the bed, hands in his lap, closed his eyes, let his mind clear, and took in a long sniff.

Nothing.

The house was still clear. There was nothing, no doorway to there.

He opened his eyes, and then took in another deep breath. He eased out of his shoes without untying them, took off his belt, then his tie, undid the collar button, then stretched out on the bed with an almost silent groan.

Clear. Safe. Then: God I'm so tired of this.

In minutes, though, he was snoring.

A shower and change into a fresh suit did wonders with the cobwebs between his ears and the ache in his lower back. The grandmother clock in the downstairs hall was just striking six when he entered the kitchen. Becky was by the sink making a salad. Max lay in a little portable hammock-type bed in the middle of the breakfast table, gnawing on his little fists as he watched the spinning fan light overhead.

"So," Becky said over her shoulder, "how was the nap?"

"Necessary." He sat down at the breakfast table. Max ignored him, preferring the fan to an old fart in a grey suit smelling of Ivory soap and Old Spice.

"It bounces," Becky said.

"This hammock thing he's in?"

"The wire frame is springy. Max likes it when you bounce him a little."

Fran did as directed, and Max raised both fists straight out, and said something very much like "Goo."

"How was the drive?"

"Well, I took 209."

She whistled. "The long way."

"It was fine. Very scenic." Then he cleared his throat. "I saw someone when I got here. A Phil Gully. Know him?"

"Retired school teacher. Chemistry, I think." She pointed. "He lives right up the road."

An alarm bell went off. "So he's your neighbor?"

"He's got the big house near the top of the mountain."

"The Dubois House," Kevin said, entering the kitchen, slapping the mail down on the table and taking a seat on the other side of Max. He gave his son a kiss on the forehead. "All the really old places around here are named after famous former owners."

Becky chuckled. "Then we should call our house the 'Nobody Important Ever Lived Here House'."

"Why are you asking about Phil?" Kevin asked.

"No special reason." Fran shifted in his chair. "So he's just … retired?"

"Apparently so." Becky picked up the salad bowl. "Like this former police detective I know. Kev will you get Max? Dad, the salad tongs?"

"You'll get to meet Phil tomorrow night," Kevin said, lifting the hammock and baby.

Another alarm. Different, but an alarm just the same. "Oh?"

"At the party."

Fran managed not to groan aloud. He found the tongs on the counter and followed everyone out of the kitchen. "What party?"

Becky glanced over her shoulder. "I didn't mention the party? Just a few people. Neighbors like Phil. Max's official 'coming out' bash. I figured it beat lugging him all around the town to show him off. Show you off too Pop, you old dust mop."

"Quoting Shirley Jackson is not going to fix this young lady."

"Ahh, you're gonna love it."

"Great," Fran said, frowning. "Can't wait."

The faint, intermittent sound of Max crying woke him up. He was totally disoriented for a moment, terrified not knowing where he was; but then the ache of fear in his gut subsided, and he turned over in the new bed, in the dark of the small sleeping porch at the end of the upstairs hall, and listened to his fretting grandson. I wonder, he thought, should I—? Then, next door, he heard a muffled voice, the squeaking of bedsprings, then a bedroom door opening, and Becky, in the hall, saying softly, "Coming honey." Max's crying peaked as the door to his nursery opened, then subsided.

Fran rolled onto his back, knowing it was wrong to do so, knowing he would turn back onto his side before attempting sleep again, but wanting to keep both ears free of the pillow, wanting to *hear*.

Eventually he heard his daughter's bedroom door creak and close.

"He okay?"

Their bed squeaked. "He's fine. Just a little hungry."

"Good you took that one, then."

Silence for a minute.

Becky said, "You can't sleep? What's up?"

"I'm worried."

The bed squeaked again. "About what?"

More silence. Fran blinked in the darkness.

"Your father," Kevin said, finally.

"What about him?"

"You know."

Fran brought both hands up to rub his face, to cover it.

"He hasn't even mentioned—" Becky began.

"He says he sees ghosts, Beck. Monsters."

"He hasn't talked about that in years, Kevin, you know that. Give him a break, will you?"

"I can't help it. He's like a ticking time bomb."

"He's not. He just had some very bad cases when he was on the Force. Really bad ones."

"Monsters in The Boneyard."

"Kevin."

"It was in the papers. I'm not making it up. You could google it for chrissakes."

More silence. Fran brought his hands down, stiff, staring upward.

Kevin: "You're mad, now."

"I'm not mad."

"I'm just worried about Max."

The bed squeaked loudly, "*Now* I'm mad. How could you say something like that?"

"I'm just—"

"My father would never hurt Max! My father loves him!"

"I know, of course. I'm just—"

"Good night, Kevin."

"Really, Beck—"

"I said good night."

4

Enjoying the fact that his son-in-law was still in the doghouse the next morning, Fran took his breakfast coffee into the morning room where Kevin sat alone, still in his pajamas, reading the paper. "Getting the cold shoulder I see. Something wrong?"

Kevin rustled his newspaper, frowning at it. "It's nothing."

Fran settled into the love seat caddy-corner to the sofa Kevin had commandeered. Time to throw him a bone, he decided. "I finished your book. The one on Aaron Burr." He took a sip of coffee. What the hell was in it, cinnamon? "I never knew about that Texas deal. Or the whole Electoral vote mess with Jefferson. Reminded me of the Bush-Gore craziness."

"History is never new." Kevin turned a page of the newspaper with a sharp snap. "It just repeats, and repeats, and repeats."

Fran forced himself to take another sip of coffee. Yep, cinnamon; Jesus Christ. "So what are you working on now?"

"A biography of Rufus King."

Fran and Kevin turned. Becky stood in the doorway to the hall, Max on her hip. "First draft is done, right Hon?"

Kevin blinked, his frown dissipating. "Um, yeah. Now the real work begins."

Fran looked from one to the other. "Who's Rufus King?"

Becky shook a finger at him. "Exactly."

Fran had always been proud of being able to remember names of people, particularly a sizable number, all at once, like at a crime scene.

Becky, of course, read his mind. She leaned close to whisper in his ear, "This isn't a murder investigation, Daddio, it's a party."

He took the bottle of beer she held out, and gave her a benign smile. "The only thing missing is the body."

Her eyes went round in mock indignation. "Thanks a lot!"

He pointed with subtle nods of his beer bottle, "Those four by the window, Bill and Katy Moyer, neighbors down the street, and Greg and Susan—not Sue or Suzy—Landis, also neighbors down the street. All four of them are making a big deal about what great friends they are, but what I'm seeing is how much they really hate each other's guts."

"Dad—"

"I'm just observing." He took a swig of beer. "Can't help it. Take the gentleman by the fireplace talking to Kevin. That's the Reverend James Goodhall, the pastor at the First Presbyterian Church in town. He is fine with Jim. His wife Gloria, whom I think I should not call Glo, is in the kitchen spiffing up the hors'd'ouvres platter she and the Reverend brought. They live in the big Dutch colonial across the road. Now, Gloria and Jim—"

Becky raised a warning finger.

"—Gloria and Jim are a truly loving couple with no obvious agenda other than they are here for a good time. Very rare, but nice to see."

"Just remember, none of them are suspects in any crime."

"Yet," he said, and took another swig of beer.

His daughter patted his shoulder as she rose. "Mingle, please."

Fran was gathering his energy to rise himself when they all heard a short burst of static from the baby monitor on the mantle. Then the baby gave a cry, and then another.

"I'll get it," Kevin and Kate Moyer said at once, then she laughed. "Daddy first."

Kevin went for the hall.

"Here, I'll help." Fran looked up; Reverend Goodhall was beside him, offering an arm. Fran took it, surprised at the other man's strength as he was assisted to his feet. "Didn't even spill the beer," he said.

"Heaven forbid." The Reverend smiled. "Becky tells me you're a police detective."

"Was. I'm retired now."

"Down in Philadelphia?"

Fran nodded. "I moved to the suburbs."

Kate Moyer joined them. "She's very proud of you, you know. I bet it must have been exciting, investigating crime in a big city."

"Well," Fran began.

"What kind of detective were you Frank?" Bill Moyer put an arm around his wife.

Fran gave him his full attention. "It's Fran, short for Francis. Named after my grandfather."

"And at least one saint," Reverend Goodhall added with a smile.

Bill saluted Fran with his beer. "Fran it is."

Kate asked, "Were you a homicide detective, Fran?"

"Yes I was. Five years as a beat cop, then twenty in the Homicide Division. They don't let you do that anymore, though. Now they mix it up. Better to move people around, learn different things."

"That's sounds so exciting!" Susan Landis hugged herself. "Just like those shows on TV!"

"Actually, it was pretty boring most of the time. Hurry up and wait kind of thing. More paper pushing than anything else. And most criminals weren't the sharpest knives in the drawer as a rule. That's why—"

"—They were criminals!" Kate laughed again.

Fran gave her a nod and a wink.

"But you did have some notoriety, didn't you? One very famous case?" That was from Greg Landis, joining the group at last. "Unless there was another Detective Lomax in Philadelphia back in the early 80s I remember reading about it."

"Famous and notorious!" Reverend Goodhall turned to Fran with raised eyebrows. "I'm intrigued."

At that moment Kevin appeared in the doorway from the hall, holding Max face front against his belly. Max was waving both arms and kicking furiously, staring wide-eyed at all the faces turned to him.

Susan Landis clapped her hands in front of her throat, "What a cutie!"

"He should be in a Gerber commercial," Gloria Goodhall gushed. "What does his onesie say?"

"That's his 'Hide Your Daughters' number," Becky said, entering from the kitchen with a platter of finger food. She put the platter down on the sideboard and reached for Max.

"Oh no," Katy Moyer said, "Please let me take him! I haven't held a little one in so long."

Within ten minutes everyone had held Max at least once, without any serious incident. Max took all the manhandling stoically, with a wide-eyed expression and occasional smile for all. Reverend Goodhall had him last, and he proceeded to raise Max up high, over everyone's head, then come down with a slow, gliding, "Whooo!"

Unfortunately, that was it for Max, who promptly broke out with a wail of his own, accompanied by instant, astonishing crocodile tears.

That was the moment the front doorbell rang, and Max was just as suddenly quiet, blinking hugely at the new sound. Kevin went to answer it. "Must be Phil," Becky said. And so it was.

The man at the gas station came in from the hall with Kevin behind him. He had two bottles of wine, one in each hand. "White and red," he said, "like Billy Joel, I can't make up my mind."

Several people chorused, "Phil!"

Susan Landis whispered to Fran out of the corner of her mouth, "Now the party's started!"

Phil gave Kevin both bottles, then his coat. "So where is your son? Where is little Max?"

"Right behind you."

Phil turned, and Becky was there, holding Max up. "What a wonderful wonderful little man!" he exclaimed. "May I—?"

Becky handed him over.

Fran stood motionless, watching his grandson settle against Phil's chest.

"Oh my, he's so warm and soft! I don't remember the last time I held a little one."

"Word of warning, though," Becky said. "If he grunts, that means he's giving you a present."

Gloria laughed. "Love those baby presents!'

"If Max is in a gift-giving mood," Phil said, "then it is back to Mama he goes." He lifted Max with both hands. "Right, little man?"

Max blew some bubbles, grinning, to everyone's laughter.

Fran forced a small smile.

"Here." Katy took Max from Phil. "My turn."

Phil saw Fran then, and crossed the room. "You must be Becky's father. Proud Grandpa, eh?" He extended a hand.

Fran shook it briefly. Warm, soft, and no calluses. "Fran Lomax," he said. "Pleased to meet you."

"Fran saw you at the gas station yesterday when he was coming in," Becky said.

"Really." Phil locked eyes with Fran for a beat, then two. You know me, Fran thought. You know me like an old friend. He continued the stare. And I know you.

Then Phil winked at Becky. "Only one gas station in town, we all run into one another sooner or later, eh?"

"I was just making conversation," Fran said.

"Fran is a famous police detective," Greg said.

"Well," Fran said.

"In Philadelphia." Phil nodded. "The Butcher murders, remember them? Five people flayed and de-boned."

"What?" Kate Moyer handed Max over to Becky. "Did you say—"

"A bona-fide serial killer case." Phil reached over and wiped some dribble off Max's chin with his finger. "1983, wasn't it, Fran? At least one book was written about it."

"Unauthorized," Fran muttered.

Greg snapped his fingers. "That's right! Something about bones."

"Up In The Boneyard," Phil said. "I own a copy, as a matter of fact."

Katy turned her wide eyes toward him. "Can I borrow it?"

"Certainly. I'm sure I can dig it up for you."

"Before the night is out," Katy told Fran, "I want all the gory details."

"Well I'm taking Max up to bed," Becky announced to the room. "Any last kisses or hugs, now's your chance."

Max did one more circuit. When it was his turn, Fran took his grandson's hand in his own and gave it a gentle squeeze. Even with eyes half open, halfway to dreamland, Max matched Fran's quiet smile with one of his own.

"What a wonderful child," Phil said, beside him, as they watched Becky take him upstairs. "A wonderful gift."

Fran was close enough to smell him. Just an anonymous aftershave, a hint of Ivory soap. "You married, Phil," he asked. "Not now I see, but ever?"

"No, unfortunately. Never found the right person." His expression was serious, Fran saw, but laughter danced behind his eyes. Laughter and…something else.

What the hell, Fran thought. I'll play. "We've met before."

"At the gas station yesterday, apparently."

"No." Fran looked at him calmly. "Before that."

Phil shook his head. "I don't think so. I've never been to Philadelphia."

"Really."

"Well you're both about the same age, aren't you?" Katy put her arm around Phil and squeezed.

Phil laughed. "I'm not sure who she is complimenting with a comment like that! I just turned sixty-seven last month."

"And my father-in-law," Kevin chimed in, "is coming up on his what, Dad? Seventy-third in April?"

"Well that's close enough." Katy looped her other arm around Fran. "Long enough for you two to have met somewhere, sometime, right? Now what's this new Internet game you made up, Phil?" She steered them both across the room as she spoke, heading for the sideboard.

"I did not invent it. I heard some students talking about it. It's called Can You Believe this Shit."

"YouTube," Gloria said, "right?"

"What's a you tube?" Fran asked.

Later in the evening, after Phil's game had run its course, someone (Fran suspected Kevin) produced a well-worn Trivial Pursuit box game. Fran was instantly everyone's choice for partner, which made him blush. "Your father is a serious cutie," Susan said to Becky.

"Maybe," the Reverend said, "but I've got dibs. Old men against the couples. We will mop the floor with you all."

"And I'm out," Phil said, "because I am terrible at this game. Embarrassingly terrible."

Katy protested, "But you're good at the science questions."

"Whoopie," Phil said. "You guys have fun. I will just pour myself another glass of wine and, what's the word? Chill."

Gloria linked arms with him. "I will join you."

The Reverend extended his hand to Fran. "Partners?"

Fran shook it. "Let's do some floor mopping."

Half an hour later, Fran looked up from reading the card, about to say "I have no idea what this question means," when his reflex snapshot of the room registered, and he said instead, "Where's Phil?"

"Upstairs I think," Katy Moyer said.

The Reverend nodded. "Duty calls, I expect."

Somehow, above all the other sounds in the room, Fran heard a creak from the ceiling overhead. "And Becky?"

"Upstairs too," Kevin said, regaining his seat, passing Bill Moyer a new beer.

Fran rose too quickly, grimacing at the sudden spike of pain at the base of his spine. "Excuse me."

"Here." The Reverend took the card from him, "I'll take over. We've got them on the ropes anyway partner."

Kevin said, "There's the half bath off the kitchen, Dad," but Fran waved it off. "Need to ask Becky something." He maneuvered around the Landis's and the Reverend's wife and made it into the hall without whimpering aloud. Damn I should have taken those pills. Staying sharp at the party for Becky's benefit was one thing, but this was ridiculous.

He took the stairs one step at a time, gripping the rail, each slow, thudding step bad, but doable. The ceiling light in the upstairs hall was off, but he saw light under the closed bathroom door at the end, and the faint wash of a nightlight over the threshold of Max's partially open door on the left. He reached the nursery and paused to calm his breathing, and to compartmentalize the pain. Then he pushed the door open.

In the blue semi-dark, nearly in silhouette, he found Gully standing next to the crib, holding Max out with both hands, like he was inspecting a melon at the supermarket.

"What the hell—!" Fran was in and across the room despite the pain, his only thought the safety of his grandson. Both of them, Gully and Max, turned their heads at his voice and movement, Max in mid-giggle, Gully with a wide smile, now frozen in place.

"Dad!"

Becky's voice behind him stopped him. He closed his eyes as he felt her hand on his shoulder. "What's going on?"

"Your father was concerned," Gully said.

Fran turned, glad the half-darkness of the room hid the flush of embarrassment on his cheeks. "I was concerned," he said.

"I was mixing a fresh bottle of formula. Phil was keeping Max occupied for me."

"And I just couldn't resist one more goodnight hug," Gully

said, his dancing eyes for Fran and Fran alone.

"Right," Fran said. "Sure."

"Everything okay up there?" Kevin, at the bottom of the stairs.

"Yes honey! We're fine." Becky looked at Fran. "We're fine, right?"

"Yeah." Fran wiped his forehead. "Just peachy."

Kevin was in the kitchen, loading the dishwasher and dealing with what was piled in the sink. Becky sat next to Fran, holding his hand. She said, "Phil is just a retired school teacher."

"I know."

"Lived here forever, everybody says."

He cocked his head slightly. "You sure?"

"Sure I'm sure. He's harmless. Everybody is. Everybody's nice. This place is nice."

He could see she was trying very hard not to get upset with him.

She said, "It's not here, Dad."

The Boneyard.

"In the house," she persisted. "Our home. In our town. It's just not here."

"I know it's not," he said.

"I checked myself, you know. The smell, the door and window moldings. If it was—"

"If it was, I would have made sure you never came anywhere near this place." He managed an awkward smile. "Nice as it is."

Becky reached across and gave him a hug. A big long one. "You should go to bed. Kevin and I will deal with all this."

He made an effort to rise. Grinning, she offered her hand. "So you're okay with Phil?"

"Absolutely," he said.

5

He slipped out of his shoes, lay down on the bed on his side, pulled the top cover up to his chin, and pretended sleep. He listened in the darkness to his daughter and son-in-law downstairs making a tired, half-hearted effort to clean up the worst of the party remains. Then Max made a noise, live for Fran, baby monitor for them, just a small cry that maybe promised more, and Becky immediately came upstairs to comfort him. Kevin did a round of the rooms, probably checking locks, then came up himself.

Quiet murmurings down the hall. Fran took in a long breath, held it, then let it out. Damn, this bed was perfect for his back. Too bad he wasn't going to sleep in it.

He heard movement in the hall, then heard his door open; a strip of soft light fell across him. "'Night, Daddio," Becky whispered, and his door closed without a sound.

He waited ten minutes, then ten more past the time of the last creaking of bedsprings, clicking off of bed-lights, whispered kisses goodnight. The old house had its own sounds, but the silence, the night silence, the sleep silence, finally came. He pushed the cover off and got up. The pain in his lower back was just a dull throb, thanks to the double dose of pain pills. He straightened his pants, re-tucked his shirt, redid the top button, then brought his tie up, snug. He found his shoes and slipped them back on without having to untie them first, good old broughams. The Browning was where he had put it, wrapped in an undershirt on the top closet shelf. He took it down, checked it by touch alone, then holstered it and clipped the holster to his belt, right side. His suitcoat was hanging on a bedpost; he shook it briefly, held it out, then slipped it on. Then, on feet trained thirty years to be as silent as necessary, he went downstairs to the kitchen, and out the back door, into the night.

"... Honey?"

"Hmm?"

"I thought I heard something."

"Mmm. Prob'ly Max. You want me to ...?"

"No, It'll be okay. Go back to sleep."

"Mmm."

Fran went up the gently sloping curve of the road under the black overarching trees. The darkness was formidable, but enough of the Moon's thin silver sliver penetrated to keep him from tripping into a ditch, or walking into a tree. The darkness made him cautious, but the presence of what was ahead of him, the power of it, made him slow. It entered him, filled him, weighed him down. And it was crafty: it found where his pain lay twisted through his lower spine like barbed wire, and twisted it more, tighter and tighter with each step. But he didn't stop. Oh no. This was real, dammit. This was real.

The cars that passed were all on the other side of the road, coming up behind him. His shadow materialized at his feet, stretched out and up on the gravel and asphalt, then vanished as the cars rushed by. Three times in as many minutes that happened, then he saw a break in the trees and the ghost of an open field beyond. "Phil's place is just a quarter mile up the mountain," Becky had said. He stumbled through the under-growth and stopped at the edge of the lawn, for that was what it was, and caught his breath. The wind in the trees made a shushing sound, building to a crescendo, then subsiding. Ahead of him, beyond a thick wall of trees, was a glimmer of yellow light. As branches and leaves moved it resolved into a rectangle, a window. Gully's house; it had to be.

Fran waited a little longer, looking, listening, then with a groan of pain he struck out across the lawn.

The bulk of the house separated from the trees as he approached. The light was indeed a side window, toward the back. The kitchen, maybe. A low garden edged with bricks emerged on the left, then slate flagstones, and he followed them to a front door set under a shallow portico and flanked by two wood benches. The screen door was unlocked, giving him access to a big lion knocker. He knocked twice, lightly, then again, with force. The sound echoed back from the trees.

After a moment the portico light came on, and Fran brought his hand up to shade his eyes. A lock snapped, then another, and the door swung inward. Fran saw Gully in silhouette against a diffused light somewhere down the central hall. "Detective." Gully's voice held no surprise. "Fran. It's late."

Fran said nothing.

"Here." Gully stepped aside. "It's also cold. Please come in."

Fran entered, looking left to a library, right to a living room. The stairway before him was wide and massive, and he could see that the hallway beside it led all the way to the rear of the house because there was a window there, reflecting light from the kitchen. Gully pushed the front door closed, and secured it with one of the locks. "Here," he said again, moving into the library. "This is where I keep the bourbon." He turned on a floor lamp between two large leather chairs, and motioned Fran into one of them.

"I'll stand," Fran said.

"Ahh. I see. Well I'll sit, then." Gully took the chair on the right.

Fran put his right hand on the chair back of the other. Gully glanced at his other, buried in his coat pocket, and smiled.

"You know why I'm here," Fran said.

"I have a clue." Gully gestured to Fran's pocketed hand. "Go ahead, please."

Fran took the Browning out, but kept it pointed down.

Gully looked at it with an amused expression. "Impressive. Police issue?"

"No. It's all mine." Pain suddenly shot through Fran like a burst from a flamethrower, and though he thought he hid it, Gully's smile broadened.

"That old injury," he said. "From when, 1983? The damage

to that old apartment house on Cherry Street was incredible, yet you survived it." He reached over to a tantalus on the other side of his chair and poured himself a drink. "Are you sure you won't join me? It would do wonders for that back of yours."

"So you studied it. The murders. The Boneyard. The whole thing. Me."

Gully nodded vigorously. "The true history of it goes back well before your involvement, as you discovered in your own research. And even long before that. There is actually a Lenape Indian myth that talks of it. But the Boneyard was not just there, in and around Philadelphia. The interface, the doors, occurred in many places, many times."

"With murders."

"Oh no, not at all. That was unique to your case. It was the unfortunate involvement of two young boys, Pitcairn and Alton, and what they unknowingly took with them when they escaped." Gully's voice went flat. "What needed to be returned, Fran. That was what sparked the murders."

The names, spoken, chilled Fran. He hadn't heard them in decades, hadn't even thought of them: Pitcairn, gone, and Alton gone with him. Into the mouth of it, swallowed. Gone. And him nearly gone with them.

God I am tired. I am just so damn tired of this.

He said, "So you are saying the Boneyard is really benign? Harmless?"

"I firmly believe that all they really want is to be left alone. Just that. Left alone."

Fran looked at Gully's drink, then up to meet his steady gaze. "So people like me are—"

"Troublesome. A problem requiring a solution."

Fran re-gripped his weapon. "When it comes to protecting my family I'm more than happy to be someone's problem."

"Indeed," Gully sat slowly back, smiling. "The great Francis Lomax, dragonslayer."

Fran chose not to respond to that. "You're one of them," he

said instead.

Gully picked up his glass and pondered it. Then he looked up, the smile still there. "From the Boneyard you mean? You think I have a Bone Worm in me?" He held out his free hand. "What is it they all had? Those who were taken? Scars? Do you see any scars?"

There were none, of course. That had been the first thing Fran had looked for, even at the gas station. "You've gotten better, over the years. More sophisticated."

"I'm just a fan," Gully said. "That's all. Surely you believe that."

"The molding," Fran said.

Gully's smile faltered. "The what?"

"I never reported that. Never put it in any report." Without turning, he went over to the room's only window, reached out and ran his hand over the molding trim. Then he raised the Browning up to point at a spot between Gully's eyes.

Gully's voice was regretful. "I wish there was some way to stop that from happening."

Fran brought his right hand up, cradling his left.

Gully put his drink down, then stood. All semblance of kindness and concern, anything human, was suddenly gone. "Do you think it would matter? Killing me?" He raised his arms briefly, taking in the room, the house, the world outside. "Do you think it would stop any of this?"

"It would be a start."

"Ah Fran. Fran Fran Fran." Gully took a step. "You're tired. I can see it. So tired. Of the pain, of the chase. Of this. Of everything."

Fran blinked rapidly, his eyelids suddenly with minds of their own.

"It's okay." Gully took another step. Fran saw subtle movement to the side, in the hallway. Shadows suddenly became more than shadows. "Really," Gully continued, "I understand more than anyone." He extended his hand. "More than anyone could, actually."

"I have to do this," Fran said.

"No," Gully said, "you don't."

6

Dawn sunlight slanted across the driveway and up the steps, just touching Fran's muddy shoes.

"Dad?" Becky closed the front door behind her. "Dad?" She crossed the porch to him. "Are you okay? Why are you out here?" She put a hand on his shoulder. "My God, you're wet and you're freezing! Have you been out long?"

His face was in shadow. He didn't turn, didn't look at her.

Her voice gentled. "We should go inside."

He turned his head toward her finally, but not all the way. "What?"

"We'll get you into dry clothes. Kevin can get the fireplace going."

He nodded slowly.

She helped him up. He touched his tie knot, loose, pulled partway down, then a shirttail hanging out. She took his arm. "What have you been doing out here this early Daddio, huh? Here." She tried to help him with his shirt. "Why is this buttoned wrong?"

He looked down. Then back up. "Oh," he said.

UP IN THE
BONEYARD

*This story had several inspirations. The first was my love of airplanes, the older the better. The next was a short story by Ray Bradbury called "Skeleton", the one he re-wrote for **The October Country**. A third was the Merricat poem from Shirley Jackson's **We Have Always Lived in the Castle**. The final and most important influence was Fritz Leiber's poem canon "The Demons of the Upper Air" as well as his short story "The Hill and the Hole" from **Night's Black Agents**. The trick was making all of these influences into something that was my own: the idea of a doorway to a dark place, in this case The Boneyard, that could only be accessed at a particular height (and therefore pretty much a secret until airplanes were invented, skyscrapers were built, and mountain-climbing became a tourist sport). This story was one result of that idea. Another, written a few years later, was the novel **The Bone Worms**.*

1

October 1985

Most mornings, when the weather wasn't too cold, and almost always by nine, he went down the street from his small apartment to the fast food restaurant on the corner for a muffin with egg and cheese, and a large coffee, black. Depending on the change in his pocket that day, he picked up the Post as well, and read by the glass window next to the sidewalk until his coffee was gone, or until it was too cold to finish.

The counter people knew him on sight, and they always gave him a smile or a friendly nod, a polite "Good morning, sir," or a "Nice day we're having, hm?" By nine o'clock, most days, the only other customers he had to deal with were old people like himself, who didn't give a tinker's damn about how they looked, and mothers with little children too young yet for school. These were sometimes a problem.

"Look at that old man, mommy!" a chubby boy of four or five exclaimed, and pointed with a finger dripping pancake syrup.

"Shush, honey," the mother whispered, careful *not* to look his way.

The little boy imitated her whisper: "But his face looks *funny*."

His mother put her finger to her lips and frowned elaborately. "I said *be quiet*, Jake. Just eat your pancakes."

But the little boy persisted. "His hands, too. He's got marks and lines and boo-boos all over. I think...I think he was in a fight and got hurt."

"*Jake*."

The old man turned sideways, concentrating on his newspaper.

"Yeah." The little boy nodded. "Musta been in a fight. Hey mister, were you in a fight?"

He raised his paper up, like a curtain, like a wall. The little boy was talking about his scars, of course, the ones that showed above his collar and across his face, and below his jacket cuffs, all the way to his fingertips. After seventy-odd years, they still showed plainly against his pale and wrinkled skin as vivid brown lines, razor-thin, and just as straight.

"Maybe," the little boy suddenly exclaimed, "maybe he's a pirate! Hey mister!"

Enough. His coffee was finished, anyway. The old man shook his paper out, folded it, and tucked it under his arm as he rose.

"I'm *so* sorry," the mother said to him as he passed, "but he's only four..."

A cutting breeze ruffled the end of the newspaper, but the bright sun made him squint, and was warm on his face. He pulled at his jacket cuffs, squinting even more. Little children be damned, he thought, and decided to complete his morning ritual by walking the two blocks to the park.

He passed Mr. Lupe arranging fruit outside his bodega, who smiled and waved as he approached, "Be-u-teeful morning, Mr. Spangler! Be-u-teeful day for the park."

The old man nodded, and smiled back. He paused to pick up a tangerine. "Are these new today, Mr. Lupe?"

"Just in!" The grocer waved him on. "Go, take it, eat it while you watch the boats in the harbor, then come back and buy a bagful!"

The old man lifted the tangerine in thanks, then crossed the street and went carefully up the stone steps into the park. It was an old city park, with large gnarly beeches, and wandering, rumpled concrete walks. The park followed the edge of one of southern Brooklyn's many low bluffs, and most of the benches had a grand view over endless rows of brownstone tenement roofs that made up the old neighborhoods below. The Verrazano Narrows beyond was a shining blue arc to the Atlantic, framed by the immense suspension bridge to Staten Island that carried its name.

His favorite bench was empty, in full, warm sunlight, and he slid onto it gratefully. He looked to the two blue-grey arches of the Verrazano Bridge, wondering yet again how high they were, and deciding, again, that he should look it up in the library. Surely they were higher than two hundred and fifty feet. His gaze wandered across the borough skyline, such as it was, the tenements, apartment houses, water towers, warehouses and scattering of low office buildings. Nothing as high, nothing high enough, *there.*

He remembered his very first visit to the Woolworth Building after his release from the hospital in the Spring of 1914, avoiding the shiny mahogany and brass elevators, taking the stairs instead, one floor at a time, all the way to the top. My God, he thought, the courage that had taken! And then the Empire State when it opened a decade and a half later, one of a vast crowd of people that first day, again, avoiding the elevators so he could linger on every floor, from the twentieth to the thirtieth stories...but there had been nothing there, in either building.

They had not been there.

He had tried other tall buildings through the years, wherever in the city they sprang up, all with equal failure. No, it had to be *here*, in the southwest neighborhoods of Brooklyn, where the Cow Meadow had once been, *here*, above the tangled and dirty streets now laid out before him.

Then his eyes suddenly darted. Movement, in the jumble of tenements near the Fort Hamilton recruiting center, just east of the Belt Parkway, something rising. A crane boom, a construction crane, a big one he had not seen before, its spidery tower camouflaged against the hills and suburbs of Staten Island beyond. He counted the streets as anxiousness rose like a bloody bubble from his stomach to his throat. It was there, the exact spot, where this crane now raised its spidery finger, higher and higher, *there*...the site of the old Cow Meadow.

It took him almost a half hour, walking a block, resting, and then walking a few more, to reach the neighborhood of the crane. More than once he stopped, more out of defiance than fear, to turn around and go back to the safety, silence and sanity of his apartment. Oh, the bones in his body ached so!

So what? He argued with himself. So what that they were finally building a new building, and that they were building it *there*. So what? It would probably mean nothing. It would probably mean nothing at all. It probably wouldn't even be *high* enough.

But in the end, even though his joints pulsed with pain, he managed the entire distance from the park on the bluff to the construction site, and he stood across the street from it, using a light pole for support, and slowly regained his breath.

The site was a full city block square, surrounded by a garishly painted plywood sheet wall. The only thing inside that was visible was the yellow and blue crane that soared overhead, its boom swinging slowly against the glare of the morning sky.

The old man dared his legs to move, to take him in for a closer look. Left to themselves, they would have jerked him, danced him away from this place, back up to the safety and sanity of his quiet neighborhood, to the bag of tangerines waiting for him at Mr. Lupe's bodega. But he crossed the street instead and went to the wall, to one of the peephole slots cut into it, and looked through.

On the other side was a vast excavation, even larger than he had feared, filled with shouting men and rumbling construction vehicles and huge, jutting concrete pilings rooted down through the sand and gravel to the bedrock below.

"That's gonna be a big one, all right."

The old man started, then turned. A stout, middle-aged woman in a loud, cheaply cut coat and faded paisley scarf turned from her own peephole and winked at him. "Another thirty story steel and glass refrigerator." She shook her head in disgust. "This is *Brooklyn*, for chrissakes. Since when do we want to look like *Manhattan*, eh?" She looked to the old man for moral support, but he was already speaking. "Thirty?" He was unable to mask the underlying tremble in his voice. "Did you say *thirty* stories?"

The woman jerked a calloused thumb in the general direction of 14th Avenue. "The big sign at the other corner, hotshot, says it's gonna be a thirty, THREE-OH, story condo, with million dollar views of the Narrows and the Bridge." She grunted. "Fat chance you or I will ever have seeing the inside of it when it's done, either. You can bet your cardiac arrest on *that* one, pops."

The old man touched his fingers to his lips. Thirty stories was more than two hundred and fifty feet, wasn't it?

"I remember," the woman continued, "my dad told me this part of town used to be just one big weedy lot, all the way down to the water. Used to have circuses here my dad said. Circuses. Used to call it the Cow Meadow, can you believe that? Cows and circuses in Brooklyn?"

But the old man was no longer listening. Instead, he was looking up, at the crane in the sky over the building site. "Oh my God," he whispered, as the sudden, certain reality of it sank in. The bones within him began aching anew, and he knew why. "Finally," he whispered. *Finally*.

2

May 1913

For a penny a person was led by one of the ground crew through the tall grass of the Cow Meadow to the aeroplane perched like a huge wood and cloth beast in the middle of the open area beyond the carnival tents. No one was allowed near enough to touch the flying machine, of course, but the sight alone of such an exotic device, so close up, was well worth the copper.

An extra penny bought an introduction and handshake with the young aeronaut himself. He was Anthony Spangler, twenty-two years old, tall and spare, with dark eyes and even darker hair. His wide, friendly smile was set in an open, unlined face, and he smelled of castor oil, leather, and healthy sweat. More than one young lady swore they almost fainted, putting their laced and gloved hand in his, warmed by that smile.

"How high will it go, Mr. Spangler?" a brazen voice asked from the crowd.

"High enough to dance with the clouds," the young aeronaut replied at once, grinning.

"Now that," the reporter from the Sun said, "is a quote!" He scribbled for a moment in his notebook, and then regained Spangler's attention. "How long will take you," and he drew a circle in the air with his pencil, "to fly to the Bridge and back in that aeroplane of yours?"

"I only have fuel enough for about twenty minutes," Spangler said, pulling a white linen towel from his jacket and wiping his hands. "I guess I'd better make it back by then, eh?"

"You sound very sure of yourself, sir," the reporter continued, squinting his eyes and pointing his pencil shrewdly. "How much do they pay you to put your life in the hands of a machine like that?"

The aeronaut laughed. "I'm not doing this for the money, sir!"

"For what, then, Mr. Spangler? If not for the money, then for what?"

"Ahh!" Spangler's grin was electric. He leaned close to the reporter. "Have you ever flown in an aeroplane, sir?"

"Not hardly! I get giddy enough on the Broadway train."

"Well let me tell you," and Spangler motioned the reporter even closer, close enough to growl roughly in his ear, "it's even better than *sex*."

The reporter blushed, just as the chief of Spangler's ground crew interrupted, "We won't have this weather for long, boss." He pointed to the clouds building up in the southwest over Staten Island.

"You're right, Bill." The young aeronaut reached out suddenly and shook the reporter's hand. "For free," he said. "Wish me luck."

"Of course, sir," the reporter said, still blushing. "Luck...."

The aeroplane bounced twice as it raced down the field, then leaped into the air with a roar, all but drowning out the cheers of the crowd as it banked and circled low over the carnival tents.

"He'll need more height to get over the Bridge," the reporter yelled into the ear of the ground crew chief, gesturing to the gothic towers and spider web cables of the Brooklyn Span up the East River.

The chief shook his head. "He's not going to fly over it," he yelled back, "he's going to fly *under* it, like Mr. Lincoln Beachey did. You watch."

They all did, hundreds of faces lifted up, following the slow, stately flight of the fragile biplane as it climbed over the streets and farms of Brooklyn.

The mass of clouds shrouding Staten Island moved across the Narrows more quickly than anyone could have guessed. The aeroplane skirted the edge of them as it circled up, one hundred feet, one hundred fifty, two hundred...

Then the cloud bank engulfed the machine, and the sound of the motor took on a different, almost querulous note. The crowd waited expectantly for the plane to emerge, but the sound of the motor grew faint, tenuous. Someone cried out, after a moment, "He made a wrong turn!"

"He's headed for Jersey!" yelled another.

The drone of the motor dwindled to nothing.

Moments became a minute.

The crowd was transfixed, then began murmuring.

One minute edged toward two. The reporter sought out the crew chief. "What is happening here?"

Then, abruptly, the aeroplane dropped out of the clouds, silent, gliding down in a tight, dangerous spiral with its motor off. Several people screamed as the crowd surged forward, following the police, the carneys and Spangler's ground crew, all to be near the spot where the machine would surely crash.

They found it in the tidal mud at the edge of the Cow Meadow, a crumpled wreckage of torn linen, looping piano wire and splintered spruce.

The police and carneys kept the spectators at bay as the ground crew threw pieces of the aeroplane aside to pull Spangler clear.

"He's alive!" one of them called out, and a collective sigh ran through the crowd.

Spangler was laid on a blanket spread over the mud to wait for the hospital wagon.

Panting, wiping his forehead with his handkerchief, the

reporter found and accosted the crew chief standing over the unconscious aeronaut. "How is he?"

"He's cut up bad, but nothing's broken, I think."

The reporter gestured to the wreckage. "Will it burn? Will it explode?"

The grim-faced man shook his head. "The magneto's off; the fuel tank isn't ruptured; everything's cold; it's safe enough."

The reporter looked from the crash to the crowd of men around the fallen aeronaut. "But what happened? Why was the motor off when he came out of the clouds?" He grabbed the other man's sleeve. "Why did he crash?"

The chief glanced over his shoulder to the aeroplane, then cleared his throat. "There was something in the motor; clogged it; shut it down."

"What do you mean? A broken part? A bird? Did he fly into a flock of birds, perhaps?"

The chief hesitated. "You're going to put this in that damn paper of yours, aren't you? Anything I say?"

The reporter looked up from his scribbling, pencil poised.

The chief cussed under his breath. "The motor." He gestured behind him, then lowered his voice. "The damn motor's full of bones. Little white bones."

"Bones? So it was birds, then."

The chief shook his head again, violently, this time. "No blood, no feathers, no nothing...*just bones*." He raised his hands, and they were shaking noticeably. "That's all I'm saying." Then he turned away, and went to kneel in the mud by the aeronaut.

The reporter stepped awkwardly through the muck to the craft; the police knew him, and let him pass. He crouched by the hot, oily metal of the motor, pushed a flapping remnant of shellacked linen aside, a piece of splintered strut...

And he saw the bones for himself, just as the ground crew chief had described. Tiny, delicate, pristine in their whiteness, lodged in every slot, every hole, every crevice of the steaming motor.

The clanging of the hospital wagon interrupted his inspection then, and he was hustled out of the way of the horse team. He stayed close enough, however, to see Spangler open his eyes in his bloody face when they lifted him into the wagon; he opened them wildly, like a madman, and everyone in the Cow Meadow heard him scream. *Shrieked*, the reporter wrote in his notebook, *shrieked because he had flown straight into the mouth of hell, shrieked because he was now awake, because he now realized it had been no dream, but a nightmare made real...*

In the umber shadows of a private hospital room that reeked of Witch Hazel, sheet starch, and urine, the broken young man in the high, rumpled bed said, "I read what you wrote in that paper of yours." He gestured to a pile of newsprint on the chair beside him. "I never said those things."

At the end of the bed, his hands resting lightly on the chipped enamel rail, the reporter shrugged. "I thought you came off rather well, Mr. Spangler." He noted the extensive stitching on the young man's face and arms, the oddly straight and regular wounds. "Reaction has been almost entirely positive in your favor."

The young man in the bed was stonily silent.

"You're a hero, Mr. Spangler," the reporter continued, stepping around the bed to stand beside it. My God, he was cut up *every*where. "Even better," he said, "you're a *tragic* hero."

"My tragedy sells your newspapers."

"And builds reputations, sir."

Spangler shifted under the stiff, wrinkled sheet, and a quiet groan escaped him. "Lies sell your papers."

"But what's the lie here? I saw the bones for myself. They clogged your engine and caused your flying machine to crash. Do you deny that?"

Spangler stared at a sliver of light beside the brown window shade. "They stopped the engine," he said, almost whispering, "but they didn't cause me to crash. I could have flown my machine with the motor off; I could have glided it down safely."

"Then why didn't you? Why did you choose to crash?"

Spangler turned from the light. The stitched wounds made him look like a crudely constructed cloth doll (Lord, the reporter thought, he must have a thousand stitches or more, the poor wretch!) but what he saw flash in the aeronaut's eyes was what made him shiver, was what made him want to take a sudden step back. "Because," Spangler said, "there was one part of your article that was true."

"What part was that?"

The aeronaut hesitated. "The part about...hell. The part about gazing into the mouth of hell." He raised his head from the pillow, his eyes bright with fever, pleading, almost. "I...*interrupted* them. They...*noticed* me." He strained against the pain, and the contours of his neck stood out in trembling cords. "They looked up from their work, from their evil, secret plans, and they *saw* me...the hatred in their faces, the *madness*...." His head fell back, and he closed his eyes with a silent shudder. "You were right, Mr. Reporter: I gazed into the mouth of hell up there, in that cloud, and it...took away a part of me that I'm not sure I will ever get back." He gathered up the sheet in his clenched fists, shaking, shaking (more wounds, there, on each hand, more stitches), then dropped his head back to the pillow, and looked away. "Until I can return there," he whispered, "I will never get that part of me back."

"But who are these people, these people with so much hatred? How can they be up there, in the sky? What did you really *see* up there?"

Spangler brought his shaking hands up to cover his face.

The reporter pulled something small and white from his waistcoat pocket and held it up. "The bones, then, Mr. Spangler, what do they mean?"

Spangler slowly dropped his hands, focused on the thin, curved bone the reporter held between his fingers, and his already pale face drained of all remaining color. "Where did you get that?" he hissed.

"It was wedged into the engine of your flying machine. There were hundreds of these--"

"*Dear God*," Spangler suddenly cried out, bringing his hands up to hide his face again, "dear God in Heaven get it away from me! Get it OUT!"

The nurse in the hall came around the doorjamb. "That's enough for now," she said flatly.

The reporter turned to her in annoyance, but checked himself when he saw in her expression that she was more than ready to match him.

"At least I'm a sympathetic ear, Mr. Spangler," he said, turning back. "They won't all be, you know."

"Visiting hours end at four o'clock sharp," the nurse said formidably. "It is now four-oh-two."

The reporter reached for his watch fob, but then thought better of it. Instead, he pocketed the bone. "I wouldn't dare to disagree, madam," he said then, and placed his bowler firmly, if not rakishly, on his well-oiled head. "Not for a moment. Not for the *moon*."

The circus, minus its air show, finally packed up and took the rails to Philadelphia. And Anthony Spangler, the next Lincoln Beachey, the next Glenn Curtiss, the next Captain of the Clouds, was never heard from again.

Until 1986, when he made the newspapers one last time.

But for a very different reason.

3

October 1986

The condominium high-rise had already been finished for a few weeks before the old man named Anthony Spangler summoned enough courage to finally visit it, and to actually go inside.

To go *up*.

To go *back*.

He knew he had to; he had known since that first day a year ago, sitting in the park with his tangerine, when he had discovered it was being built; and then, when he had visited the construction site, when he found out how *high* it would be. And he knew *they* were waiting for him. *They* had always had been there, in the air above that part of Brooklyn, waiting for him, so patient in the hot, acid darkness, whispering their evil secrets, drawing their wicked plans, waiting for him to return. It had only been a matter of time, after all...

Come back, Mr. Spangler, they whispered, *you have something of ours...and we have something of yours, too....*

From the park, throughout the Spring and Summer, he had watched the building go up, a steel skeleton slowly skinned over in brick and glass, growing inexorably above the rows of tenements and brownstones that separated *it* from *him*. Slowly, steadily, into the autumn, the building rose to fill the empty air.

On the bureau in the bedroom of his second floor walk-up, neatly arranged, were the newspaper clippings he had collected over those long months, mostly from the Post, because they lived off that sort of thing. *Construction Worker Takes Fatal Leap*, was one, *High Rise Mishap Results in Near Death*, another, and a third, most telling: *Oh Dem Bones, Dem Bones*.... The construction company, according to this last article, had been finding bones, little ones, always picked clean and bleached white, on the floors of the uncompleted upper stories, most on the twenty-eighth floor, but, tellingly for Spangler, none below. Some of the workers on these highest floors had even found the little bones in their lunch boxes, and the contents, the sandwiches and packaged snacks, oddly disturbed. Rats, bats, stray hawks or owls littering with the debris of their kills...*something* had been depositing the bones up there. Beyond that, even the Post had not dared to speculate. Just odd; very odd.

Beside the clippings on the bureau were a wooden crucifix, a vial of blessed water, and a silver-bladed knife with a carved ash handle. He had no way of knowing if any of them would help, or what real purpose they might serve; there had been no one to ask, no book in the library to read, nothing to research.

Every day, during the past year, every day after the day he *knew*, he had felt his body begin to fail him. Sometimes it was just his joints aching, and a few aspirin and a nap had been enough to deal with it. Other times, though, his limbs and fingers actually throbbed with pain. Those times, aspirin and sleep had not been enough, and he had been forced to drink himself into a stupor to dull all feeling. Today, this final day, his legs shook, his feet tapped the floor, his fingers danced, all on their own, his entire body seemed to do a rock-and-roll boogie to some mad, macabre beat. But it did not stop him; it only made his resolve that much more certain. I have to do this, he said to himself. I can't live this way any longer. I have to do this. I have to. Spangler shifted his gaze from the bureau to the bedroom window. It was a good day, warm and clear. A good day to—

He nodded his head. Today. It had to be today. If he waited any longer, he might never summon the nerve, the courage...

He struggled into his best suit and tie, and, after several attempts with fingers that rebelled at tying the knots, a pair of shiny new black oxfords. He placed the crucifix, vial and knife into a soft nylon satchel. Standing before his bureau mirror, he saw a very old man in an ill-fitting suit, but a man with no outward fear, a man with sober resolution, resignation, almost; a man with a singular, inexorable purpose. Somehow, he knew he was ready, ready in every possible way, to finally face *them*. Somehow, he knew he could do it.

Finally, after seventy-three years.

The entrance to the building was set back from the street behind a line of newly potted trees. Beyond the taped, spindly trunks he found a soaring wall of black glass punctuated by a revolving door and two flanking swing doors with brushed aluminum bars that said PUSH in subtle, polished letters. He hesitated before the revolving door, then chose the swing door on the right, and pushed. A gentle breeze of sweet, conditioned air washed over him as he entered. A uniformed security guard stood behind a podium immediately to his left. He appraised Spangler's clothes and satchel in one sweeping look, then nodded, "Good afternoon, sir."

Spangler said, "I want to look at one of the units."

"Certainly, sir." The guard gestured across the lobby to a woman behind a desk. "Right over there."

Spangler made his way across the wide sea of green print carpet to the young woman in the smart suit dress seated behind the mahogany desk. UNITS STILL AVAILABLE! announced a placard beside her; the letters of the sign were the same shade of red as her lipstick and long, manicured fingernails. She smiled brilliantly. "Good afternoon, sir!"

"I would like to see a unit," he said, holding his satchel up in both hands, tight against his chest. "Please."

She nodded briskly. "Of course! How many bedrooms were you interested in? We have a furnished two-bedroom sample on the second floor—"

"I need to see something on the twenty-eighth floor, miss."

Her perfectly smooth cheeks creased for the briefest moment in a pretty frown. "I'm afraid we have no samples that high, sir. I can assure you, however, the ones we have on the second floor have exactly the same layouts and amenities—"

"I'm sure they do, miss. But I need to see one on the twenty-eighth floor."

Her frown deepened, then suddenly cleared. "For the views, you mean?"

He nodded. "Yes. Exactly. For the views."

"Well, in that case..." She looked down at a small computer screen and tapped a few keys on the keyboard before it. "There are actually several vacancies on that floor. How about...." She hit another button, then ran a plastic card through a swipe slot in a small device beside the keyboard, and offered the card to him, "Number 2803? Faces east, with a wonderful view of Sheepshead Bay and the Rockaways."

He took the card. She saw his hesitation. "That's the key card to the elevator, and to the unit itself. There is a slot beside the doors." She touched a scarlet fingernail to the card. "See? When you put it in the slot, this arrow has to face up."

"Like a money machine at the bank?"

"Exactly! Now, please remember, 2803 is unfurnished. All appliances are unplugged. Just bare white walls."

"I understand."

"Give me a few minutes here to secure the system, and I will meet you in the apartment."

"Meet me—?"

"Of course! I wouldn't have you inspecting a unit all by yourself!" She smiled again. "And on our way back down, we can look at one of the furnished samples if you like."

"Yes. Thank you." He looked at the card dubiously.

She smiled again. "Slot beside the elevator door. Just push it in, and the doors will open. Give me five minutes here...."

The elevator doors closed slowly, silently, on the building representative's smile and wave from across the lobby. Five minutes. Would that be enough? He closed his eyes for a moment, then pushed the button for the twenty-eighth floor. He didn't feel the car as it rose, but a glowing red number display told him he was going up: 10...20...23...27...then a soft *ping*, and the doors whispered open.

Before him, against the wall, a brass bowl held a spray of expensive, artificial flowers on a narrow table; above, a forgettable Impressionist print of a French coastline leaned out in a gilded frame. The hallway began on the right. He took in a deep breath...and stepped out of the elevator car, into the hallway.

Nothing.

No sound except his shoes on the carpet, his breath through his nostrils.

At the far end of the hall, a translucent window let in a rectangle of muted daylight. There were six doors. He went to the third one, 2803. There was a slot device exactly like the one he had used to open the elevator doors, just as the young woman had said. He went past the door, however, all the way to the end, to the window. There, bathed in the diffused light, he stopped, turned, and looked back the way he had come.

Nothing.

No one home.

The only sound was the hammering of his heart in his chest, his temples, and behind his eyes. The only feeling: the pounding pain of his bones that had been ceaseless ever since he stepped inside the building. Calm down, he told himself. You still have time. You must be ready.

He went back to the third door, turned the card so that its arrow faced up and in, and inserted it. The door lock made an audible *click*. He pushed, and the door opened easily, swinging in to the left. He entered the empty apartment, stepping first on blond parquet, then soft grey carpet as he moved into the long, high-ceilinged living room, A narrow, chrome appointed kitchen glittered beyond a butcher-block island bar on the right, but he was drawn to the other side of the living room by the view of Long Island through the balcony doors. He saw street after street of Brooklyn marching off into the haze that was Queens, with the green of Nassau County just a smudge on the horizon.

He went to the glass doors and put a hand up to a handle, but stopped short as a sudden shock of pain pulsed through his head. It felt like his skull had suddenly contracted, squeezing his brain. He stood there with his eyes tightly closed, hand still on the door handle, until the pain eased.

He went over to the butcher-block counter, opened the satchel, and fumbled out the silver knife, the vial of holy water, and the crucifix. His hand hovered over each of them for a moment, then he took the vial up, uncapped it, and returned to the balcony doors. He put a thumb loosely over the vial's mouth and shook it out, sending a few drops of the blessed water splattering against the glass.

Nothing.

He tossed more water against the glass, enough to send it dribbling all the way to the floor.

Nothing. Just like the Woolworth Building, the Empire State, the Twin Towers, just like all the other tall buildings he had tried through the years. Nothing.

No one home. Not even here.

Maybe I dreamed it.

There, the thought that had plagued him for so many years. It had been 1913, after all, over seventy-two years ago. Maybe he had dreamed it, and over the years had just embellished a particularly hideous nightmare. Maybe—

"No!"

The scars on his body were real. The memory of what had caused them was real too. *This*, was real.

He only had moments, now, before the building representative joined him. He moved his thumb from the bottle's mouth and flung his arm out, splashing most of the holy water against the glass. He shouted, "Do you feel that? Do you hear me, calling you?" He threw the vial to the floor, where it bounced harmlessly off the soft carpet. "Where are you? WHERE ARE YOU?"

Nothing.

No one home.

Inside his body, he felt his bones screaming.

You're crazy. You dreamed it. You're just a crazy old man....

But his bones... *His bones*... He whirled about, went back to the butcher-block, grabbed for the silver knife--

Something bounced on the carpet behind him, bounced and rolled, and came up against he sole of his shoe. He looked down, saw it there, pristine and white against the black leather.

A bone.

A small, impossibly white bone.

He turned, looked up, across the room to the balcony doors.

But they were no longer doors.

His feet jerked then, all by themselves. He cried out, suddenly aware that his body was moving itself, and that he no longer had any strength to stop it. He realized that it was his bones pushing him forward, his bones controlling his movement, finally...his bones, moving with a power all their own, dragging their shroud of flesh across the carpet, to the gaping maw of hot, acid night that now yawned beyond the balcony, to the same endless, irresistible darkness he had flown into so many years ago, now grabbing at him, hooking him, tearing at him....

"YES!" He screamed. "Take them back! Get them OUT of me! You BASTARDS! TAKE THEM *OUT OF ME!*"

Like an unfurling flower, then: his flesh opened up, ripped along every single scar that he had carried on his person since 1913. Like blood-stained worms wriggling free from damp earth, his bones danced forth, all of them, femur, rib and knucklebone alike...and skull too, shedding its old, tattered wrappings, and shitting its contents, reaching, gaping, *biting*....

A few minutes later, the door lock clicked, and the building representative entered the apartment. "So, sir," she began, "how do you—" but then she saw what was on the carpet before her, and splattered, *flung* on the walls, ceiling, windows and balcony doors...and she began screaming, *shrieking*....

Although the main carcass locations and fluid splatter patterns were large, Detective Hendrix, the Primary, was able to lay the plastic tarp back over the majority of the victim's remains. He stood there, studying the gentle humps and folds of the tarp, then, swishing softly in his tissue booties, walked the kraft paper path the CSU crew had put down to the relative cleanliness behind the kitchen island. Goldberg, the Assistant Medical Examiner, was leaning against the butcher block, making notes on his clipboard. He looked up as Hendrix approached, and gave the detective a wan smile. "Twenty-three years on the job, Frank," he said, "and I never worked a scene like this."

"I know, I know." One more time, Hendrix took in the blood and tattered viscera pieces still clinging to the living room walls and ceiling, his gaze coming to rest, finally, on the rumpled tarp before the balcony doors. Then he looked beyond the doors, to what lay outside. "This is just fucking *crazy*."

"Lafferty and the rest of the CSU weren't too talkative. How soon was the vic discovered?"

"I have witnesses who got *rained* on, Irv, twenty-eight stories down."

Goldberg grunted. "That must have been pleasant."

"The building rep says the vic came to look over an empty apartment. He took the elevator up alone. She followed in five minutes, she says, eight minutes tops...and she found this."

"*Eight minutes?*" The Assistant M.E. put his clipboard down, shaking his head in frank disbelief. "No way, Frank, no frigging way. Do you know how long this must have taken to do? Full disembowelment, complete evisceration, every single bone, every single one—"

"It was driving the CSU guys nuts—"

"This would have taken me *hours*, and I know what I'm doing."

Hendrix cursed softly. "And the perp left nothing behind, in here, in the hall, the elevators... It's like he just jumped up on the balcony rail, spread his wings, and flew away." He nodded toward the balcony. "At least he left us those."

Goldberg looked up from his notes again. "That's another thing, though."

"What do you mean?"

Goldberg pushed off the butcher block. "Follow me."

As they crossed the room to the balcony doors, side-stepping the tarp, Hendrix said, "I know, they're completely clean, like they've been steamed and bleached—"

"There's that, sure. Bones are pretty messy, pretty bloody, when you rip them out of a fresh carcass."

"And the perp arranged them in a circular pile, like a tee-pee. Like he's a fucking Boy Scout or something."

Goldberg nodded. "There's that, too."

They reached the doors. Outside, on the balcony, they looked out at the bones, all perfectly white, perfectly arranged, with the skull perched neatly on top. Hendrix said, "I know: in five minutes he kills this old guy, debones him, steam-cleans the skeleton, then sets the bones out there like a tinker-toy set. Makes no fucking sense whatever."

Goldberg hesitated. "Just how old was this guy, Frank? I heard late seventies, maybe even eighties."

The detective frowned. "The building rep said he had to have been that old, easy. Maybe even older."

"Well then, that's the thing."

"What's the thing? What are you trying to tell me, Irv?"

"Those bones out there," Goldberg pointed, "they're from a twenty-year old. Twenty-five, tops."

"Bullshit! How can you—?"

"Lots of ways. Calcification at the joint ends, condition and wear of the teeth...." The Assistant M.E. shrugged. "Lots of ways."

The detective looked out at the pile of bones, so neatly, so carefully arranged; the skull on top, with its bright young teeth, seemed to leer at him. "Then who the hell bones are *those?*"

ETC.

Bio

Keith Minnion sold his first short story to *Asimov's SF Adventure Magazine* in 1979. He has sold over two dozen stories, two novelettes, an art book of his best published illustrations, two story collections, and one novel since. Keith was a book designer and illustrator from the early 1990s to the 2010s, and also did extensive graphic design work for the Department of Defense. He is a former schoolteacher, DOD project manager, GPO printing contract specialist, and officer in the U.S. Navy. He currently lives in the Shenandoah Valley of Virginia, pursuing oil and watercolor painting, and sometimes even fiction writing.

Colophon

This book was designed on an iMAC utilizing the Affinity publishing software suite, Ver. 1.7.2. The type was set in Baskerville and Futura. The cover art was created in acrylic polymer with maybe a little bit of digital manipulation in Affinity Photo. The interior illustrations were created in pencil, and india ink.

The Bone Worms was originally published as an ebook original by CD Publications in 2011.

"Up in the Boneyard" was originally published in **SHIVERS IV**, CD Publications, 2006.

Curious about other Crossroad Press books?
Stop by out site:
http://store.crossroadpress.com
We offer quality writing
in digital, audio, and print formats.